The
First
Word

The

First

Word

Isley Robson

Montlake
Romance

Published by Montlake Romance, Seattle

www.apub.com

Amazon, the Amazon logo, and Montlake Romance are trademarks of Amazon.com, Inc., or its affiliates.

ISBN-13: 9781503943674
ISBN-10: 1503943674

Cover design by Diane Luger

Printed in the United States of America

For Rob, Max, and Immy: the reasons I do what I do.

CHAPTER ONE

Andie Tilly peered at the walls of her cubicle through a gathering mist of tears. The colorful patchwork of photos, mementos, and cards from the families of the children on her case list rippled and blurred. *I won't cry.* For more than two years, the bustling offices of Metrowest Early Intervention had been more home to her than her small, silent apartment. She never thought it would come to this—her job snatched unceremoniously from beneath her feet.

Budget cuts, her boss explained after he dropped the bombshell. A couple of big grants had fallen through, and as their most junior occupational therapist, she was the one they would have to let go.

Now she had just a few more hours to pack the most rewarding years of her life into a file box. She took down the giant inflatable baseball bat that hung over her desk: a gift from Ramón, a preschooler with autism who, with her help, was finally able to tolerate crowds well enough to have recently attended his first Red Sox game. She'd leave the bat for another client, Jade, who always giggled when she saw it.

"Ms. Tilly?"

Andie turned, brow furrowed and bat in hand, as a stranger filled the entrance to her cubicle. He was a stocky, pleasant-looking man, with a thatch of red-gold hair and lively blue eyes that were an uncanny match for his chambray button-down.

"Yes?"

"I'm sorry to interrupt," he said, raising his hands in mock surrender. "My name is Tom Reardon. I work for Rhys Griffiths, Will's father."

Will. Andie let the bat drift down to the floor. Of all the children she'd evaluated recently, Will had grabbed her heart like no other. He was a gorgeous toddler with soulful blue-gray eyes who had been referred for an autism screening by his preschool director in the upscale town of Concord, Massachusetts. As if fulfilling a prophecy set in motion by his name, he was a force of pure will—affectionate and often hyperfocused but capable of being tipped into inconsolable meltdowns. He'd never spoken and could spend vast stretches of time spinning the wheels of the blocky little wooden trains he carried around like personal totems.

"Of course I know Will. Is he—is everything okay?"

"Yes—I mean, no." Tom smiled apologetically. "That is, the answer to that question depends on you."

"On me?"

"Yes, Ms. Tilly—"

"Andie, please."

"Andie." He offered another nervous smile. "When Rhys was told Will would be seeing a new therapist due to layoffs, he chased me out of my office with orders not to come back until I'd talked you onto his payroll."

"Mr. Griffiths wants to offer *me* a job?" Andie frowned in confusion.

Tom nodded, glancing at his watch. "That was almost two hours ago. I'm expecting him to call any minute and check up on whether I've accomplished the task."

"He's serious, then." Andie raised her eyebrows. "You'd better come in."

She couldn't help but soften toward the man when he tripped over the baseball bat on his way to the guest chair sandwiched beside her desk.

"You do realize Mr. Griffiths was resistant to Will's evaluation from the beginning?" she asked once he was safely seated. "He dodged my phone calls. He stalled on the consent forms. For weeks he made it practically impossible for me to do my job. Now he's hell-bent on saving me from the unemployment line?"

Even when Will's appointments were finally scheduled, his father never once deigned to enter the Metrowest facility. There was no Mrs. Griffiths in the picture, so a buttoned-up British nanny accompanied Will to the center for the evaluations in his stead.

"Are you certain Mr. Griffiths is feeling okay? No recent bumps to the head?"

Tom's mouth twitched at the left corner. "I'm sure you're familiar with the concept of denial?"

Andie nodded. Sometimes her enthusiasm ran away with her. Even if it was anticipated, an official autism diagnosis was news every family needed to process in its own way.

"It may have taken Rhys some time to come to terms with the situation," Tom said, "but now that he's on board, there is *nothing* he will not do to tackle this."

"I suppose it's safe to assume Mr. Griffiths is used to getting what he wants." Andie was reminded of the Internet search she'd done on Will's father while waiting on the consent forms.

Rhys Griffiths was a thirty-four-year-old engineering wunderkind whose company, Zephyrus Energy, had blazed onto the scene with an initial public offering that shattered market expectations. The media seemed to view him with a kind of puzzled awe, buzzing with stories about the quirky genius who insisted on taking most of his meetings barefoot. It was a detail that made Andie wonder whether Griffiths himself had sensory issues, just like his toddler son. She remembered a *Forbes* photo spread showing a lethally handsome man with eyes the color of blue smoke, flanked by his innovative wind-turbine prototypes.

"Rhys is . . . driven," Tom conceded. "But there never was a more devoted father. He's determined to beat this thing, even if it means having a therapist on call around the clock."

"On call?"

"Yes, you will be expected to live at the Griffiths home for the duration of the engagement," Tom confirmed. "Your own report identified sensory challenges that are interfering with Will's feeding and sleep. Rhys will need you to be on hand to provide whatever therapies you see fit, day or night."

Andie's scalp prickled. *Rhys Griffiths wants me to stay in his house?* "Now I'm sure there's been a misunderstanding," she said. "I'm a clinician, not an au pair." Did he not realize that professional OT appointments were measured out in forty-five-minute increments? She'd never heard of anyone having their own occupational therapist in residence.

"You will, of course, be more than fairly compensated for your inconvenience."

She gulped in astonishment at the sum Tom named as her proposed base salary—more than four times her pay at Metrowest, and free from the administrative hassle of having to collect from health-insurance companies like most solo practitioners did. She'd be able to hold on to her apartment and even pay off a significant chunk of her student debt. Best of all, she'd be working with Will.

But none of that mattered. Because the idea of living in the family's home like some glorified nanny or nursemaid constricted her chest like an iron band. It wasn't just professional pride that made her resistant to the proposition. It was that Andie simply didn't *do* family.

She turned away, trying to block out the memory of screeching tires on a long-distant night, and a small navy rain boot with red trim flung to the gutter. *No.* The casual interdependence, the implicit trust, and the intimacy of domestic life were off-limits to her now. She couldn't insinuate herself into the heart of a family. She couldn't risk it, even as an employee.

"They need you, Andie." Tom chipped away at her fraught silence. "I'm not just making this offer as Rhys's lawyer but as his friend. He needs you. And Will—my godson—does, too."

Her breath escaped in painful splinters. She loved working with children. She had thrived at Metrowest, supported by the clinic's routines and protocols, and the camaraderie of her more experienced colleagues. But caring for a child in a private home? It was a responsibility she could never take on.

"I have to be honest with you, Mr. Reardon . . . Tom. Living at their house, being on call . . . I'm really not comfortable."

"Rhys understands the request is unusual," Tom said. "But he can't wait for you to find a job with another practice and then try to get on your case list. He needs your help now."

Andie's nails carved painful crescents in her palms. *You're allowed to say no. For Will's sake, you* must *say no.*

"I'm sorry. I love Will and I appreciate his father's urgency, but I'm afraid I can't take the job." Just uttering the words eased the hot pinpricks that tingled at the nape of her neck.

Tom sighed, massaging the bridge of his nose. "I'm going to have to throw myself on your mercy, Andie. I don't want to think about the grief I'll suffer if I go back to Rhys without yes for an answer."

"But there are plenty of other therapists out there. I'm sure Mr. Griffiths could afford a battalion of experts. I don't see why it has to be me."

Tom paused, looking abashed. "There's something else. Three days ago, Will spoke his first word. It was quite clear, and he's said it a number of times since."

"That's great!" Andie cried, her heart leaping at the enormity of the breakthrough. "But what does it have to do with—"

"It was your name, Andie." Tom raised a beseeching gaze to her face. "The only word Will has ever said in his life is your name."

~

Andie stood in her tiny one-bedroom apartment in the Jamaica Plain neighborhood of Boston, assessing her interview outfit. Jeans and practical tops were her usual uniform when working with her young clients, and she saw no reason to present herself in any other way.

Tom was due in five minutes. Determined to ensure that she accepted the job, he'd offered to drive her to the Griffiths house and back.

Her stomach fluttered. She'd surprised herself by saying yes. Not to the job, as yet, but to a meeting with Rhys Griffiths. How could she not, when her pulse raced with elation at the news of Will's first word?

He said my name. The thrill of it galvanized her. Maybe this was it—her chance at absolution. She could make a difference in the life of this child. Prove that she was worthy. That she was wanted. That, after all these years, there might be a way to wipe the slate clean.

Her cell phone trilled, and she rushed into the living room to find it, only to see an ID on the screen that turned her excitement to ashes. Her mother. On the rare occasion that Susan Tilly called, it usually heralded nothing good. In the years since Andie's father's decline and eventual death, her mother's *physical* bruises had healed. Where her youngest daughter was concerned, however, Susan's outlook remained perpetually bruised and pessimistic.

Andie stared at the jangling device, her hand retracted in indecision. Should she take the hit now or defer it? Not that Susan was ever forthright in her jabs. She preferred a campaign of attrition—a subtle barb here, a long-suffering sigh there. Sometimes Andie thought it would be easier to assert herself if Susan would just come right out with it and voice her accusation that Gus's death could be laid at her door. Then at least she'd have something to brace herself against.

"Andrea?" The thin thread of Susan's voice echoed through the small apartment. Nobody but her mother called her by her proper first name.

"Hi, Mom."

"You're not at work."

"No, I'm actually not with Metrowest anymore. I was laid off."

Andie could feel her mother's negativity—her assumptions—gathering like a storm cloud.

"What happened, Andrea?" Susan's tone was heavy with awful possibility, as if no failure of Andie's would surprise her.

Oh, you know, I burned down the clinic. Or, I accidentally left three disabled toddlers on a bus with an escaped ax murderer. What did the woman expect?

"There were budget cuts." Andie forced brightness into her voice. "As a matter of fact, I'm about to go to an interview, for a job that looks like a sure thing."

She cringed, wishing she'd been able to resist the small flame of self-assertion that always flickered to life in response to her mother's lack of faith in her. She should have known better than to reveal too much.

"Oh? What's this new job?" Susan's cynicism vibrated across the airwaves.

"I'd be working with a nonverbal autistic boy in Concord."

Susan had one question, guided as if by instinct: "How old is the boy?"

"Almost three." Andie's voice faltered. All of a sudden she had to battle a scalding fullness in her throat. Her beloved younger brother had been three on that terrible night of sleet and fog.

She was struck by the memory of police lights strobing through the gloom; the sweet, still curve of Gus's foot in its white sock; and the stark image of her mother on her knees by the curb, everything familiar about her face swallowed by a rictus of horror and grief so desperate it still clutched Andie's heart in panic. She squeezed her right hand into a futile fist—the hand that should have held on, kept Gus safe.

Susan made a small, inarticulate sound that combined both pain and censure. Mother and daughter had never been able to share their sorrow. They'd been on lonely parallel tracks since that long-ago night when Andie's fatal lapse in focus had brought disaster down upon them—never openly clashing but never reaching rapprochement, either.

"Mom . . ." The yearning to connect was always there. She only wished her voice didn't sound quite so plaintive.

"Yes, Andrea?" Susan sighed. Her tone always managed to imply that it was somehow reckless, or at least unseemly, for Andie to have built her career working with young children after what had happened.

"Is there anything I can do for you, Mom?" Andie gathered her composure. "You must have called for a reason."

"I was going to go over plans for the maple-sugaring party," Susan said. "But you obviously have other things to worry about."

"Okay. Well, then . . ."

"Good-bye, Andrea. I hope you'll take care."

The curt click in her ear signaled the end of the call, and Andie sagged into the couch cushions, the familiar crevasse of self-doubt widening. It was incredible how one call with her mother could somehow negate years of hard-won maturity, a master's degree, and countless hours in the trenches working with children who needed her help. One word from Susan and she was transformed back into that hapless girl, a creature too absorbed in make-believe to focus when it counted. And what was the idea of a job with the Griffiths family but another foolish fantasy?

What was I thinking? She flushed with shame, disgusted at the thrill of validation she'd felt at being the subject of Will's first word. What hubris to think a single word could erase her past. Will deserved better than to be used as a test case for her redemption. *What if I screw up again?* She had no business installing herself on the front line in the Griffiths household, without the safety net of a large, bustling practice around her.

The penetrating bleat of the buzzer set her teeth on edge. *Tom.* She should just send him on his way. But she owed Mr. Griffiths the courtesy of a fair hearing. Or at least the appearance of one. She'd go through the motions, hear him out, and then politely decline the offer. It was the only acceptable outcome—for her, for Will, and for his father, although he might not know it. She'd hold firm and face him down. Then she'd go back to her tiny apartment, cut her foolish hopes back down to size, and put the pipe dream of absolution behind her.

CHAPTER TWO

Rhys steeled himself as the headlights cut a slice of brightness through the gap in the wine-colored velvet drapes. It seemed like hours that he'd paced back and forth across the den, compulsively checking the sweeping driveway, where a row of young maples stretched spindly branches to the darkening February sky. Finally, she was here—the elusive Andie Tilly, who'd refused to take the job without first vetting her prospective employer.

Andie. For a name that had turned his whole world upside down in an instant, it was surprisingly lightweight. Who was she, this person who held the key to his son's inner world? He imagined a frumpy preschool-teacher type. Cheerful, uncomplicated, spouting an endless stream of indulgent baby talk.

The nonsense words that had once come so easily to Rhys, pulled from him by the magnetic charm of his smiling infant son, had dried up as the months ticked by and one developmental milestone after another fell by the wayside. It wasn't that he loved his beautiful boy any less. In fact, it was in the darkest moments that his love for Will burned the most acutely. But somewhere along the way, Rhys himself, exhausted, had subsided into a wordlessness that paralleled that of his child.

When Will first uttered the name, the significance had been lost on Rhys. "An-dee." It was just a random pairing of syllables. But Will repeated the word with apparent intent. "An-dee." As he produced the sounds, he brandished a small blue squeeze ball. Rhys's first thought was to wonder whether there was a child named Andy in Will's preschool. Perhaps they'd played with the ball together.

The formidable Mrs. Hodge cracked the mystery when Will, enunciating the word with increasing vehemence, grasped her wrist and pulled her to the door, clutching the ball in his other hand. Andie was the young woman who worked with Will and had given him the ball, the nanny confirmed. The occupational therapist. She uttered the job title with suspicion, as if occupational therapy were some occult art.

Rhys remembered the barrage of voice mails and e-mails from the earnest therapist. *Andie.* He'd blocked both her name and her dogged determination from his mind. Those had been difficult days, when an official diagnosis loomed like a line in the sand. Now he stood on the far side of that line. And this time, instead of threatening darkness, Andie's name—on Will's lips—brought the promise of light.

One thing was certain: he would bring her into his household for as long as it took to help his son. His entire body hummed with urgency. He thanked heaven he'd heard about the layoffs at Metrowest before she'd disappeared for good.

Rhys paced into the foyer. *Where were they?* He stalked across the gleaming expanse of marble and flung the front door open. And there, almost nose to nose with him, stood a figure on the threshold, poised to knock.

He took in the flash of emphatic hazel eyes, and the perfect symmetry of dramatic winged brows set against pale, fine-grained skin. Her face was delicate, heart shaped, and framed by a lush cascade of dark hair. The reality of this woman was so different from the image he'd conjured that it felt like an ambush. She was striking. Beautiful, by anyone's definition.

"Oh, I'm sorry." She took a step back and offered her hand. "You must be Mr. Griffiths. I'm Andie Tilly."

"Yes, I suppose you are." Rhys realized the words were inappropriate as soon as they passed his lips, but there was no biting them back. It was a dilemma he often faced when meeting new people. Overcome by the barrage of sensory input in those first few moments, he could become unmoored and lose his way in conversation.

With Andie Tilly, the problem was magnified tenfold. His gaze skated over her soft pink mouth—full but unsmiling—and the elegant stem of her neck. Eyes. Lips. Skin. Throat. Each feature vied for his focus, like the scattered pieces of a puzzle he had yet to solve.

Too late, he noticed that he'd grasped her hand and neglected to let it go. He gave himself a swift mental kick and released his grip. Sometimes it seemed his entire history with the opposite sex was nothing more than a series of pratfalls brought on by a kind of interpersonal dyslexia. Time and time again, he'd failed to read the cues.

Now, for Will's sake, he'd given up trying. He could no longer risk the damage. It was a good thing this woman was only here for a job.

She was stalled on the doorstep, waiting for an invitation, so he waved her inside. Well padded in a bulky winter jacket, she slipped by him and into the foyer with an elegant economy of movement. A frigid blast of New England air followed her in, but the chill dissolved in a warm ripple of sensation where her sleeve brushed his chest.

Shrugging her jacket into his waiting hands, she stood there in hip-skimming jeans and a simple T-shirt, exuding a fresh, lemony scent and an unassuming grace.

"Where's Tom?" he asked, groping for a conversational anchor.

She shot him a searching look. Her eyes were mesmerizing, their shape as cleanly etched as an Egyptian hieroglyph. Against the flawless backdrop of her skin, they sent potent signals. Anxiety. And something more profound.

"He's in the car, taking a call. He said I should come in. I hope I didn't disturb you."

"Not at all," he said, working to collect himself. "I was expecting you, of course."

He guided her through the glittering, formal foyer, careful to maintain a pleasantly neutral expression. But as he ushered her into the den, his focus unintentionally riveted to the subtle swing of her denim-clad hips, he was forced to acknowledge that he was indeed disturbed. More disturbed than he cared to admit. Not least by his toddler son's staggeringly good taste in women.

"I confess I was curious to meet you," Andie said as he showed her to the cluster of leather club chairs grouped by the fireplace. "Your son really made an impression on me."

"The feeling seems to be mutual." He gestured for her to take a seat. "Which makes me even more curious to get to know you."

She gave an uncomfortable smile, polite but locked down, her gaze skittering away as she settled herself into the leather upholstery.

Rhys was too restless to claim a seat for himself. "Tell me how you did it," he prompted. "How you got through to him."

"There's no secret to it," she demurred. "I interacted with Will the same way I would with any client. It's just—"

"Yes?" Rhys pressed.

She dipped her gaze and drew a deep breath.

"This might sound strange," she confided, "but I understand kids like Will. I know what it's like not to feel at home in your own skin. To experience the world as an unforgiving place. Not in the exact same way they do, of course. But I get it, and I want to help. Maybe he could sense that."

Rhys stilled, his pulse pounding at his temples.

"That doesn't sound strange at all," he said, his voice raw. He cleared his throat. "But I have to admit I'm pretty ignorant about what you occupational therapists actually do. Will strikes me as a little young to have an occupation."

"Don't worry." Andie's posture loosened a fraction as the flicker of a smile played across her lips. "Occupational therapy isn't about putting Will to work."

"Well, that's a relief. I was a little worried about finding a business suit for him that would work with the diaper."

He enjoyed her look of shy surprise and the creamy flash of her throat as she laughed. Her eyes were a liquid swirl of gold, green, and brown.

"That's a common misconception," she said. "What OTs mean by 'occupation' is really any kind of fulfilling, purposeful activity. For young children, it means exploring through play, managing their sensory responses without melting down, and learning to perform the simplest tasks of daily living."

"Such small steps." Rhys's smile crumpled as he thought about the long road ahead. The familiar sadness loomed, settling like a boulder on his chest.

"That may be, but they're important steps. It's about building a foundation so Will can go on to face bigger challenges."

Rhys nodded mutely. He would never give up on the essential things he wanted for Will's future. Family, love, and intimacy, most of all—the enduring sources of happiness and human connection this disorder was trying to steal from his son. Rhys had forgone those things for himself long before his ex-wife, Karina, left, but he would never stop fighting to secure them for Will. Because, at the heart of it, wasn't it the essence of parenthood to want more for your child than you claimed for yourself?

$\sim$

The desolation in Rhys's eyes pierced her, and Andie averted her gaze, surveying the opulent room. The den was more like a traditional gentlemen's club than a domestic living space, with its rich colors, heavy beams, intricate mahogany moldings, and antique carpets. For someone used to apartment-scale living and assemble-it-yourself furniture, the overall impression was as disorienting as being dunked in a cut crystal decanter of expensive scotch. Rhys's accent—upper-crust British but with a subtle, rhythmic lilt—only added to the effect.

She watched him pace before the fireplace like a big cat in a small cage. He was tall and broad shouldered, with a presence so vivid that the air was charged with it, but his sculpted features were softened by a look that was more hobo chic than captain of industry. His black hair, so sleek and cropped in the *Forbes* photos, was longer and had been raked into a haphazard tousle. The ragged hems of a pair of old jeans trailed down over bronzed insteps and toes. Andie forced herself to wrench her gaze away from the curious intimacy of those broad, bare feet padding across the Persian rug.

"You'll help us?" His tone told her he was simply looking for confirmation. It wasn't truly a question but more of an incantation. How could she refuse, when she was their lifeline—their link to a world beyond the walls of Will's diagnosis?

Andie felt her resistance slipping. Did he have to use those eyes on her? She'd never seen anything like them—the way they caught the light and turned to blue haze. Even Will's eyes weren't tinted with quite the same wood-smoke hue. A curious sensation expanded in her chest, a mingling of empathy, fascination, and a nameless impulse that made her want to reach across the room and fold him in her arms.

But it was impossible, the idea of living under the same roof as this man and his son. Accepting their trust when she knew, in the deepest corners of her soul, that she wasn't worthy of it. If Rhys Griffiths really knew her—knew her flaws and her failings—he wouldn't even be making this offer.

She drew a long breath, quivering with regret on the exhale. "I'm honored that you sought me out, and I couldn't be happier Will has started to speak," she said, choosing her words delicately. "But I'm afraid I can't take the job."

She tried to keep her head aloft as the betrayal and incomprehension began to register on Rhys's face, but the pressure was too great, and she found herself staring at her clasped hands.

"You won't help us." The incriminating words hung in the air. Rhys came to an abrupt halt mere feet away. She could almost hear something inside him disintegrating as he reached to steady himself against the fireplace mantel, his breathing ragged.

"I'm so sorry."

"You won't help us," he repeated, half-dazed.

"I shouldn't have come," Andie whispered. "It was a mistake." Shame suffused her. Tears pricking at her eyes, she launched herself out of her chair, striding blindly for the door.

Her progress was arrested by the hot band of his fingers around her wrist, and the reversal of momentum sent her stumbling off balance toward the stern pillar of his body. She collided with him, her hand coming up to reclaim an inch of space between her torso and the powerful wall of his chest. For untold seconds they stood locked in place, his hand still imprisoning hers.

His shock too raw to be pacified, he forced her to see him as he was, laying his emotions bare. She took in the full impact of his distraught eyes, shallow breath, pounding heartbeat, and barely contained power. A strange detonation resonated deep within her. *How on earth am I going to get out of here intact?*

She wasn't, she realized. A part of her had already sheared off, like the immense wall of a calving glacier, and had floated off in solidarity with Rhys Griffiths, oblivious to the safeguards she'd spent her entire life erecting.

The den door burst open, and Tom, fresh off his phone call, barged into the room.

"Oh," he mouthed. "I'm sorry . . . er, I think I hear my godson in the kitchen. I'm going to go and say hello." He hightailed it with such comical speed, slamming the door in his haste, that the tension broke, and Rhys and Andie collapsed side by side into adjoining club chairs.

"I shouldn't have touched you. I'm sorry." Rhys looked in confusion at the hand that had grasped hers.

"It's okay. I understand."

"Do you?" he asked intently. "Because I want you to understand." He shifted, allowing his head to drop back against the burnished leather. "Can you imagine what it has been like for me to wait almost three years for my son's first word? Three years of holding him, coaxing him, teaching him, loving him."

"No," she replied. "I can't imagine."

"Usually a child's first word is 'mama' or 'dada.' The person they love and depend on most in the world. But Will's first word was 'Andie.' And yet you refuse to help us."

"I can't . . ." There was no way to make him understand.

"Why not? If I increased your salary, perhaps?"

"It isn't about the money," Andie protested. "If I could help Will, I would do it."

Then what is it about? The unspoken question hovered between them.

"Three months," Rhys proposed, his voice imbued with deliberate calm, like a trainer approaching a terrified prey animal. "All I ask is three months of your time."

Just three months. Could she manage that? She sat immobilized by the weight of his stare as opposing impulses warred for the upper hand. Could she face her demons? Could she trust herself to function here as a professional, the way she had at Metrowest? She wanted to, she realized with a jolt that took her breath away. She wanted to very badly.

"At least let me show you where you would be staying," Rhys volunteered. "You'd be right next door to Mrs. Hodge, the nanny, in your own wing on the second floor."

She shook herself back to reality. "No, I really must go." She rose, heading back into the foyer, where the facets of an enormous crystal chandelier cast prisms of light in every direction.

She noticed a small pair of Thomas the Tank Engine rain boots sitting neatly beside the front door. Her heart squeezed painfully. *Gus's rain boots were barely bigger than those on the last day he wore them.* She felt the blood drain from her face. Then came the warm pressure of Rhys's hand at her elbow.

"Are you okay?" he asked gently.

She nodded but froze as the sound of squawks and giggles filtered in from a nearby room, along with Tom's good-humored murmur. It sounded like the voices were heading their way.

"Maybe I'll see the room, after all," she conceded, panic constricting her chest. She couldn't let Will see her—not when she'd resolved to turn down the job. It would be wrong to appear before him, an apparition from another world, and then vanish. Besides, the sight of his shiny baby cheeks, each carved with a dimple, just might be her undoing.

Rhys raised questioning brows but led the way up the sweeping staircase. They crested the rise to the second floor as Will, Tom, and the nanny emerged into the foyer and headed for the stairs. The crescendo of voices echoed up from below.

"It's bathtime for you, young man," the nanny said, over Will's strenuous objections.

"Don't worry, Will," Tom soothed. "If you're good for Mrs. Hodge, I'll read you a bedtime story before I go."

Andie regarded Rhys, his eyes shadowed with the solemn responsibility of doing right by his son. The desire to help them was like an inexorable tide in the pit of her stomach.

She gazed at the dark corridor that beckoned to her right. If she hurried, she could beat a rapid retreat and avoid being seen by the small group. Was she going to take the coward's way out? From her vantage point, she could see the dark crown of Will's head bobbing as he took the stairs one at a time. His hands were like small pink starfish, clasped by Mrs. Hodge on one side and Tom on the other.

A familiar sense of vertigo kicked in. She was standing at the brink of a precipice, not just a staircase. In Will's sturdy form she saw echoes of Gus. And there were those dimples. Seeing them, she knew. *I can't run away. I can't leave him.*

She steadied herself with one hand on the balustrade, composing her features into a smile and willing her legs to hold up their end of the bargain. The group reached the landing, and all three turned their faces to the apex of the staircase. Suddenly, a squeal burst from the pint-size toddler, followed by a cascade of babble: a jubilant parade of vowels and consonants, each sound pregnant with delight. One pair of syllables stood out from the rest, forming a word infused with wonder. "An-dee!"

Instantly, Andie was in motion, striding down the stairs. She swooped down to Will and bundled him into a fervent hug.

"Hello, Will," she laughed, breathless at her own audacity. "It looks like I'll be staying awhile."

CHAPTER THREE

Andie's hands froze in a white-knuckle grip on the steering wheel as she pointed her ancient Honda Accord up the long driveway. If anything, the Griffiths house was even more imposing in daylight than it had been on her first visit to meet Rhys two weeks ago. She'd needed the interval to find someone to sublet her apartment, to render her already-neat space immaculate, and to gird herself for life with the Griffiths family. Not that she would ever be truly ready.

A gentle, snow-covered slope fell away from the mock-Georgian mansion, which dominated the surrounding acres. Careful landscaping tried to marry the enormous redbrick facade to its setting, but the immature plantings couldn't compete with the scale of the building. With its multiple gables, matching Juliet balconies, central portico, and white stonework trim, the gleaming structure boasted a bewildering array of architectural features to justify its no-doubt-astronomical price tag.

Andie thought wistfully about her neat little apartment. About her bookcases, their contents all arranged in alphabetical order, not one title out of place. About the small table that could seat no more than two, and rarely did even that. And about her painstakingly organized home-office space, where she could always lay her hands on the folder she needed because there was no one there to inadvertently sabotage her system—to insert chaos into the equation.

That was what she needed. A universe where you could put something down and count on it to be there when you returned. A world where the stakes were manageable and the entire bedrock of your existence couldn't open beneath your feet from one moment to the next. Not this gigantic house, with its unpredictable inhabitants and its daunting responsibilities. She suppressed a sharp pang of anxiety as she juddered to a stop outside the front door.

Deep breaths. She closed her eyes and inhaled, only to be startled out of her skin by a jaunty rap at her window. Frowning, she pumped at the manual window crank, muscling the troublesome pane down a couple of inches.

"You scared me half to death," she complained as Rhys's eyes, in all their blue-smoke glory, loomed in the narrow opening.

"Sorry. I just wanted to let you know there's a garage bay around the side you can use."

He jammed his hands into his jeans pockets against the cold and gave the Honda an assessing look.

"That is, if you can get that thing to start up again."

"Hey!" she protested. "That's Ernie you're talking about."

"Hmmmm, I hate to break it to you, but I don't think Ernie's long for this world."

"He's in perfect running order. He passed inspection with flying colors."

Rhys leaned forward, peering at an odd, pale spot on the paintwork on the driver's door.

"What's that? Glitter?"

"Nail polish," Andie said. She turned the key in the ignition, annoyance flaring as she fired Ernie up with a sputter. "I didn't want to leave the rust exposed, and I couldn't afford to have it treated professionally. It works fine for now."

"Yeah, until the entire thing corrodes to dust. Having your car disintegrate on the Mass Pike is bad for your health."

"You should move," she advised with a scowl. "If you want to keep your toes."

She pulled the Honda into the spacious parking spot and pushed the creaky driver's-side door open.

"We can't all drive BMWs," she announced as Rhys appeared and popped the trunk open.

"What on earth makes you think I'd drive a BMW?" He looked genuinely perplexed.

Andie had to smile at his stark literalness. "I used BMW to mean luxury sports cars as a class, generally. As far as I'm concerned, they're all the same."

"Okay, no they're not. And I drive a Porsche Carrera."

"Must be handy, getting Will in and out of his car seat, in a practical family car like that." It was only fair that she got her own jab in, if he was going to take her to task over the car that had served her so long and so well.

"It's my commuting car."

"And Ernie is mine," Andie said firmly, hoping to close the door on any further criticism. Ernie was what she could afford, and she wasn't about to apologize for that. Rhys could butt out.

"Fortunately, your commute just got a whole lot shorter," he said with a grin, lifting her suitcases from the trunk. "Let's get you settled in."

She followed him up an interior staircase, left with nothing to carry but her lightweight tote and a couple of pillows. It was amazing how her irritation evaporated in the afterglow of his smile. Actually, it was enough to make her irritated all over again to think that she could be so easily manipulated by a quirk of genetics. Surely he didn't need to be quite *that* attractive. It was overkill. *Freakish, actually.* And she wasn't about to be taken in by it.

She stomped along, eyeing the deep V formed by the tapering of his lean frame from his broad shoulders to his trim waist and hips. Adding the definitive dot to the exclamation point was a show-stopping rear end, lovingly encased in worn denim. *Nope,* Andie told herself firmly. *I'm impervious. Completely immune.*

"We'll drop off your things upstairs first, and then I want to show you a project I've been working on," Rhys announced as they emerged into the foyer and he took off up the main stairs, bearing her suitcases as if they weighed next to nothing.

"Will's still napping," he whispered as they walked past a closed door that spelled out Will's name in decorative letters painted red, blue, and yellow.

He led her down a wide corridor to the guest room he'd shown her on the evening of their first meeting—an oasis decorated in touches of delft blue and crisp white, with a plush queen-size bed festooned with pillows; a high-pile, cream-colored rug to soften the dark hardwood floor; and a writing desk in antique white tucked into an alcove. The room looked as serene and welcoming as it had upon her first viewing.

"You didn't need to bring your own pillows," he commented as she tossed the soft bundle on the bed.

"I'm a creature of habit," she said. It was impossible to explain how even something as insubstantial as a pillow could feel like an anchor when she was this far adrift.

It was oddly intimate to be standing with Rhys in the room that was supposed to be her private refuge.

"So what's this project you want to show me?" she prompted, gesturing to the door.

A smile lit up his entire face, and he lost no time in leading the way back downstairs. Andie's curiosity was piqued as she trailed after him, wondering at the decided spring in his step.

"I feel like I'm in *Gone with the Wind*," she marveled as they descended the sweeping staircase. She slapped a hand over her mouth, way too late, realizing how gauche she sounded.

"This place *is* huge," Rhys agreed with a laugh. "My ex-wife's choice. But don't worry. On weekdays, my housekeeper, Jillian, is here, and of course, Mrs. Hodge, so you won't feel as if you're rattling around like a lone penny in a jar."

"Mrs. Hodge lives in full-time, right?"

"Yes, but every other weekend she goes down to Connecticut to visit her daughter."

He took the stairs down to the finished basement area where she'd be doing Will's OT sessions, a space they'd toured at their first meeting. The sizable room was impressive, carpeted and painted in neutral tones, with a view of the large sloping yard and pond through double glass doors that let in plenty of natural light. She would have to set up some equipment, but it was a far cry from the dingy, functional spaces she'd occupied at Metrowest.

Rhys paused at the door.

"Are you ready?" he asked.

"I guess," she admitted. His irrepressible smile made her lips curl upward in response.

"Close your eyes," he urged, taking her hand.

She froze for a moment. Normally she wouldn't allow herself to be left at such a disadvantage with a stranger. But something about his good-natured enthusiasm compelled her to lower her lashes and allow him to lead her gently inside, his fingers exerting a warm pressure as they clasped hers.

"Okay, here it is!"

She opened wide eyes to the most exquisite OT room she'd ever seen. The walls were painted a serene blue gray, with accents in midnight, scattered with a constellation of stars that gleamed under a strategically placed black light. Metal panels mounted to one wall were covered in heat-responsive paint, so Will could watch the imprints of his hands appear in rainbow colors, which would then fade out.

There were swings of many types mounted to a ceiling crisscrossed with a latticework of reinforced metal bars with sturdy eyebolts. There were thick gym mats, squishy inclined ramps, and exercise balls she could arrange into obstacle courses. She saw stretchy hammocks hanging like colorful cocoons, a ball pit, a trampoline, and a low table for fine-motor exercises. There were even partitions Andie could use to fashion either a small, cozy space or a large, open one.

"Like it?"

"*Like* it? It's so incredible you could actually charge admission," she breathed, gripping Rhys's arm. "How did you do this?"

"I got on the phone with a contractor as soon as you said you'd come. It took a few days to track down equipment and supervise the installation.

"And I only finished painting this morning," he added, brandishing fingernails still outlined in blue latex.

Rhys had called her a couple of times over the past two weeks, asking about equipment she might want to order upon her arrival, but she couldn't have guessed that he was working to pull this off. Something about the earnest joy on his face and the blue paint smearing his cuticles opened up a shaft deep in her chest, and his smile brought light to its farthest reaches.

"I've never worked in a space this gorgeous," she confided. "I don't know what to say."

"You don't need to say anything. Honestly, doing this helped me. Until now there hasn't been much I could do for Will, you know. But working on this . . . gave me a chance to stop feeling so useless."

"Tom wasn't kidding," Andie laughed, feeling winded by his forthright stare. "He said once you set your mind to something, you don't quit."

She eyed him as a wayward little laugh burst from her lips and echoed around the room.

"What?" he asked.

"I get the impression that if I'd said Will needed elephant-assisted therapy, I'd be looking at an elephant pen right now."

"*Elephant*-assisted therapy? Is that a thing?"

"Yes, they have programs in South Africa and Thailand for kids with autism." She darted a suspicious look his way. "Please don't get any ideas."

"You're Will's program director, not me," he protested, smothering a smile. "No elephants unless you specifically say so."

"Okay, then, we're agreed."

"Seriously, Andie," Rhys began, suddenly tentative, "anything you need, you let me know. I want you to know how grateful I am that you decided to come here. Really, thank you."

"No problem," Andie mumbled, tongue-tied by the earnest intensity of his gaze.

Eager for a diversion, she wandered over to a heavy bolster swing hung at hip level and settled her weight on it. She kicked her legs out and set the swing in motion as Rhys explained how to safely adjust the height of the swings and hammocks.

In her flustered state, she misjudged her momentum as she swung forward, the arc of the swing bringing her so close that her knees brushed against his hips, their faces only inches apart. All of a sudden she was acutely aware—at almost a granular level—of the nubby softness of his plaid shirt, the healthy animal sheen of his neck, and the warm scent rising from his skin.

The strong column of his throat met the line of his jaw at an angle that perfectly satisfied her aesthetic sense. She felt a treacherous jolt in the pit of her stomach as she studied it, a sharp spike of sensation piercing her and holding her close for a seemingly endless instant before the swing arced away.

Okay, calm down, she chided inwardly, gripping the cables and dipping her glance. *It's just pheromones or something. Smoke and mirrors.*

Nature playing its tricks. Good job, biology. You've made your point. He's attractive, okay? I get it. Now, leave me alone.

"If you're up for it, I was thinking we could start working on Will's bedtime routine tonight," Rhys suggested, seemingly oblivious to her discomfort.

"Sounds great." Maybe if she turned her attention to the actual reason she was here, she'd stop being knocked off balance by Rhys's presence.

"Of course, you should take the afternoon to settle in. But then you can watch what I'm doing with his bedtime routine and let me know where I'm going wrong."

"I should be able to come up with some strategies."

"If you can, I'll put a statue on the front lawn in your honor," Rhys said. "You have no idea of the toll sleep deprivation has taken on this household." He gestured at the subtle bluish shadows under his eyes.

"I can only imagine," she said sympathetically. Anxiety started to dawn as she thought through the actual logistics of the exercise—bumping around in the dark confines of Will's room in close proximity to Rhys.

"Come on, you should unpack and relax a little," he prompted, leading the way back out into the corridor. "Will is going to put us through our paces later."

"I'll be ready," she assured him. And she would be. She was determined to help Will in any way she could, regardless of the presence of his absurdly attractive father.

Her cell phone trilled as she approached the entrance to her room, and she ran to silence it before it interrupted Will's nap. It was Jessica, her beloved sister, the closest in age to Andie of all the Tilly siblings. The one person who'd stood by her when everything had fallen apart.

Unlike her two eldest sisters, Louisa and Rose, who had married young and settled in their hometown in western Massachusetts, Jess was an associate creative director at an ad agency in Boston. She and her husband, Ben, a copywriter, lived in a small apartment in the

Charlestown Navy Yard, perched right on Boston Harbor. They were the linchpin of Andie's social life, apart from a few friends she'd gathered on her way through grad school and at work.

"Jess," Andie said warmly. In her rush to get ready for the temporary move to Concord, Andie had needed to skip out on their usual coffee dates over the past couple of weeks.

"How's the first day going?" Jess asked. "How's the house? How's your boss?"

Andie could picture her sister lolling on her crimson custom sofa. The tallest of the Tilly girls, Jess was angular and stylish, with a frame like a greyhound, a passion for designer clothes, and a gift for accessorizing that had sadly bypassed her siblings.

"The house is big. The boss is . . . nice, so far. You should see the OT room he set up for Will."

"I Googled him," Jess confessed. Her voice sounded close enough to be in the same room. "And, holy crap, Andie! You never mentioned he was that gorgeous."

"He's moderately attractive," Andie conceded with caution.

"Says you," Jess said with her trademark snorting laugh. "I've set a photo of him as the wallpaper on my desktop at work. Ben hasn't noticed yet."

"I heard that!" echoed a voice in the background. Given that Ben and Jess worked for the same agency and lived cheek by jowl in a one-bedroom condo that was six hundred square feet only in its wildest dreams, they didn't keep too many secrets from each other.

Jess laughed. "That 'Blue Steel' stare gets me going each morning."

"Stop it," Andie ordered, suppressing a chuckle of her own as she recalled her sister's fondness for *Zoolander*.

"I can't help feeling there's more to this situation than meets the eye," Jess probed.

Andie had told her very little about how she came to accept the job—certainly nothing about Will's first word. The last thing she needed was for her sister to start nosing around for hidden significance where there was none.

"It's a job, Jess," she said. "No different from my job at Metrowest."

"Except you're installed in the house of the most beautiful man east of the Mississippi."

"Jess—"

"Okay, okay, I'll table this discussion for now," Jess grumbled. "But only because there's a more pressing issue at hand. The Oscar party. Are you in?"

Jess and Ben had made their annual Academy Awards celebration, with its ritzy dress code, flowing champagne, and Hollywood trivia games—complete with Lindt gold bunnies as prize statuettes—a sought-after event. Tomorrow was the big day, and Jess had been petitioning Andie to make a sooner-than-expected visit back from the burbs.

"I can't, Jess. It will only be my second day at the house, and as of tonight we're getting started on Will's sleep issues. I can't duck out so soon."

"I can see I'm getting nowhere with you today," Jess harrumphed. "Well, I'm planning a trip out in your direction very soon. We're going to hit the outlets and pick out our Oscar gowns for next year. I'm not taking no for an answer. Fortunately, I'm a lot more persuasive in person."

"It's your freckles," Andie said fondly. "They're irresistible."

"Damn straight," Jess confirmed. "Now, get back to work. I'll save the killjoy statuette for you this year."

"You do that," Andie laughed. "Love you, Jess." For the first time in their conversation, she felt a bit wobbly. Being at Rhys's house did feel different, and it was disingenuous of her not to share that with the sister who meant everything to her. But there were some doors she wouldn't open. Not even for Jess.

"I love you, too, you gorgeous pain in the ass." Jess's declaration enveloped Andie like a hug before they disconnected, leaving Andie to face her new world alone.

CHAPTER FOUR

When Andie retired to her room to rest and unpack, the silence that settled over the house was enough to jar Rhys's thoughts onto a far less promising track. He stared pensively at his phone before tapping back into the e-mail message from his ex-wife that had dinged into his in-box earlier that afternoon. For probably the hundredth time, he studied the inscrutably brief missive, trying to make out its subtext.

> I'm back in Concord. We need to talk about
> our son.

There were so many things wrong with those two short sentences he hardly knew where to begin.

I'm back in Concord. What the hell did that mean? For someone who'd been incommunicado for close to two years, Karina offered surprisingly little context. Was she announcing her permanent return to Massachusetts? Or was this simply a fly-by-night visit? The last thing he knew, she'd been shacked up in Silicon Valley with Lance Bello, their former department chair at MIT, who'd been lured away to join Stanford's engineering faculty.

Karina, brilliant but notoriously flighty, was still finishing her doctorate and transferred to Stanford when she'd walked out on Rhys, seeing Lance's West Coast job offer as her chance to escape the confines of motherhood. With their on-again, off-again affair definitively on again, she and Lance had taken off for warmer climes, leaving his wife and two children in the dust.

Our son. Our son? He skipped back to the phrase that really blew his mind. Did she really think she had any kind of claim on Will when she'd walked away and not looked back?

Rhys still couldn't understand how Karina had failed to see it: the manifest glory of the small being they'd created together. For her, the pregnancy was more of a dramatic flourish than the beginning of a lifelong commitment. Just one more live grenade dropped on the battlefield of their relationship. But, by the ninth month, the scene-stealing impact of it was not nearly enough to compensate her for the insults and inconveniences of her changing body. By Will's fourth month of life she'd announced that she still wanted to be the star of her own story, and "a baby"—she wouldn't focus on the particular wonders of their specific baby—would make that impossible. Her defection to California had followed shortly after.

For Rhys, parenthood hadn't effaced his identity. It only enriched it. From the first moment he saw the miracle of Will's face—the wonder in his hazy, unfocused eyes, and the adamant point of his tiny chin—he knew that being this child's father would forever define him.

We need to talk. What could they possibly have to say to each other? And why now? A flicker of unease rippled through him as he thought about the timing. Could she have somehow heard about Will's diagnosis? But why would that have prompted her return? Rhys doubted that a woman who ran away from the demands of a perfect infant would come rushing back to take on the challenges of a toddler with autism.

And who would have told her? He'd planned to tell her himself, of course, once the reality of Will's diagnosis stopped tripping him up all over again every time he thought about it. But her return had preempted his plans, and now he'd have to deal with it.

They'd set up a meeting on neutral ground for the following morning: a café in the center of town, where they'd once spent leisurely Sunday mornings. Even in a crowd of unflappable New Englanders, Karina had always turned heads, with her flawless skin, long black hair, and feline ice-blue eyes. Eyes Rhys had taken such pleasure in admiring but had never been able to read. He still cringed to think how easily he'd been dazzled by the drama that clung to her like a signature scent.

Suddenly the baby monitor crackled as Will let out a passionate yell. He almost never woke up calmly but was instead racked with emotions larger than the small body that contained them. Rhys knew the feeling. Like his son, he experienced life at a high-torque intensity, his central nervous system simply generating more heat and force than the average person's. His senses delivered the world to him in vivid Technicolor, gifting him with deep jewel-toned moments of great passion, joy, and focus. If they occasionally extracted their cost in sharp-edged sensations of dissatisfaction or intense disquiet, when life seemed to crash in on him—loud and insistent—then that was a price he'd learned to pay. He only hoped Will would one day find the same balance.

He ran up to Will's room, noticing as he approached that Andie's door was open. She peered around the doorway as Will's next scream echoed down the corridor, and Rhys waved to signal that he had things under control as he hastened to the rescue.

Will stretched out his arms as he entered, and Rhys gathered him up, struck as always by the perfect sense of rightness that settled over him when he held the sturdy little toddler against his chest.

He stroked Will's hair, letting his fingers slip into the soft, dark waves at his nape. *He needs a haircut,* he thought with foreboding. Will had suffered through his first little-boy cut at fifteen months. The strokes of the comb, the brisk snipping sounds of the scissors beside his ears, and the synthetic fabric of the cape fastened around his neck sent him into paroxysms of distress. Since then, Rhys had spun out the weeks between trims. Another thing Andie might be able to help them with.

They moved out into the corridor, and all too soon Will wriggled to be set down, captivated by the shaft of peach-colored light slanting into the corridor from Andie's doorway. He ran to explore but was brought up short by the surprise of seeing the normally empty room occupied. Rhys hung back, suddenly afflicted by a creeping reluctance, knocked off balance by the strange—disconcertingly attractive—new person he'd invited into his space.

He'd brought this woman into his home for Will's sake, but personal interactions sapped his energy. Too often he was confounded by the petty games and mixed messages that complicated most dealings with fellow members of the human race. He'd learned from hard experience that others didn't necessarily engage with the world the same way he did: always saying what he meant and meaning what he said. For some, the thrust and parry of communication was a sport, with words and gestures delivered to win a point, to obfuscate, or to resound simply for effect. He'd always needed a refuge, a place to process and recover. A place where he could simply *be*, without the need for constant vigilance.

"Andie!" Will cried, pulling Rhys's attention back to the moment. Will was so excited that the exclamation ended with his classic pterodactyl shriek, and he practically danced in Andie's doorway.

Rhys smiled ruefully. *Say my name*, he willed for the millionth time as the familiar chasm yawned in his chest. It still confounded him that this woman had moved Will to speech where he had failed. Nothing could quite erase the sting, not even the balm of gratitude that she'd agreed to help them. And it *was* a big request, expecting her to uproot herself from her home and her life in the city . . . from friends, family, and a possible boyfriend. A woman like Andie Tilly didn't walk through the world without gathering something of an entourage.

Perhaps that was what accounted for her initial resistance to taking the job: some guy she cared about. But that hypothesis shed no light on the fear—the near panic—he thought he'd glimpsed in her eyes at their first meeting. *What was she hiding?* Unless her anxiety had simply been her first, honest reaction to Rhys himself. He knew he could be brusque, intimidating, graceless.

He halted in Andie's doorway as he came upon a sight that was unlikely to diminish the woman's almost supernatural appeal in his son's eyes. The late-afternoon sun burnished her west-facing room with a copper glow, and she knelt on the floor by an open suitcase—the long, loose waves of her hair limned in light. She looked like some kind of sylph, her slim body arranged in a casually graceful posture, her legs neatly tucked under her. *Who are you?*

"Will, have you come to help me unpack?" Everything about her seemed to glow.

"Be careful about extending that kind of invitation," Rhys warned, propping himself awkwardly against the doorframe. "It's one of his favorite pastimes, although he usually ends up *inside* the suitcase, so the 'help' factor is debatable."

"Oh, I don't know," Andie responded gamely. "Let's see if he wants to put these shirts in the drawer."

Taking Will by one hand, she took a folded shirt in the other and led him the few feet to the open bureau.

"Like this, Will," she demonstrated, laying the garment flat in the bottom of the drawer.

Rhys watched in fascination as Will followed Andie back to the suitcase, accepting the shirt she placed in his hands. Taking another, she scooted back over to the drawer and demonstrated once more. The tip of his tongue sticking out in concentration, Will lifted the shirt over the lip of the drawer and let it fall on top of the pile. The neat folding unraveled as the silken garment came to rest, but Andie praised him effusively.

Will's lack of speech made it all too easy to forget how much he was really taking in, Rhys reflected. Too often he gave up on asking him to perform tasks for himself, wary of the bleak depression that swamped him when he came up against the limit of Will's abilities. The fear was always there, an alien presence trying to annex him from the simple pleasure of being with his son.

He forced his thoughts to be still and immersed himself in the scene in front of him: Andie's gentle patience and Will's earnest focus. Not to mention the sheer sweetness of his son's face as he stole sidelong glances at her, unable to quite meet her gaze but soaking in her approval.

"When I came back from the Caymans last month, Will insisted on being zipped into my carry-on," Rhys commented idly.

"A lot of kids with sensory issues crave the joint compression they get from squeezing into tight spaces," Andie observed. "Just be careful there are no places around here that he can get stuck. No toy chests with heavy lids. Nothing airtight."

"Yeah, I'm pretty paranoid about that kind of thing," Rhys said. "Nothing is more important than Will's safety."

"Of course," she responded hoarsely, turning back to her task.

"The Caymans, huh?" she commented a moment later. "You entrepreneurial types with your offshore tax havens and white-sand beaches."

"I was there for a conference," Rhys hastened to explain, not sure why he suddenly felt embarrassed.

"Well, it explains one thing I was wondering about."

"What's that?"

"Your feet," she said, gesturing across the room to where his bare toes sank into the high-pile rug. "You were barefoot when we first met as well, and I couldn't figure out how on earth a Massachusetts resident would have tanned feet in the middle of February."

He glanced down at his own toes, habitually bare and even more bronze-toned than usual in the afternoon light, and looked back at her, surprised she would have noticed such a detail. Rhys hated the

confinement of shoes—their close, humid pressure a constant aggravation. He didn't feel grounded, fully at ease, unless he could dig his toes
into sand, wet grass, or the silken fibers of the Persian rugs he selected
for their rich plushness.

Averting her eyes, Andie handed Will another folded shirt and
turned her back to Rhys, busying herself with arranging the drawers.

Soon the stack had been dispatched, and Will straddled the side of
the suitcase, trying to slide into the empty spot vacated by the shirts.

"Careful, Will," Andie said gently, removing a hair dryer from his
path before he could sit on the prongs of the power cord. Will plunged
his hands into the soft contents of the suitcase that surrounded him,
his chubby forearms emerging festooned with scraps of satin and lace.

"Ahem." Andie cleared her throat. Yes, that was definitely a blush
riding high on her cheeks as she stared pointedly at Rhys. "You should
probably turn around."

"Turn around?" Rhys repeated, clueless until he looked more
closely at the fabric adorning Will's wrists. If he wasn't mistaken, that
was a black lace thong, and the raspberry-colored confection beside it
was another garment of the same type. Now it was Rhys whose cheeks
were flaming as he turned to face the corridor.

"I'm sorry," he gasped. "I didn't mean to let Will rifle through
your . . . unmentionables."

"Unmentionables?" Andie couldn't restrain a giggle. "I'm sorry,
Rhys. I know you're British, but I didn't realize you were a nineteenth-
century Quaker."

Rhys rested a hand against the doorframe, gripped with embarrassed laughter.

"You're the one who made me turn around," he protested weakly.

"Okay, then, maybe I'm a Quaker, too," she admitted, still convulsed with giggles.

Their laughter was matched by a delighted squeal from the direction of the suitcase, and Will was chortling, too, each cheek imprinted with a dimple, his laughing eyes narrowed to twin crescents.

The sight almost brought Rhys to his knees. It was so rare for Will to be able to join in with the hilarity of those around him. He was so often emotionally off-kilter that this moment of connection was ineffably precious. Rhys wasn't quite sure what to expect from Andie's tenure inside his home, and he reflected upon this as he swallowed down the lump of emotion rising in his throat. But her stay with them was certainly off to a promising start.

CHAPTER FIVE

It was too easy, Andie thought as she observed from the shadows of Will's room. Too easy to slip into a comfortable familiarity with this man and his son. Perhaps it was the surprise of the beautifully outfitted OT room that had knocked her off guard. Or maybe it was the unexpected intimacy of the afternoon, with both the nanny and the housekeeper off duty. Whatever the reason, her first few hours at the house had felt like a moment out of time. And that was not a good thing.

She had to remember herself and not get lost in the intimacy of her new role. Rhys seemed all too willing to treat her as if she belonged. But she knew otherwise. *You're an impostor, and don't you forget it.* She had to keep her walls up and make sure Rhys butted up against their hard contours, too. Because she was afraid of the kind of expectations that might develop if he became too comfortable with her, started to trust her in all the ways that felt only natural when an employee began to fit in like one of the family. She didn't deserve that kind of trust. She wasn't one of them, and she never would be.

It didn't matter that her heart seemed to turn over as she watched Rhys hold his sleepy son against his shoulder as he readied him for bed, his large, capable hand cupped gently under Will's head. It made no difference that the sight of Will's serene profile and his dimpled fists, clasping handfuls of his father's shirt, stirred her in ways she'd never experienced. Those feelings were all the more reason for her to lock her happy-families fantasy back in the lead-lined box where it belonged. She was here as a professional, and even now the clock was ticking down toward a three-month expiration date, at which point she vowed she would leave with her peace of mind intact.

Andie watched from across the room as Rhys read Will his customary three stories, letting the rhythm of his voice wash over her. She was observing their nighttime routine, learning how Rhys usually settled Will to sleep.

It quickly became apparent that Will was wired with some kind of subliminal alarm system that went off when Rhys moved more than a few inches away from his body. Will appeared lost in peaceful slumber before Rhys's first attempt to leave the bed, his eyelids at half-mast, his arms flung out. But the minute Rhys shifted his weight to get up, the alarm tripped. Will's eyes flew open, his fists clenched reflexively around the nearest part of his father he could grab, and the screaming started.

Bloodcurdling was a fitting description of the inhuman sounds coming from Will's small body. Rhys shot Andie a ragged look and scooped Will up, swaying on his feet. Then, to her immense surprise, he began to sing.

The room vibrated with a rich, unearthly baritone shaping a melody that sounded almost hymnal. Strange, guttural consonants mingled with pure, elongated vowels in a language that was utterly indecipherable to Andie—except for one recurring word that sounded oddly like "saucepan." There was love in every twist of the melody, in every mystifying phrase, and she held herself utterly still, somehow abashed to be witnessing an interlude between father and child that felt primal, transcendent.

Rhys sang on, modulating his volume as Will's cries tapered off. Then, for a seemingly endless succession of minutes, he hugged and soothed, his gaze occasionally meeting Andie's across the room as the darkness deepened and a strange communion bound them. Her breath seemed to synchronize with Rhys's as time slowed. Every now and again, an aftershock racked Will's body with a sleepy half sob, but the tears were drying on his cheeks, and his eyes finally drifted closed again.

Slowly and with infinite care, Rhys bent low and angled his upper body toward the toddler's bed, trying to deposit Will on the mattress without breaking the spell. Andie could tell almost immediately that it wasn't going to work. She raised her hands in warning, but it was too late. Rhys missed the signal and continued in the attempt. There was no way that kind of movement was going to avoid tripping Will's internal alarm. Suddenly the room was filled once again with discordant sound. Rhys wiped his eyes weakly, shooting a traumatized smile Andie's way.

"This is how it usually goes," he said softly over the top of Will's head. They'd already been in his room for more than an hour.

Andie regarded him sympathetically. "I have an idea," she said. "Hold on a sec."

Within a minute, she was back, bearing an item from her OT tool kit.

"It's a weighted blanket," she explained in response to Rhys's raised eyebrows. "I think you need to start off with him lying down. He seems to respond really well to being hugged, having your arm around him. Let's try this and see if the extra pressure helps. Then, if he drifts off, you can remove your arm, and he'll still feel the consistent weight of the blanket."

"At this point I'll try anything," Rhys sighed. Kissing Will's head, he lay down and draped his arm around him, hugging softly and humming the same melody, as Andie lowered the blanket over Will.

The toddler offered no response to the extra weight, except to shift contentedly. Soon Rhys's humming wound down, and he closed his eyes, encouraging Will to do the same. The only sound in the room was the gentle murmur of water sounds coming from the sound machine on the bookshelf. The calm deepened, and Andie found herself drifting into an almost meditative state.

She stretched to dispel the tension that had gathered in her shoulders in response to Will's screams. Time took on a strange unreality as she waited, sneaking occasional peeks at the handsome matching profiles of father and son facing each other on the pillow.

Finally, when she was certain Rhys had fallen asleep, he stirred, letting one arm drift out so he could brace his hand on the floor and shift his weight from the low toddler bed with as little impact as possible. Andie held her breath as he executed the smooth roll, peeling himself off the bed in one fluid movement. Wincing in anticipation of more screaming, he looked back at the bed to see Will still sleeping peacefully.

With an exhausted thumbs-up, Rhys trod carefully to the door and waited for her to follow. He felt around the doorway for the hallway light switch on the other side and clicked the light off to avoid a shaft of brightness falling onto Will's bed. Finally, they tumbled out into the dark corridor.

"Thank you," he said, performing a small "I'm not worthy" homage in the shadows. She let out a tense breath and smiled at the vintage *Wayne's World* reference, inclining her head in the direction of the stairs.

"Don't talk yet," she whispered urgently. "It's not safe."

They crept along to the top of the staircase, and Rhys let out a laugh of disbelief, reaching out to gently grip her shoulders. Andie had to command herself not to jump out of his grasp. His touch was so warm and his presence so large that it seemed to exert a magnetic force.

"Amazing," he said. "It actually worked. We're out!"

"I have to ask. What was that song you were singing?"

"Oh." Rhys gave a sheepish smile, attractive laugh lines etched at the corners of his eyes. "That was 'Sosban Fach.' Little Saucepan. It's a folk song. All Welsh children can sing it in their sleep. It was a favorite at my local rugby club, but when I slow down the tempo, it helps Will nod off."

"Well, I think it must have magical properties. I almost went into a trance myself."

"Not as magical as your bag of tricks. That blanket worked wonders. Now you must have dinner with me to celebrate."

"Um . . ." Andie shifted uncomfortably, looking back toward the small kitchenette near the nanny's room. "I was actually going to look around for a can of soup or something and get an early night."

"After what Will and I just put you through, I'm not about to let you go to bed with nothing more in your stomach than a cup of Mrs. Hodge's Bovril."

"Bovril?"

"Yes, it's a concentrated meat extract. Comes in a jar and you dilute it with water to make a broth. I happen to know Mrs. Hodge takes a cup of it now and then. Horrible stuff."

"Any chance you have a can of chicken noodle in the kitchen downstairs? I haven't had time to shop for anything yet—"

"Don't be ridiculous. You're going to eat properly or I'll feel so guilty I won't get any sleep. Plus, it's your first night here. You should get a welcome dinner, and I want to hear your thoughts on what else I'm getting wrong with the bedtime routine."

Andie nodded. That she could do. "Okay, then. Thanks."

She followed Rhys down to the kitchen, peppering him with ideas about how to calm Will before bedtime: perhaps a massage after his nightly bath, and a chart with pictures detailing every aspect of the bedtime routine, so it would always unfold with utter predictability—something kids like Will thrived on.

"Bathtime is always a three-ring circus," Rhys confessed. "Tantrums, tears—you name it. I skipped it tonight because I couldn't deal with it, but you'll see."

"Well, we're going to have to work on that, too," Andie said. "Probably sooner rather than later."

Rhys gave a heavy sigh. "Sometimes I feel like all I do is force Will to go from one calamity to another."

"Don't worry. It'll get better. I have plenty of tricks up my sleeve." Andie smiled reassuringly. "You've been on the front lines for a while."

They reached the cavernous great room and kitchen, and she was once again struck by the scale of the house and its empty, echoing spaces.

"So on weekends, you're it—with Will, I mean. Just the two of you?"

"Yes. Nights, weekends. Every moment it's possible for me to be around. Why? Does that surprise you?"

"Having seen you in action with Will, it doesn't surprise me at all. But it wasn't necessarily what I expected."

"Because I stalled on the evaluation forms," Rhys supplied, his eyes lighting with challenge. He opened the fridge and started pulling out dinner items. Some steaks in a marinade. A large bowlful of salad greens. A collection of other sides. "You expected me to be a hands-off dad."

"I didn't say that," Andie protested.

"But you thought it."

"I might have wondered. Before I met you. But even then, I wouldn't presume to judge. I don't have children. I can't pretend to understand what it's like."

Rhys looked down at the countertop, his expression unreadable. After a beat, he glanced back up, his face open, neutral. "Do you like steak? Green beans? Mashed potatoes? Salad?"

"Let's skip the salad," Andie said decisively. After the evening they'd just had, she wanted her calories delivered as efficiently and indulgently as possible. Besides, on a frigid February evening, there was little that appealed less than the idea of chewing her way through a hedgerow's worth of greenery.

Rhys nodded and lit the broiler.

"You must have thought I was a complete ass," he mused as he busied himself with preparing the steaks and heating the side dishes. "And I don't blame you."

He shot her a chastened glance, spotlighted in the warm glow of the task lighting above the kitchen counter. "First I act like the big-shot CEO, refusing to return your calls, and then all of a sudden I'm bulldozing you into coming here."

Andie watched his hands as he seasoned and stirred. They were large and bronzed, with big, square palms, and fingers that were straight and capable. She imagined them wielding the paint roller down in the OT room, preparing the space for her to work with Will, and her throat thickened with emotion.

"You're not so bad," she said, looking up to find him watching her. She cleared her throat, her lips forming into a wry smile. "Although the media profiles had me a little concerned. Fancy acoustic panels and such."

"Oh, no, you didn't read the *Wired* article?" He stared at her in dismay as she gave an amused nod and whisked past him to find a pair of oven mitts to liberate the mashed potatoes from the microwave.

"Perks and Quirks at Zephyrus Mogul's Upscale Headquarters" the headline read. The journalist had gone to town with her descriptions of the amenities and upgrades Rhys had insisted on adding to the Zephyrus workspace. There had been a number of column inches devoted to a lingering meditation on the state-of-the-art, Swiss-imported curved ceiling panels he'd installed in the company's largest meeting rooms.

"Concert-hall-quality acoustics?" Andie teased.

"It was an emergency," Rhys explained. "I literally couldn't lead our all-hands meetings because the din was messing with my head. The sound of all those voices at once—it was like hot pincers being individually applied to every one of my synapses."

"That's quite an image." Andie regarded him quizzically, thinking how like Will he was, with his powerful sensory responses. Except that

Rhys had the power to enshrine his preferences in the very architecture of the Zephyrus offices.

"And the swanky game room?"

Rhys had reportedly given up the space initially earmarked for his own office—taking a modest interior office for himself—and turned it into an all-access gamer's paradise with sweeping harbor views.

"We're trying to attract the best minds out there. We have to compete with Google and all the really cool start-ups. Having a place to decompress is practically mandatory, and it helps the creative process."

"But what about your office?"

"I go inward when I'm working. Really working, I mean. I don't need a big space or expensive views."

According to the write-ups, Rhys eschewed traditional conference-table meetings and encouraged his staff to collaborate on the move. Rumor had it that there was an ad hoc cash bonus waiting for the employee who generated the best idea while hanging, batlike, from an inversion table in the gym. Andie stifled a smile as she reflected that, in many ways, Rhys had turned his company headquarters into a grand version of Will's OT room.

There were also company nap rooms, with individual sleep pods like a Japanese capsule hotel, and a complimentary laundry service for those stuck at the office after hours—a particular favorite with the single, workaholic city dwellers among the ranks. And it wasn't only about naps, video games, and free laundry. Andie had been impressed to read about the generous parental-leave policies Rhys handed down, including paid time off for parents to attend school meetings, field trips, and volunteer events. But she had to admit it was the colorful oddities that made the biggest splash.

"How about Blue Food Monday?" She couldn't resist.

Rhys smiled sheepishly, and Andie caught a glimpse of the child he once must have been.

"Can't a guy have a thing for blue food? I was on a creative bender that week, and I thought, *Why not set the caterers a challenge?*"

"Is it like the corporate equivalent of musicians demanding green M&M's in their dressing rooms?" Andie asked, realizing that the profiles she'd read on Rhys did indeed view him with a certain puzzled awe, as if the journalists were dazzled by the rock-star magnetism he exuded. His honed features and startling blue-smoke eyes probably accounted for a good part of their fascination.

"Not really," he laughed. "The media trots out the blue pasta, the acoustics, and the sleep pods when they want to paint me as a finicky eccentric, and maybe they're right. But why not make the most of the things you can control?"

Andie thought she could see purplish shadows gathering in the depths of his extraordinary eyes as he thought about the things he couldn't control. Namely, the reason why she was installed in the Griffiths household.

He plated their steaks and gestured to the array of warmed side dishes. They helped themselves, buffet-style, and carried their plates to a table bracketed by built-in banquettes. Rhys invited Andie to sit, and he retrieved a bottle of red wine and two glasses. His legs didn't quite brush hers as he settled on the bench opposite hers, but she could sense his every movement like it was etched on her skin.

"When did you first suspect it?" she asked. "Will's autism, I mean."

"Probably at about six months. Will was always more . . . explosive than other infants. I mean, they all cry and hate to be put down to sleep, but he was on a hair trigger. He would go on these legendary crying jags."

"His screams are so raw it hurts to listen to him," Andie said.

"I know." Rhys looked up, his tormented expression giving way to a kind of jaded humor. "Once he was crying in the background when I left a phone message, and Tom suggested patenting the recording and licensing it to the military as a weapon."

"I guess you have to laugh, sometimes."

"You do."

His vivid energy enveloped her, the air crackling with warmth and electricity, as he tilted the wine bottle and the ruby-dark liquid burbled pleasantly into her glass. She watched, conflicted. This meal was taking a path that led further from the solitary cup of Bovril than she'd meant to go.

She should probably shield her glass with her hand, protesting the idea of drinking alcohol with him—essentially drinking on the job— but something about his open expression made her hold her peace. It was kind of like taking a case history, she told herself. *Yeah, except case histories don't usually involve a generous glass of Merlot and a man with a lethal, scorched-earth charisma.*

"I kept finding reasons to reject the truth," Rhys admitted. "But I knew."

He swiped a restless hand across his brow and up through his hair in an unconscious gesture that left a clump of dark strands pointing skyward.

"By the time he turned one, he still had no interest in waving bye-bye or playing peekaboo. Sometimes when a stranger would make eye contact with him, he'd pull back like it caused him physical pain."

Rhys gave a tormented half smile.

"I was obsessed with those developmental checklists," he said. "I'd get e-mail updates on what Will was supposed to be able to do. I'd watch him like a hawk, and I'd fret and agonize."

"I sometimes send those checklists out to clients," she confessed. "With only the best intentions, of course."

"Some of the milestones were less black-and-white," he said. "I could fudge them a bit in my own mind, or round up. And he was doing some skills just fine."

"But there were no words," Andie said softly.

"No." His voice echoed. "I thought I could fix it. I thought that just by trying harder, taking him out more, talking to him, I could unblock the words. But they still wouldn't come. You should have seen me. I was a lunatic, carrying him around the neighborhood, frantically pointing and naming everything in sight. Performing a pantomime in front of his high chair at every meal. Grinning until my face hurt."

Andie took a remedial gulp of her wine, shaken by the pain etched in the tense lines of his face. Here was a man who appeared to the outside world to have everything—genius, success, and a combination of physical traits that was indecent for nature to bestow on one person. But he reveled in none of it, consumed, instead, with worry for the small boy who slept upstairs.

"Out in public, I'd see other families with toddlers who were pointing and chattering," he told her. "I'd follow them down the street, trying to figure out how old they were—why they were able to do something that was apparently so natural, and Will wasn't. I got a few strange looks, believe me."

Andie could imagine. Rhys was hardly inconspicuous. No doubt there would be plenty of eyebrows raised if he chose to tail a stranger's child down the street, hair standing on end, eyes blazing.

"Did you have anyone you could talk to?"

"Tom, of course, and my techie friends from MIT and my start-up days, but none of them have kids, and it was tough for them to understand what I was going through. I could have looked elsewhere for support, but the idea didn't appeal. I'm not much of a joiner."

"More of a lone wolf?" Andie suggested, his frankness touching her.

"That's one way of looking at it, I suppose," Rhys conceded. "I've been called lots of things. Odd, reclusive. Just plain weird. And I came in for much worse as a kid. But, yes, I've always been a bit of a loner."

"You were bullied?" Andie blinked. So much for Rhys's charmed life.

"Kids can be vicious, and I was goofy and awkward, at least until I grew into my height. Crazy good at math and science but dismal when it came to hand-eye coordination and girls."

Andie eyed him, unable to keep the incredulity from her face.

Rhys smiled. "Oh, I was a disaster, completely inept at reading the signals. I thought they actually wanted help with their quadratic equations. A touch of Asperger's, I'm pretty sure."

"Not diagnosed?"

"No, back then it wasn't a thing, and I might have flown under the radar even if people had been looking out for it."

"These days, it's so common."

"Yeah." Rhys gave a rueful laugh. "You walk into any tech company and you can't swing a cat without knocking over half a dozen engineers with Asperger's. They're my tribe, but it took me a long time to find them. And it made for some lonely years."

Andie nodded soberly. She understood loneliness. After Gus's death, it was almost as if her classmates could sense her parents' rejection of her, and they shunned her, too, like starlings avoiding a chick thrown from the nest. She let a sad smile tug at her lips as a thought bubbled up, unfiltered, from the depths of her memory.

"When I was a teenager, I used to love it when it rained," she blurted. "It was the only time I felt comfortable—knowing everyone was going about their business, separated by a wall of water. The heavier the better. That way, I wasn't the only one alone."

She swallowed, shocked that she'd let such an unguarded comment slip past her lips. It was as if something about Rhys's vulnerability gave her immediate access to her own. Either that or the wine was more potent than she thought. She fought to gather herself, but dark memories and powerful sensations shimmered perilously close to the surface.

～

Rhys looked at her searchingly. It was a curious image: the idea of a multitude of individuals shuffling around under their umbrellas, each one a roving oasis of dry space, separated by a transparent barrier. But he got it. The difference was he didn't feel the same unfulfilled longing she obviously did, the yearning to be a linked part of the larger whole. He might have when he was a child, confused as to why he was different. Shut out by his peers at school. But he'd made his way, thanks to the support of parents, who'd accepted his quirks, allowing his confidence to grow, along with his drive and ambition—paving the way for the friendships he'd eventually found at Vision, Inc., the start-up incubator where he and Noah, his engineering protégé from his postdoc teaching days at MIT, had worked to get Zephyrus Energy off the ground.

"I've always loved the rain, too," he said. "But I have to make an exception to the theory."

"Oh? What's that?"

"Well, when you're a parent, you automatically have someone else under your umbrella. It's a bond that's inviolable, rain or shine. And I can't imagine it changes until they're independent, out in the world. Maybe not even then."

He was startled at the expression that came over her. It was like a windshield in an explosion, a thousand cracks and fissures expanding across its surface. It was in her eyes, the set of her mouth, and her posture as she visibly bowed inward. He watched, fascinated, drawn in by the clarity of her pain, the sheer transparency of her emotions.

And that was when the rarest of sensations struck him: the conviction that he was in the presence of someone he could read. He couldn't shake the feeling that this was a person who wore no masks.

He'd been in grade school when he first learned that reading people was a necessary skill—one that had somehow been left out of his repertoire. Even now, he was sometimes so focused on the content of a person's speech that he failed to interpret the twitch of an eyebrow or the curl of a lip that was directly at odds with the spoken message. The world was—as the saying went—a stage, and he could never know for certain whether the player opposite was expressing an innate truth or inhabiting a role, telling him who they were and what they thought, or simply what they wanted him to hear.

With Andie, though, he sensed a breathtaking transparency. Perhaps it was her close acquaintance with solitude that had deprived her of the facility to conceal her emotions. Whatever it was, he'd never been able to understand anyone like this, never been made to *feel* like this while simply talking to another person—not even, at first, with Tom, or with the close-knit group of techies and scientists Tom affectionately referred to as the Visionaries. The sensation was like a hit of pure oxygen.

"Not all parents feel that way," she said, her voice strained.

Her eyes were huge, turbulent. Her cheeks flooded with deep color, making her look fifteen years old. The girl who loved the rain. He wanted to pull her under his own umbrella, shelter her from the callousness, the indifference, or whatever it was she'd faced from her own family.

It took him a few grinding seconds to go from intuiting to reacting. The psychological machinery was halting, rusty. "I'm sorry, Andie. There I go again. It's one of my faults, to assume my experience is universal. Tom is always taking me to task. I know it makes me an insensitive clod."

"No, it makes you a good father—that you can't imagine it any other way," Andie said. "It's as it should be."

He was still reeling, high on the sense of connection. Kind of ironic, given what they'd just been discussing. Was this what other people felt all the time? This immediate access to another's emotional state? It was an intimate topography he'd never had the opportunity to explore. He felt like a voyeur, a vampire, drinking in the unfamiliarity, the intensity of it. And if this was what it was like to share her pain, what kind of high would it be to share her happiness? Not that he was likely to find out. Not when he'd inserted his foot so firmly in his mouth he doubted he'd be able to extract it.

"Just ignore me," he mumbled, abashed. "I get a bit carried away sometimes."

He was the last person who should be spouting lofty ideas about parenthood, he reflected. After all, he'd failed to give Will the one gift he most wanted to provide: a happy home with two loving parents, like he'd had growing up.

"I lucked out in the parent department," he told her. "Which makes me privileged in ways that go beyond all of the stuff people usually think about." He gestured around him at the grand house.

"That doesn't surprise me," she said. "It's pretty clear you learned how to be a parent from people who knew how to do it right."

Rhys was speechless for a moment, struck by the generosity of her comment. Something in him burned to find out what made her experience so different from his—why that fathomless hurt lurked in her eyes—but he could sense her withdrawing from her spontaneous revelation. And yet the startling sense of connection remained.

"Tell me about your parents," she encouraged, her posture loosening as she ushered the conversation safely away from herself.

"Well, my dad is a bit of an oddball, like me," Rhys said fondly. "He's a professor in theoretical physics at Oxford."

There was no question where Rhys had inherited his mathematical, systematizing mind. His physics-professor father was endowed with striking aptitudes but without the social instinct that made human interaction second nature. Of course, he got by. And Rhys did, too. But, like his father, he had to work at it, grasping at social cues like a child snatching prize tickets out of the air in a carnival wind tunnel, certain that—all about him—important messages were fluttering to the floor unread.

"Wow, okay," Andie responded. "I don't know quite what to say to that. It's impressive."

"He's way out of my league," Rhys laughed. "It's hard to measure up to a father whose job is to understand the fundamental nature of matter. It's one of the reasons I moved to the US, to establish my own identity in a place where he doesn't cast such a long shadow."

"And your mom?"

"She's an English teacher. She's brilliant, in a different way. It's always been her job to run interference between my dad and the rest of the world, to act as his translator."

In truth, his mother, Diana, had performed that role for Rhys as well. Both he and his father reveled in the abstract, able to pick complex patterns out of data, to envision sophisticated theoretical models in three dimensions. His dad, Simon, could construct algorithms from thin air but couldn't navigate a cocktail party to save his life. His bookshelves were littered with many of the highest awards granted in his field, but he became helpless at the first whiff of department politics. Diana navigated all that for him, helped him through it, in her frank, insightful way.

"They sound like a great pair," Andie said with a shy smile. She looked wistful, but her distress had retreated. Maybe it was the effect of the wine, but his gaze was drawn to the soft curves of her lips—the lower one full and pillowy, the upper one a classic bow. He admired the silky weight of her loose, wavy hair as it snaked over her shoulders and tumbled halfway down her back. He could imagine the cool brush of it against his fingers and how it would contrast with the hot satin of her cheek.

She was so pretty it was almost like an optical illusion. He blinked, and waited for her image to resolve itself again, the planes and angles, crests and hollows of her face resuming their ideal form beneath his gaze. Exactly as he would have designed them if his eye for form and symmetry extended beyond the realm of physics and engineering, and into the divine. He couldn't believe she was sitting across from him, in his kitchen, digging into her mashed potatoes.

Nothing felt more important in that moment than to keep her there, smiling that tentative smile. So Rhys told her about his childhood growing up in the Teifi Valley in southwest Wales, with its emerald grass and low gray skies. About the crumbling former rectory that was his family home, a money pit his parents could never quite bear to sell, despite the necessity of their being in Oxford for much of the year. And about the gut-wrenching trips he'd taken with Will each Christmas since his birth, trying—not always with great success—to manage his outbursts on the transatlantic flight.

"It must be hard, doing it all alone," Andie remarked.

"I can't complain. Most of the time I'm lucky enough to have reinforcements." Rhys shrugged. "Mrs. Hodge, for one. She might seem like a bit of a curmudgeon, but she loves Will like family.

"And, for better or worse—" He broke off for a moment, not having planned to confide in her about Karina's return but suddenly compelled to do so. "Will's mother has actually made a surprise reappearance."

"Oh?"

"I heard today that she's back in the area, and she wants to meet, and I'm not altogether sure why. She walked out when he was barely six months old, and I'm not putting him through that again."

"What are you going to do?" Andie's eyes were wide, her curiosity mixed with concern.

"I'm meeting with her at a café in town tomorrow morning. I can't let her near Will until I know what she's up to, so I'm not comfortable with her coming to the house."

"You have full custody?"

"Yes. It was a clear-cut case of abandonment. She bailed on us without a backward glance. I tried several times to get her to come back for Will's sake, but the most contact I've had with her since then is through Tom sending legal documents back and forth to California."

"What do you think she wants?"

What, indeed? Rhys tried to douse the spark of unease in his gut with a smooth mouthful of Merlot. "I really couldn't guess."

"Is there anything I can do to help?"

"I'm expecting Mrs. Hodge back midmorning to look after Will while I meet with Karina, so no. But thank you." He smiled, trying to convince both himself and Andie that he was calm in the face of whatever potential crisis his ex-wife might manufacture. "I'm not about to rope you into an impromptu babysitting gig on your first morning here. Besides, I'm sure you'll be plenty busy setting up for Will's OT sessions."

"I can't wait."

Her smile reoriented him, drawing his focus mercifully away from the apprehension that filled him at the thought of Karina's return.

He glanced down at his plate. He had worked his way through his side dishes as they talked, but his steak still sat there untouched. He hadn't even been aware of eating the rest, so distracted was he by the novel experience of being the most talkative person in the room.

"What's wrong?" Andie asked. "You don't like your steak?" Her own plate was bare, Rhys noted approvingly. He could never understand people who picked nervously at their food, as if it was liable to jump up and throttle them.

"Something's missing," he said. He went to rummage in the fridge, coming back to the table with three of his favorite brands of hot sauce: one from Vietnam, another from Jamaica, and a third from Louisiana.

"Sorry, I should have put these out before," he said. "I was distracted, I guess."

Resuming his seat, he worked intently, dropping large dollops of all three types of sauce on his steak in a combination that looked like a Jackson Pollock painting, until he was startled by a strange hiccup from Andie's side of the table.

She was laughing, and it was as heady a sensation as he remembered from their shared mirth over the contents of her suitcase. The pitch of it zipped through his blood, and the air felt warmer, denser, as she flung her head back, exposing the creamy expanse of her throat.

"What's so funny?" he asked, his voice tight with longing.

"You're just like Will," she told him, her eyes flashing gold and green. "With your bare feet and your hot-sauce habit, you're definitely a sensory seeker."

"A sensory seeker, huh?" he pondered, taking in the translucence of her skin, the high color in her cheeks, and the small dimple at the left side of her mouth. "Okay, you might be right about that." More right than she could possibly know, he realized uncomfortably. It was something he was going to have to watch.

CHAPTER SIX

It took Andie several moments to orient herself when she woke the next morning, cushioned by the sumptuous pillow-top mattress in her room, savoring the unaccustomed smoothness of high-thread-count sheets. Her bed at home was utilitarian by comparison. Trust Rhys to own sheets that delivered nothing less than an indulgent sensory experience. But she had no business thinking about her new boss's taste in sheets. The previous night's dinner had done nothing to bolster the professional barrier she intended to preserve between herself and Rhys. From now on she'd do better, starting with giving him a wide berth for the rest of the weekend.

Drifting back to sleep was an appealing option. She'd been roused by one of Will's night awakenings at about 3:00 a.m., staggering sleepily into the corridor to offer to help soothe him back down, only to be urged back to bed by a contrite Rhys.

She'd just fallen back into a blissful doze when a jarring noise penetrated her warm cocoon. The insistent chime of a doorbell sounded, once, twice, and then, after a brief pause, clanged repeatedly, as if someone were leaning on the button. The noise was sure to disturb Will, even if he was already awake. So why wasn't anyone answering the door?

Perhaps Rhys had already left for his meeting and Mrs. Hodge was busy with Will. Maybe it was an overzealous deliveryman, in which case it would be mean-spirited not to answer, now that she was awake.

As the ringing continued, she swung her legs over the side of the bed and padded out into the corridor, pulling her striped flannel pajama top closed over her camisole tank. Still groggy, she made her way down the stairs. The black-and-white checkerboard marble was cold underfoot as she shuffled to the front door. In her sleepy haze, it was all she could do to push the unruly strands of her hair back from her face before reaching for the door and tugging it open.

A woman who looked to be in her late twenties—very close to her own twenty-eight, if she had to guess—stood framed in the doorway. She was clad head to toe in stylish black, a shade that emphasized eyes of fiery ice blue—reminiscent of a Siberian wolf, glacial and assessing. The smile on the woman's lips faded quickly as she took in the spectacle Andie presented: rumpled pajamas, flyaway hair, bare feet. The stranger herself was immaculate, from the high collar of her wool cape to the tips of her slim boots. A glossy curtain of straight, dark hair flowed past her shoulders.

The machinery of her thoughts clogged with sleep, Andie struggled for context. The obvious answer was that this was Rhys's ex-wife. But Rhys had been clear that he and Karina were meeting in town, not at the house. In fact, he'd stated outright that he wasn't comfortable having her anywhere in Will's vicinity.

The woman's eyes narrowed as she looked Andie up and down and then craned to see past her, that startling, pale gaze scanning what could be seen of the more-distant reaches of the house. For a moment she looked almost crestfallen when her search turned up no further signs of life. No one but Andie—awkward, tongue-tied, and rather wishing she'd decided not to answer the summons of the doorbell.

"Can I help you?"

"Is Rhys in?" The smile was back, brittle and ominous, and the woman took one step over the threshold, casting an incredulous look at Andie's flannel pajamas, apparently perplexed as to how such a dowdy creature could be taking up space in Rhys's house.

Was this a current girlfriend of Rhys's? She was, aesthetically speaking, the kind of woman Andie could picture with him. A world-class beauty. In which case, should Andie clarify her role here? And should she try to avoid mentioning that he was meeting with his ex? *Domestic politics.* Just one more reason why taking up residence in the Griffiths house had probably been a big mistake. The woman took another step forward, forcing her to yield yet more ground, and Andie was enveloped by a distinctive scent—the seductive sweetness of jasmine, combined with a more piquant note that reminded her of Earl Grey tea. *Bergamot.*

She straightened, squaring her shoulders. She wasn't going to allow herself to be cowed by this woman, no matter who she was.

"You'd better wait here," she said decisively. "I'll see if I can find Rhys."

She turned on her heel but broke in midstride. She should probably get the woman's name, at least.

"And who should I say is looking for him?" The question came out rather artlessly, Andie had to admit, but it hardly justified the boiling rage that surged behind the woman's eyes, almost as if she were affronted at not being instantly recognized and given her due. An awful, sinking feeling tugged at the pit of Andie's stomach. *Maybe this is Karina, after all.*

"You can *say* it's his wife," the woman snapped.

"Ex-wife." Rhys's retort cracked like a whiplash, reverberating in the expansive space as he emerged into the foyer from the garage stairway, wiping his hands on a greasy rag. He bore down on the surprise visitor, his expression thunderous.

"Ah, there you are, Rhys. Aren't you going to welcome me back?"

"Karina." Rhys shook his head in disbelief. "What the hell do you think you're doing here?"

"We're meeting this morning," Karina responded blithely. "Or had you forgotten?"

"You're an hour—and three-quarters of a mile—off target."

"Well, you know how busy that café gets. There were no tables, so I thought a slight venue adjustment might be in order."

"A slight . . . venue adjustment?" Rhys's jaw was so tight it was apparently a struggle to get the words out. His gaze slid to the upper floors of the house, in the direction of Will's room.

"Well, now that I'm here . . . ?" Karina gave a charming smile, seeming to blossom in the glare of Rhys's irritation. This was a game she obviously enjoyed.

Andie caught the sound of tires crunching on gravel and looked out to see Mrs. Hodge, back from Connecticut, pulling up to the house.

"Now that you're here, you can turn right back around and keep the arrangement we agreed to," Rhys told Karina. "Get your car, and I'll be a few minutes behind you."

Accepting no argument, he crossed in front of his ex-wife and swung the door open. A muscle pulsed near his jaw as he stood and waited pointedly for her to take his cue. After several pregnant moments, the woman gave a long-suffering sigh and stalked out.

"Sorry about that," he said to Andie once the sound of footfalls had retreated. "I didn't mean for you to get dragged into this. I should have guessed it would be beyond her power to resist showing up here."

"I'm fine," she assured him.

"I hoped you'd be able to get some sleep, after last night. You're probably not used to being woken up by toddler screams at three a.m."

"Don't worry about it. I went right back to sleep afterward."

"I was fiddling around down in the garage just now. Trying to psych myself up for this meeting." He scrubbed absentmindedly at the back of his hand with the rag he still held. "I was thinking about giving that jalopy of yours a once-over. Wouldn't want it breaking down in the wilds of suburbia. That okay with you?"

"Um, sure," Andie agreed. "Why not?"

Rhys gave a satisfied nod. "I'd better get cleaned up and deal with this." He gestured vaguely to the driveway as his ex-wife started up her car.

"Good luck."

"Thanks. I may need it."

~

By the time Rhys reached the café and patisserie that sat across from the commuter rail tracks in Concord's town center, the first morning rush had dispersed. He hurried into the warmth of the store—redolent with the aroma of coffee and croissants—his collar turned up against the icy blasts of air that howled under the awning.

He spotted Karina at a corner table and bristled like a herding dog scenting a predator in his territory. It was hard to believe she'd had the gall to show up at the house. His skin prickled at the idea of her coming face-to-face with Will. Until he knew why she'd come back, there was no way he was letting her near his son.

He was also unsettled by her brief confrontation with Andie. His first instinct, upon hearing their voices and emerging to find them at the front door, had been to fling himself between them, covering Andie before Karina detonated whatever piece of nastiness she had up her sleeve. The "wife" comment was an effective opener, but he sensed she'd just been warming up. Andie's arrival at the house had sparked a tenuous but infinitely precious flicker of hope for the advent of something good and positive in his and Will's lives. It was too soon to have that small flame smothered by Karina's demands and misrepresentations.

"I had no say in how you walked out of Will's life," he said, marching up to the table. "But I will damn well have a say in how, and whether, you get to walk back in."

"Have a seat, Rhys." She had already procured their coffees—a cappuccino for her and a shot of espresso for him. Just like old times.

He sat stiffly, his hackles still raised.

"You shouldn't have come to the house."

Karina shrugged. "This place was mobbed. You know my motto: 'Always have a plan B.'"

Rhys's head began to throb. Yes, he knew his ex-wife's motto all too well. Brittle, paranoid, and unaccountably insecure for one so brilliant and beautiful, Karina had always felt the need to shore up her position by hedging her bets. Try as he might to read her cues and provide ample reinforcement, she'd apparently never felt certain in his affections.

At first, he'd been too besotted to mind the grandiose fights she staged—the constant accusations of infidelity. He'd actually been charmed at first, thinking it a symptom of their passion. Lust and adrenaline were a volatile mixture, sweeping him along on a runaway roller-coaster ride as he'd clung on for dear life, drunk on terror and uncertainty. But that was no way to live, and it wasn't real love. He later found out that she'd started an affair with Lance Bello just six months into their relationship. *Her plan B.*

"What happened to us?" Karina mused, with her usual impeccable timing. Over the rim of her coffee cup, her preternaturally blue eyes gleamed.

Rhys felt a blood vessel bulge at his temple. "Well, you might recall, you walked out on me and our son . . ."

He stared across the table at the woman who had borne his child. It seemed so unreal that the two of them, almost strangers to each other now, had created his beautiful boy. Their relationship had already tolled its death knell by the time he learned he was to be a father. Several weeks after he'd broken things off with Karina, she showed up on his doorstep with the news that changed everything. *A baby.*

As it turned out, the child was his, and—no matter what the emotional climate between them—he'd been determined to support her, to make it work. He proposed to her, hoping that such an irrefutable signal of his commitment would be enough to reinforce their perpetually ravaged peace. And he bought her the house on Monument Street. But even its sizable footprint was apparently not enough to finally help her feel anchored. Safe.

He took a bracing sip of espresso. "Plenty has happened to us," he said, striving to keep his tone level. "But even more has happened to Will, who never asked to be brought into this mess we created between us. So let's just focus on his best interests, okay?"

"You're talking about his diagnosis?" Karina leaned forward in her seat, her expression avid.

"How did you find out?" Unease clawed at him and would not let go.

"Well, it should have been from you," Karina huffed. "But apparently you thought it was appropriate to tell practically everyone at your company before you informed your son's mother."

Ah. It was true that most of the engineers at Zephyrus were his friends, and Rhys had done nothing to conceal his struggles from them. He'd met many of them when he and Karina were both at MIT, and she'd presumably retained her links with some of them.

She was entitled to keep her friends in the wake of the divorce. But it was unsettling that she still had a direct line to connections that wove throughout the fabric of his current life. Not that he could be angry that someone had told her about Will. He hadn't sworn anyone to secrecy, and they probably made the reasonable assumption that she knew.

"You're right," he conceded. "It wasn't what I intended to have happen. I've been pretty shaken up about this whole thing. The diagnosis hit me hard, and I suppose I wanted to get my head on straight before I broke the news to you. I'm sorry."

"Tell me, Rhys. Tell me about Will. I need to know about my son."

My son? There she goes again. But Rhys decided to let it pass. It was the most interest she'd ever shown in Will, after all.

"Will is wonderful," Rhys said. "He's sweet, affectionate, strong willed. And so beautiful that once you look at him, your eyes are spoiled for anything else."

To her credit, Karina smiled, her expression wistful.

"But how is he affected by his autism?" she asked. "What does he do? What can't he do?"

"I'll be honest," said Rhys. "Sometimes it seems like he feels the whole world as an assault. Often he'll disappear inside himself to some place I can't reach him, where he can't even hear me call his name."

"And he doesn't talk at all?"

Rhys gave a guarded smile. "A few weeks ago, that would have been correct."

"But he's started speaking?"

"Yes—one word," he told her, watching her face. Now was his chance to signal, in no uncertain terms, Andie's vital place in Will's world.

"What is it?" Karina's eyes were wide with curiosity.

"It's 'Andie,'" he said briskly. "The name of the woman you tried to scare away this morning when you arrived at my front door."

He wasn't sure quite how to interpret the subtle narrowing of her eyes and the miniscule twitch of a muscle at her jawline.

"So our son said your girlfriend's name before he said yours?"

She sure knew how to go for the jugular.

"Andie is an occupational therapist, not my girlfriend," he said. "She's been able to reach Will in ways no one else has."

"And you have her installed at the house? How convenient." Karina licked cappuccino foam from her full upper lip, clearly not buying Rhys's demurral.

Rhys ignored her snarky comment and pressed on with what mattered.

"Even with her intervention, and the best speech and behavioral therapists in the area, Will's progress is going to be slow. His autism spectrum disorder is severe. Andie is starting a new regimen with him. She'll be working with him every day, as a supplement to his therapeutic preschool and other supports."

Karina leaned forward in her seat. "That's all very well, Rhys, to have all these strangers working with Will, but *I* want to be in my son's life. I want to get to know him. I want him to know who I am. Shouldn't Will's main attachments be to his parents?"

"That would be difficult, considering you washed your hands of him and have been three thousand miles away for the majority of his life so far," Rhys pointed out. "Will has had to depend on a different kind of family. Those he can count on to stick around."

"I deserve that," Karina conceded. "But I'm serious, Rhys. I want to get to know Will. I plan to stay in Massachusetts and see where it goes."

"You'll 'see where it goes'?" Rhys choked the words out. "You come barging back in here with some vague intention of perhaps following through? You'll forgive me if I'm not jumping at the chance to let you see Will, based on that kind of assurance."

"I know you're angry," Karina said, a tinge of pink appearing around her eyelids and at the tip of her nose. "And you're right to be angry. But I wasn't myself after Will was born. You remember how detached I was? How irritable?"

"Yes," Rhys responded cautiously. He would never forget her agitation, the tension that vibrated through her, her reluctance to hold the newborn Will, and the near panic that clutched her at the idea of being pinned down to the drudgery of breast-feeding. She'd seemed disoriented, almost wired, and consumed with jumping straight back into her academic work without so much as a pause to draw breath. It was Rhys who cradled Will in the quiet hours, feeding him his bottle and gazing into wide blue eyes of such heart-stopping beauty that everything else in the world fell away.

"I couldn't handle it," she sighed. "Being responsible for this tiny, perfect creature. It was hard to believe he actually came from my own body. It was too much."

Karina paused, darting him a tremulous glance. "You know about . . . postpartum depression?"

Rhys nodded. He felt a pang of compassion for her. Not enough to displace the smarting pain he felt on Will's behalf but enough to admit a new dimension of understanding. A sense of puzzle pieces falling into place.

It wasn't as if his behavior toward Karina during those critical months after Will's birth would have helped her mental state. He'd been business-like, polite, but not emotionally supportive. Because she'd broken his trust, in more ways than one. He should have been better than that, he thought with chagrin. More perceptive. More considerate. And he might have been, if he hadn't been so panicked by her rejection of Will.

"I wasn't in my right mind," she said. "I made a mistake. A terrible mistake. And I hope one day you'll find it in your heart to forgive me."

"My forgiveness is irrelevant. You disappeared when Will was *this big*." His hands shaped the ghost of a six-month-old Will. "You know he'll be three in a few months?"

"That's why it's so important that I'm here now. He needs his mother."

If only you'd come around to that conviction two years ago. Now it all smacked of too little, too late. And there was something about her abject demeanor that just didn't sit right. He wanted to believe she was sincere, but he'd fallen for her faux remorse too many times. Where Karina was concerned, he could no longer afford to take anything on faith. She would need to demonstrate her newfound commitment to Will through actions. Words were no longer enough.

"How are things with Bello?" Rhys asked, not really wanting to know the answer.

"We broke up," Karina admitted. "It started going wrong almost as soon as we got to Palo Alto."

Her eyes darted to where Rhys's right hand rested on the table, his index finger loosely hooked through the handle of his espresso cup.

"I realized . . ." She gave a theatrical sniff, her eyes shimmering. "I realized it was never about Lance. You were always the main event, Rhys. I'll admit, I used Lance as a weapon to hurt you and to prop myself up when I felt you turning away from me. But that's all he was to me. A sideshow to the only thing that really mattered—my relationship with you."

Her words sounded rehearsed. But Rhys was distracted from parsing her argument by a strange tickle on his lower arm. It was only when he was able to tear his horrified gaze away from her face that he realized her hands had crept forward and she was touching him, tracing seductive little trails over the underside of his wrist.

"What the hell are you doing?" He snatched his hand away, his skin smarting as if he'd been stung.

"I realized what's important," she continued, undaunted. "It's you and Will. I know that now."

She looked up from under her lashes, the luminous, overchlorinated blue of her eyes making her expression seem almost contrived.

"We meant something to each other once," she said, her tone soft and packed full of contrition. "Maybe one day we could again."

Is this what she was like all along? How could I have been taken in by her? He had to suppress a shocked tingle of admiration at her sheer nerve. She'd always known how to play to her strengths. Even now, she made a compelling picture as she sat across the table from him, her eyes large and tragic, her curtain of smooth dark hair making a bold backdrop for the riveting tableau of her face. Her lips trembled subtly as she heaved a ragged sigh and gazed toward the window, the harsh wintry light lending drama to her profile.

He'd been sympathetic when she alluded to her struggle with postpartum depression. But Karina never knew how to quit when she was ahead. She was always intent on pushing for more. Her assertions about their relationship were so preposterous that they called into question everything else she'd said. Any attempt to rebuild a romantic connection between them could be nothing but a farce. What mattered now was Will.

"I'll always be grateful for our relationship because it produced Will," Rhys said, trying for diplomacy. "But I think we both know better than to think there could ever be any more between us now than a shared interest in his well-being."

Karina's throat convulsed, the motion accentuated by the stark light pouring through the café window, and she turned back to face him, her expression raw.

"But can't we—"

"No, we can't," Rhys said firmly.

"I see." Her eyes flashed dangerously before she feigned a sudden interest in the dregs of her cappuccino. When she looked up at him again, her face was composed, the set of her lips righteous. She'd regained her pristine mask, which guarded her responses while broadcasting a calculated set of signals.

He thought back to the previous night at dinner, to the sheer relief of sitting across from Andie, freed from the maddening confusion that so often sabotaged his interactions. With her, there had been no delicate juggling act, no weighing words against facial expressions, no painstakingly fine-tuning his interpretations based on nuances of tone. He'd been able to just be, and somehow he could read her anyway. Andie's face was an open book.

"I *had* hoped we could come to some sort of agreement so I can at least get to know Will, but I can see now you're determined to make this difficult," Karina said crisply, jolting his attention back to the matter at hand. "Although I am a little surprised, as I'm sure you'd prefer to avoid going through the courts?"

Rhys blinked, trying to keep hold of his reaction as alarm surged beneath his skin. It would be a mistake to underestimate his ex-wife.

"It's never been my intention to keep you from Will," he said, making his tone calm and deliberate. "You'll remember how I pleaded with you to come back from California."

It was true. He'd always intended for Will to have both of his parents around. When Karina left, he'd been single-minded about it—prepared to declare a truce and swallow his pride just to bring her back into Will's orbit. But Karina had refused, and now everything in him protested the idea of exposing Will to her. Will enjoyed a stable, well-ordered life, filled with affection. The last thing he needed was an infusion of Karina's brand of volatility.

He had to be strategic, however. He needed to prevent her from escalating her demands.

He passed a restless hand across his face, pressing blunt fingertips to tired eyes.

"I'll think about it," he told her. "But if I do agree to let you see Will, it's going to be on my terms. No more showing up at my house unannounced. That was a violation of my privacy, not to mention that of the rest of my household."

She tensed, absorbing his words like a blow, and he wondered whether his last comment had been ill-judged. When she narrowed those crystalline blue eyes a fraction, he was sure of it.

"Of course," she conceded prettily, but there was something brittle in the smile she flashed as she set down her empty cup. Her expression reverberated through him like stress fractures spreading across the icy surface of a pond, and it occurred to him that danger and fragility were not opposites but mutually reinforcing states. His ex-wife was a study in both, and he'd be a fool to forget it.

CHAPTER SEVEN

Karina had barely stalked off down Thoreau Street when Rhys pulled out his phone.

"How did it go?" Tom asked, as Rhys watched the woman's slim, dark shape disappear around the corner.

"It was about as disturbing as you might expect. It looks like she's back here to stay for a while, and she's determined to get access to Will."

"What did she say?"

"Well, she's already mentioned going to court. Of course, she might have been bluffing or saying it just to get a rise out of me."

"That wouldn't surprise me."

"How worried should I be? Can she really do anything?"

"She *can* file for parenting time or a change in custody."

"She can?" Rhys fought the urge to open his door and retch into the gutter.

"Well, she can try. But she'd have to show a significant change in circumstances. And it would be a tall order for her to prove Will's current arrangement isn't meeting his best interests."

"Bloody hell, Tom. I thought we were watertight on this." Even a hint of risk felt like a deluge.

"Don't panic. She'd have to have a good angle. Abandonment is a steep hurdle for her to overcome."

"How about postpartum depression?" Rhys said bleakly. He had visions of her barreling in with a team of experts claiming she'd signed away custody of Will in a postpartum fugue state and was now asserting her parental rights. He couldn't let that happen. He wouldn't. "She's already forming her argument. She wasn't in her right mind at the time, and so forth. What am I going to do?"

"I wouldn't freak out just yet."

"That's your considered legal advice? Don't freak out?"

"Yeah, it is, actually."

Rhys didn't know whether to feel relieved or riled by his friend's calm tone.

"Come on, Tom."

"Seriously. She'd have to prove she's settled back here and making a go of it. A house. Gainful employment. Stability. That sort of thing. And, you know, solid, dogged application is not Karina's strong suit."

No, Tom was right. Impulsivity, instant rewards, and shortcuts were more to her taste. Which was not exactly reassuring when he thought about her spending time with Will.

"She wants to see Will sooner rather than later."

"You should probably humor her. The courts don't like it when the custodial parent tries to cut the other parent completely out of the picture. Unless there's a very good reason."

"Is not being out of my mind a good enough reason?"

"Just take it slow," Tom soothed. "Supervise. With Karina, it's impossible to know whether this is a temporary whim or serious intent."

"Neither one sounds terribly encouraging, to be honest." But, yes. He would do as his friend advised and set up some visits under terms he could live with. At the library or the indoor playground. Neutral ground. He'd think of it as an inoculation. Measuring out Karina's interactions with Will in limited, supervised doses to prevent the situation from veering out of his control. An unpleasant jab but worth it in the long run.

"Oh, and Tom?"

"Yes?"

"Keep your ear to the ground, would you? Karina still has some friends at the company, apparently. Someone told her about Will's diagnosis before I had a chance to. Probably one of the engineers she knows from way back. It worries me."

"Say no more," Tom said. "I'll see what I can find out."

"Thanks, mate."

Rhys pulled his car away from the curb and shot off toward Monument Street, spurred on by a piercing eagerness to have Will within his sight again.

~

Andie took refuge in her room and the OT gym for much of Sunday, unable to wipe the penetrating stare of Rhys's ex from her mind. The woman was beautiful, assertive, and clearly back to stake her claim. It was a good thing, Andie told herself. Anything that took her mind off the surprising rapport she felt with Rhys was surely a positive development. If Karina had come to her senses and realized she belonged with her child and his father, then who was Andie to argue? True, she couldn't love Karina's manner or what she knew of the woman's history with Rhys and Will. But, after all she'd been through, Andie was a staunch proponent of second chances. At least the woman's fierce possessiveness upon finding Andie at the door suggested deep-seated feelings for her erstwhile husband.

Andie tried to ignore the sharp frisson of disquiet she felt every time she remembered the pale fire of Karina's stare. Her discomfort was surely due to the fact that the woman had mistakenly pegged her as a rival—an assumption so outlandish that it made her head swim.

Presumably Karina's hostile attitude would shift once she began to make amends and bond with her son.

Rhys had confided in Andie in general terms about the outcome of the café meeting, and she knew a visit among Karina, Will, and Rhys was on the horizon. Not that Rhys seemed terribly happy about the development.

As Sunday turned into Monday and the workweek began, it wasn't her handsome employer who was the most visible presence in the house but the ubiquitous Mrs. Hodge. Margaret Euphemia Hodge, to be exact. Her full name was an intimate tidbit Andie never would have known had it not been inscribed on the bookplate inside the cover of a Brother Cadfael mystery left in the TV room. And it was a detail that didn't immediately leap to mind when she lurched blearily into the small upstairs kitchen on Monday morning, eager to make her coffee, only to find that the room seemed to have blossomed overnight with a profusion of little yellow sticky notes, all bearing the insignia *MEH*.

At first, in her sleepy haze, she thought the nanny was offering a lukewarm review of the contents of the kitchen. *"How do you like that marmalade?" "Meh—I could take it or leave it . . ."* But, as the coffee machine gurgled and hissed, depositing its dark nectar into her mug, the obvious finally dawned on her: the woman was staking her claim to the objects marked with yellow flags.

Apparently, by doctoring her cup with milk from the open container she found in the fridge when she'd first arrived at the house, Andie had crossed some kind of line. And she was quickly learning that, in the world of Margaret Euphemia Hodge, lines were in plentiful supply.

There were lines marking off mealtime, playtime, naptime, and therapy time for Will—lines that set the contours of each day. There was also a line for personal space, and a line for acquaintanceship, which—as far as the woman's relationship with Andie was concerned—apparently stopped far short of first-name familiarity. But the biggest line drawn by Mrs. Hodge was the one that separated Rhys from the rest of the household.

"Mr. Griffiths is a very busy man," the older woman confided in hushed, reverent tones as she and Andie crossed paths in the small kitchen while Will spent the morning in his new behavioral therapy–based preschool program.

"I like to think we, the household staff, play a small but critical role in making his lot easier," Mrs. Hodge opined.

Andie balked for a second, pausing in the act of raising her mug—filled with black coffee—to her lips. Her egalitarian streak throbbed painfully at the upstairs-downstairs hierarchy that governed this woman's view of the world.

But, on second thought, wasn't that exactly what Andie wanted: to cordon herself off from the seductive intimacy of the little family unit Rhys and Will presented? If her professional veneer wasn't proof against their charms, then maybe Mrs. Hodge's caste-based schema would provide extra reinforcement. Whenever she was a bit too taken by Rhys's smile, she could remind herself to get her upstart butt back down to the scullery to black the stove, or whatever it was the residents "below stairs" still had to do in the declining years of the British Empire.

"That's what we're here for," Andie agreed staunchly.

"Lord knows he has enough to worry about, running that company of his." Mrs. Hodge let her teaspoon ding-ding-ding against the porcelain walls of her teacup as she stirred in a cube of sugar. The aroma of bergamot drifted in the tail of steam that curled lazily from the dainty cup, conjuring the image of Rhys's ex, as if the ghost of her presence still lingered in the house.

When Mrs. Hodge finally raised the cup to her lips, she had a faraway look in her eyes. Perhaps she was caught up in the image of herself as some kind of domestic goalkeeper, preventing the bothersome details of daily life from hurtling into Rhys's net so he could focus on his greater role in the public sphere.

"Um, how did you come to live here and work for the Griffiths family?" Andie asked. "Clearly there's the English connection, but . . ."

"I trained as a Broad Haven nanny," Mrs. Hodge said with a beatific smile, as if Andie should instantly understand the significance. "For the early part of my career, I worked on a large estate in Suffolk, for an earl and his family."

The woman paused, scanning Andie's face as if to monitor it for the appropriate level of awe. Andie pasted on a polite smile. She had watched William and Kate's wedding. *How could I pass up the fashion commentary?* And she'd leafed through pictures of their growing family in the gossip rags at the supermarket checkout, but she knew precious little about the ranks of British nobility. *Are earls still a thing?*

"You've been with Will since almost the very beginning," Andie said. "It must have been upsetting for you as well when his diagnosis came through."

Mrs. Hodge drew herself up to her full height and regarded Andie with a suspicious look.

"Yes, well, these medical fads have a way of working themselves out, don't they?" she said briskly. "One month all behavior problems can be chalked up to attention-deficit whatsit, and the next month it's autism. All the wee ones really need is a good, firm hand and a chance to learn a bit of self-control."

"I . . . dah." Andie was reduced to incoherence as Mrs. Hodge reached for an orange, yellow, and blue cellophane package on the counter—"Hobnobs," according to the brightly colored plastic. The woman shook two cookies from their nesting place and laid them delicately on her saucer, before heading for the TV room.

"My cousin Ronnie didn't talk until he was almost four," she said, pausing in the doorway, "and from that moment on, one couldn't get a word in edgeways. Never did him any harm. Although he did turn out to be a confirmed bachelor . . ."

She raised her eyebrows ominously and disappeared, the sound of her footfalls soon replaced by the soft murmur of the television.

All the breath whooshed out of Andie's body as she doubled over, swallowing a bubble of incredulous laughter. *Did that really just happen?*

Jillian, the other weekday inhabitant of the house, was a sporty dynamo of a woman with a sandy-blonde ponytail and an exercise tracker strapped to her wrist. Her daughter had just gotten engaged, she confided to Andie, and she and her husband were engaged in a friendly weight-loss duel so they could cut a dash at the wedding as the proud parents of the bride. She'd worked for Rhys since before Will was born, she told Andie as she organized the contents of the large, stainless-steel fridge, getting in a few extraneous squats and lunges along the way.

Andie took to her immediately. The woman's cheery energy seemed to chase the shadows out of the huge house. It was reassuring to see her at random times during the day, power walking behind the vacuum cleaner or bustling back and forth to the laundry room, which was right next to the OT gym. Jillian's salt-of-the-earth practicality helped Andie rein herself in when her anxiety started to skyrocket.

Sometimes she'd walk through one of the large, elegantly furnished rooms and stand sniffing for a moment, utterly convinced she could detect mysterious notes of jasmine and bergamot in the air. She would turn suddenly, heart racing, expecting to be confronted by a flashing pair of aquamarine eyes. But, every time, her fears would prove unfounded, as Jillian or Mrs. Hodge would pace by, or Andie would find herself spooked by nothing more than an empty room. It was Mrs. Hodge's Earl Grey tea that was playing tricks with her, she decided, and maybe a touch of guilt as well. Because, try as she might, she couldn't completely suppress her ill-advised admiration for her new employer, even with the specter of his ex-wife looming so large in the shadows.

On Thursday evening, Andie and Mrs. Hodge were sitting together in the large downstairs kitchen, attending Will as he finished his dinner, when Rhys strode in.

"Tonight, we tackle the bath," he announced, looking exquisitely handsome in a slate-gray suit offset by a crisp white shirt that brought out the warm tones of his skin. A magnetic shiver pulsed down Andie's spine as everything in her oriented toward him like a compass to north.

"A suit today," she commented, used to seeing him come and go from work in his usual jeans and button-down shirts. Now he looked almost as he had in the *Forbes* spread she'd pored over before they'd met. She remembered how she'd thought him so fierce and imposing, the dramatic lighting and cavernous space of the warehouse backdrop emphasizing the chasm that separated him from ordinary mortals. How different that man was from the Rhys she'd seen with Will—so tender and indulgent.

"Board meeting," he explained with a self-deprecating smile that did strange things to her insides. The scent of night air, citrus, and warm skin washed over her as he leaned in close to unlock the high-chair tray and scoop Will into his arms.

Will pressed against Rhys's chest, his solid little body relaxing into home base. His small hands fluttered around his father's face like doves released from their cage, gently pecking and brushing Rhys's stubbly chin and the crisp, dark waves of his hair. Immersed in the rich textures, Will chortled with glee.

"You're off the hook for bathtime tonight, Mrs. Hodge," Rhys said. "Andie and I are going to see if we can figure out how to deal with Will's aversion to water."

"Well, if you think that's a good use of your time, Mr. Griffiths." The nanny sniffed. "I'm more than happy to soldier on as I have been. It's no trouble."

"You're a trouper, Mrs. Hodge, really," Rhys assured her. "But I'm sure you, more than any of us, could use a break."

"You're a dear. I wouldn't object to putting my feet up for a few minutes with a good mystery."

Mrs. Hodge boosted herself out of her chair and walked to the sink with Will's plate and cup, her orthopedic shoes squeaking on the smooth floor.

"Well," Rhys prompted, turning to Andie with a breathtaking smile. "Shall we?"

"Let me just run up to my room and get a few things." Andie, after thinking through the bath conundrum, had set aside a few props she thought might help. She gathered a couple of squeeze balls; a chewy, stretchy spiral bracelet; and some nontoxic foam bath tiles printed with ornate, repeating jewel-toned William Morris wallpaper designs. Barnyard animal bath toys were probably more Will's speed, but it was all she could find on short notice.

After grabbing the assortment of toys, she stepped out into the hallway. Rhys, his suit pants swapped for jeans, had stripped off his business shirt so that his torso was swathed in nothing but a fresh, white, short-sleeved T-shirt.

Andie busied herself gathering towels and readying her props as the water roared out of the tap into the sleek tub in Will's bathroom. She turned off the blazing overhead light, switched on two shaded wall sconces instead for a gentler ambience, and lined the toys up on the edge of the tub.

"Brace yourself," Rhys warned as he entered the bathroom with Will in his arms. At the sight of the tub, Will flinched and tried to scramble farther up Rhys's body, seeking a higher perch. His faint whimpers echoed against the walls, answered by his father's deep, soothing tones.

"Why don't you put him down, and we'll see if we can get him to put his hand in the water?" Andie suggested.

It was almost comical to watch Rhys trying to peel his son from his torso. The moment he detached the toddler from one point of contact, Will managed to latch on somewhere else, clamping with every available part of his body—from teeth to toes—in order to stave off the inevitable. Finally, Rhys had Will dangling from only his hands, and he deposited his son onto the soft nest of towels by the side of the tub.

Andie couldn't help but notice the woven muscles of Rhys's upper arms, where they emerged from the short sleeves of his T-shirt. They looked edible, like braided loaves baked to golden-brown perfection in an artisan's oven. But they weren't puffed up or showy. No, she observed with a detached sense of appreciation. They looked capable. Perfectly proportioned, like a da Vinci sketch of the ideal male form.

Her mouth went dry, and she felt slightly aghast at her own susceptibility. She wasn't going to fall for this, was she? It was just nature up to its old tricks again—trying to scatter some more of those blue-smoke eyes through the gene pool. Just as well she and Rhys were separated by Mrs. Hodge's trusty class divide. Harboring an illicit crush on the lord of the manor would be just plain tacky.

"Here, Will," she said, holding up one of the brightly colored foam tiles and floating it in the warm bathwater. "Can you touch the square?"

Will looked longingly at the bobbing object, small whimpers trapped in his throat. Rhys leaned closer to help him reach, but Will was startled by the movement, and instead of touching the toy, he flailed at the surface of the water, sending a wave sluicing down the front of his father's shirt.

Yikes, Andie marveled as the white shirt turned translucent, molding to Rhys's chest and abs like a second skin. She found herself transfixed for a moment by his deep chest and flat stomach corrugated with muscle—all of it apparently the same even-toned caramel shade as his face, neck, and arms. His Cayman Islands tan.

Will's cries saved her from herself.

"It's okay, Will. It's okay," Rhys soothed, picking him up once more.

"Have you ever tried getting in the tub with him?" Andie asked. She peered skyward, expecting a bolt of lightning to flash from the bathroom ceiling and strike her down. But this was no lustful scheme. There really was no other way she could think of to get Will into the tub at this moment, and she wanted so much for this attempt to be a win for him and Rhys.

"When he was really little, I used to sit him on my lap when he got too big for the newborn tub."

"And how did he do?"

"Well, he was less reactive about quite a few things back then. He actually did okay. Should we try it now?"

"Um, yes. Okay." Andie wanted the floor to swallow her up as she felt her cheeks flood with lurid color.

"Oh, don't worry," Rhys reassured her, no doubt unable to miss the flaming tomato shade that suffused her face. "I have no intention of stripping down to my unmentionables." His grin was pure magic.

"God forbid," Andie said faintly, fanning limp tendrils of hair away from her heated face.

"Here." Rhys held out his arms. "If you take him for a minute, I'll go and put on some swimming trunks."

To Andie's surprise, Will submitted to being passed into her arms, clamping himself onto her with his arms and legs. She had to brace her feet on the bath mat and exert a conscious effort to hold firm as Rhys leaned in close, his scent lighting up traitorous pleasure receptors in her brain as he transferred Will into her embrace. Finally, he disappeared from the room, and Andie rubbed her cheek against the baby-soft waves at Will's crown.

"Don't worry," she said softly. "With a dad like that, you'll have a great life. You'll see."

She shushed and soothed him, improvising a bobbing dance on the balls of her feet. From her vantage point, she could see Will's impossibly long little-boy lashes fluttering against the curve of his cheek as his cries wound down. He was so beautiful, so perfect in his innocence. It was already becoming difficult to imagine a time when she would no longer see him every day, and she hadn't even been at the house a week. Still, three months was a long time—time enough for him to make great advances, if all went according to plan. At least she would have that.

Andie looked up from her reverie to see Rhys in the doorway, clad in nothing but board shorts and a smile, a towel draped over one shoulder.

"Nice job," he commented. "I can't believe how quickly he calmed down for you."

"Beginner's luck," she murmured.

Her gaze bounced from Rhys's naked chest and shoulders to the feral grace of his lean hips and the tantalizing line of dark hair that arrowed under the low-slung waistband of his shorts. Suddenly it seemed there was no safe place to rest her eyes. As Rhys stepped into the tub, she forced herself to train her sights on Will's plump right hand, his fingers threaded through hers like they belonged there.

~

Rhys felt faintly ridiculous folded into the bathtub in his hibiscus-patterned board shorts. Andie knelt by the side of the tub, holding Will, her face level with Rhys's. The humidity had put roses in her cheeks, and a few distracting loose ringlets clung to the sides of her elegant neck.

"Okay," she said, her gaze touching his and skittering away. "I'm going to pass him to you. Make sure you're ready to grab him, so he doesn't dangle."

She leaned in close, Will held securely against her chest, until she was slotted into Rhys's hovering embrace. Her breath against his neck was an electric current as she pressed Will into his arms and waited an eternal millisecond for him to complete the transfer of his son's familiar weight. He supported Will's compact body against his chest, humming soothingly.

As Will's weight settled, Rhys let his arms relax slightly. A surreptitious look confirmed that the toddler's feet had entered the water and were now submerged almost up to the ankles. His disgruntled squawks didn't intensify, which was a positive sign.

"Did you see how he clutched at me when I leaned over to pass him to you?" Andie asked.

"Yes, he doesn't like being tipped. He never has." Rhys recalled all too well how Will would always startle awake when laid down on his mattress, even if he'd been slumbering peacefully in his arms moments before.

"He definitely has some vestibular integration issues," Andie mused, pushing a tendril of damp hair from her forehead.

"Come again?" Rhys cocked an eyebrow, unfamiliar with the OT jargon.

"The vestibular sense deals with movement, gravity, and balance through input from the inner ear," Andie explained. "I've noticed Will doesn't like swinging or spinning motions, either. He can't orient himself, and he feels like he's falling. It's really scary to him."

Rhys saw himself at age seven trapped at the top of a slide by a group of boys cruelly amused by his reluctance to leap cavalierly to the ground like they did. He sucked in a breath, remembering the hurt and anxiety that were his constant companions on the playground. Now he finally had a name for the overdeveloped physical caution that had made him the object of those boyish taunts. He'd gradually made his peace with the idea of hurling himself through space, forcing himself to muscle through his anxiety, until he ultimately became a star winger on the school rugby team and at university. But he'd never reconciled himself to roller coasters or boating. And air travel was no picnic, either. He still loathed being bucked and tossed by forces outside his control. *Is that what Will feels all the time?*

He ruffled Will's hair sympathetically. "Okay, so he's not going to be a trapeze artist or an ice dancer. No big deal, right?"

"Not in its own right," Andie conceded. "But the vestibular system affects all our other senses and our development generally. If it's disordered, it can cause delays in speech and language, among other things."

"Will's speech delay might have something to do with his problems with balance?" The idea was challenging, yet Rhys found himself trusting her assessment implicitly. A few weeks earlier he'd shared Mrs. Hodge's opinion of OT as pseudoscientific mumbo jumbo, and now here he was, practically eating out of the hand of the high priestess. How things had changed.

"It's only part of the picture, of course," Andie added. "But it's best to cover all the bases."

Will's cries dwindled to halfhearted murmurs, and Rhys settled him on his lap so he could see the foam tiles Andie had placed along the rim of the tub in a simple pattern: blue, red, blue, red. Rhys felt Will's hair brush his cheek as he turned to watch Andie's progress, and soon the toddler was straining to look more closely. Andie floated the remaining tiles in the water, selecting one at a time to add to the lineup snaking along the stretch of porcelain.

Suddenly Will cried out in protest, slapping at the tile Andie had just placed into the sequence. A few foam squares fell back into the water, and Will pored over them as they floated around him. With his small pink tongue protruding between pursed lips, he examined the pieces and, safe on the island of his father's lap, began to configure his own pattern on the edge of the tub.

At first, Rhys saw no logic to it, as Will lined up a gold tile followed by a blue and two reds and then a green, but as the rest of the pieces eddied in the water and their patterns resolved before Rhys's eyes, realization struck.

"The patterns," he rasped, grabbing Andie's wrist.

"Ye-es," she said with exaggerated care, looking at him like he had a few screws loose. "Aren't they gorgeous? I think they're based on William Morris designs—"

"No, not that." Rhys gestured helplessly, the words locked in his throat. Finally the logjam cleared, and his excitement came pouring out in a torrent. "Don't you see? He's alternating the patterns, rather than the colors."

He pointed at the gold tile, tracing an elaborate, scrolling acanthus leaf pattern in which the leaves curled predominantly to the left. The next tile, the blue, showed the exact same pattern printed in reverse, with the leaves—buried deep within a complex, interlocking design— arcing right. The next tile, with a red background, mirrored the left-facing pattern of the first, and Will followed it with a right-facing red tile, then a left-facing green tile. He continued the pattern until all the tiles of that type were used up.

Will was looking beyond the overall color of the tiles to the complex design of leaves and vines beneath, and he was able to discern the subtlest distinctions among them. A subset of tiles with similar, but not identical, patterns was left floating in the tub. Andie had inadvertently set up a visual-spatial intelligence test, and Will had just aced it. Unequivocally. Rhys could hardly think over the pounding of his heart.

He was suddenly struck by the memory of his own fascination with a set of prints that had adorned his sixth-form homeroom— architectural photos showing infinite repeating patterns from the ceiling of Istanbul's Blue Mosque.

The piquancy of those intricate, mathematically precise designs had affected him like a drug, geometry and artistry mingling to open up a whole new world of perception. On the way through the corridors of the school, he'd find himself preemptively tracing the kaleidoscopic patterns in his own mind, eager to rest his eyes on their graceful lines— much as he'd later delight in mapping wind-flow patterns in computer simulations. The arabesque mosaics spoke to him more eloquently than the gruff voice of his homeroom teacher, who was forced to call Rhys's name in progressively more demanding tones. *Griffiths. Griffiths! Oh, for God's sake, boy, stop your woolgathering!*

"Oh my God, I see it!" Andie cried. "That's brilliant! The way the leaves weave through in different directions. I hadn't compared them that way before." She pushed the tiles together so the sinuous leaf patterns lined up, snaking closer and then arcing away in precise, repeating rows, and raised bright eyes to Rhys's face.

"Do you know what this means?" he asked, hardly daring to move.

"It means he's smart," Andie said, with a warm, exuberant laugh. "Really smart. Not that I doubted it for a minute."

Rhys had to concentrate to stop his hands from shaking as he reached up to stroke Will's hair. He had worried about Will's intellectual functioning. Of course he had. It was his job as a parent to worry about everything, and Will's lack of speech made it next to impossible to gauge the nature and acuity of his awareness, the way his mind worked. Rhys had begun to despair of ever finding a way to truly communicate with his son. But Andie and her toys had given him a window into Will's thoughts, a glimpse into the kind of mind he understood. A mind like his own.

He took in her lovely face, alight with pure happiness as she reached out to give Will a fond chuck under the chin. *You had faith, where I didn't.* He locked eyes with hers. *You did this.* The awareness pulsed in his blood. Words weren't enough. He wanted to sweep her and Will into a shared embrace. He wanted to spin her in his arms.

He wanted to . . . kiss her. And it wasn't a friendly peck on the cheek he wanted to give her, either. No, he realized, drinking in the sight of her flushed cheeks and the dazzle of excitement in her eyes. He wanted to kiss her with the irrepressible, rapturous hunger of a man who has just had his life handed back to him. Will could think in visual analogies. Through their shared ability, Rhys could find a way to communicate with his son. The thrill was like a drug, sweeping all compunction from its path.

It might have been half a minute before Rhys realized he was staring, gazing at Andie with a devouring intensity. She broke their eye lock, the color draining from her cheeks as she pushed back from the edge of the tub and got to her feet. *Oh God. What must she be thinking?*

She must have seen it, he realized as she cleared her throat uncomfortably and wiped her wet hands on a nearby towel, obviously preparing to leave. She actually looked upset, he realized. And no wonder. She'd brought him a near miracle, and here he was, eyeing her like she was the main course at a banquet. For some reason, his urge to connect with her—to share his jubilation with her—was powerfully visceral, sensual. He needed to rein it in before he sent her fleeing from the house for good.

"I . . . um . . . I'm going to leave the two of you to finish up." From her standing position, she leaned in to drop a kiss on the top of Will's head. "You did great tonight, Will."

"Andie," Rhys said, his voice hoarse as she halted by the door, "thank you."

"Of course," she said with a cautious smile, one hand on the door handle. "I'm so proud of him." With that, she slipped from the room like a shadow, leaving Rhys and Will both staring at the space in the doorway where her image had vanished.

Rhys leaned forward and gathered Will close for a hug. Andie was Will's lifeline. Having her in the house was a godsend, a fragile and precious gift he sometimes sensed would evaporate if he put a foot wrong. She was strong and capable, but she was fragile, too. And here he was, slavering over her like some badly behaved large-breed puppy.

He'd seen the discomfort dawning in her eyes when he'd stared at her so openly, his yearning written all over his face. She seemed to find it hard enough to accept even his gratitude—but his desire? It was something that had no place in their working relationship. He needed to get a grip on himself. He couldn't blow this. He couldn't do that to Will, he realized as he dried the toddler off and readied him for bed. His attraction to Andie was his own burden to bear. He wouldn't make it anyone else's problem.

He waited in the shadows until Will settled down to sleep, then gathered himself and headed downstairs to the den, where two generous fingers of whiskey had his name written all over them.

~

Andie wasn't sure how she made it back to her room. She was too busy unraveling precisely what had happened between her and Rhys in Will's bathroom. One minute she'd been helping with Will's bath while fending off the admittedly not unpleasant buzz of attraction that lingered below the surface of her interactions with Rhys. The next, she'd been filled with sheer delight at Will's breakthrough with the patterned bath toys. All had been well until her gaze met Rhys's and panic sliced through her chest at the crushing intimacy of his expression.

She couldn't even put her finger on exactly why it had happened. All she knew was that sharing Rhys's joy in Will's achievement felt so shockingly parental that the wrongness of it robbed her of breath. In that instant, it was as if she'd slipped into some crazy time warp, hurdling over the first stirrings of desire, fast-forwarding through courtship, leaping over the first couple of years of marriage, and landing somehow at a place where she and Rhys were able to exchange significant looks over Will's head like a long-established couple doting on their child. It was madness! And the worst of it was that she found herself enjoying the sensation. No—more than that—she found herself unsettlingly euphoric at the merest taste of the idea.

No wonder she'd gone into an immediate tailspin. She hadn't even been able to speculate about what Rhys was thinking as she backed away from the tub and beat her fast retreat. She couldn't do this, couldn't get sucked into the heart of this family. Not when there was a thousand-foot barrier preventing her from making good on the promise that kind of closeness entailed. She was usually so capable of reining in her impulses, controlling her emotional responses, but there was something about the Griffiths men that got under her skin. Way under.

There was no harm in feeling for Will, she told herself—bonding with him to the extent her professional role, and her own affectionate nature, demanded. But sharing goofy, besotted grins with Rhys over Will's accomplishments was so far over the line that she'd need a GPS and a seven-day food supply just to navigate her way back to it.

She crossed to the recessed window by the writing desk in her room and flipped the latch, sliding the window open so wide that frigid air tumbled into the room. She inhaled sharp, icy lungfuls, bracing herself against the frame as her mind raced. All she could see was Will's smile and Rhys's fond, joyful expression, infusing life into a remote chamber of her heart she thought she'd locked down for good. The sensation hurt, like warm blood rushing back into frostbitten flesh. *I didn't ask for this. I was fine with things the way they were.*

There had to be some way to restore her equilibrium. It must be the intimacy of the setting that was messing with her head, she reasoned, as the cold air stung her face. Nothing more. She must simply be starved for her usual contact with colleagues and friends. She obviously needed to get out more. And to remember that Rhys and Will might be on their way to reconstituting their family, with Karina at its center. She forcibly pushed aside the image of Rhys's smile and took herself off to the bathroom to brush her teeth before she was sucked back into fantasyland.

CHAPTER EIGHT

Her chance to get out came the very next day, but not exactly in the way she might have wanted. A freshly showered Rhys, dressed for work in his usual beat-up jeans and casual button-down, greeted her as she headed downstairs to the kitchen.

"Mrs. Hodge has an emergency dentist's appointment this afternoon, and she was supposed to take Will to his speech-therapy session right after preschool," he said after offering her a cappuccino from his fancy chrome espresso machine. "Any chance you could take him instead?"

"Oh." Not what she'd expected. She collected herself. It wasn't an unreasonable request, considering the number of hours she had free before Will's OT session. "Sure, I can do that. What time should I pick him up?"

"One o'clock. You can use the Range Rover. Mrs. Hodge is taking her own car to her appointment."

"Um, okay." It was exactly the kind of expectation she was leery of. Minding Will while operating heavy machinery. A Range Rover. *Sheesh! The thing must be three times as big as Ernie.* But it would have been churlish of her to refuse. Who was she to be that precious, when Rhys was paying her very generously for her time?

"Thanks. You'll be saving my life at work today."

"No problem at all." It was the kind of thing a grown-up would do. A normal, reasonable request of the kind functional adults took in their stride every day. She was functional, wasn't she? Sure, she'd had stuff happen in her past, stuff that demanded some modifications to her expectations, to her life plan. But she prided herself on making it work, on operating successfully within the parameters she set for herself. She sealed her agreement with a resolute nod.

"Great!" Rhys smiled. "I'd better hit the road, then."

"Right. See you later. I won't forget Will's appointment."

All morning, the thought of the behemoth vehicle ate away at her. It was stupid, but she never drove anything but Ernie, and she didn't like the idea of being at the wheel of something that cost a small fortune and probably maneuvered like an aircraft carrier. Worries kept flaring up to plague her. Would she hop into the vehicle only to find that the steering wheel was on the wrong side? Rhys was British, after all. Maybe she'd open the back door to discover that someone had uninstalled Will's safety seat and she had to rig up the whole thing using only paper clips, string, and Scotch tape. She actually snuck down to the garage to check midmorning, while Mrs. Hodge was busy doing Will's laundry.

Mrs. Hodge made herself some soup for lunch, while Andie hovered nervously, dreading the moment when the older woman would leave. Was her dentist's appointment really all that important? She was able to eat soup, after all. Maybe she should just blow it off and chaperone Will as usual.

"So, having some problems with the old teeth?" Andie couldn't resist inquiring as the woman seated herself at the small table in the upstairs kitchen. Mrs. Hodge glanced up, a slightly affronted expression crinkling her brow. Andie didn't mean to refer to her teeth as old, per se. Well, no older than the average fifty-something-year-old's teeth anyway.

"Yes, as a matter of fact. A crown popped off last night."

"Ah. That must hurt," Andie observed, hoping Mrs. Hodge would issue a contradiction.

"Actually, it does. But I'm getting it taken care of in an hour, so I expect I'll be right as rain in no time."

"Perfect. Lucky the dentist could fit you in."

"Yes, quite."

There was nothing more to be said about it, but Andie tracked Mrs. Hodge's departure with wistful eyes as the nanny headed to the laundry room once more before leaving for her appointment. She admired the woman's solidity, her workmanlike efficiency.

Andie entered the garage with a good half hour to spare before she was due at the preschool. She took her place in the driver's seat, noticing that the doors of the Range Rover were about twice as thick as Ernie's, and closed with an expertly engineered clunk that oozed money. At least in this tank, Will would be well insulated. She started the car and adjusted the mirrors, floating out of the garage bay. *You can do this.*

The floating sensation continued as Andie pointed the car down the driveway. It was actually quite refreshing, seeing the world from this vantage point rather than hugging the road at close range. She drifted toward the town center in the plush, climate-controlled bubble, her comfort level growing with every turn. Soon she reached the preschool, where she managed to find a spacious parking spot. *So far, so good.*

She went inside a few minutes early to chat with Will's main behavioral therapist and to pack up his bag before leading him back out to the car. So far this mission was turning out to be a piece of cake, she thought with satisfaction as Will sank obediently into position in the car seat, and she fed his arms through the straps and snapped the buckles into place.

The speech-therapy clinic was only a mile away. Andie's heart sank as she approached and saw that the small parking lot was full. Sighing, she kept going until she located a metered spot on the opposite side of the road. She hadn't packed the stroller, so she'd have to walk Will across, or carry him, she realized, as she fiddled nervously with his hat and mittens and unbuckled his seat belt. He'd walk, she decided, as he complained and thrashed in her arms, slithering down her body to the edge of the curb.

She took one small hand snugly in hers and stood at the edge of the nearest crosswalk, fighting a surge of nausea as passing cars swished by. *Don't be silly. You've got this.* A woman in a minivan drew to a stop in the nearest lane, ushering them across. Andie smiled and waved. She stepped into the road, stooping to encourage Will's dawdling progress. *One step at a time.*

They were a couple of paces into the far lane when Will's hand jerked in her grip. Andie's heartbeat jolted as she looked down to find herself holding an empty fleece mitten. She turned in slow-motion horror to see Will darting back in the direction they'd come, back toward the lane where the minivan had just started to move into the crosswalk. A gust of freezing wind had caught the brim of his deerstalker cap and blown it backward, and he'd slipped her grip to retrieve it.

"No!" The scream tore from her throat, and she flung herself in front of the minivan before she even realized it. The bumper was up against her shins, her hands splayed on the warm hood as if she could hold back one and a half tons of lurching machinery. The frenetic strobing of police lights cut through the shadows of her memory. *Not again. Never again.* Her fingers burned where she should have held on—to Gus, to Will—and the thin thread of Susan's long-ago scream vibrated through her.

Several seconds passed before she registered that the minivan had halted, and Will—huddled behind her legs—was miraculously safe. The driver's look of concern melted into relief, and she flung Andie a commiserating smile. Children clamored in the back of the van, and small hands waved behind the tinted glass as the harried mom shuttled her charges on their way.

"Will! Oh God!" Andie snatched him up and propelled them both out of the crosswalk with inhuman strength, not stopping until they came to rest on a bench near a brick walkway leading to the speech therapist's office.

"Andie, Andie, Andie," he murmured, pressed against her chest, content to wait for her grasp to slowly, reluctantly, loosen. She ran her fingertips through the pixie-fine waves of his hair, over his shoulders, and down to his feet, double-checking that he was, as he had to be, all in one piece. The hot wave of terror was receding, and as it ebbed away, a chilling dread was creeping in to take its place.

Somehow, they made it up the path and into the sterile, fluorescent-lit waiting room, Andie's chest still heaving with painful, splintered breaths. Will let go of her reluctantly to accompany the therapist into her office, and Andie searched for the nearest bathroom.

So, this was it: the end of her run at the Griffiths house. She shouldered through the door of the women's restroom, bile rising in her throat. Clutching the edges of the mercifully clean porcelain sink, she retched until her throat felt scalded, and the waves of nausea finally subsided.

She would have to tell Rhys. There was no way around it. He deserved to know, and she needed to hand back the responsible adult badge she should never have been issued in the first place, fraud that she was. It was probably for the best, she told herself. That weird thing with Rhys in the bathroom the night before had probably been some kind of karmic warning. So why did she feel so desolate? Her eyes were huge and ringed with shadow in the harshly lit bathroom mirror, and she couldn't fight back the sob that rose in her throat when she thought about leaving.

She'd felt so elated over Will's success last night, before things had taken a turn for the strange. She couldn't imagine leaving him now. Maybe there was a chance she would be able to continue to work with him—not from the house, of course, but under a different arrangement, back within the safe, institutional walls of a practice, if she could find herself another job. But, no, she had to be realistic. Rhys would likely never let her within five miles of Will once he learned what had just happened.

She trudged wretchedly back to the waiting room but found that she couldn't sit. All she could do was pace and fret, clutching at the damp tissue she had to keep pressing to her eyes. She could hardly wait for Will to reappear so she could wrap him in her arms. But at the same time she dreaded the end of his therapy session because it would bring her one step closer to the moment when she would see the loathing in Rhys's eyes and hear the contempt in his voice.

She'd been fooling herself. In spite of her misgivings, and over the strains of her own stern self-reproof, she had harbored the secret hope that her stint with Will would be a turning point. That working so intensively to build Will's skills would engineer some kind of transformation in herself as well—opening her up, priming her for something more than the cramped half life she'd been living for so long. But it wasn't to be.

She wondered what would happen to her now, wondered if she could keep going on the same treadmill she'd been on, pouring her energies into helping children she would grow to love just before she had to say her inevitable good-bye. She rubbed at her swollen eyes, certain of nothing except for the sobering fact that there was no sensation on earth worse than the whisper of a child's fingers slipping from her grasp.

~

The door to Rhys's den had never seemed so imposing, Andie mused as she stood on the threshold that evening. To her feverish eye, the door-frame itself looked at least twelve feet high. Rhys had only just arrived home, and Mrs. Hodge was with Will in the kitchen, starting his dinner. Better to get this over with right away, Andie figured. She'd already started collecting her things, hoping to make the process of packing her bags as quick and painless as possible.

She could hear Rhys moving around inside as she inched forward and reached out her hand. *It's now or never.* She knocked decisively, and straightened. If she had to do this, she would at least try to keep her dignity.

"Andie?" Rhys craned to see her framed in the doorway, and a broad smile broke over his face. As she moved into the room on numb legs, she couldn't help but notice that the midgray shade of his button-down brought out an almost purple-heather tint in his eyes. God, he was just so . . . devastating.

"There's something I need to talk to you about," she began. The warm curve of Rhys's mouth straightened into a line, and his brows drew together in concern. *Say good-bye to the last time he ever looks upon you with goodwill.*

The pain of what she had to confess lodged like an icicle in her ribs. She'd drawn out Will's OT session when they returned that afternoon, delighting in his progress as he tackled simple obstacle courses and worked on puzzles that tested his fine-motor skills. Then they giggled and played on the floor, and Andie had swiped away tears when Will, panting happily from exertion, laid his head in her lap, looking straight up at her with his sweet blue-gray eyes that tipped down at the corners like he was in on some eternally amusing secret.

"There was an incident this afternoon," Andie said. "I take full responsibility, and I understand that after what happened, you won't want me to continue on here. I've already started packing."

"Andie." Rhys shook his head in confusion, doubt blooming in his eyes. "What happened? Is Will okay?"

"He's fine, thank goodness." Andie's right hand drifted up to hover over her heart. "But he could have been hurt."

Rhys stepped toward her, his eyes haunted, urgent. "For God's sake, tell me what happened."

Andie relived the moment as she spoke. Her heart quaked as she saw the image of Will's hand clasped in hers. In her mind's eye, she watched him twist free from the mitten, her own fingers tightening around the empty scrap of fleece. She closed her eyes, letting the flood of sensation rush back in. She felt the cold blast of air on her face that had sent Will's cap flying back across the road. The awareness of the looming shape of the minivan as it began to move across the crosswalk. The warmth of its hood under her bare hands as she'd screamed.

"So I turned and jumped in front of the minivan, and the woman saw me and stopped," she finished, her voice smaller than she would have liked it to be. "I reacted as quickly as I could, and it turned out okay. But . . . things could have been different." She turned to the side as she felt her brave demeanor buckle and crack. All of a sudden there were tears pricking at her eyes again. *What was with all these stupid tears?* "Like I said, I'm packing my bags. I'm so sorry. I'll be out of your way tomorrow morning at the latest."

Rhys kept his eyes trained on the floor near her feet. Any moment his fists would clench, and he'd look up with venom in his gaze. He'd call her incompetent, a waste of space—just like Susan had. She stood frozen, waiting for the verdict to be delivered. *Guilty. Worthless.*

Instead, he did the strangest thing. He raised his eyes to her face. They were warm, open, and full of compassion. His mouth tried for a smile, but it half collapsed under the weight of some emotion she couldn't identify.

"Oh God, Andie." He reached out toward her and suddenly he was close, and moving closer. She felt the warm pull of his arms as she was drawn up against the broad expanse of his chest, her damp cheek pressed into the soft, slightly nubby fabric of his shirt. He smelled like heaven—the familiar citrus of his soap or aftershave mingling with a warm scent all his own, firing up those greedy neurotransmitters that seemed to rouse from their slumber whenever he was around.

"I'm so sorry." He exhaled into her hair, the errant jets of his breath sending jolts of sensation ricocheting across the nape of her neck and down the length of her spine. "I should have warned you when I asked you to pick him up. You've become a part of things so quickly, I guess I forgot."

"Forgot?" she murmured insensibly, her wits dulled by the cocoon enveloping her senses.

"Yes, Will has a bit of a reputation. In fact, his name should really be Will 'Houdini' Griffiths. It was unforgivable of me not to give you fair warning. He's done the same thing to me—or tried—at least ten times in the last six months alone."

"But that doesn't mean . . . I still should have—"

"You were perfect," Rhys soothed. "I don't know many people who would have thrown themselves into oncoming traffic to save him."

"But you don't understand," she protested. "It was horrible. All of a sudden he was just gone, and I didn't know what was happening. I should have been more on top of things. He could have . . . I wasn't alert enough. I wasn't . . . enough."

The tears were flowing freely now, slipping down her cheeks in rivulets that left a darkening patch on the front of Rhys's shirt. Whenever Andie closed her eyes, she saw her little brother's outflung hand, so small and pale. She even heard the tinny strains of Christmas music floating on the air. *I must be losing my mind,* she thought as she clung to Rhys like a shipwreck survivor.

"Andie, you didn't mess up. I did by not providing you with critical information." His deep voice reverberated against her chest. He felt so strong and solid and good. "In fact, you've shown yourself to be a woman of impeccable reflexes.

"And you've done more than that," he continued, his voice low, reassuring. "You've done more for Will than anyone. You can't leave. You're his connection to the world."

"Maybe I've helped a little," she conceded with a loud sniff. "But while he's out in that world, he's entitled to a minimal level of safety. You can't have some hapless employee endangering—"

"Of course Will's safety is paramount, but Andie, you're hardly hapless." He lowered his head and spoke next to her ear, the current of his breath stirring her hair and lighting up nerve pathways that sent odd little quakes vibrating through her belly. "And I don't think of you as just an employee."

"Oh?" Her mouth formed an astonished shape as Rhys's hand stroked her shoulder and trailed down her back in motions that were not sensual but comforting. Somehow, heat bloomed under his touch anyway, and she felt that she could easily stand there all night, as long as he kept drawing those trails of fire beside her spine.

"No," he said, his tone thoughtful. "You're more like a . . . a miracle worker, or a mythical creature. At least, I think that's how Will sees you. But, more importantly, you're a friend."

"A friend." It seemed that all she could do was provide an echo.

"Yes." He smiled, his lips moving against the sensitive lobe of her ear. "My friend."

Now she really was melting. Her head had come to rest in the crook of his neck, and when she tilted her face up, the satiny skin of his throat was millimeters from her lips. She inhaled deeply, mainlining phero-mones, or some quintessential chemical he alone manufactured—heady, addictive. Even more narcotic, though, was the almost incomprehensible fact that he somehow didn't condemn her for what had happened. It was too much for her to wrap her head around. Far from blaming her, he was standing there with his arms around her, comforting her, offering her his friendship.

"And as much as you've done for Will," Rhys continued, "I think you're doing even more for me. Being able to talk to you about him, to see him through your eyes . . . dealing with this autism thing, sometimes it feels like I'm trying to dam up an ocean by tossing in one pebble at a time, just trying to get some solid ground under my feet, you know?"

"Yeah, I think so."

"Well, with you here, helping me, now I have someone tossing pebbles by my side—only you're much more effective. You're hurling boulders—or building a whole island or something. I think I've mangled this metaphor."

"So, wait," she said. "You really don't want me to leave?"

"No, Andie. I really don't want you to leave."

He laughed—a short, warm outburst that told her he didn't understand her uncertainty, her lack of self-assurance. To him, the incident at the crosswalk was a small thing, already receding in his rearview mirror, and he couldn't understand why she didn't see it that way, too.

She imagined having that ability, the power to shrink the incident back down to its proper size. Life was full of such forks in the road, she supposed, when worst-case scenarios loomed for an instant in all their awful potential. For the lucky majority, those moments became near misses, fleeting interludes of glimpsed horror that receded as quickly as they'd appeared—catastrophes averted so normal life could resume in all its happy obliviousness.

Andie no longer had the luxury of being able to shield her eyes. She saw every sinister possibility, every snare, every lurking calamity. She couldn't explain her perspective to Rhys. Nor did she want to. She couldn't infect him with her knowledge, because being a parent meant trusting that all the things that could go wrong wouldn't. Being a parent was the ultimate act of faith.

She held herself perfectly still within the circle of his arms. His warmth, his kindness, and his regard were almost palpable things, swirling around and through her. Her first instinct was to reject them before he could snatch them back, realizing his mistake. But she forced herself not to move. *Will wasn't injured. Rhys doesn't hate me. I can stay.* At this moment, those truths were enough. In fact, they were pretty damn incredible.

"Okay," she said. She pulled back from his embrace, shocked to discover that she felt robbed of the contact and wanted nothing more than to slide right back up against the solid wall of his chest. "I guess I'll stick around. See if I can help you toss a few more pebbles."

"Thank you," he said fervently. "That's all I ask."

Funny, she thought, as she cast a wistful glance back at the sculpted line of his jaw, how he thought she was the one doing him the favor.

CHAPTER NINE

Rhys woke early the next morning to find the world transformed. Snow had fallen overnight, cloaking the landscape in a quiet, glistening mantle. He stood by the kitchen window, sipping his first espresso of the day as the rising sun painted the crest of the hill behind the house in warm apricot hues. The shadowed slope below it glowed more subtly in purple-blue tones, turning the scene into an Impressionist masterwork. It was Saturday, and despite the fact that Will seemed to be enjoying an uncharacteristically late morning, Rhys couldn't sleep. He was too preoccupied by thoughts of Andie.

He couldn't shake the memory of the deadly serious expression on her face as she'd stood in the doorway to the den the previous evening. *There's something I need to talk to you about.* At first he'd been convinced she was going to call him out for the hungry way he'd stared at her in Will's bathroom. Surely that was the reason for the bruised, distrustful look in her eyes. But then she'd launched into her confession about the near accident in the crosswalk.

She was within her rights to feel shaken. There was little in his experience that was more frightening than one of Will's impromptu escape attempts. But what he didn't understand was the terrible trepidation that darkened her eyes and bowed her posture as she stood there waiting for his response—trembling like a whipped puppy afraid of the next lash.

Taking her in his arms had been natural, automatic, and her distress had been enough to distract him from the thumping of his own heartbeat as he folded her against him. She felt slight, but she was deceptively strong, every muscle coiled in wait. Even when she'd sighed and accepted the relief of his embrace, she held a part of herself firm and unyielding, stretched as taut as a bowstring against the length of his body.

He wondered what it would take for her to relax into softness. Probably more finesse than he would ever be able to muster. She was so skittish, wary. Right now, he just needed her to feel secure in his home. Keeping her there, working her magic on Will, was paramount. So he'd done what his instinct had told him to do right from the start: declare his friendship.

He liked her. He admired her. It was that simple. Now all he had to do was draw a big, fat line underneath their friendship and leave it at that. No more getting carried away by the fizz of elation that eddied through his bloodstream when she smiled. No more dwelling on precisely how it had felt to tug her close, the silkiness of her hair brushing his jaw, her body charged with tension as she wrestled internal forces he could only guess at.

With the world nestled beneath its white blanket, the other residents of the house took longer to wake than usual. Even Will seemed to be lulled by the calm. For once, his waking was not announced by plaintive wails from the monitor but by just a gentle rustling, followed by a sequence of murmurs with a contented, inquisitive cadence. Rhys went to collect him, and they settled in the kitchen, where a train table sat by the French doors. Will's eyes went wide at the diamond-bright landscape beyond the windows, and he settled to play, casting furtive glances outside as if awed by the drama of the scene.

Andie was the next inhabitant of the house to appear, her booted feet drumming jauntily on the stairs before she emerged in the kitchen wearing jeans and a cherry-red sweater that made her look about seventeen. Her hair was pulled back from her freshly scrubbed face in a ponytail, and her skin and eyes gleamed. He was relieved to see that she looked happy, relaxed—a world away from how she had appeared the previous evening.

"Wow!" She looked out at the sunlight setting individual crystals ablaze across the unblemished expanse of snow. Above the brilliant whiteness, the sky was a serene blue band. "It's gorgeous," she declared.

She turned to Rhys with a broad smile that made something within his rib cage shift. Making way for . . . what? *Nothing you should even be considering.*

"Yeah, but it looks like nobody's getting in or out until the snowplows arrive," he pointed out. "Tom's supposed to be coming later to visit, but we're snowbound for now."

"No problem," she said, sinking to her knees beside Will at the train table. "We can settle in for a while."

Rhys picked up a dark-green wooden train with a bronze dome, one of Thomas the Tank Engine's pals. "Care to be Emily?"

"I'd be honored," she laughed. "But can I have a coffee first?"

Soon they were ensconced in an elaborate game. Will giggled uncontrollably when Emily and Percy crashed and had to be hauled off to Tidmouth Sheds for repairs. Then Sir Topham Hatt was called into action to clear the tracks when an escaped herd of aliens—from a completely different play set, naturally—wandered across the express line to Knapford Station. Rhys and Andie kept the game play going, modeling for Will how the engines interacted with one another. It was actually fun doing this when he had another adult to riff off, Rhys realized. Much less exhausting than when he had to perform all the roles single-handedly, waiting for the long-deferred moment when Will would take up the pretend play himself.

Eventually the adult knees began to suffer from being pressed into the polished hardwood of the kitchen floor, so Rhys and Andie took a break to fix some pancakes. Will devoured his as he sat in his high chair, pulled up to the edge of the banquette table, while Andie and Rhys chatted about favorite breakfast foods of their childhoods. Andie confessed a secret passion for Froot Loops, while Rhys tried to explain the virtues of the rather-more-exotic Welsh delicacy laverbread, a seaweed concoction spread on hot buttered toast or mixed with porridge oats and fried into savory cakes. When he offered to ransack the pantry for a tin he thought he'd brought back from his last trip to Wales, she demurred rather quickly, declaring herself already stuffed to the brim.

Mrs. Hodge made an appearance by midmorning, her hair arranged in curlers above a tweed skirt and high-necked blouse. She was meeting one of her expat friends and going into Boston to see a show, so she was especially eager to hear the roar of the snowplows.

"Well, I don't know about anyone else," Andie declared, after her third coffee, "but my day won't be complete until I've made some tracks in that snow."

"I can do you one better," Rhys told her. "I think I can find our sled in the garage. How about we take it out for a spin?"

The red plastic sled was pretty basic but would work well enough on the slope beside the driveway, he figured. He and Andie bustled about, locating gloves, scarves, hats, and boots, while Mrs. Hodge zipped Will into his snowsuit, promising hot chocolate upon their return.

Once outside, Rhys felt like they were enclosed in an idyllic snow globe. The hill behind the house blocked the wind, and the sky stretched overhead in a pristine blue dome. Andie's red puffer jacket and Will's blue snowsuit were bright splashes against a field of white. Will stomped around gleefully, poking holes in the clean snow and lifting it up to his mouth to enjoy the cold sensation on his tongue.

Rhys chose a launching place and took a test run to make sure the route was safe. Then he snuggled Will between his legs, and they sailed down the hill, Will squealing in delight, apparently not bothered by the fine spray of snow crystals that flew up and stung their flushed cheeks.

"Mind if I take him down?" Andie asked, as Rhys dragged the sled and its remaining occupant back to the top of the hill. She fixed him with a look that contained a flicker of the uncertainty that had undone her the prior evening.

"Be my guest." He handed her the rope and helped her settle Will securely in place before waving them on. A lump formed in his throat as the sled took a small turn at the bottom and tipped them out into the snow. They both turned to look up at him, bright-eyed and laughing, their faces side by side, and suddenly there wasn't enough oxygen in the world to fill his lungs.

Rhys, you're a goner. He sucked in a sharp, painful breath, his boots crunching crystalline drifts of white powder as he trudged down the hill to help Andie to her feet. He was still overwhelmed with relief that she'd decided to stay. He felt both depleted and elated, as if he'd just run a marathon and was floating on endorphins. How was it that after only a week, her presence had become essential to him? To Will, too. He reached out, his gloved hand enfolding hers as he helped her up. Huffing out a breath of laughter, she straightened, steadying herself against him for a moment before she turned, seized the sled's rope, and—issuing a playful challenge—bolted for the top of the hill, with Will chortling and exclaiming in her wake. Rhys didn't know which of the two of them would suffer more when her time with them came to an end.

~

Jess made good on her threat to drag Andie out shopping for Oscar-party gowns, calling later in the week to lure her away from Rhys's for an afternoon prowling the aisles at a Nordstrom Rack outlet in the suburbs, not far from Concord. Ever since Jess had moved back up from

Rhode Island and Andie had registered at Boston University for her bachelor's and master's degrees, the two sisters had begun the tradition of meeting up regularly to indulge their passion for bargain hunting.

It was the afternoon of the first meeting between Will and Rhys and Karina, and Will's usual OT session was canceled in honor of the occasion. Andie had felt a small quake of trepidation on Rhys's behalf, picking up on the latter's tension as the morning wore on, but Rhys had shooed her out of the house to visit with her sister. She hoped the reunion between Will and Karina would go well, and the stress would transmute into harmony, for all their sakes.

"There they are!" Jess announced in satisfaction, pointing her cart in the direction of a tall rack of evening dresses topped with a sale sign. "This may take a while."

Andie laughed, her spirits soaring. She still felt slightly giddy, as she had ever since her encounter with Rhys in the den, when she'd confessed to the incident in the crosswalk. From that moment, it felt like her life had been jolted from its customary track and was unfolding as if in a parallel universe.

The snowy day spent with Rhys and Will had been another revelation. The ease of Rhys's acceptance and the joy she'd felt riding down the hill on the sled with Will felt altogether different from anything she'd ever known before. Halfway through the afternoon, Tom had arrived to hang out, and the way the afternoon segued from sledding to pizza to—later in the evening—a bottle of wine opened in front of the fireplace had been the purest pleasure. This was what it felt like to be included as a matter of course, to participate in the quotidian happenings and rhythms of a household as a legitimate member. Not as some reprehensible shadow, ashamed to tread too heavily or to make one's presence felt.

The experience sat on her shoulders like an ornate cloak, its sumptuous folds and ostentatious gilding a tremendous luxury, but still an awkward fit. Her smiles, jokes, and interjections had come as if from some deeply buried muscle memory, her conversational maneuvers still stiff and heavy but gradually loosening as she stretched and moved beneath the mantle of their regard.

It was Rhys's pledge of friendship that had made all the difference, she knew, putting some kind of platform back under her feet, rescuing her from the free fall she'd started the moment they'd shared that fond glance above Will's head in the bathroom. Tom's presence helped still further, diluting the hothouse intimacy she felt with Rhys. Her chest still knotted when she thought about how it had felt to stand wrapped in his arms that night in the den, her entire body galvanized with electricity. It had been too good, too much. As if she were standing on the edge of the Grand Canyon and someone had snatched away the safety rail.

"I'm going to grab a selection, and we'll see how things shake out," Jess declared, intruding on Andie's thoughts. She looked like an elegant, freckled praying mantis, with her long, angular limbs and that acquisitive gleam in her eye. "But we're not leaving until we've bought something."

"Jess, I don't need an evening dress," Andie protested, but her heart wasn't really in it. She felt a rare thrill of pleasure at the idea of actually buying one of the beautiful garments, after all those years of simply looking.

"Of course you do." Jess set her straight. "For next year's Oscar party, which you're not missing."

"It's almost a year away." She felt her resistance fading.

"You won't find better prices than these. Unless you're too fancy for last season's style, now that you're staying in that mansion and all."

"You're impossible." Andie flashed a long-suffering look at her sister but had to smother a secret smile as she sifted through the rack, her fingers drawn to the rich colors and silky fabrics. They headed for the attendant, bearing a heap of garments that far exceeded the dressing-room limit.

"We'll wait for rooms side by side," Jess told the woman.

Once ensconced in a changing-room stall, Andie peeled her jeans down to her ankles and smoothed the dresses over the top, hobbling out into the aisle to show Jess each selection. They each had their merits, but none quite lived up to the elusive vision that swam in the back of her mind. Her sister, of course, looked effortlessly chic in the avant-garde styles she preferred, particularly one bronze silk asymmetric creation that combined a daring neckline with intricate, cascading pleats that grazed the floor.

"I have large dry-cleaning bills in my future," Jess laughed. "Now, what about you?" She fixed Andie with her sherry-colored stare and reached into her changing room to fish out a dove-gray lace gown with a lavender grosgrain-ribbon belt. The silvery overlay was intricate and gossamer fine, and a swirl of gray tulle began where the fitted lace ended at midthigh. "I found this for you to try."

Andie stood in the stall with the delicate garment in her hands. This one might warrant actually taking the jeans completely off. She gave in to a shiver of anticipation as she kicked her feet free and wriggled into the dress, feeling the satisfying slither of the zip as she reached to fasten it, and the gown encased her like a second skin. A dizzyingly gorgeous second skin that made her original skin glow the color of fresh cream. *Wow. Just wow.*

She pulled her hair from its elastic and shook it over her shoulders before stepping out to show Jess, who slapped her hand over her mouth in a display of awe.

"If Monica Bellucci and Rachel Weisz had a love child, she could only hope to look like that." Her appraisal swept lower. "Minus the plaid socks. You have to buy this."

"No." Andie demurred from long habit. "It's so expensive."

~

Fifteen minutes later, Andie was being steered toward the nearest Starbucks, a garment bag knocking against her hip.

"You could sell jockstraps in a nunnery," she complained as she snagged a table.

"You deny yourself things, Andie," Jess commented, with a look that spoke of more than evening gowns. "It's high time you gave up your sackcloth and ashes."

"What can I get you to drink?" Andie pointedly ignored her sister's confrontational glare but allowed her words to resonate.

"Let me get it," Jess insisted. "After all, I'm the one who forced you to buy a Badgley Mischka."

Andie relaxed back into her seat, pushing back the urge to peel open a corner of the garment bag and pay homage to the glory of the silver-gray gown. There was something to be said for the adrenaline rush of a purchase made purely for pleasure.

"Do you realize this is the farthest west I've been since last year's maple-sugaring party?" Jess mused as she placed their cups down on the table. These days, she was far more likely to go to New York for work than to travel more than five miles west of Boston.

"You'll be getting a nosebleed next, we're so far out in the sticks." Andie smiled, rippling the surface of her coffee with the plastic stirrer.

"I talked to Susan the other day." Jess's voice dipped low. Jess always referred to their mother as "Susan," usually in a brittle, ironic tone. Never "Mom." The more familiar appellation was a courtesy that Andie continued to bestow, more out of wishful thinking than anything else.

"Oh God, it's almost maple-syrup time, isn't it?"

"Yup. She's determined to rope us in again."

Every winter, their mother tapped the maple trees that grew on her fifty-four acres and threw open her doors for a maple-sugaring party and pancake breakfast to celebrate the first batch of syrup for the season. Andie and Jess generally shared the role of sugar-shack assistant, waitress, and all-purpose lackey at the community event, where Susan drummed up customers for her farm stand. Louisa and Rose were always honored guests, too busy tending to their spirited broods to offer much help.

"You don't have to go, you know," Jess pointed out. "You don't owe her anything."

Andie opened her mouth to speak but then snapped it shut, the glow rubbing off her mood. That was where Jess had it wrong. Andie couldn't escape the notion that, in fact, she did owe her mother. That if she couldn't restore her son to her, the least she could do was to show up each year and perform her public penance in her mother's virtual morality play. With the Tilly family's Christmases and Thanksgivings having been abandoned seventeen years ago, Susan's pancake breakfast was her one big celebration of the year, the one ritual Andie was still a part of. Her role was a necessary foil to her mother's star turn as martyr and plucky survivor. She couldn't deny her mother the satisfaction. Besides, there was always the chance—a slim one, admittedly—that she and Susan would finally find their way to reconciliation.

"No, I'll go," Andie said with what she hoped was a reassuring smile.

Andie was secretly proud of her mother for the entrepreneurial spirit and fierce drive that had made the farm a local attraction and a pillar of the Camden economy. After she had emerged from her husband's long shadow, Susan had demonstrated that there wasn't much she couldn't overcome. If only she weren't so determined to deny Andie's ability to do the same. In her mind, her youngest daughter was perpetually hapless, tainted by tragedy.

"Andie," Jess said gently, "there's something else I wanted to tell you."

Time slowed down as Andie looked at her sister across the wobbly café table and finally took in the significance of two things that had pinged at the edge of her consciousness since Jess had sat down. Rather than evoking the dark-roasted richness of her sister's favorite coffee brew, the steam rising from Jess's cup gave off the fragrant, grassy scent of green tea. And, instead of waving her free hand around to punctuate her speech, Jess had draped it over her stomach in a protective, cherishing pose that women have adopted since time immemorial.

Andie knew, in that moment, exactly what it was her sister was about to say.

"I'm pregnant," Jess confirmed, and Andie tried to hold on to her senses as the room spun and the bottom fell out of her world.

There was something her lungs were supposed to be doing. *Oh, yes. Breathing.* The chatter of the crowd and the intrusive whine of the steam nozzle on the espresso machine filled in the silence for a beat, giving Andie a chance to gather herself.

Jess. *Pregnant.* Of course, it made perfect sense. That was what people did when they grew up, right? They settled down and had kids. Women like Jess didn't settle for the boyfriends that were Andie's usual fodder—pretty, commitment-phobic boys with stupid facial hair and an air of perpetual irony. They married kind, serious men like Ben. Men with commitment enough to launch a new generation into this world and stick around for the duration. Men like Rhys, in fact. Although he was so far beyond the usual run of guys that he might as well be from a different species.

"Oh my God!" Andie shrieked, holding on to her wits long enough to give Jess the excited reaction she deserved.

Jess and her devoted, funny husband would be the very best of parents, and Andie was truly happy for them. Or, at least, she would be, as soon as she managed to smother the almost-debilitating fear that this would alter her bond with Jess. Throughout their adult lives, Louisa and Rose had been the ones who hunkered down in Camden and popped out Susan's grandchildren, while Jess and Andie pursued their careers in the wider world and served as each other's staunchest supporters. Would Susan now try to sink her claws into Jess? Andie couldn't let that happen.

"You're on notice that you're my go-to babysitter," her sister said firmly. "And you're already the baby's favorite aunt."

Andie felt an irrepressible rush of warmth. It was so like Jess to effortlessly intuit Andie's fears and dispatch them without a moment's hesitation. She took a deep breath, infusing her tone with every ounce of the warmth she felt toward the sister who'd picked up the pieces after Susan had done her worst. "I'm so, so happy for you, Jess."

Jess gave a little hiccup, her surfeit of emotion spilling over. "I sometimes wonder whether I have it in me to get it right. Raising kids, I mean. You know . . . after the example *they* set for us?"

Andie had no doubts. She could never do it, but Jess . . . well, Jess was strong. There was something vibrant and untouchable in her nature that had always enabled her to hold herself above the rank bitterness of the Tilly household.

"Look at Louisa and Rose," Andie said. "If they can manage it, you certainly can."

"Yeah, they're doing fine, apparently. But they got out sooner than we did."

"You're fine, Jess. More than fine, actually. You're perfect." Andie meant it. After all, out of the four Tilly sisters, it was only Andie herself who had really gotten away too late. "Does anyone else know?"

"Are you kidding?" Jess laughed. "I literally just peed on the stick this morning. You're the only one we've told. We're going to wait until the end of the first trimester to tell Susan. Or maybe until the baby turns eighteen."

Andie chuckled grimly. "Well, if she's still in the dark, at least she won't try to co-opt you at the pancake breakfast. Promise you'll stick with me?"

"Of course I'll stick with you. Always. And hey, you should invite Rhys. Will would love the petting zoo. Susan posted on the farm's Facebook page that they got some alpacas and a couple of miniature horses. Blond ones. They're so cute they'd make your eyes bleed."

"Maybe," Andie equivocated. The very idea of bringing Rhys within spitting distance of Susan was likely to give her hives.

"Okay, I have to pee," Jess grumbled. "It begins! But I'm not going to be one of those high-maintenance pregnant women. I promise."

"All right, go!" Andie laughed. She sat motionless at the table as Jess swished into the restroom, letting this new reality settle over her, delicately feeling out her reaction as if she were probing her mouth for a new tooth. After the initial shock subsided, she was surprised to discover that what she felt—far more acutely than the fear that had always surged at the idea of Jess having children—was a gentle buzz of excitement. The optimism that had lifted her over the past few days reasserted itself, and warmth bloomed in her chest.

When Jess returned to the table, they chatted about ultrasounds, maternity clothes, and outlandish contenders for baby names. Persephone emerged as the day's top pick for a girl; Silas, for a boy. Andie had never had the chance to experience this with Louisa or Rose.

As she and Jess hugged and finally went their separate ways, Andie's eyes pricked with tears. She found Ernie and had to sit for several minutes before she was able to fit the key into the ignition. Her eyes brimmed and overflowed as she was gripped by a blend of happiness and grief so confusing that she lost track of what she was even crying about. She shook her head and started Ernie with a businesslike flick of the wrist, wondering at the power of those warm tears that seemed intent on carving inroads in the glacial lump in her chest that had been her touchstone for so long.

CHAPTER TEN

"Ugh." Karina gave a shudder as she paused on the threshold of the indoor playground. "Is this where people come to die when they've entered the terminal phase of style-deficit disorder?" She gazed out at a sea of moms wearing spit-up-stained T-shirts and sweats.

"Because God forbid that raising a new life should be any reason to let one's *Vogue* subscription lapse," Rhys commented drily. He probably should have been angered by her wildly impolitic remark, but it was almost reassuring to see that Karina couldn't fully suppress her true colors, even when it was critical that she make a good impression. She cut a striking figure in her high black boots, tailored black pants, and a silky-looking black blouse sure to harbor a dry-clean-only tag somewhere within its folds.

Will clung to Rhys like a limpet, not at all sure what to make of this exotic-looking stranger. Karina's first few moments with her son weren't the poignant, theatrical reunion she might have wished for. She'd met them at the entrance to Imagination Station, and when she'd leaned in too close to greet Will, he'd buried his head against Rhys's shoulder, hugging his favorite wooden Thomas train to his chest and running a compulsive finger across the worn disk of the train's animated face.

Tears were still drying on Will's cheeks from a showdown that had erupted only minutes before, when Rhys tried to persuade him to leave the toy in the car. It was an unwritten rule at the venue that personal toys were best left at home, as sharing wasn't exactly the forte of the playground's young clientele. But Rhys had eventually backed down, figuring that the meeting with Karina was enough of a challenge that Will might need his precious comfort object.

Looking a little nonplussed that the playground's policy required her to surrender her boots at the entrance, Karina tucked them into a bright-yellow cubby next to Rhys's and Will's shoes.

Imagination Station was a large warehouselike space, with areas marked out for different kinds of play. There were blocks, ride-on toys, a crafts-and-puzzles corner, a slide, a ball pit, a rose-covered cottage stocked with toy appliances and plastic food, and a replica fire truck for the toddlers to climb on. The scent of diapers, sweaty feet, disinfectant, and rubber was overlaid with eau de juice box and the faint aroma of stale Goldfish crackers.

"This place must be an incubator for some kind of super virus," Karina said, her nose wrinkling as they stepped onto the bouncy flooring.

"When it's twenty degrees outside and your toddler needs to blow off some steam, there aren't a huge number of options."

"Well, do they at least serve coffee?" Karina asked as she whisked out of the way of a grimy-faced little girl bearing down on her with a plastic lawn mower.

"It's strictly bring your own," Rhys said, gesturing to his stainless-steel commuter mug.

"Where do we sit?" Karina was surveying the area as if to locate a lounger from which to view the action. She craned her neck, perhaps hoping a drinks waiter might still emerge from behind the miniature country cottage at the end of the large room.

"We don't." Will was already toddling off toward a large, orange twisty slide, and Rhys lost no time in following him.

Making his determined way up the ladder to the apex of the slide, Will began to fuss when he got stuck behind a little boy who'd come to a dead stop three rungs from the top. Sure enough, the vertigo-afflicted toddler started backing down, stepping perilously close to Will's fingers. Rhys ducked in and supported Will, moving him far enough to the side so that the other child could climb back to safe ground.

Karina, a game look on her face, positioned herself at the bottom of the slide to meet Will as he came down. But as soon as he saw her there, her gaze a little too avid, her arms outstretched to block any escape route, Will began to cry, furiously working his chubby little legs against the plastic chute as if to scrabble his way back up to the top.

"Maybe we should build something instead," Rhys suggested quickly, moving to the front of the slide to scoop Will up. He lifted Will onto his shoulders to distract him and strode toward an enclosure filled with colored blocks, Karina trailing along behind.

"Will, would you like the blue block?" she asked once they were settled in the new space. Her voice was shrill, her manner too insistent, as she knelt on the floor and waved a plastic brick before Will's eyes.

"Will?" she pressed, her aquamarine eyes so close that Will recoiled from their intrusion. A pit opened up in Rhys's stomach. She reminded him of how *he'd* been in those agonizing months after Will's first birthday, when speech should have started to blossom, and Rhys had dogged his small son—constantly pointing and naming, prowling over him with a strained smile in an attempt to elicit a response, performing a virtual cabaret of communication skills at every turn. But where Rhys knew his son through the everyday intimacy of being there, Karina had no way to read the nuances of his behavior or to know when she was overdoing it.

He had prepped her on the phone a few days before and sent her some of the parenting books and articles he'd found most helpful, but there was no substitute for face-to-face experience, and Will and Karina were still, for all intents and purposes, strangers to each other.

Will, brow furrowed, turned pointedly away, selecting his own blue block from the jumble on the floor.

Karina dipped her head, her silk-swathed chest rising and falling rapidly as she struggled to control her breathing. She brushed away what might have been a tear, and a pang of compassion tore through Rhys. *She's really feeling this.*

"I'd hoped . . ." She trailed off. "I don't know what I'd hoped."

He reached out a hand and placed it tentatively on her shoulder but withdrew it quickly, disconcerted by the tense fragility of her form and her body heat warming the silk. Her frame felt small and slight, as if it were made of sparrow bones, and it was almost inconceivable to think they'd once been physically close.

"You can't take it personally," he said. "Will operates according to a logic all his own."

"I know." Karina swallowed hard and flashed a quick smile. "I'm fine, really. I'll just keep trying."

"Take it slow," he suggested. "There'll be other days."

"Thanks. I appreciate that."

She sniffed and hesitantly met his gaze. "I'm sure your girlfriend has no trouble bonding with him."

Frustration welled up at Karina's willful misunderstanding.

"Andie isn't my girlfriend," he said. "I already told you she's Will's occupational therapist, and she's staying with us for three months." He decided not to mention his hope that he could prevail upon Andie to stay longer.

"Rhys, I'm not an idiot. The woman answered the door in her pajamas—"

"For the last time, she is Will's therapist, and I'd appreciate it if you would stop casting aspersions."

"Oh . . ." Karina broke off, her demeanor already brightening as the message finally sank in.

In fact, by the time Will took off in the direction of the ball pit, her expression was so happily preoccupied that Rhys already regretted clarifying the situation. He could practically see the lavish schemes hatching under cover of Karina's sweeping lashes. With a deep sigh, he tossed back the dregs of his coffee and took off after his son.

Will left his train on the wide ledge around the ball pit and maneuvered himself into the enclosure, where another toddler boy wallowed delightedly in a sea of red, blue, and yellow plastic orbs. The boy's mother sat on the ledge, a harried expression knitting her brow. In addition to the toddler who played in the ball pit, she had an infant tucked against her chest in one of those stretchy fabric wraps. She looked exhausted, with dark shadows under her eyes and wisps of red hair escaping from a haphazard ponytail. Rhys gave her an awkward nod as he hovered nearby.

Will was more interested in the tactile novelty of plowing through the pit than he was in the other boy—until the boy reached for Will's train. Rhys saw the conflagration looming as the plump little hand closed around Thomas's familiar, weathered sides. He cursed himself for not persevering with Will in the battle to leave the toy in the car. Anyone who got between Will and Thomas was asking for trouble.

"Um." Rhys hesitated, unsure of what to say to the mother, who whipped her head around to face him.

Rhys's mind went blank. He'd seen these negotiations play out before, usually between parents who conducted a saccharine, singsong one-way dialogue that modeled dispute resolution for their offspring, sometimes with a decided edge. *We share our toys, don't we, Beckham? But seeing as the other little boy doesn't want to share, we'll give the toy back.*" But there was no way Will would be a compliant participant in such a ritual. Not when Thomas was in a rival's hands.

Will uttered a throaty squawk and started thrashing his way through the slippery sea of balls to get to the other child.

"I think . . ." Rhys started again but was distracted by the way the mother's eyebrows had rushed together, deepening the furrow between them.

"He thought it was a playground toy," she said defensively. "Jack, the train belongs to the other little boy. Mommy needs to take it back now."

"Thomas! Thomas!" Jack said passionately, clutching the train to his body.

Oh, no. Will was getting closer, and judging from the expression on his face, he was about to do something desperate.

Will has autism. He just doesn't understand . . . The words quivered on the tip of Rhys's tongue, but when the moment of truth came, he found that he simply couldn't bring himself to say them. Why should he announce the achingly personal fact of his son's diagnosis to a perfect stranger?

He was about to lean in and retrieve Will when a black shadow flitted by. Swooping in like a bird of prey, her sleeves a flutter of silk, Karina wrenched the train from the hands of the astonished Jack. Rhys was horrified to see that she pulled hard enough to create a recoil effect. As soon as the toy was torn from his hands, Jack flew backward and crashed down hard in the slippery mass of balls. He appeared unhurt, but if there was anything less becoming than a full-grown adult skirmishing with a diaper-clad child over a toy, Rhys had yet to see it.

"There," Karina said with satisfaction, just as the boy's shrill scream split the cavernous space. Dozens of alarmed faces turned their way to witness the sinister black-clad woman triumphantly brandishing the toy purloined from her pint-size victim.

With Thomas still in Karina's grasp—out of the frying pan and into the fire, as far as Will was concerned—Will added his voice to the commotion.

Jack's mother's face looked bloodless, her stricken expression making Rhys want to fold in on himself in a penitential origami sculpture, growing smaller and smaller until he wasn't there at all.

"That woman manhandled my son." The aggrieved parent raised an accusing finger at Karina as the infant in the wrap began to stir and whimper, small fists balling against his mother's shirt.

"I'm sorry," Rhys said thickly as he stepped over the edge of the ball pit, bracing his weight on both sides of the barrier so he could haul Will into his arms. "I'm really sorry."

Karina drew herself up indignantly. "I—"

"Not another word," Rhys said through gritted teeth. Holding a still-shrieking Will against his chest, he stalked to the door, stepping into his shoes and stooping to grab the rest of their gear before they escaped into the frigid winter day, pandemonium erupting in their wake.

Karina hobbled out after them seconds later, her boots still unzipped. She passed the toy into Will's hands, causing a minor reduction in the decibel level issuing from directly beside Rhys's ear. Will was past the point of being immediately soothed by the return of the train.

"I don't believe it," Rhys fumed, storming across the parking lot to the Range Rover.

"What?" Karina demanded. "While you were standing there dithering, I did what had to be done."

"You practically assaulted a child." Rhys swung Will's door open and began to buckle him into his car seat. "I wonder if this is the first time a family has been blackballed from the indoor playground."

"That boy took Will's toy. I got it back. Plain and simple." Karina flounced around to the passenger-side door and took a seat instead of retreating to her own car. Clearly, she wasn't going to let them escape to lick their wounds but, instead, wanted to stay for a while and push their aggravation to the limit.

"I know you haven't spent much time in parenting circles," Rhys said, unable to contain his exasperation, "but conflicts generally aren't settled gladiator-style. The goal is to model self-control and diplomacy."

He started the ignition and turned the heat way up, trying to take the edge off the chill.

"Well, maybe I haven't spent much time in parenting circles," Karina asserted, the tip of her nose going pink and her eyes starting to shimmer. "But just then I *felt* like a parent. I felt like a mama bear."

To Rhys's consternation, Karina was apparently so moved by the idea of reclaiming her maternal role that passionate tears were flowing down her cheeks. The only positive development was that Will's cries were tapering off as he turned his attention to the familiar cluster of toys on the backseat.

"I failed him when he was little," she sobbed. "He needed me, and I failed him. I was in no state to parent him, and who knows what effect my leaving had on him?"

Am I now supposed to comfort her for abandoning him? A desperate, suffocating frustration seethed in Rhys's chest. *And must she always turn the narrative to put herself in the center?*

"Autism is a neurodevelopmental condition," he said, his voice tight. "Will's autism has nothing to do with your leaving."

"Well, I'm here now to fight for him," Karina continued. "He needs his mother."

The implication being that I haven't been fighting for him every day of his life? Rhys bristled. *And that the mysterious void in his existence should now be filled by a fickle heroine whose superpower is vanquishing toddlers and stealing candy from babies?*

Karina turned wide, wet eyes on him. "Rhys, I think I should move back into the house."

"What?" Rhys sucked in a stinging mouthful of air, and all of a sudden he was coughing, his incredulity leaving no room for breath.

"I should be on Will's team," Karina said with almost religious fervor. "I want to be there for him every day."

"Karina, you are *not* moving back into the house," Rhys wheezed, once his speech returned.

"Why not?" she countered. "You have plenty of room, and you've already installed *employees* there to take care of Will. Shouldn't helping him be more important than any hard feelings between us?" She readjusted the drape of her silk blouse, perhaps wanting to perfect the magnanimous picture she believed she presented.

"Let me be clear." Rhys pinched the bridge of his nose, trying to restore his equanimity. "You will not now, and nor will you ever, occupy the position you once did in our lives or our house. You deserted us, and even if we don't look too closely at the sordid details of that particular betrayal, there's no going back."

"I know it will take time—" Karina began.

"No," Rhys intoned. "Time won't fix it. Sad puppy eyes won't fix it. Hell, the bloody Dalai Lama wouldn't be able to fix it. I'm offering you the chance to get to know Will under my conditions. Take it or leave it."

"Fine. Be that way." Karina reached for the door handle. "We can talk more next time I see Will." She swung the door open and angled herself to leave.

"Karina?"

"Yes?"

"Where *are* you staying?" He figured he should know, if they were going to persevere with her visits.

"With a friend," she spat. "I've been reduced to sleeping on a couch and sharing a bathroom. Last night her boyfriend clogged the toilet. Are you happy?"

As she slammed the door, he wasn't sure whether to laugh or cry. But it did occur to him to wonder whether she'd already blown through the very generous settlement he'd given her. And, as she stalked away across the parking lot, he couldn't help but observe that she hadn't even bothered saying good-bye to Will.

~

It was closing in on dusk when Andie turned up the long driveway toward the house after her shopping escapade with Jess. As Will's therapy session was off the day's schedule, she'd had plenty of time to linger on the return trip. She stopped in the center of Concord to browse in a bookstore and pick up a few groceries—small, mindless activities that kept her mind only half-engaged, allowing her to thoroughly enjoy the mood of optimism that still buoyed her.

Her attention would stray for a moment, and then, returning to herself, she would be surprised anew by the astonishing circumstances that had shifted her outlook. *Rhys trusts me. Rhys is my friend. Plus, I'm going to be an aunt—for real, this time.* It was as if she had to become acquainted with these facts from different angles, to come upon them almost by surprise over and over again to reassure herself that they would hold firm. Firm enough to become the scaffolding for her dream of a different kind of life.

As she drove up to the house, she spotted a dark figure outlined against the pale stone of the front steps. *Who is that?* As she drew closer, the image resolved itself into Rhys's lean shape, swathed in a well-cut black wool coat and jeans. He sat with his usual casual grace, leaning against the stone balustrade, his long legs crossed at the ankle. She slowed as she pulled into the turning circle, and he raised one hand in greeting. *It's almost as if he's . . . waiting for me.*

She pulled Ernie into the garage bay but decided to walk around the outside of the house rather than take the interior staircase.

"Aren't you freezing?" she asked as she reached the front entrance, her shoes crunching on the gravel. To the west, behind the house, the sky was darkening from lilac to deep purple. The front of the house, with its jutting portico and overhanging Juliet balconies, was somewhat sheltered from the wind, but the air was still cold enough to make Andie's nose and ears tingle.

"What, me?" Rhys smiled. "I don't feel the cold. I have this." He warmed his fingers around a large coffee mug. "Besides, I needed to clear my head."

"Care for some company?"

"Actually, I would."

"How did it go today?" She set down the shopping bags looped around her fingers.

"Before I open that can of worms, do you want to grab yourself a coffee to stay warm?" Rhys asked. "There's a fresh pot."

"No, thanks. I'm fine. Adding more coffee to my system would just give me palpitations."

Instead of sitting on the step beside Rhys, she decided to hop up on the balustrade above him.

"I see you're fond of the high perch," Rhys commented wryly. He fixed her with a curious look that made her legs all quivery.

"Just like *Yertle the Turtle*," Andie agreed, referencing the book she'd overheard Rhys reading to Will the night before.

"Dr. Seuss, teacher of life lessons," Rhys sighed.

"So, what life lessons have you learned today?"

"Beware of Karina, for one," he said. "But I knew that already."

"How did Will do with her?"

"Not terribly well. She's so impatient to connect with him that she's sabotaging herself."

"Poor Karina." There was something ineffably sad about the fact that Will couldn't understand the significance of the gorgeous, lonely, high-strung mother who'd come back to reconcile with him.

"And there was an incident at the playground. A hostage situation involving Thomas the Tank Engine."

"Oh, dear. That sounds unpleasant."

"It needn't have been a big deal. Will left his train for a moment, and another boy picked it up, perfectly innocently. Of course, Will wanted to take the kid down—"

"But you stopped him?"

"Karina did it for him." Rhys shook his head ruefully. "She tackled him. It was unbelievable. I don't think we'll be able to show our faces there again."

"Oh, no. She put her hands on someone else's child?"

"Yup. Left him sitting on the seat of his pants with a stunned look on his face. And then the screaming started."

"Yikes."

"It was quite a scene." Rhys took a gulp from his cup. "But I blame myself."

"How could you have known what she was going to do?"

"I couldn't. But the problem is that I froze," he said softly. "The other kid's mom thought I was pissed off that he'd taken the toy. But I was just worried about Will having a meltdown."

He took a deep breath. "That was the moment I should have come right out and said it: 'Will has autism.'" Rhys shook his head, an expression of ineffable sadness settling in his eyes. "This woman had no idea why we were so stressed out about the train, and I could have helped her understand. But I couldn't say it."

Rhys's hands clamped tighter around his mug, his knuckles forming pale peaks. "I physically couldn't make the words come out of my mouth. It would have felt like this . . . this *steamroller* riding right over the top of Will's life, his future."

Rhys swept a hand through his hair, leaving ruffled strands pointing in all directions. "So, as I stood there brooding, Karina took it upon herself to save the day."

"With dramatic consequences."

"Quite."

"You know," Andie said gently, lowering herself down from the balustrade, "mentioning Will's autism in public is perfectly okay."

A field of energy seemed to engulf her as she squeezed in beside him on the step, almost shoulder to shoulder.

Rhys sighed. "I know—and it's not like it's any kind of secret. It's just that I don't want to attach some kind of label to him—some kind of disclaimer: 'This is my son, Will. He has autism, so you'll just have to excuse him, because he can't *do* any better.'"

His voice cracked. "I don't want him to hear me talking about him to some stranger. Reducing him to a label. Dismissing him. Dismissing all he will be—and all that he already is."

"There's no requirement for you to announce his autism to everyone you meet," Andie said, nudging Rhys's shoulder with her own. Every molecule in her body seemed to jangle and jump at the contact, and she had to fight to regain her focus. "But even if you did, so what? Will is still Will."

She turned to look at him. "Remember, he's not even three yet, Rhys. Anything could happen. By using the word 'autism,' you're not making his outcome a self-fulfilling prophecy. You're just helping people understand, in the moment—like you said, about the mom at the playground. It's not a stigma. It's a tool. It gives you explanatory power."

"You're right." Rhys buried his head in his hands for a moment.

"Speaking of explanations," he said, sighing again, "Karina has decided to cast herself as the heroine in Will's story. She's attributing his autism to her absence, and now she thinks miracles will accompany her triumphal return."

"Seriously?"

"She even announced that she wants to move back into the house."

"And what did you say?" Andie asked, skewered by a pang of anxiety.

"That it's not going to happen." A note of incredulity colored his response. "But, at the same time, I can't deprive him of knowing his mother."

"No."

"I just want to do what's right for him."

"You're not doing so badly." Andie wondered whether she ought to hook a comforting arm around Rhys's shoulders. *Would a friend do that?* But those shoulders looked so dauntingly high and wide from this angle. She'd have to stretch awkwardly to maneuver herself into the right position. And if merely sitting beside him caused this dangerous tug of attraction, she didn't see how she could increase the contact and not jump right out of her skin.

"At the end of our café meeting the other day, Karina was going on about 'Why us?'" Rhys said, lifting one hand and pressing his fingers to his temples. "I was so furious with her. I know she was talking about autism, but it was like she was wishing some quintessential part of Will away. And then I realized I'm not much better. All that self-pity."

"It would be pretty unusual if you didn't feel that way," Andie pointed out. "In fact, it would be unnatural. You're not expected to be a saint."

"But there's a certain amount of ego involved, you know? I assumed, just like Karina, that because we're relatively fortunate people—healthy, reasonably intelligent, with all of our fingers and toes—that our child would get a free pass on the hard stuff. But, really, why the hell not us?"

"No reason at all, I suppose, statistically speaking," Andie said. "And I can tell you one thing for sure."

"What's that?"

"If I were Will, I'd be thanking my lucky stars it *is* you and not someone else who gets to have him."

Rhys looked away for a moment, and when he turned back, his expression was so raw that she felt her heart lurch.

"It takes one quirky mind to know another," he said. "After all, if you're looking for a reason for Will's autism, I'm half of that puzzle."

"Maybe so," Andie said. "But it's your love for Will I was talking about, your dedication. Just look at your connection with him and all you've already done for him."

"I'm lucky I have the resources to give him what he needs," Rhys reflected soberly. "Imagine what it must be like for a single parent on minimum wage. They sure as hell can't hire their own personal Andie."

"Well, no. Aside from the fact that there's only one of me—"

"And you're taken," Rhys interjected. He turned back to her and smiled, and something in his expression sent a pulse of warmth all the way to her toes. There was an intimately proprietorial ring to his comment that only days before would have made her heart quail. But now she was able to let it vibrate pleasantly through her veins. Rhys was her friend, and right now she was where she was meant to be.

Rhys looked down at his hands still clasped around his coffee mug. When he looked up, his expression was slightly sheepish.

"Sorry, Andie," he said. "I'm such a sad sack. I can't help fretting about Will's future. Who will he be? What will become of him? Will he be happy? Will he be loved?"

"He will be exactly who he is," Andie said. "And you'll just have to try to keep up."

Rhys laughed ruefully while getting to his feet. "You're probably right . . . wait, I just noticed my coffee is stone cold, and one hand may, in fact, be frozen to my cup."

"Yeah, my teeth are chattering," Andie agreed.

Rhys reached out and took her hand, tugging her to her feet. "Thanks for listening," he said as they climbed the stairs to the front door.

"My pleasure," she said as Rhys stooped to help her gather her shopping bags.

And it was, she reflected. In fact, this time with Rhys and Will was turning out to be one of the most fulfilling periods of her life. The question was no longer how she was going to settle in here without sacrificing her peace of mind. It was how she was ever going to leave.

CHAPTER ELEVEN

Andie paused on her way down the staircase, picking up an almost subliminally slight waft of bergamot and jasmine in the air. Rhys and Will were out with Karina now, on her fourth visit, and Andie couldn't help but wonder how they were doing. She always felt slightly queasy until they returned. She was getting way too attached, she reflected grimly. Somehow they had taken up an immutable place on her psychic-radar screen. Her awareness of them glowed luminously against the black field of her customary solitude.

Her friendship with Rhys had deepened in recent days as they'd ventured out into the world with Will, working to expand his tolerance for the incursions of daily life. They'd taken him for a haircut, made one memorably awful trip to the grocery store, and even went out one evening to brave a meal at a family-friendly restaurant. They'd almost made it through their entrées before Will's patience ran out, and they had to beat a quick retreat. It was all therapy in action, but somehow Andie suspected she might be the one being most profoundly transformed.

She emerged into the kitchen to find Jillian huffing, lunging, and jogging on the spot as she unpacked groceries, occasionally stopping to nibble on a thin slice of ham from a rolled-up selection on a plate.

"Having a meaty snack?" Andie asked as she pitched in to help.

"Early dinner," Jillian corrected morosely. "Geoff and I are going bowling tonight, and if I don't have something now, I'll cave and eat french fries."

"Are you sure that's enough for a meal?" Andie looked dubiously at the small, slippery stack of deli meat.

"Yup, it's on the Dukan diet." Jillian performed a squat as she stowed a bag of peas in the freezer. "I'm upping my game. Geoff lost four pounds last week. Four! And he works a desk job. I'm on my feet all day, and all I lost was a lousy half pound."

"Not fair," Andie agreed. "But you look great."

"A friend is coaching me. Next week Geoff will be eating my dust."

Andie laughed. "It probably beats protein powder."

Just then, the sound of murmurs and footsteps heralded the arrival of Rhys and Will. They swung into the kitchen looking tired, rumpled, and altogether too good to be true.

"How did it go?" Andie asked.

"Okay." Rhys shrugged. "We had to brave the indoor playground again because Will was too noisy for the library. The only person who knew us from last time was the woman who runs the place, and she stopped giving us the evil eye after a while."

"Nice."

"But the peace didn't last long," Rhys said. "Karina trod in some wet stuff. Probably apple juice, but the jury is still out. Her foot was soaked. She didn't take it well."

"I'm sorry," Andie commiserated.

"I *hope* it was apple juice," Jillian chimed in.

"Now we're really banned." Rhys grimaced, putting Will down so he could toddle over to the train table. "Mrs. Hodge can still take Will there, though, I suppose."

Rhys started searching through the cupboards. "Will's starving. He ate his way through two bags of Goldfish crackers and was ready to start on a third. I'd better feed him."

"And I'd better be off," said Jillian, popping the last piece of ham into her mouth and chewing efficiently as she surveyed her fitness tracker. "At least I'll get some more steps in at the bowling alley."

Soon, Will had been fed, and Andie and Rhys whisked him upstairs for bathtime. If his happy squeals were any indication, the nightly ritual was quickly becoming one of his favorite activities. And why not? He now had enough bath toys to sink a battleship, and he had Rhys and Andie wrapped firmly around his little finger. Despite their best efforts, he still insisted on Rhys actually getting into the tub with him each time.

Andie had hoped the sight of Rhys in his swimming trunks would lose its impact by virtue of sheer repetition, but her central nervous system wasn't getting the message.

"This is starting to feel pretty high maintenance," Rhys said, laughing as he lowered himself into the tub for what, by her count, was the fifteenth such exposure. *Oh, those arms. And whoever had installed the lighting in this bathroom deserved some kind of medal.* The warm glow set off his skin tone to perfection. Andie swallowed down the lump in her throat and tried to ignore the far-more-dangerous ripple of heat in her belly. *He's your friend, remember?*

"He obviously doesn't like having to sit directly in the tub," Andie said. "I'm not sure if he feels safer being on your lap because he's held a little above the water, or because it's you."

"Maybe a little bit of both?"

"We could try him in an adaptive bath chair. They're pretty comfortable, and it would sit him up higher but still give us the access to bathe him properly."

"Sounds perfect." Rhys nodded as he soaped up Will and rinsed him off. "Why don't you order one?"

"They're pretty expensive, and I'm not sure if insurance covers it."

"Andie, if I need to, I'll sell my Porsche." He shot her an ironic look. "Really, it's not a problem."

"Okay, then." Andie grinned.

Rhys lifted Will up and into the fluffy bath towel she held in her outstretched arms, and she hugged the damp, fragrant bundle of little boy, setting him down so she could dry him off.

Rhys looked at her intently through the steam. "How about joining me for dessert or a drink after I put Will to bed?" he asked.

Her reply was out before she'd even processed the idea. "I'd like that." *Of course you'd like it. Just look at the man!* But, as lightning fast as her response came out, some quiet part of her was aware that something between them was shifting. Or at least that it might, if she were to allow it. Rhys's invitation opened the path to new territory, even as she was still trying to find her footing on the old. A stab of panic tore through her.

Rhys made matters worse by choosing that exact moment to unfold his lean form and step from the tub. Rivulets of water trickled down the planes of his chest and stomach, and heat rose from his skin, diffusing his clean scent into the steamy air. Andie inhaled deeply, trying not to show outward evidence that he lit up her senses like a city switchboard.

"Meet you down there in half an hour?" Rhys suggested. "I'll read this guy a few stories and hope he drifts off."

"All right. Thanks, Rhys. I'll see you there." *Breathe.* She diverted her attention to Will, reaching out to ruffle his hair before letting herself out of the bathroom. "Good night, Will. Sleep tight."

By the time she walked tentatively down the staircase toward the den half an hour later, Andie thought she'd done a pretty good job of dousing the embers of her attraction to Rhys. She'd splashed cold water on her face, thrown open a window, and meditated cross-legged on the floor until her pulse had gone back to normal. It was quite simple, she told herself. She just had to remember where the line was in their relationship.

She repeated a decisive mantra as she drifted down the stairs to the foyer. *You're simply eating ice cream with your friend Rhys. Nothing to see here.* Fortunately, he'd probably be clothed by now. If there were any mercy in this world, he'd have covered those glorious arms with long sleeves.

Nope. No mercy. She paused in the den doorway, from which she could see Rhys adding another log to the fireplace. He'd dressed in a charcoal-gray burnout T and old jeans, and had set out a tray on the coffee table, stocked with pint containers, bowls, and glasses.

He looked up, spotting her. "Andie, come in. I rustled up a few flavors to choose from."

As she walked over to him, bathed in the warmth of his attentive smile, she could have sworn some evil sprite had snuck into her jeans and hooked up a live wire that led directly to her groin. *Okay, that was weird.* Rhys reached out to grab another log, his arm tensing and flexing in the flickering, coppery light. Andie sat down, training her gaze on the fireplace and its licking flames.

"So . . . ," she began, until she realized that every thought had flown from her head, apparently chased away by her nervous system's electrical-wiring problem. She searched her reservoir of small talk and came up empty. *What is happening to me?*

Rhys regarded her curiously. "Would you like a glass of wine?" He picked up a bottle of red that had been breathing on the sideboard and splashed a good measure into a glass.

"Um . . ." *Adding alcohol to this live-wire situation may not be the best move,* Andie fretted. Then again, wasn't alcohol supposed to lower psychological arousal? Or, wait . . . was it the other way around? Did it increase psychological arousal but lower physical arousal? Was this problem in her groin or her brain? *Oh, what the hell!* She was never going to get through this evening if she didn't do something about this evil-electrician sprite.

"Yes, please," she said, accepting the glass. She took a generous gulp, her tension loosening a little as the wine worked its warming magic. "This is such a great room," she said, gesturing at the huge fireplace and the ornate wood moldings.

"It did turn out pretty well," Rhys agreed. "Although I hated it at first."

"Really? Why?"

"It felt so fake, trying to create a nineteenth-century-British-gentlemen's-club feel in a new-construction house. Karina brought in a decorator as soon as we moved in here. It just felt weird, like she had this *GQ* idea of how to style me, and this room was my set."

Andie viewed the room with wide eyes. "But you have to admit she nailed it."

"I know," he said. "For the whole time she lived here, I kept a white laminate desk and orange office chair in that corner to mess up the ambience." He gestured to the end of the room, where an elegant array of built-ins sat beside a tall window framed by wine-colored velvet drapes. Andie could imagine the jarring effect.

"Psychological warfare, interior-design edition," she said in a deep mock voice-over. "Ouch."

"Yeah, not my finest moment, but it was satisfying at the time." Rhys gestured to the ice-cream-and-gelato selection on the coffee table. "Have some ice cream and try to forget I told you that."

He cast her a humorous, appreciative look as she piled some salted caramel and peanut butter brownie into a bowl. In the muted light, his eyes took on that purplish wood-smoke hue that made her want to stare. The live wire lashed and fizzed, spraying warning sparks.

"So, what happened between you and Karina anyway?" she asked, trying for a casual tone. *Did friends ask each other these kinds of questions?* "I know she left, but—"

"I'm embarrassed to talk about it," Rhys protested. "If you Google 'relationships' and 'clueless,' my name probably pops up."

"I've made some pretty awesome relationship blunders myself," Andie said encouragingly. "How about I tell you one of mine, and you can tell me yours?"

"Sounds fair." Rhys took a bracing gulp of his wine. "You go first."

"Okay, let me think." She closed her eyes and ran through the catalog. She hoped digging up one of her more humiliating examples would be enough to keep the sprite at bay. When she'd finally made a selection, she smiled beatifically.

"Picture this," she said, setting the scene. "Hipster Boyfriend Number Two. Skinny jeans. Goatee. Weird obsession with the hurdy-gurdy."

"Sounds like a complete tool." Rhys's brow furrowed slightly, but he seemed willing to play along.

"I met him at an indie coffee shop in my neighborhood," Andie said. "When not crafting artisanal instruments, he was a barista."

Rhys narrowed his eyes.

"Oh, it's true," Andie insisted, laughing. "So, we were together for a few months, and we got serious enough that I let him keep a toothbrush at my place."

"Let me guess," Rhys interjected drily. "It had to be your place because he still lived with his parents."

"With his mom," she confirmed with a wicked grin. "Anyway, I was just starting to develop a fondness for the tortured strains of the hurdy-gurdy. I think I was even considering asking if he wanted to move in, when he sent me this text dumping me."

"Why?"

"He was watching TV at his mom's, and he heard a song I liked being played on a *car commercial*. He said he couldn't be with someone who had 'sold out' so completely. Besides, he said dating was—and I quote—'a cliché.'"

"Okay, that's pretty great." Rhys leaned over to clink his glass against hers, but there was a turbulence in his gaze that she hoped she was imagining.

"Yeah, that's one of my favorites." She wasn't about to admit that Hipster Number Two had been one of the more serious boyfriends in a string of lightweight relationships deliberately chosen for their built-in self-destruct button.

She had always steered clear of dating grown-ups. Men who took on big commitments and accomplished things that meant something, men whose passion and energy struck an answering spark within her. Because men like that deserved more from her than she could ever offer. They deserved family, commitment—the whole nine yards.

Just such a man sat in front of her right now, and for a moment it pained her to look at him. It occurred to her that, in trying to keep things light, she had revealed more about herself than she'd intended. An uncomfortable thought. She ducked her head and cleared her throat, before presenting him with a face that was composed once again.

"So, tell me about Karina."

"Ah, well," he said soberly. "I'm afraid that's not a story that polishes up so well. She cheated on me. With my department chair at MIT. The same guy she ran off to California with when Will was a baby."

"Oh, no, that's awful. So it all happened after Will came along?"

"No, that's where it gets complicated." Rhys took another generous sip from his glass. "She actually started cheating on me with Lance pretty early in our relationship. Not that I knew it at the time."

"Okay, first of all, what kind of scumbag professor sleeps with his graduate students?" Andie shook her head disparagingly. "Do people still do that?"

"Lance is a bit of a walking cliché." Rhys flashed her an ironic glance that shot electricity down to her toes. "But a very married one. With two children."

"Oh, that's not good."

"Yeah, well, Karina's arrival in the department caused quite a stir. There still aren't enough women in engineering, so she kind of stood out."

And not only due to her statistical rarity, Andie was prepared to wager. Karina had a presence that would stand out anywhere. She felt a shriveling sensation inside. Was that . . . *jealousy?*

"Even I noticed her," Rhys said, shaking his head ruefully.

"Even you?"

"Well, I was pretty absorbed in my research at that point. I was studying large-scale flow structures around wind turbines—"

"Large-scale flow structures," she repeated, testing the words on her tongue. Somehow it sounded sexier when he said it.

"We were trying to measure velocity fields caused by blade-generated motions—"

"Uh, Rhys?" Andie said with a smile. "You can skip that part."

"Oh, right. Sorry." Rhys gave a self-deprecating grin. Andie moved her chair a fraction closer to the fire. Maybe if she focused on the warmth on her skin, she could ignore the fact that she was melting on the inside.

"Anyway, it would have taken a bomb going off to get my attention, but somehow Karina managed it. Things unfolded between us pretty quickly. It was a thrill to be able to discuss my research with someone I was getting so close to. She's brilliant."

Brilliant. *Check.* Supermodel good looks. *Check.* Andie found herself feeling a little less kindly toward the genetically gifted Karina with the Slavic cheekbones and Mensa IQ.

"But she was also much more insecure than I realized at the time," Rhys continued. "It wasn't easy for her, looking like that and being in a male-dominated field. She copped some pretty unsavory comments."

"That's horrible."

"She was really brave about it, but I know it ate away at her—all the 'Get back in the kitchen' crap and worse. A couple of times I came pretty close to clobbering some of the guys."

She could practically see the glowering Rhys swooping in like a vengeful archangel to defend women in the STEM subjects. She cast a furtive sidelong glance at him, trying not to notice the way the soft fabric of his T settled against the flat plane of his abs as he leaned back in his chair. She wondered what it would be like if a man like that were ever to defend *her*.

"I think because Karina felt threatened, she wanted everything all at once," Rhys continued. "Publications. Acclaim. She started pestering me for coauthorship credit on a research paper she had nothing to do with. There was no need for her to take shortcuts like that, but she was completely obsessed with the idea."

"But wouldn't that risk both your careers?"

"I realized later that was the point. It was the risk she loved as much as anything. She had to be right on the edge, or she didn't feel alive."

"Oh my God. It sounds completely exhausting." Andie's focus faded in and out. She was riveted by his story but also mesmerized by the beautiful shapes his lips made as they formed the words. *Those lips.* They were generous but not pouty, the upper one wide and well cut, the lower one fuller and almost indecently sensual.

"By that point we were already fighting constantly," he went on. "I said no to her request, of course. I wasn't a complete imbecile . . . and I didn't realize it until much later, but that's when she started her thing with Lance. The research paper was some kind of test, and I failed."

Uncertain what to say, Andie reached out and placed a tentative hand on Rhys's shoulder, giving a companionable squeeze. At the merest contact with him, the live wire spawned little live-wire tributaries. They ran everywhere, buzzing at the base of her spine, over her scalp, behind her knees, and back up to the hot spot between her legs. She drew her hand back in shock.

A thought jarred her. *What if I just leaned in and kissed him?* A few more inches and it would be done. He'd taste of red wine and salted caramel and . . . Rhys. She could already anticipate the hot jolt that would leap down her throat at the touch of his lips, his tongue electrifying every cell in her body, probably short-circuiting her entire system.

The only problem was that Rhys was off-limits. Her sad little anecdote about Hipster Boy had driven home a point she hadn't even realized she'd been making. A man like Rhys could never be just a dalliance or the punch line to an anecdote. He was so beautiful, so real, and so good. *Too good.* Besides, he was her friend, and throwing that away for the sake of a quick fling would be an insult to him and a betrayal of Will.

Not that the realization made it any easier. She had never felt like this—hypercharged, unsettled, and filled with the utter certainty that if he didn't touch her, and soon, she would simply flame out and fade into decrepitude from sheer neglect. Battling her impulses, she shrank farther down in her chair and turned her attention back to his tale of woe.

~

"So, how did you find out about Karina and Lance?"

Huh? Rhys had to force himself to focus. It felt like the height of irrelevance to be narrating the dead history of his relationship with Karina when Andie was near. *The way that woman licks a spoon! It ought to be outlawed. The way she . . . breathes.*

It was wrong of him, but she had inched down in her chair to bring her feet closer to the fire, and he had the perfect vantage to see right down her shirt, into the tantalizing valley between her breasts. Farther south, the hem of her shirt had ridden up far enough to expose a taut band of skin, ivory-pale and lustrous, above the waistband of her jeans. He felt the hot rush of blood to places he'd just as soon not think about, under the circumstances.

What if I just leaned in and kissed her? He imagined cupping the smooth curve of her cheek and parting her lips with his tongue to explore the sweetness within, his fingers twining into the heavy veil of dark hair that spilled over the back of her chair cushion. The air around him seemed to quiver with intention.

But the very subject of their conversation was enough to remind him that his relationship decisions had always left a path of destruction in their wake. Acting on impulse now would surely be the worst move he could make. Andie was an employee living in his house, and the linchpin of Will's treatment. He couldn't screw that up. Not for anything.

"A friend tipped me off after walking in on them one day in Lance's office," he said, picking up the thread of the story. "I was completely gutted. I ended it with her right away . . . then, several weeks later, she turned up on my doorstep announcing that she was eleven weeks pregnant, and I was the father."

"But how could you know for sure?"

"She swore blind she'd been in an off-again patch with Lance when it happened. I remembered the particular weekend. I didn't know it at the time, but she was finishing up a course of antibiotics for a sinus infection, and she'd forgotten about the potential for birth-control interactions."

"Oh, dear."

"Yes, well. She's brilliant, as I said, but flaky. She seemed contrite, vulnerable. What could I do? I wasn't about to abandon a child that could be mine," Rhys sighed. "I had a paternity test done, of course, once Will was born. But I knew the minute I laid eyes on him that he was mine. More mine than hers, in the end."

"She didn't want him?"

"Being a mother wasn't her top priority, but I take my share of the blame. We got married. I was pretty set on it. But I wasn't exactly a loving and attentive husband. She'd broken my trust, and it wasn't as easy to get over that as I'd hoped. Pride is one of my main faults, as it turns out."

He exhaled. "I wonder whether we might have been able to hold it together for Will's sake if I'd been a little easier on her."

His comment seemed to galvanize Andie, propelling her bolt upright in her chair. "Oh, no," she said, her eyes dark with intensity. "It might be a noble idea, but my mother stayed with my father until the bitter end, and it poisoned her. It poisoned everything . . ."

Rhys let out a controlled breath. At last, some insight into what lay behind Andie's bouts of reserve.

"Your father was a difficult man?" he asked softly.

"You could say that." Andie let out a pained laugh that made Rhys want to take her hand and enfold it in his. "He had problems with alcohol. He was a cop. Very macho and . . . domineering. He wasn't exactly overjoyed to find himself surrounded by five women. He spent the last six years of his life in a wheelchair, which took the fight out of him somewhat."

"I'm sorry. How did that happen?"

"He was shot while responding to a domestic-violence call when I was thirteen," Andie said. "Fate has a keenly developed sense of irony, apparently."

Ah. So Andie's father was abusive. He felt a powerful surge of indignation on her behalf.

"Yes, it does," he agreed. He turned to regard her, just as she did the same. Her breath whispered across his cheek. He could see so far into her eyes that he was overcome by a rush of vertigo. How did a woman like this emerge from a family like the one she'd come from? He would have kissed her at that moment, except he still felt like he was falling, gathering velocity like an avalanche as layers of desire, compassion, admiration, and tenderness added their weight to the sum of his feelings for her.

"Did he . . . hurt you?" He remembered her flinching on the night she'd shown up to confess to the almost-accident in the crosswalk.

"Me? Not physically, no." She gave a small shudder. "It was my mother who bore the brunt of it."

His fists unclenched, and he let out a sigh of relief. Her father hadn't laid his hands on her. Not that she could have felt safe in an environment like that, always waiting for the other shoe to drop. He wanted to make it up to her somehow, to console and nourish her, filling her world with good things, crowding out the bad memories until the pain had nowhere left to hide.

"Your bowl is empty," he pointed out. "You should try the hazelnut."

"I couldn't," she protested, her eyes warm. "I'm way too full."

"Another drop of wine, then?"

"No." She rose to her feet with a laugh, and he felt compelled to rise, too.

"Well," he said, with an ironic twist of the lips, "I don't know about you, but to me there's nothing more conducive to a good night's sleep than running through a list of my worst memories and romantic failures. I'm sorry, Andie. I meant for you to have fun tonight."

They were standing close together, and the sparks in her eyes kindled with amusement. She laughed again, her shoulders tilting so that her hair swung forward in a dark curtain. When she looked up, her expression was bright, fond.

"I did have fun." She was inches away, her cheeks pink from the warmth of the fire, her lips twisting wryly. "It's like the fortune cookie says: 'Happiness shared is doubled. Pain shared is halved.'"

"You're generous to say so. I feel like I've rather failed as a host."

"No, Rhys. You and failure are two things that don't belong in the same breath." Her expression grew more serious. "Somehow it doesn't hurt so much when I tell you things."

That was ironic, because his heart hurt as he looked steadily back at her. Actually ached, as he took in the sweet candor of her expression.

Longing surged through him, pushing against a tidal wall that was cracking at the seams. Of its own volition, his right hand drifted up to touch her cheek, her skin like sun-warmed velvet to his fingertips. Her lips parted in surprise, and his thumb drifted across to brush the bottom one, his pulse leaping as he felt its moist plushness.

Everything in him strained toward her, like a vine unfurling its tendrils toward the sun. He steadied himself, trying to imagine his feet rooted to the floor, his spine unbending—a giant oak rather than a vine. Firm and unyielding. He forced his hand back to his side. His yearning was so obvious she must have been able to see it.

They stood stock-still, gazes locked as time seemed to slow. Heat spread through his veins as she regarded him, her lips still slightly parted, her breath coming faster. Her lashes swept down, and she moistened her lips with the tip of her tongue, swaying almost imperceptibly toward him. But she stopped herself at the last instant, her left hand coming up between them, her fingers spread against his chest.

"It's late," she said, her cheeks suffused with color as she leaned away to place her almost-empty wineglass on the tray. "We'd better get some sleep. Based on Will's track record, one or both of us is going to be woken up in about three hours' time. Do you want me to take night duty tonight?"

"No, I'll do it." The empty space she'd occupied moments before left him feeling bereft as she turned and walked to the door. "Mrs. Hodge gave me the monitor. I'll bet she's putting in her earplugs tonight."

"Okay, then. Good night, Rhys," Andie said from the doorway.

"Good night, Andie," he responded, mentally levitating out the door and following her. He forced himself to stay still, his features as deliberately composed as if his world hadn't just tilted on its axis.

CHAPTER TWELVE

Coward. Andie berated herself as she brushed her teeth, making faces in the bathroom mirror. Part of her had wanted to prolong the pleasurable torture of her fireside confab with Rhys, but her nerve had failed when he'd looked at her in that unsettling way. Like she was somebody worthy of his esteem. His desire. And then when she stood to leave, and he'd risen with her, standing so close with his hand against her cheek, his intention to kiss her all but emblazoned on his forehead, the intensity of her reaction had startled her.

When his thumb had brushed her lower lip, her stomach had turned over. She'd leaned in, swayed by instinct and the powerful pull he exerted, but she'd been frightened by the answering rush of heat in her blood. The huge room had suddenly become too confining, too humid, too *close*, and their contact too honest. Too real.

I made up my mind to resist him, and I did. It should have felt like a triumph. Or at least a relief. So why did her escape weigh on her like the bitterest disappointment?

She put herself to bed with brisk efficiency, eager for unconsciousness to claim her. Of course, because she wanted it, her brain allowed her no such respite. When she tried to read, the words jittered across the page. When she closed her eyes, a powerful restlessness took over her limbs, making her toss and turn. When she finally did lapse into a shallow sleep, a dream tugged her back to a place she'd rather not go: her childhood home.

She saw Susan perched in her favorite nook in the kitchen, the yellowed stain of a fading bruise riding high on her left cheekbone. It should have been a scene of domestic harmony. Soup bubbled on the stove, and the voices of the older girls faded in and out. They giggled over something on TV in the den before drifting back into the kitchen to check on how soon dinner would be ready, only to be shooed away again by their father, Jim. Susan clutched a cup of coffee, her knuckles white and her eyes hollow as she stared across the room at her husband, who held Andie on his lap.

Andie could feel the solidity of her father's arms around her and the gentle tug of his fingers as he stroked her hair, but her body vibrated with tension. She tilted her face up to his, eager for an approving glance, only to see his narrowed eyes beaming their challenge across the kitchen at his wife, his lips curled into a lazy smile. Their silent exchange wasn't about her, yet Andie was trapped at its center, a particle suspended in a charged field.

It was one of those dreams where you need to get out, but your surroundings are as sticky and intractable as taffy. Jim's arms, muscle-bound and sheathed in his dark-uniform shirtsleeves, locked around her like the bars of a cage. She smelled the sour blast of alcohol on his breath, felt the malevolent energy that rippled through his body, although his fingers in her hair were deceptively soft.

Susan's stare flicked over her, and she might have imagined it, but she thought she saw darkness gathering in her mother's eyes. Andie shivered, in spite of the humid warmth of the kitchen and the furnace of her father's lap.

It was then that Will's raw, penetrating wail cut into the dream. Andie struggled to sit up, her heart pounding. She squinted at the clock:

1:57. Superimposed over the afterimage of her dream, Will's screams made her throat constrict in panic. *I have to get him.* She swung her legs out of the bed and moved toward the crack of light under the door to the hallway. The sound in the corridor was much louder, hastening her steps. She entered the room to the sight of Will marooned on his bed, tears soaking his face.

The screams abated a little as he saw Andie and reached out his arms to be lifted from the bed. She folded his small body against hers as if it belonged there, bobbing soothingly on the balls of her feet. Tenacious toddler fists gripped the straps of her camisole tank top. The straps were her tether, ensuring that she couldn't leave him until he released her. She danced in a small circle around the perimeter of the rug, bouncing and weaving, murmuring and hugging him with a steady, reassuring pressure. The soothing motions and the comfort of his solid form snuggled so resolutely against her chest began to work their magic on her as well.

A shaft of light illuminated them as the door swung open, and Rhys, barely awake, swayed at the threshold of the room. He wore flannel pajama bottoms, a loose T-shirt, and a sleepy expression that was disturbingly sexy.

"What are you doing?" He yawned, swiping a hand through hair that stood endearingly on end.

"Will woke up," Andie stage-whispered, motioning for Rhys to stay quiet.

"I can see that," he said, padding into the room and gently rubbing the toddler's tousled curls. "You didn't need to get him. I said I would."

"It was automatic. I heard him, I came in." She continued to rock and sway, angling her head to press her cheek to Will's sweet-smelling hair. "I was only half-awake, and I forgot that you planned to do night duty."

"Well, thank you." Andie could hear, rather than see, his smile. He stood close, his scent magnified by the recent warmth of his bed.

Will gave a faint hiccup as he relaxed against her shoulder, his eyelids at half-mast.

"I can take him," Rhys said. "You should get some sleep."

Rhys held out his arms, and she angled toward him, beginning the delicate maneuver of transferring a barely sleeping child from one adult to another. Andie hiked Will higher and tried to pry him from her torso, but his body molded tenaciously to her own, sheltering against her in a comfortable doze. Rhys moved to the side, trying to shift his son's weight. He found some leverage but had to place one hand between Andie's body and Will's.

All of a sudden she felt the cool rush of air against her left breast, and a shock of sensation as a warm hand grazed the peak of her bare nipple. In the dizzying mix of confusion and outright embarrassment that overtook her, Andie had to struggle to support Will's weight before he was lifted out of her arms. *What the hell just happened?* She took a step back, fumbling to rearrange her tank top.

"I'm sorry, I didn't mean to . . ." Rhys faltered. "I don't even know what . . ."

Will must have tightened his fists around her straps and gripped hard, pulling her tank top from her body just as Rhys reached in.

"Uh . . . don't worry about it. Will has a strong grip." She laughed uncomfortably, but Rhys had turned away, applying himself with exaggerated focus to the task of settling Will on his bed.

Andie stood rooted to the spot as a scorching flush inflamed her cheeks. She didn't want to leave the room with things still so unsettled between them. But how could she stay? The accidental touch made a mockery of the stark longing she'd felt for Rhys in the den earlier, and of how right it had felt to hold Will in her arms for those brief, comforting moments.

She could imagine two loving parents involved in the close, physical work of caring for a young child. There would be a kind of beauty to it: the ebb and flow, the casual touches, the affectionate dance of

146

domestic intimacy. If the situation had been different—if she hadn't backed away from their almost-kiss in the den—the accidental brush might have been nothing but a blip. Easily forgotten in the onrush of their deepening intimacy.

But she had cut and run. And now the atmosphere in Will's room was thick with mutual embarrassment. *It's a good thing,* she reminded herself. *That kind of intimacy is off-limits to you.* But, at that moment, all the arguments she'd ever mustered to barricade herself from Rhys were no more than dust. She couldn't even remember why they had mattered. Now she wished—more fervently than anything—that she had kissed him. It had been a crossroads, she realized, and now she was careering down the wrong road, powerless to halt her momentum and find her way back.

"I'm happy to stay and help," she offered, her voice sounding feeble to her own ears.

His expression, faintly discernible in the dim light, made Rhys look like he would rather be anywhere but there.

"No, please," he insisted, the lines of his face tense. "You should go. I've got this."

A knot formed in her throat as she shuffled to the door and let herself out into the corridor. That was that, then. The only way Rhys would ever touch her was by accident, and she'd have to make her peace with it.

CHAPTER THIRTEEN

Five days later, Rhys was stuck, in more ways than one. He cursed as an Audi boxed him into the parking spot he'd just started to back out of. He'd given Mrs. Hodge a couple of hours off and left work early to pick Will up from preschool to spend the afternoon with him. It was becoming increasingly difficult to find any quality time at all with his son now that Rhys had effectively barred himself from the shared areas of the house during waking hours.

Unable to face Andie, he'd buried himself in work ever since the incident in Will's room. He'd handed bath duty back to Mrs. Hodge, who, with raised eyebrows, had agreed to work with Andie on the task.

Rhys felt he was the worst kind of coward. He'd left extra early for work the morning after the brush in the dark. He hadn't been ready to face Andie—hadn't known how on earth to finesse the strangely intimate screwup that threw the unacknowledged tension between them into such stark relief. It was easier not to deal with it at all.

The problem was that each moment of avoidance drove the wedge between them that much deeper. If he'd shown up at dinnertime on the first evening after the snafu, he now imagined, they might have been able to laugh it off over a casual glass of wine in the kitchen. But he hadn't manned up, and the longer the void stretched between them, the more impossible it was for him to imagine bridging it. This afternoon he couldn't just head home with Will, because Andie would probably be there, and he'd be struck mute with excruciating self-consciousness the moment he fell under the spell of the woven spokes of gold in her eyes.

If only he'd followed his impulse and kissed her that night in front of the fireplace, tasted the mellow red wine on her lips. He thought he'd read her signals correctly, that she wanted it, too, but then something had spooked her. He'd missed his window. And what had he done next? He'd blundered into Will's room like some sleep-addled zombie and *groped her. Way to go, Griffiths. Talk about suave.*

He burned to think of the careless touch in Will's room, to recall the incomparable softness of Andie's skin, still imprinted on his clumsy fingertips, and her gasp of shock. Occasionally, he would stare in disbelief at his own hand, as if to disavow its traitorous presence on the end of his arm. But the critical problem was not with his fingers, he thought wretchedly. It was with *him*, with whom he was to the very core. *I've botched it all.*

With Andie barred from him, he took no solace from the fact that he *was* able to see Karina. A couple of days into his self-imposed exile from the house, he fidgeted and fumed through another visit between Will and her, this time at a local children's museum. She was doing a little better with Will and seemed to be making a genuine effort to engage with him, but their meetings still had the uncomfortable habit of devolving into tears—either Will's or Karina's.

Now Will squirmed and hummed in his car seat as Rhys finally backed out of the parking spot and pulled the Range Rover into the stream of traffic heading for the center of town. But where would they go? It was with a little flash of inspiration that he remembered the ice-cream shop near the commuter-rail station.

"Want to get some ice cream, Will?" he proposed with exaggerated jollity. The truth was he'd become so dependent on Andie's company that without it he felt off balance, insular, morose. There was something transformative about the sessions they had spent working with Will—those engrossingly practical efforts that swept away sadness with action and progress. She brought to their world a life-giving buoyancy. Without her, he could feel the pull of the dark current that had consumed him in the weeks surrounding Will's diagnosis.

At the prospect of ice cream, Will had started to babble animatedly, injecting the stream of sounds with a richer range of vowels and consonants than he usually used. Following the advice of the speech therapist, Rhys tried to mimic the complex vocalizations and reflect Will's excited inflection right back at him. Like two prehistoric birds, they squawked back and forth as they pulled into the lot by the station.

Rhys leaned in and placed a kiss on Will's forehead as he unbuckled the safety seat. He swung the toddler into his arms and went up the steps into the store, which was actually more crowded than he had expected on a sleet-ravaged winter weekday. People waiting for the train had sheltered inside to avoid the cold and—ironically—wound up buying ice cream.

As soon as they were inside, Will struggled to get down. Rhys resisted for a few seconds but recognized the danger signs in the increasingly frenzied flapping of Will's hands and his shrill tones of protest. He reluctantly lowered his son to the floor. Will immediately toddled into the forest of jean-clad legs of the moms, kids, and teens scattered around the open space of the store.

Rhys tried to fix one eye on the board of ice-cream flavors and coffee drinks, but Will was making a beeline for a couple of middle-school kids playing with the door in the corner that let out right onto the commuter-rail platform. They were idly opening and closing it, oblivious to the cold blast of air that poured in with each arc of movement. Rhys was forced to leave his place in line and dash over to scoop Will up before he got outside and headed right for the target of his fondest obsession: train tracks. Maybe this hadn't been such a great idea, after all.

An older woman and her daughter had unknowingly taken his place in line by the time they returned to the front of the store, Will voicing his disapproval. Rhys bounced Will in his arms, bobbing in place as he examined the flavor selections, trying to halt Will's thin squeal of displeasure. Rhys was dying for a coffee, but with Will to wrangle, he knew he'd have to cut his losses and focus on the vanilla soft-serve. He could caffeinate himself later.

Will's cries gradually dwindled, to Rhys's immense relief. But there was a middle-aged pair at the front of the line who seemed determined to sample every ice-cream flavor in the lineup. They held their little white plastic spoons with pinkie fingers extended, like connoisseurs, deliberating as if the choice between Moose Tracks and Peanut Butter Cup was a decision of national significance. Too irritated to watch them, Rhys let his gaze wander around the cluster of small tables. His eyes lit upon another pair seated at a table for two.

They were just another local father and son—the dad in jeans and a casual button-down shirt, with a toddler boy who appeared only slightly older than Will—but they enjoyed their ice creams, and each other's company, with a conspicuous ease that drew Rhys's attention like a magnet. *What must it be like to live in a world where a trip to the ice-cream shop was a sure thing? An instant hit.*

Rhys jiggled Will in his arms and watched as the father playfully snatched a napkin up from the tabletop and perched it on his head. The redheaded toddler giggled manically as his dad pantomimed searching for the napkin, checking under his coffee cup—because of course *he* got to have coffee—under the table, under the little boy's T-shirt, behind his ear. "No, Dada! Your head! Your head!" the boy called between peals of laughter. Taking the cue, his father rolled his eyes upward and tilted his head back, searching for the scrap of paper, which was now in the process of floating to the floor. "Down! Down!" the child gasped, doubled over in hysterics.

"Dada!" The word mocked Rhys as he stood there in line. His temples throbbed as he cataloged the series of impossible preconditions that would have to be met in order for him to enjoy a similar exchange with Will. First, Will would need to be able to tune out the sensations inundating him from every direction in the noisy space. Then he would need the calm and endurance to tolerate sitting at the table. Even more difficult to navigate would be the finer points of the joke itself—the ability to read the humor in his father's expression, the shared laughter at the silliness of a napkin sitting on someone's head, and the fiction that his father didn't "know" the napkin was there and needed to be made aware of it. The whole concept was light-years away from Will's current level of development, even aside from the issue of language. Rhys's chest was tight with sorrow.

The couple at the head of the line finally moved off to the side, licking their ice creams with self-congratulatory zeal as they looked about for an unoccupied table. Will began to whimper, not sure why he was no longer being jiggled, so Rhys started up the motion again, wondering how he would keep up the rhythm while retrieving his wallet and holding the ice cream steady when it was handed to him.

They finally made it to the counter, and Rhys placed their order, still bouncing. He somehow managed to complete the transaction, take the ice cream—a cone tipped into its own bowl for safety's sake—and move toward the seating area, only to find that there were no tables available. The connoisseur couple had taken the table previously occupied by the father and son and had settled in for a leisurely feast, trading licks of each other's cones.

Rhys couldn't make Will eat outside, and he wasn't crazy enough to let his son into the car with an open container of ice cream, so he found a spot where they could stand by the window. The sill formed a shelf wide enough to hold the bowl while he set Will back down on the floor. All it took was a brief pause for Rhys to stretch the tense muscles of his arms and back, and, almost as if in slow motion, Will reached an arm up and swiped the bowl down from its perch. The container tipped in midair, depositing half its contents on Will's sleeve, before coming to rest in a gelid heap on the floor.

Will screamed as the cold, sticky substance began to melt through the fabric to his skin. He flailed his arm to free himself from the sensation, sending a large blob of vanilla ice cream sailing into the open top of a quilted leather designer handbag that was dangling from its owner's arm as she passed by.

"What the—" the woman screeched. The tone of her outburst mingled with Will's cry in a discordant din that messed with Rhys's brain. He dabbed at Will's sleeve with one hand and tried to pass the outraged woman a handful of napkins with the other but somehow found himself mopping at her bag when she refused to take his peace offering. He was disturbed to see a distinctive logo on the bag in the shape of interlocking *C*s, which he feared was a designer label that came with a hefty price tag. Karina had had one like it—but the name eluded him.

"I'm so sorry." Rhys flung his apology at the bag owner, and at the room more generally, as every eye in the place was riveted to the unfolding scene.

"Get away from me!" the woman snapped, fury flashing in a pair of heavily mascaraed blue eyes. Will caught the full impact of her rage at close range. He scrunched his eyes closed, flinging his head back, as a full-blown tantrum took possession of his body just as Rhys knelt down to soothe him.

The force of Will's tough little head slamming into the bridge of Rhys's nose was almost blinding. He couldn't answer for the expletive that escaped his lips as he reeled in agony, feeling for the hot trickle of blood or the sickly crunch of misaligned bone. To his relief, his face seemed to be intact, but it was ringing with pain as he bent down to wrestle a rigid, keening Will into his arms.

"People who can't control their children should think twice before inflicting them upon the rest of us," the self-righteous handbag owner pronounced. Rhys had been considering trying to fish his business card out of his wallet and offering to reimburse the woman for the professional cleaning of her bag, or even to pay for a replacement. Now, in the hot rush of rage and hopelessness, he simply hugged Will close and made for the exit, leaving the ice-cream bowl upended on the floor.

What do you expect when you go to an ice-cream shop? If Designer Bag Lady wanted a mess-free, child-free afternoon, she could take her fucking bag to a wine bar or a spa, he thought as he hauled Will out to the car. Why was she risking her delicate sensibilities—and her designer gear— at an ice-cream shop? Nose still throbbing and eyes smarting, he fought the urge to turn back around and lay into the woman.

Now he was furious that his knee-jerk reaction had been to apologize. He should have had some scathing response at the ready, a pithy comment that would have made Bag Lady shrivel with shame all the way down to her designer-clad toes. And all those sanctimonious onlookers, too. *How dare they try to make me feel ashamed of my own son!*

But Rhys, like his son, just didn't have the words—or at least never at the right time. If he hadn't caused this stupid rift with Andie, for instance, he and Will never would have been roving the streets of Concord that afternoon in the first place. They would have been safely at home, probably enjoying Andie's company. The suffocating, leaden sensation in his chest flooded back with a vengeance. *Will deserves better than this.*

Shushing and soothing, Rhys finally prevailed upon a rigid, flailing Will to conform to the shape of his car seat. Finally able to start the car, his hands still sticky with ice-cream residue, Rhys gave in to thoughts that continued to circle fruitlessly from rage to sadness to self-recrimination, as Will's screams filled the car, and they turned in the direction of home.

CHAPTER FOURTEEN

Even if there was nowhere for Rhys to escape his own folly in Concord, at least there was always the Zephyrus Energy headquarters, where he could seek refuge in conclaves with his engineering team. A few days after the ice-cream shop debacle, he touched base with Noah, his friend and Zephyrus's SVP of engineering, to go over the latest modifications the team was making to a modular, midsize turbine that would soon be ready for the market.

Noah's rapid-fire talk of mixing vortices and mean-flow kinetic energy was music to Rhys's ears after too long brooding over his personal life.

"We've increased our peak energy output three times over," Noah enthused as they rounded the corner to Rhys's office, "and seriously cut down the final assembly costs."

The door to the office was slightly ajar, the room dim, its motion-detecting lights at rest. Which made the sultry voice that issued from the interior doubly jarring as Rhys and Noah stopped in the doorway.

"Well, if it isn't my lucky day," came a sensual purr. "The two tallest drinks of water I've ever had the pleasure to meet."

Not quite believing what he was seeing, Rhys swung the door fully open to reveal a figure perched on the edge of his desk. Karina, clad in a wine-colored blouse and a fitted skirt that revealed long, slender limbs encased in silky hosiery, looked right back at him, a feral glitter in her eyes.

"Karina!" Noah blurted nervously. Karina had always been amused by how easily she could fluster Rhys's former protégé. Traces of the shy, awkward kid Noah had once been rose to the surface of his leaf-green gaze, belying his sophisticated veneer. He looked truly confused by her presence here. So he wasn't one of the old friends who knew of her return.

"You didn't mention you'd be stopping by," Rhys said pointedly.

"It was a spur-of-the-moment thing," Karina responded. "I'm meeting a friend for lunch and thought I'd drop in here first to surprise you."

An odd energy vibrated from her, and as Rhys stepped closer, he noticed that—in spite of the seductive picture she presented—she didn't quite gleam with her usual polish. When she turned sideways for a moment to pluck an invisible speck of lint from her blouse, he saw that her hair was slightly matted at the back, as if she hadn't bothered to pass her brush through that section.

"I . . . uh, I should be going," Noah announced. "I have that . . . thing I need to get back to."

"It was wonderful seeing you, Noah," Karina called knowingly.

He melted from the doorway, and Rhys turned his attention back to the intruder in his space. How long had she waited there? An oily queasiness came over him as he reflected that for the lights to have deactivated, she must have lurked there motionless for several minutes at least.

Motionless, yet bristling with tension—the air was alive with it, and Rhys was cast back to the memory of a time he'd discovered her sitting in the dark, trancelike, on the bathroom floor, when Will was about three months old. She was unable to sleep, she'd told him, so she was listening to the sounds of the night. Her uncanny stillness had been its own kind of exertion.

"Karina, what can I do for you?"

She slipped from the edge of the desk and straightened, the erect set of her shoulders causing the opening of her blouse to gape.

"I wanted to see you, just the two of us," she said, stepping uncomfortably close. Her fingers grazed the front of his shirt.

She reached down to flick open the next button on her claret-colored blouse, exposing a delicate scroll of black lace. "I was thinking maybe we should get reacquainted, now that things are going so well with Will."

"So well" was perhaps the most egregious overstatement Rhys had heard to date. And there was something painful, heartbreaking, in her hopeful expression as she drew closer. Her eyes burned bright but bore faint purplish shadows of fatigue, and her lips looked chapped.

"Karina, are you okay?" Sleeping on someone's couch obviously didn't agree with her. *Maybe I should make inquiries . . .* But no, she was her own person, and he had no business trying to manage her life.

"Never better," she said blithely, sliding one hand up to rest on his shoulder.

He had to force himself not to recoil from the contact. Instead, he captured her wrist and gave it an avuncular squeeze before removing her hand and placing it gently back by her side.

"This can't happen, Karina."

"Why not? The physical part of our relationship was so good. And you said Andie isn't your girlfriend, so—"

She was right that their physical connection had once been enthralling. Karina's capriciousness and the pervasive sense of uncertainty she'd incited had kept him constantly guessing, dangling, panting after her. But the thrill had evaporated in an instant once her fundamental untrustworthiness was revealed. Now her touch inspired nothing but unease. And for all that he'd spoken the truth when he said he and

Andie weren't together, he wished there were some way he could make it so. It was the sensation of *her* skin that he craved in his restless dreams each night. Andie was the one whose presence closed some vital circuit that lit him to incandescence.

"Just because I'm not with Andie doesn't mean I'm available to start something with you."

Karina went dangerously still. "I see," she said, shutters slamming down over the hurt and speculation in her eyes.

She paced to the door and paused, her delicate hands resting for an instant on the doorframe, like small, fearful birds poised to take flight. She turned back to him with a breezy smile painted on her face. "I understand," she said with an intimate, almost conspiratorial lilt. "It's too soon. Of course, I was only testing the waters. This can wait. I do have a lunch date to keep, you know."

This can wait? When was she going to get it into her head that there was no *this?*

Throwing a final, knowing look over her shoulder, she stalked off, her fragile bravado practically shimmering around her like a reality-repelling dome.

~

What the hell is Rhys playing at? Andie shivered and adjusted the faulty heat setting on Ernie's 1980s dashboard, fretting over the strange disappearing act the man had pulled for the past several days. She'd seen little more of him than the dust his Porsche kicked up as he sped down the driveway each morning. And, other than the afternoon two days ago when he'd stormed into the kitchen, the bridge of his nose swollen and bruised, carrying a squalling Will in his arms, he'd barely seen his son, either.

That day he handed Will directly over to Mrs. Hodge and headed straight for the den, muttering something about the ice-cream shop.

Andie passed Will's room after midnight that night to fetch a water glass from the small upstairs kitchen and had been surprised to see the door slightly ajar. Peering surreptitiously inside, she'd discovered Rhys, outlined by the soft glow of the night-light, sitting cross-legged on the floor by Will's bed, his attention riveted to the serene contours of his sleeping son's face. She'd thought about planting herself in the doorway and demanding a word, but something about Rhys's expression stopped her from breaking the spell.

What is going on with him? Andie nursed her irritation like a flame because she was terrified of the alternative. What if this was about something more than the embarrassing brush in the dark? What if Rhys had finally seen through her and realized she was unworthy of the trust and kindness that had been halfway to transforming her entire world? Perhaps this was his way of withdrawing from her—taking back his friendship. Taking back his endorsement of everything she was. She knew from childhood experience that even the meanest shreds of comfort could be snatched away in an instant.

Well, she was sick to death of drifting around Rhys's big, empty house, waiting for the man himself to put in an appearance. It was soul destroying to lurk around the halls where they'd laughed and talked together, and she became more and more convinced they would never recapture that happiness and ease. That she might finish out her days here without ever again basking in the warmth of his kindness. So she'd decided to go exploring. She might as well make the most of being in picturesque, historic Concord.

She pointed Ernie down snow-lined roads that were the very picture of quaint suburban affluence, past gracious facades of historic houses in every hue—from colonial yellow to sage green, pale apricot, blue gray, and sparkling white. Pretty soon, the houses grew fewer and farther between and were interspersed with rustic red barns, fallow fields glittering with frost, iced-over ponds, and deep stands of towering evergreens.

Andie drove at a leisurely pace along quiet, winding lanes, naturally drawn to the more rural roads. Despite having turned her back on her childhood town in western Massachusetts, she was still seduced by visions of rolling acres, weathered post-and-rail fences, and the inquisitive liquid, dark eyes of horses peering out over stable doors. The scenery evoked a strange shiver of nostalgia.

A memory ambushed her, and she had to slow Ernie to a crawl as it shimmered in her field of vision and took possession of her senses. She recalled the musty-sweet smell of decaying leaves, the cold wind whistling by her ears as she bent over the neck of her chestnut quarter horse, Bingo. She remembered the swooping sensation in her chest as she took daredevil leaps over a makeshift cross-country course, through fields lined with blazing red-and-orange trees, while her father whooped in exhilaration, following on Flash, his tall off-the-track thoroughbred. She'd shone with pride when they'd finally pulled up and Jim had uttered a word or two of gruff praise.

Where did that come from? Andie took a deep breath, feeling to the very outer edges of the memory. Her parents had not had any extra money when she was growing up, but before everything in his life had narrowed to the aperture of an Old Crow whiskey bottle, her father had kept a few riding horses on their land. Occasionally, he'd even been motivated to share his interest with his kids. Only Andie had really taken him up on the offer. Louisa, Rose, and Jess had dabbled and then lost interest. Gus, of course, never reached the age to truly start—a fact that made Andie's heart lurch as she idled on the quiet road, lost, for a moment, to history.

This forgotten memory of her father, hidden for so long behind subsequent years of slurs, rejection, and plain old indifference, felt like something important. Like evidence of something. *He did care about me, once.* She wasn't sure what to do with the insight. After all, how much value could you put on the fleeting good opinion of a man like her father? But she had to concede that once upon a time she would have happily risked her neck to see the gleam of approval in his eyes.

Her mind drifted, for a few seconds, back to the dream Will's screams had interrupted on the night of the tank-top malfunction. The strange dynamic between Susan and Jim, and her role in it, as they'd sat in the familiar old kitchen. Was it truly a dream, or a memory from the days when the three of them could still be in the same room together?

After the age of eleven, Andie's main source of company—other than Jess and her sweet sympathy—was the horses. She remembered hiding out for hours on end in the tumbledown stable, where she could soak in their company, always gentle and forgiving, and the intoxicating scent of their big, warm bodies.

She could practically conjure the scent as she shook herself back to the present and pressed down on the accelerator, rounding a bend in the road that provided a glorious view of a sprawling white farmhouse.

A more idyllic setting she had never seen. The house, with its generous porch, red door, and black shutters, was flanked by a grove of majestic trees on one side and a wide lawn and overgrown English garden on the other. A sweeping driveway lined with more towering trees led to a big red barn and a complex of fenced yards. At a second glance, the barn looked more lovingly tended than the house itself. As she slowed down, she noticed the front door was weathered, the porch sagged slightly, and one of the black shutters was hanging.

A sign over the barn's wide doorway read SADDLE TREE FARM, and, on a series of smaller shingles, LESSONS, BOARDING, CAMPS, HIPPOTHERAPY. She suddenly felt as if all the air had been knocked from her lungs. Abruptly, she turned on her indicator and pulled to the side of the road.

She could see Will in her mind's eye, perched atop a sturdy chestnut pony, a huge grin making his dimples pop. Therapeutic riding could work wonders for a child's postural control, balance, and coordination. Even better, it could help build communication and socialization skills.

Hippotherapy went another step beyond that, enabling physical, occupational, or speech therapists to use a horse's movement as a therapeutic tool. Andie couldn't think of a better way to help Will progress.

Over the past week, she'd been even more intensely focused on her reason for being there, pouring ever more energy into Will's therapy. And Will needed the extra support. He was more challenging in his daily OT sessions and at mealtimes. Rhys still handled bedtime, but the change in his other routines meant Will was sleeping more fitfully again and waking everyone in the house with his nighttime cries, feeling Rhys's absence acutely. Andie kind of knew how he felt.

Gravity and a sense of inevitability propelled her down the hill. She turned into the drive. The soles of her boots crunched on the gravel as she approached the barn.

"Hello!" she called, but the only response was from a huge black mare, who ambled over and hung her massive head over the fence of the closest yard. Probably a Percheron, Andie guessed, assessing the horse's stocky build and intelligent eyes. She reached out a hand, letting the giant animal sniff her fingers before stroking the incomparably soft skin of her nose. The mare blew out in a gentle snort through huge, velvety nostrils, sending a cloud of vapor into the frigid air. Andie lay her hand on the flat plane of the horse's cheek and leaned in to her neck, inhaling deeply. That was it: the smell that had meant peace, calm, and security in the ruins of her fractured childhood.

Reluctantly, she stepped away from the fence, where the mare seemed content to linger, and walked toward the barn's entrance.

"Can I help you?" A shape emerged from the wide center aisle, in the form of a grizzled-looking man in overalls and work boots.

"Yes, I wanted to ask about your therapeutic riding program."

The man scratched his forehead and squinted, his pale-blue irises gleaming from within deep pockets of weather-beaten flesh. "Ah, well, you'd have to talk to Maisie about that."

"Is she in?" Andie asked eagerly.

"She's . . . no, not right now," the man said, rubbing his jaw and raising bushy gray brows. "You could try her at the main number in a day or two. Wait a second." He broke off and disappeared into what could have been a tack room or an office and reemerged moments later bearing a flyer photocopied inexpensively in black and white.

"Here," he offered, passing it to her with a calloused hand ingrained with dirt. Andie was relieved to see a web address listed at the bottom of the page. At least the operation had a passing acquaintance with the digital age.

"Thanks," she said with a smile, glancing into the cleanly swept barn. "I'll be in touch."

The man waved good-bye and returned to breaking up a bale of hay into individual flakes. One of the horses in the barn gave a whinny of anticipation, which widened Andie's smile as she walked back toward the road, pausing to say farewell to the big black mare.

She rested her hand on the horse's well-muscled black neck, her mind full of possibilities. *Are you really contemplating the idea of putting Will up on top of a half ton of horseflesh?* Not without an experienced instructor and at least two side walkers, she decided. And even then, she would only consider it if they used an extremely docile horse and an abundance of adaptive equipment. But something about the idea lit her up inside.

These gentle, majestic animals had saved her during her teenage years, making it possible for her to salvage a vital spark of caring and connection with the world, rather than turning on herself, losing herself in the same downward spiral of grief and recrimination that had consumed her parents. Why, then, could they not be effective in the much more optimistic task of helping Will—with his sweetness, his curiosity, and his limitless potential—connect more fully with his world? She would have to raise the idea with Rhys. That is, if she ever got to talk to the man again.

She headed back to the car, a spring in her step. She could not have guessed how much being around horses again would lift her spirits. Somehow it had reset her perspective, reacquainting her with an undamaged thread of herself from the long-distant past.

The girl she was once was not afraid to take risks. That girl still had the courage of her convictions. That girl would not just hang around the Griffiths house, waiting for Rhys to quit his Invisible Man routine. She would demand what was right, what was necessary. For Will, that meant getting his father back. And when she thought about what was necessary for her—what had become as vital to her as oxygen—her thoughts drifted inexorably back to that almost-kiss in Rhys's den.

If she possessed even an echo of the courageous spirit that had once defined her, she would admit the truth: What she felt for Rhys was not just friendship. No, what she felt was much riskier than that. And it was disingenuous to pretend otherwise. She'd been denying that truth when she'd averted their near-kiss, and the result was her current state of limbo—and Will's. So she was done pretending. Forever was off-limits, but she would accept what Rhys offered with openness, honesty, and joy, for as long as it lasted.

And if he was no longer offering, that was fine, too. As long as she didn't have to endure the waiting and wondering any longer, and as long as Rhys was back under the same roof as his son. She was going to confront him, she decided. She wasn't sure yet what she'd say or do, but she would do it at the very next opportunity.

~

"Do you have a minute?" Tom poked his head around Rhys's office doorway. Rhys had been staring, unseeing, at his screen saver as it etched fiery trails across a field of black on his monitor, his mind full of blueprints and hypotheses.

"What's up?" Rhys had spent so long in brooding solitude lately that his own voice surprised him. It sounded like it came from the bottom of a well.

"You want the truth?" Tom seated himself in his usual chair facing Rhys's chaotic desk, where sketches and formulas had recently sprouted on pieces of scrap paper.

The one silver lining to this whole Andie catastrophe was that it had forced Rhys to take refuge in invention. "I feel certain you're about to give it to me," he responded drily.

"Allison sent me an emergency text to warn me you're wearing your holey shirts again."

Rhys looked down at his plaid sleeves almost in surprise, noticing the frayed cuffs and threadbare elbows. His administrative assistant, Allison, knew him too well. Whenever he was in crisis, he would automatically reach for one of his softest, most well-worn shirts. Like Will with his security blanket or his trains.

"So? I've had nothing but internal meetings this week. Does it matter?"

"Not in a business sense, no," Tom conceded. "I'm talking on a personal level here." He surveyed his friend. "What's going on with you?"

Rhys ran a restless hand through his hair and fixed him with a weary gaze. "I'm fine."

"How are things at home?"

"Funny you should ask." Rhys laughed mirthlessly. "I actually wouldn't know. I was getting in the way, so I took myself out of the equation." He snatched up a squeeze ball that sat on his desk and lobbed it through an executive basketball hoop in the corner.

Tom's eyebrows rose. "What happened? Last I heard, things were going great. I've seen for myself that Andie's a freaking miracle."

"Yeah, she is," Rhys agreed. "I figured I should step back and let her do her thing. Stop putting my foot in it." He paused and added grimly, "Or hand."

"O-kay." Tom whistled. "I won't ask what that's about."

"It's about me," Rhys fumed. "It's about the fact that Andie's the best thing to come into my life—and Will's—in fucking . . . *ever*, and here am I, blundering around with my usual *Night of the Living Dead* clueless Aspie act, screwing things up."

"Yeah, you're such a terrible person," Tom said with a deadpan expression. "Give Andie a bit of credit here for a minute. My guess is she can probably handle you."

"Thanks a lot, asshole." Rhys bridled. "You think her training with special-needs kids might just qualify her to deal with me?"

"Oh, give me a break!" Tom collapsed in helpless laughter. "This from the millionaire PhD with the Elvis charisma, who has to beat women off with a stick every time he steps out in public. My heart bleeds!"

Rhys shot him an incendiary look and then went back to staring at his monitor. Tom, still stifling chuckles, sat back to let his words sink in.

Rhys could feel the weight of his friend's fond scrutiny as the minutes ticked by. *"What?"* he finally exploded in frustration.

"You like her," Tom observed. "Like, *like* her like her."

"That's the stupidest statement I've heard since second grade," Rhys harrumphed.

"Doesn't mean it's not true."

"Have you *seen* my track record with relationships?"

"Okay, so your college years were a bit of a roller-coaster ride. Grad school, too, I guess. And Karina was a spectacular flameout, I'll admit," Tom said. "But since then you haven't even tried."

"The stakes are too high," Rhys snapped. "I can't bring a woman into Will's life and turn things upside down, only to have it not work out. I can't put him through that." There had been no one serious since Karina. Not that he hadn't occasionally been tempted, while on a business trip, to indulge just for the physical release. And it seemed that, since his public profile had expanded, there were always plenty of attractive women angling to spend time in his bed. But, when push came to shove, the idea generally left a sour taste in his mouth.

"Andie is already in Will's life," Tom pointed out helpfully.

"And, like I told you before, my goal is to keep her there. Not to mess with her and foul things up so completely that she runs screaming for the hills."

"Ah, but there's the important thing. I don't think you *would* be messing with her."

Rhys narrowed his eyes and squinted balefully at his friend. Tom was right. If he got involved with Andie, he *wouldn't* be messing with her at all. His feelings for her—complicated as they were—were genuine. *This is real. Disturbingly so.*

Another worry intruded into his thoughts. "You know that by getting involved with Andie, I'd be putting her right in Karina's sights." He was shaken by how acute the fear was.

"So you're saying that you'll never have another relationship, in deference to Karina?"

"Not deference, exactly." Rhys paused. "She's just in a complicated place right now."

"You're all grown-ups," Tom pointed out. "And if you don't act decisively, you may miss your chance."

Yeah, like I did in front of the fireplace that night. Rhys leaned forward to pick up the squeeze ball. "You're fired!" he growled good-naturedly as he hurled the ball right at the space where Tom's head had been. But his friend had already disappeared into the corridor. His face appeared around the doorframe an instant later, a broad grin lighting up his features.

"Actually," Rhys said, "get back in here. I have a project for you."

"Oh?" Tom set one tentative foot back into the office.

"I want to look into setting up a foundation for special-needs grants," Rhys said. "For families that can't afford autism services not covered by health insurance or Medicaid."

Tom's grin seemed to widen, if that were even possible.

"Yeah, yeah," Rhys said with a conciliatory smile. "Andie gave me the idea."

CHAPTER FIFTEEN

Rhys gave a start when a knock sounded at the door that evening. He was hiding out in the wine room—another custom-built feature of the house that was surplus to requirements. It adjoined the den and connected on the other side to a butler's pantry that led into the kitchen and great room. In addition to its climate-controlled shelves, it boasted a large humidor that sat empty year-round.

The knock sounded again, and he groaned inwardly, putting down the bottle he was contemplating opening. What was with everyone today? He'd have been perfectly content to get on with wallowing in his own misery, if people would just stop trying to stage interventions.

"We need to talk." Andie stood in the doorway, her eyes blazing. It was so strange to see her in person after seeing her nowhere but in his dreams for longer than a week. He had to simply steady himself for a moment and drink her in. She was nervous, he realized. Keyed up. It touched him, making him want to fold her into a hug. But the exaggerated rise and fall of her chest, swathed in a fitted pale-pink T-shirt, also motivated him in other ways altogether.

"Come in," he offered. There was really nowhere in the wine room to sit. But that didn't matter, as she was clearly in a standing mood.

"I've made a decision," she announced. "I'm leaving."

A bolt of panic shot down Rhys's spine. *Leaving?* No. That wasn't supposed to happen. That *couldn't* happen.

"*No*, Andie. You're not going anywhere. Will needs you—"

"I'll tell you what Will needs!" she fumed. "He needs his father. And if you want to keep a five-mile buffer zone between us just because you accidentally touched my . . . uh, nipple, then that's up to you. But it should be you who stays in the house, not me. I can be gone first thing tomorrow."

The way she said "nipple" was so charmingly self-conscious that Rhys felt a lick of delight, like a small flame, in his chest. He noticed for the first time that one of her eyes had more gold spokes; the other, more green. And actually, her pupils were dilated. Maybe it wasn't only nerves she was feeling.

God, she killed him. Just destroyed him. He had to focus. Had to persuade her not to remove herself from his and Will's lives. She couldn't leave. He'd never been more certain of anything.

"This week has been a nightmare," Andie continued, taking Rhys's silence as resistance to her argument. "Will has been looking for you everywhere. He's been having tantrums. He's been more difficult with transitions—"

"Wait, Andie. Please," he entreated. "I'm sorry. I never intended to set Will back and make things more difficult for you. I didn't realize—"

"You've left me no choice," she accused, her brow furrowed. "Making such a big deal about a stupid fumble."

"It wasn't about . . ." Rhys broke off helplessly.

Andie glared at him like he was the most maddening, incomprehensible idiot she'd ever laid eyes on.

"You think this is so catastrophic that it justifies deserting your child for a full week?" she demanded, grabbing his hand and pressing it to her left breast. Her eyes snapped with determination, and she arched one brow, full of challenge.

Every trace of awareness flew to his fingertips as she held them trapped against her body. Her skin was intoxicatingly warm, the delicious curve of her breast straining against the thin fabric of her T-shirt. Under the inadequate barrier of her lacy bra, the controversial nipple itself stood to attention beneath his touch. Her heart beat its insistent tattoo against his hand, reverberating through him until his own pulse seemed to match its rhythm.

He was powerless to do anything but reach out with his other hand and close the remaining distance between them, his fingers finally weaving into the heavy silk of her hair, his mouth zeroing in on hers as she gave a start, her lips parting on a breathless "Oh!"

Pure sensation jolted through him as he plumbed the sweetness of her bottom lip, and she opened to him. His bones seemed to dissolve in response to the hot, frictionless glide of her mouth, pliant and melting under his. Her kisses were so sweet, so deep, that he could only follow where they led, even if it might mean never finding his way back. His hands wound farther into her silky cascade of hair, cupping the back of her head to anchor her to him as he tasted and probed.

If he'd felt high on the buzz he got from just talking to her, reading her face, then this was something else altogether. He thrilled to the feverish dance of tension and release as they braced against one another to prolong one moment of exploration before drawing closer to broach the next. With his senses he could *know* her. He could know her sighs, her wants, her needs—what it took to melt that familiar expression of reserve from her face.

Almost without realizing it, he had lifted her up onto the narrow counter that ran around the periphery of the room, to better explore her throat with his lips. The gathering storm in his blood crashed over him, obliterating the barriers of resolve, judgment, and good sense. He needed this, and—incredibly—she seemed to need it, too.

From her higher perch, she wrapped her legs around his hips, drawing him to her with an instinctive pull that could result in nothing less than a frank meeting of the seam of her jeans with the fly of his. If she'd been in any doubt about the force of his arousal, she couldn't be anymore. Every thought, every feeling, every pulse of his blood coalesced around one critical mission: melding with her until no distance remained. And his cock was only too happy to lead the charge.

She released her grip on his hand and let her fingers drift up to twine in his hair, sending tremors of pleasure ricocheting across his scalp. His right hand, no longer trapped in her grasp, found the V neckline of her T-shirt, sliding beneath the soft cotton and beyond the lace edge of her bra to learn the curve of her breast in a kind of feverish braille.

The heat and weight of her flesh cupped in his hand almost sent him over the edge right then. The raw physicality of it floored him, the shock of being able to capture the miracle of her under his touch. He would never forget it: the smoothness of her skin, the radiating warmth, the quintessential *Andie-ness* of her that made this contact such a revelation.

He shivered as she moaned her own longing into the crook of his neck. His teeth grazed her skin as he moved down to explore her shoulder, her collarbone, and then the upper swell of her breast. At last, his lips and fingertips converged, thrusting aside the final inch of fabric and baring the peak of the nipple in question, which he teased to a glistening point. She bucked against him, gripping his shoulders as the taut peak hardened against his lips and tongue.

He lost himself in exploration, drowning in the salty-sweet taste of her skin, her scent, and the shudder and twitch of her response to his hands as they traced a path he'd mapped in his mind countless times. Finally, he wrenched himself a few inches away, gratified by the disappointed little hitch in her breath as space opened up between them. Her cheeks were flushed; her swollen lips a deep, crushed pink; her eyes dark with need.

"Is this actually happening?" he asked. It was both an existential question and a practical one. He needed to gauge her intent.

"It's happening," she said huskily. "It's definitely happening." Her lips moved against his jaw, her mouth rising to meet his with a sensual languor that made his entire body thrum in anticipation of discovering the slick heat between her legs.

He wanted to peel her out of her jeans right then and there, his hands bracing her hips as he plunged inside her, watching her unravel as she pressed up against the wall stacked with dark-tinted burgundy bottles. But there was the issue of protection. It wasn't like he had condoms conveniently secreted around the house and could just grab one from the nearest nook or cranny.

"Come with me," he whispered, his hand sliding into hers like a promise. Their flight upstairs through the sleeping house was filled with an air of suspense as Rhys turned out lights in their wake and led Andie toward the wing that was Rhys's own domain. They passed through a corridor deep in shadow, their footfalls muffled by a thick cream-colored runner.

He paused in front of a heavy, varnished door. "I haven't slept for a week," he confessed. "Every night you've been in here with me. In my head. In my blood. I can't think for wanting you."

She gestured to the dark shadows under her eyes, which made her look vulnerable and somehow even lovelier. "I haven't slept a wink, either."

He turned the door handle and led her inside. The night sky had cleared, and moonlight poured through a trio of tall windows. A large bed, dressed in white linens, dominated the room. He drew her into the center of the space, where silvery light slanted to the floor.

"Stay right there."

～

Andie stood in the shaft of moonlight, so high on the rush of courage it had taken to confront Rhys—and so overwhelmed by the result—that it was like she'd been transported to another dimension.

She honestly hadn't known what was going to come out of her mouth until she saw him standing there in the wine room. She hadn't realized how intensely she could thirst for the sheer presence of another person. Even with their weird estrangement still hovering between them, she was like a wanderer in the desert who'd stumbled upon an oasis. Every cell in her body was infused with life and energy, a current of vitality so powerful she had to fight not to tremble.

She didn't know what had possessed her to threaten to leave. All she knew was that she had to jar Rhys out of this strange impasse. She had no intention of deserting Will, but if she had to work with him some-where outside the walls of this house, she would do it. The only thing she couldn't do was endure this peculiar personal exile a moment longer.

Grabbing Rhys's hand and pressing it to her breast had been an act of blind instinct. She'd already reached a place where all her reservations about getting closer to him were reduced to rubble. She was prepared to own her fierce longing for him. How could she not, when everything in her whirled and funneled into a singular ache?

Now she practically shook with relief. In spite of his lengthy disap-pearing act, he apparently didn't hate her, after all. He was here, in the flesh. He'd never really left. And the odds were good that tomorrow she'd wake up to a day with him in it.

He reappeared in the doorway, and a ferocious happiness roared through her veins. As he stalked toward her, she met him halfway, twin-ing her arms around his neck. Her hands were eager, her kisses hungry as he lifted her to him. She wrapped her legs around his hips, her heart leaping in anticipation as he carried her to a wide window seat.

Desperate for contact, she slipped her fingers under his T-shirt to brush across the corrugated muscles of his abs. His skin was hot, satiny, and dusted with a smattering of coarse hairs that arrowed down under the waistband of his jeans. She followed their tantalizing path, finding the long, thick ridge of contained heat that pushed at the buttons of his fly. She traced its outline through the denim, panting openmouthed against his throat as desire spun and unfurled with such force within her that she was convinced parts of her would just fly off into the ether. *Her name?* Gone. *Her history?* Vanished. There was nothing but this moment and him beneath her fingertips.

She felt a tug as Rhys drew her shirt up, and she lifted her arms to be freed from its confines. Her breasts were exposed to the silvery air as he deftly unhooked her bra.

"You," he whispered hoarsely, raking both hands from her throat to her navel in a reverent sweep before reaching up to thumb the aching tips of her nipples. "You've changed everything. You know that?"

She closed her eyes to the silent explosion of longing his words unleashed. Yes, everything was different. She, too, was transformed by the strange alchemy of their connection.

The barrier of his T-shirt was too much to bear, so she grabbed two handfuls of fabric and swept it off over his head, exposing the delectable expanse of his throat. But now that his shirt was gone, there were even greater vistas to explore: the sleek, defined chest with its flat brown nipples, the taut bands of muscle that flexed in his chest and upper arms as he reached for her. A fresh wave of heat claimed her, and she lost herself in exploration, her tongue finding expanses of satiny skin and ridges of muscle, her hands slipping under the buttons of his fly. It should have been no surprise, but she felt a shock of discovery as her fingertips found him, hard and hot beneath the thin cotton layer of his boxer shorts. A knot formed in her throat, longing and excitement mingled with trepidation.

His fingertips skimmed her belly, and she wriggled, desperate to be liberated from her jeans. Button and zipper melted open under the ministrations of his hands, and he tugged the denim down her thighs, his breath hissing through his teeth as he revealed the silk and lace of her thong underwear.

His fingers were heat-seeking missiles, following the inexorable path of that scrap of damp silk. She held her breath as they circumnavigated her curves, tunneling under the flimsy fabric. A cry tore from her throat as one relentless fingertip zeroed in where she most needed it to land, with a precision that left her gasping for breath, another finger gliding through the slick heat at the entrance to her body.

His breath thundered against her earlobe, and she bucked under his touch. She needed him inside her now, buried to the hilt. But she stood trapped by the snug denim around her thighs and the merciless strokes of his fingers, sweeping along her swollen, slippery inner folds with a ruthless insistence that made her want to sob.

He somehow knew even before she did exactly where each stroke should land for maximum effect, and what kind of touch—gentle, firm, or downright forceful—would propel her into the stratosphere. Lust had melted everything. There were no hard angles, just the perfectly choreographed rhythm of pressure and release, stroke and pulse.

"Get these off me," she begged, plucking at the denim and thrilling to the dark sound of his laughter as he tugged the fabric past her knees.

"Skinny jeans," she murmured apologetically as the denim got stuck at her ankles. "And big feet."

He yanked hard, and the jeans came off, instantly forgotten as he sat her down on the bench, parting her legs and pulling aside the silk that covered her. His tongue passed across his lips in a hungry sweep, and his eyes gleamed as he went to his knees in front of her.

"No," she protested. She couldn't take it: the soft caress of his mouth. "I need you inside me. Now." Desire made her bold, and she pulled on his shoulders, holding her breath as he slithered back up the length of her body.

"Sit down," she said, directing him to the spot she'd just vacated on the window seat. She would own this, and feel this, like nothing she'd ever experienced before.

Rhys gave her an inquisitive glance, but he didn't seem inclined to argue. He groaned as she found his fly and unbuttoned it with desperate haste, welcoming the hot thrust of him into her hands. She relished the glide of satin over steel as she wrapped her fingers around his thick circumference, her thumb skidding across the slick bead of moisture at the tip. *Of course. He's just as perfect here as everywhere else. Why wouldn't he be?*

"Hurry!" she pleaded, and he produced a condom, tearing the wrapper open. He looked like an erotic statue, reclining on the window seat with the moonlight bathing his torso, his jeans peeled down over his hips. As he rolled the condom on, she stared hungrily and flung a leg over to straddle him, her knees pressed into the seat cushion.

The air was almost grainy with heat as she reared over him and lowered herself down, gasping as she notched herself against him, the slickness of her body welcoming him inside. She raised herself a fraction and impaled herself, shuddering at the exquisite sensation of fullness that claimed her. Finally, he was seated deep within her, and she gazed into pupils blown out with desire, his irises just thin purple-blue rims circling fathomless darkness.

He growled, leaning in to graze the delicate skin of her throat with his teeth. The sharp satisfaction of it set off an explosion behind her eyes, and his clever hands went to her waist. Suddenly she was moving with a reckless urgency, and he was gripping her hips, intensifying her pleasure, helping her ride him, rising to meet every thrust of her body. She'd never felt anything like it. She was so used to having to coax out the delicate, elusive flame of her desire and hold it slightly apart so the prosaic efforts of her boyfriends didn't snuff it out. But Rhys fanned her pleasure into an inferno that possessed every inch of her body, her soul.

Her climax loomed like a juggernaut as she rocked helplessly against him, crazy with need and slick with exertion as he drove into her, parting her flesh with hard, wet, delirious strokes. She came in a series of hot, blooming pulses that radiated out and bathed her entire body in flame-bright sensation. Kaleidoscopic patterns of red and gold swirled behind her closed eyes as she heard him cry out with the explosive force of his own orgasm. Damp and utterly spent, she collapsed against him, their panting breaths synchronizing as they both drifted back to earth.

She murmured as he lifted her and carried her to the bed, where they cooled their limbs against the smoothness of pristine white sheets, one of his hands still playing in her hair. She curled toward him, pummeling his shoulder with a tired fist.

"Don't ever, ever do that again," she half laughed, half sobbed.

"What?" He drew back. "I thought it was pretty damn incredible."

"Not the sex," she gasped. "Feel free to repeat the sex. In fact, I insist on it. I meant don't ever disappear like that again."

"Don't worry. I don't think I'll ever be able to tear myself away." His tone was tender, serious.

"Would you really have left?" he asked a few moments later.

"You better believe it," she responded. "I meant what I said. If I was getting between you and Will, then I would have had to leave."

"Yeah, well, the next time I'm running around with my head up my arse, I hope you'll give me a swift kick," he said. "I'm sorry, Andie. I'm awkward. I miss things. I second-guess myself until nothing makes sense anymore."

He stretched out his legs and entwined them with hers, tugging them closer together. "But this makes sense."

Andie almost couldn't take the wave of happiness that enveloped her as they lay quiet for several minutes, Rhys's fingers still tracing delicate patterns on her skin. Some vestigial part of her brain issued a mean-spirited note of warning. *Don't get used to this.* She wrestled her demons back into their lair and snuggled defiantly closer.

Rhys's hands moved to her hair, the gentle tug of his fingers sending shivers down the nape of her neck.

"Why didn't you let me kiss you before?" he asked. "Here." His hand slid down to the delta between her legs, one finger slipping into yielding heat. She shuddered, biting back a cry as she pressed her face to his shoulder. She was aching and swollen, every inch of her already yearning to welcome him into her body all over again. His fingers found the tight, sensitive bud that was the epicenter of her desire and circled it with tantalizing delicacy.

"It would have been distracting," she panted. "Too soft."

In truth, there was more to her reluctance than that. She couldn't confess it to him, but she'd never let anyone kiss her there. She had always prided herself more on her tight command of her body than her level of comfort with it. She was glad of the shadows as he searched her face, his fingers still working in languid strokes.

"Would it be distracting now?" he asked. But the question became moot as she moaned and broke apart beneath the exquisite flicker of his fingertips, her body wrung out with pleasure.

CHAPTER SIXTEEN

Rhys woke first, to discover that the shadows in the room had moved. Dawn was creeping over the distant hillside, and Andie was still in his bed. He drank in the vision of her by his side, tangled in the sheets, her chest rising and falling in peaceful slumber. She looked like a Grecian goddess, one marble shoulder emerging from the draped fabric, the length of one lean leg exposed, her hair fanned out on the pillows, her face in repose, untroubled and breathtakingly lovely.

Hers was a face he would be happy to contemplate at any time, in any light, in any season, he realized, his gaze tracing the winged lines of her brows, the shape of her eyes with their long, sweeping lashes, the graceful curve of her cheek.

He shifted position, accidentally nudging her as he pulled the sheet up. Her eyes drifted open, and the smile she gave him made his pulse race.

"I fell asleep?" she murmured incredulously. "What a waste."

She turned on her side so they lay face-to-face, inches apart, each soaking in the presence of the other. With a barely perceptible shift, they were kissing once more. Long, slow, languorous kisses this time—perhaps even more toe-curling than their previous devouring clash of lips and tongues.

Enervated by sleep, Andie was soft, dreamy, and exquisitely responsive. He turned her in his arms so they could spoon, his cock pressing insistently against her tight curves. His blood surged as she wriggled against him, and he slid against wet heat. He needed to be fused with her again, limb to limb, cell to cell, atom to atom.

He broke away for a few torturous seconds to sheath himself, and she arched her back, rubbing against him, sinuous as a cat. Then he was sliding into her again, welcomed by a surge of wetness as she held herself achingly still. They rocked together, riding lazy crests and troughs of pleasure that had their own bewitching rhythm. Skin to skin with her, surrounded by her, Rhys was possessed by a sensation that somehow combined both peace and exhilaration. Like he'd come home—like she was home.

His orgasm built slowly, honed to a pinpoint of such exquisite intensity that he shuddered against her as she was consumed by the tide of her own release.

"What are you doing to me?" Rhys whispered against her neck moments later, his breath stirring the strands of her hair. "You're too damned irresistible."

"Like you can talk," Andie murmured, drugged with satisfaction.

They lay tangled together, drifting, until he eased himself out of bed to go deal with the condom.

When he returned, she was propped on one elbow, alert, brow furrowed. "I should get back to my room."

Rhys felt a tug of loss at the idea of her slipping away, back to her solitary bed.

"No, please. Stay a little longer. There's time." He eased himself back under the covers. "Tell me about everything I've missed this week."

Andie relaxed into chattiness as she lay back against the pillows and regaled him with news of Will's progress in the OT gym. Her eyes were bright with excitement as she described his rapid mastery of the challenges she set for him. But she reserved a special fervor for her news of the farm she'd discovered that offered hippotherapy. Her face shone as she told him about the place, and her ideas about blending equine-assisted therapy with Will's other treatments.

"It could be the boost he needs," she enthused. "We have so many expectations, and we so desperately want him to speak, but with the horses he can just *be*."

"Can you call the farm?"

"I'll do it today. I checked their website, and they'll need a pediatrician's statement and Will's medical history."

"No problem. I'll organize it." He smiled lazily and stretched, luxuriating in a moment of utter contentment.

Andie turned to him, her expression suddenly solemn. "Rhys, you should know that when this thing between us runs its course, I won't let it affect my work with Will. I'll be there for him as long as he needs me."

Rhys halted midstretch, pleasurable tension replaced by disappointment. *When this thing between us runs its course? What? Aren't we just getting started?* The room seemed to dim, as if she'd erected a utilitarian tarp in front of his window when he was still trying to soak in the view of the sunrise.

The baby monitor on the nightstand issued a troubled squawk that sounded as disgruntled as Rhys felt.

"Oh, no!" Andie sat up, clutching the sheet to her breasts. "Mrs. Hodge will wake up. She'll figure out I'm not in my room. I left the door open when I went to find you in the den last night, not thinking—"

"She doesn't have the monitor. So it sounds louder in here," Rhys pointed out. "I'll get Will, and she probably won't even notice. It's still early." The urgent secrecy seemed unnecessary. In fact, Rhys was surprised by how accepting he felt about the prospect of Mrs. Hodge picking up on the new development in his relationship with Andie. But

Andie herself was clearly anxious, and it would be impolitic—not to mention tone-deaf—not to follow her lead. *Right?*

"I'd better get back." She swung her legs over the edge of the bed and started collecting her clothing from the floor. Rhys barely had time to take a last, wistful look before she zipped herself into her jeans and shrugged on her T-shirt, wadding her underwear and socks into a ball in one fist. She was ready before he'd even put on a pair of pajama bottoms and tied his robe.

Rhys led the way down the corridor, Andie shadowing him like a SWAT-team member intent on concealment. He paused at the door to Will's room, reaching out to squeeze Andie's shoulder. She nodded, tiptoeing to her own door and gesturing for him to be quick about entering Will's room. Rhys swung the door open, and Will's cries filled the corridor just as Mrs. Hodge appeared outside her own room. Her eyebrows rose as she saw Andie, still dressed in yesterday's clothes, about to sneak into her bedroom, and Rhys in his bathrobe. The nanny's jaw dropped, her face settling into an appalled expression.

Andie lost no time in putting the door between herself and the scene in the hallway. All Rhys could do was smile sheepishly and complete his rescue of Will. He heard Mrs. Hodge's door close with a crisp click as he lifted his son from his bed, his mood suddenly bleak. His unbelievable night with Andie had come to a hurried, utterly unsatisfactory conclusion.

When this thing between us runs its course . . . Her words rotated through Rhys's brain on a static loop. How could she make such a pronouncement? She'd said it with such matter-of-factness that he could almost imagine her picking detritus from the kitchen drain and holding it between gloved fingers.

Not that her words were entirely callous. In fact, they were paradoxically considerate. Hadn't the potential impact on Will been his main concern about starting something with her? Just as it had been his reason for abstaining from any personal entanglements over the past couple of years. It was only after she'd offered her reassurance that he realized that, where Andie was concerned, it was a spurious argument from the first. Andie loved Will. If he could trust anything in this world, it was that she would never hurt him or compromise his therapy. It was the damage she might cause Rhys himself that now stood out in sharp relief.

And yet, for all that, he trusted her. No matter what she said, he would not believe she could be so cynical as to slap an expiration date on the extraordinary connection that had sprung to life between them. After all, she was the one who'd stood up for it, brought it into the open, by breaking through his defenses with her courage, her refreshing candor. If it were up to him, he'd still be slinking through the shadows, confounded by his own doubts and insecurities.

He'd been the one who was too quick to underestimate their affinity. So now it was his turn to demonstrate his faith. The weekend was upon them, so he took Will down to the kitchen for another early morning of snowy vistas and leisurely make-believe at the train table, listening for the tread of Andie's feet on the staircase.

She didn't appear until late morning, looking vulnerable once more, her hair restrained in a braid that snaked over one shoulder, her eyes large and luminous. She'd called Saddle Tree Farm, she reported with a shy smile. If Rhys would rustle up the paperwork, they could stop by for an introductory session the following Friday. He agreed readily and offered her a cappuccino, relieved when she gradually settled into the relaxed rhythm of the morning, playing with Will and lingering over breakfast.

Mrs. Hodge left before noon to drive down to Connecticut to visit her daughter, and Rhys was aware of a certain tension lifting as soon as her car disappeared down the driveway. After lunch, when Will went down for his nap, he went in search of Andie, craving her company.

He found her in the laundry room, sorting her clothes into piles for washing, the washer already churning one load. She gave him an inquisitive smile as he walked to her.

"I missed you," he explained, touching her shoulder, savoring the warmth of her skin beneath the thin fabric of her loose gray T-shirt. He stepped closer and dipped his head to plant a kiss at the corner of her mouth.

She leaned into his kiss, turning as his arms closed around her so they were melded together from chest to thigh. She moaned as he teased her lips apart with his tongue, giving in to instinct, opening to him with unconcealed need. *Is she regretting her earlier comment?* He could only hope. Or was she trying to hasten its conclusion by working the hunger out of her system, expelling it in the frenzy of their mutual desire?

Within moments, his jeans and her sweats formed a pile on the floor. He was thankful for his prescience in tucking a condom into his back pocket today, and at her urging he covered himself, lifting her onto the washing machine so he could fulfill his fantasy of the evening before in the wine room.

He'd never seen anything as erotic as her, spread for him, her eyes wild with abandon, her T-shirt sliding off one perfect shoulder, dark tendrils of her hair escaping from her braid. He plunged into her, mesmerized by the place where their bodies connected, knowing she, too, was captivated by the frankly carnal image of their coupling. He pulled out with unearthly control, her body giving up inch after inch of him until she claimed him again—hot, tight, and as inexorable as a force of nature. His control unraveled as he watched her biting down on her lower lip, bracing herself against the washer as it switched to the spin cycle.

The machine knocked and thumped, oscillating as he stroked into her, his pace and pressure building as her body gripped him and evoked a pleasure so intense that afterward he was speechless with the wonder of it.

"I missed you" became Rhys's mantra. Over the weekend, they settled into a happy routine, gravitating together to tend to Will and share meals, bundling up for sledding expeditions and snowball fights, and thawing together in front of the fireplace, seeking each other out when Will was asleep to slake a thirst that seemed to intensify and demand relief more quickly each time.

Andie made no more ominous statements about "things running their course," and Rhys's contentment would have been just about complete if it weren't for the air of hesitation and reserve that came over her whenever an outside party intruded into their spellbound state.

After Mrs. Hodge returned at the conclusion of the weekend, Andie didn't back off from her next forthright physical encounter with him. She seemed powerless to resist that, at least. But she shot back to her room afterward, as if she'd been fired from a gun. *Is she embarrassed by what our relationship has become? Does she regret it? Does she not feel it the way I do?* All he could really be certain of was how strangely off balance and incomplete he felt without her sleeping by his side. It was impossible to deny it: he was completely in her thrall.

CHAPTER SEVENTEEN

Over the next few days, the stretch of bone-chillingly cold, crystalline days gave way to a comparative thaw. When the mercury rose to right around freezing, it felt so balmy that Rhys—home unexpectedly early before a scheduled meeting with Karina—suggested that he and Andie take Will to the playground.

"This can be in lieu of his therapy session today," Rhys suggested as he stood in the kitchen, stowing a variety of toddler snacks in bags for the proposed outing. "The poor little sprog could use some fresh air after being cooped up inside at preschool all morning. If we run him around a bit, he'll probably do better when we meet Karina at the library."

Jillian, who was in a buoyant mood after trouncing her husband's weekly weight-loss tally by a few precious ounces, waved them cheerily out the door.

"Don't let Will get a chill," she called as they filed out. "Bundle up!"

Andie shrank away from Rhys as they piled into the Range Rover. *He looks so much like a proud dad taking his perfect little family out for a drive.* She swallowed grimly. *You idiot! He is a proud dad. You're the one who doesn't belong in this picture.* The problem was she was almost certain that the air of fulfillment Rhys currently projected had something to do with her.

Somehow, this trip away from the house together made it all so much more real—forced her to own up to the fact that the sensuous haze she'd drifted around in for the last few days would have to give way to reality sometime.

She gripped the grab handle above her window. *I never meant for this to happen.* But she knew that claim was disingenuous. She'd made this happen as surely as gravity caused an object lobbed into the air to plummet back to earth. Just one sidelong glance at Rhys's serene profile was enough to clog her throat with a pent-up sob. *Don't depend on me. If it's a future you're looking for, you're with the wrong woman.*

Lost in his daydreams, Rhys didn't even seem to notice how quiet she'd become. He pulled into the lot beside the playground and applied the parking brake. When she joined him at the rear passenger door to help retrieve Will and all their gear, he slid a warm hand up between her shoulder blades, over her tingling nape, and into the wavy curtain of her hair. His fingers were magic, she realized hopelessly, trying to ignore the lightning bolts of pleasure that seared her down to her toes. She wondered if there had ever been a case of spontaneous human combustion in this suburban parking lot.

"Don't," she murmured, shaking him off. "Not here."

He shot her a look of consternation and withdrew his hand guiltily, making her want to catch it with both of hers and return it to that place just above her nape—a previously unrecognized hotbed of sensation. Instead, she focused on belting her coat against the cold and unbuckling Will from his car seat.

I need to set limits, that's all. She shouldered the large bag of Will's supplies and stepped away from the car. *Just because we've started this physical thing doesn't mean I've promised him forever.*

They crunched through iced-over slush and put the snack bag down on a dry bench on the sunny side of the playground and chaperoned

Will over to the object of his desire, a green plastic tunnel slide that let out onto a gray-brown puddle of snowmelt.

"If you take him up, I'll catch him when he comes down," Rhys suggested.

Andie nodded and shadowed Will as he climbed the stairs to the top of the slide, ready to catch him if his snow boots lost traction on the perforated metal surface. Will kept up a constant stream of murmurs, which ascended to curious squawks as he reached the opening of the chute. He sat himself down and then scrambled to his feet again as if to abandon the project, until Rhys's comforting face appeared in the opening at the far end.

Giggling, Will ventured onto the slide, going down so slowly that "slide" was probably a misnomer.

"Gotcha!" Rhys scooped him out of the way of the puddle and set him on relatively dry land.

Will's attention soon switched to a hanging log bridge connected by chains, which sat on the opposite side of a stretch of mushy snow. Taking one of Will's hands each, Andie and Rhys half directed, half carried him over the slippery expanse. Andie looked to Rhys to see whether he wanted her to shepherd Will onto the bridge, but his gaze was fixed on a point in the middle distance, over by the parking lot.

"What the—"

She followed his frown to its target. A slim figure in a tailored black wool coat and a swirl of long, dark hair was picking her way toward them.

Andie was unprepared for the sense of dread that swelled in her chest. Her brain conjured the sweet, blanketing scent of jasmine wrapped around its spike of bergamot. Astonishing, given she'd only crossed paths with the woman that one memorable time. It felt as if a simulacrum of Karina were an ever-present fixture in the house.

Rhys squinted at the approaching figure.

A tense smile flickered across Karina's face.

"Well, hello," she drawled, taking in the scene, Will still half-suspended between Andie and Rhys, gripping their hands tightly.

"Karina." Rhys gave her a look that could have stripped paint. "We're not meeting until three thirty, and we decided on story hour at the library. I thought we agreed, no more surprises."

His concerned, proprietorial glance lingered on Andie, and she saw Karina take in the two of them and frown slightly.

"I can take off and leave you two to have your visit here, if you like," Andie offered.

"No." Rhys looked bothered. As always, he'd offered Karina an inch only to have her grasp a mile. Suspicion flickered in the look he gave her. "Andie and I were giving Will some outdoor time before the library. How did you know we were here?"

"Oh, I was in the area and spotted you from the road," Karina declared. "I must have a sixth sense as far as Will is concerned."

Rhys's mouth tightened into a grim line. "We're going to finish our playtime here as we intended. Stay or go as you wish, but we're not changing our plans."

"I'll stay," Karina announced with a determined smile and a brisk, stilted nod of acknowledgment to Andie.

"Hello, Will," she crooned, bending down to his level. Andie slid her hand from Will's to let Karina take it, but he shook free of his mother's grip and patted fretfully at Andie's coat. Relief swamped her as he slid his hand into hers once more. A tense vibe emanated from Karina, which was completely understandable given the circumstances, but it aroused Andie's protective instincts toward him.

Rhys took Will and helped him onto one of the platforms that anchored the log bridge, carefully ushering him onto the bridge's swaying path. The structure was not easy for him to manage, given that the logs undulated and tipped underfoot. Andie actually liked it as a new test for his confidence, and she strode to the opposite platform to offer support.

She was so intent on monitoring Will's progress across the bridge that Karina took her by surprise as she stepped up beside her. *What are you doing?* There was a challenge in the gaze Karina flicked her way as they stood side by side.

Rhys looked thunderous as he followed Will across the bridge, well aware of the zero-sum test Karina had just set up, forcing Will to choose which of the two women to go to. Andie swallowed nervously. *Why would she do it? Of course he's going to come to me. Isn't he?* She cast a sidelong glance at Karina and was disturbed to see a turbulent sort of pleasure in her expression. *Of course. She loves the drama.*

Will squinted at Andie and Karina as he approached, an uncertain look on his face.

"Come on, sweetie," Karina called, kneeling down with open arms.

It was then that a streak of pure, unalloyed want gripped Andie. She knew in some rational part of her brain that she should abdicate this absurd contest and ensure that Will would cross the bridge straight into his mother's arms. But she didn't want to. It was more than just protectiveness. It was possessiveness. *Mine. Mine. Mine.* Karina felt like a rival.

Andie didn't bend down and call to him. She had enough self-control to refrain from that, at least. But she visualized Will's sturdy little form pressed up against her. She mapped out the path of his steps even before he took them, as if by doing so she could influence his course. She thought about the texture of his hair against her cheek and his sturdy shape in her arms.

She needn't have fretted. All those hours of games and cuddles laid out his trajectory as if guided by a compass.

"Andie!" Will capped off her resounding victory by bellowing her name as he advanced toward her. She was overcome by an intoxicating tide of emotion as he wrapped his arms around her legs. *Joy. Gratification. Love. Pride.* The same complex blend of responses she'd felt when he'd first said her name. The same ego-driven sense of reward that had first launched her on the path that led to this very point.

Then realization dawned. *I'm a monster!* Sweat prickled at her hairline, and her whole body went hot with mortification in spite of the chilly day. She stood stock-still, letting the full implications of her folly sink in. She'd crossed an ethical line into a no-man's-land. Of course, she'd always loved her clients. Particularly when she got to work with children long-term, it was impossible not to become invested. To revel in their successes. To cry, always in private, over their frustrations and the tough road they faced. *But this?*

Why did I let this happen? But she knew why. Ever since she'd taken this job, she'd been pinning her hopes for redemption on this one small boy. She'd thought she could prove something to herself and then step neatly away at the conclusion of the designated three months. She'd never expected to become this entangled.

"Well!" Karina huffed, turning to Rhys. "You see what happens when you give an outsider more access to our son than you give his own mother."

Andie, still queasy and aghast at her own hubris, almost burst into hysterical, horrified laughter when a wet eruption from Will's diaper region signaled the need for some quick attention. Karina blanched as Rhys fixed her with an ironic look.

"Care to take diaper duty?" he asked her, then hauled Will into his arms as she hesitated. "No, I didn't think so."

"Andie and I can stay here and chat," Karina said. "Perhaps she can give me some tips for exercises to do with Will."

Rhys looked at Andie questioningly, and she nodded. It was the least she could do, despite the fact that the idea of talking with Karina filled her with apprehension. Guilt was a powerful motivator.

"I'd be happy to show you some games he likes," she offered. Her mind was still racing. She had to make this right. She had to step back and facilitate Karina's bond with Will.

"It won't work, you know," Karina said as Rhys bore Will off to collect the diaper bag.

"What won't work?" Distracted by her own thoughts, Andie had to force herself to attend to the woman. "The games for Will?"

"No, I'm talking about that butter-wouldn't-melt-in-your-mouth, child-whisperer act you've got going on. Rhys isn't one of those men who falls for the nanny, you know?"

"I'm not 'the nanny,'" Andie said, oddly calm as resolution overtook her. Her fears that the woman had instantly detected the chemistry between Rhys and her were apparently unfounded, and Andie wasn't about to enlighten her. "I'm your son's occupational therapist, and I actually have some advice I'd be happy to give you, if you'd care to listen."

"Call yourself what you like," Karina responded dismissively, tossing her hair back over her shoulders. "But I saw the way you looked at Rhys. You should know, though, that on that front, we're both out of luck."

Karina surveyed Andie archly. "At first I assumed that you and he were together. I *was* a bit confused, as you're not his usual type." She gave a commiserating smile before launching her next salvo. "But he set me straight on the fact that there's nothing between you. In spite of that, he tells me he's not romantically available."

Karina paused, a glimmer in her eye. "I suspect he's romancing someone at work. He always did have a thing for women engineers."

For one fleeting instant, Andie wondered, *Is it true? Is there someone else?* But the seed of doubt Karina wanted to plant simply wouldn't take root. Andie could still feel the echo of Rhys's touch at her nape and the protective warmth of his gaze. *Nice try, Karina, but if you're trying to faze me, you're going to have to do better than that.* The fact that Karina thought the ploy stood a chance of working only highlighted how little she really knew her ex.

Andie was distracted by a hint of bergamot and jasmine, its dispersion contained by the cold air but still discernible as Karina leaned closer.

"I will get him back, you know," the woman confided with lethal softness. "However long it takes." Close-up, the delicate skin below her eyes looked dry and fatigued under a careful layer of foundation. In the stark outdoor light, her irises were eerily pale turquoise rings around encroaching blackness.

I can't be having this conversation. I have to get things back on track. Andie gave a noncommittal smile and took a few steps back in the direction of the car, where Rhys was finishing cleaning up Will. When Karina fell into step with her, she launched into a mini lecture on Will's triggers, sensory aversions, and cravings, and how to recognize opportunities to connect.

Rhys was standing by the car with a harried look on his face as they approached, holding Will, whose lower half was now swathed in a blanket rather than padded in snow pants.

"Will had a blowout," he announced, causing Karina to recoil subtly. "It's poop central over here. We need to take him home and change him. Then I'll bring him to the library."

Home. Andie realized with a shiver that she was starting to think of it as her home, too. She'd barely thought about her little rental apartment since she'd arrived in Concord, but now she reflected that it might have been better if she'd never left. How was it that good intentions and subterranean motives could aid and abet one another, sweeping a person along until she found herself in a place she'd never intended?

Andie was dimly aware of Karina watching as she swung into action and helped Rhys finish packing Will and his supplies back in the car, working as smoothly together as a well-oiled machine. Soon they were done, but Karina continued to stand there, a dark figure against a dappled landscape of winter beige and white, following them with a basilisk stare as they pulled out of the lot and headed for Monument Street.

∼

Andie looked troubled as they drove toward the house. Rhys was tempted to attribute her mood to the encounter with Karina, but she'd appeared out of sorts ever since they'd headed out to the playground.

"Is everything okay?" he asked mildly, his gaze focused on the road ahead. He had the sense that interrogating her too closely would spook her. He remembered how she'd pulled away in the parking lot, her withdrawal a sucker punch to the gut. *Don't. Not here.*

"I'm fine," she responded, reaching back up for the grab handle and peering out the window as if to make a thorough study of the scenery as it flashed by.

"I don't know how the hell Karina tracked us down out there." His ex-wife was making such a habit of ambushing him at odd times that he was beginning to wonder whether she'd somehow secreted a tracker on his person. It was a ridiculous thought, of course, but her preoccupation with him was unsettling.

"You do know that Karina's master plan is for the two of you to get back together."

"I've told her it's never going to happen."

"That may be, but I'm not sure she's received the message."

They drove for a minute in silence.

"I do think it's important that she bond with Will," Andie said as they passed the Civil War obelisk and the old courthouse.

"He'll come around to her if she puts in the work," Rhys responded.

Andie swallowed convulsively, as if steeling herself, and turned to peer at him.

"Rhys, you do know that I have my own life to get back to when my time here is over?"

There it was again. Her persistent focus on the end of their relationship, just when things were getting started.

"Of course you have a life," Rhys agreed, although her implication worried him. Wasn't what was happening between them part of her life, too? Or did she regard it as something hidden? Throwaway. Separate.

"But presumably you're not just going to leave us, cold turkey, at the end of the three months?" he said carefully. "Like you said, I would expect that you'd keep working with Will. And I hope that you'd continue to see us, you know . . . generally." *Generally.* If that wasn't a completely pathetic way to sum up all that Andie was coming to mean to him.

"I'm worried," she said. "With this thing we've started between us, we've really upped the ante. Now there's so much that can go wrong. And when it does, it will be an awfully long way down."

"Andie, we were friends first," Rhys said with an exaggerated confidence he suddenly didn't feel. "Why should anything go wrong? Must we be all doom and gloom? Can't we just take it a day at a time and not second-guess ourselves?"

"You're right. We were friends first. That is, we *are* friends. But I was Will's therapist before that." She fixed tormented eyes on him. "I've crossed a line, Rhys. I've done the very thing I swore to myself I wouldn't do when I came here."

"If you're worrying that you've done Will a disservice, then please stop," Rhys beseeched her. "Look at how happy he is. Look at how he's progressing."

She turned to look over her shoulder at Will, who had fallen asleep, lulled by the motion of the car. The expression on her face as she watched him made Rhys's heart lurch.

"I trust you, Andie," he said, his voice thick with feeling. "We both have his best interests at heart. We won't let him down. We wouldn't do that."

"I know," she said pensively as they pulled up to the house. "But I don't want you getting crazy ideas, Rhys. We're friends who happen to have an . . . attraction. That's all."

As soon as Rhys cut the engine, she jumped out and bustled over to Will's door.

"Hey," Rhys said, reaching out to touch her shoulder as she started to gather Will's bag and toys. She turned, her cheeks flushed, and allowed herself to be folded against him. *There.* There was nothing like the charge that passed between them when they touched. *Trust in that,* Rhys willed silently.

"Don't worry." He spoke into her fragrant hair. "There's nothing bad here. It's all good. Let's just keep moving forward. We get started on Will's hippotherapy tomorrow. We'll keep working together just as we have been."

She nodded and sniffed, and he tried to take comfort from the instinctive way she leaned into him, like she never wanted to leave.

CHAPTER EIGHTEEN

"Would you look at that?"

Andie laughed—actually laughed out loud in delight—when Will's hippotherapy mount ambled into the yard, led by the older man she'd met on her first visit to Saddle Tree Farm.

The creature, a stocky Haflinger horse short enough to comfortably nestle its head in her armpit if it so desired, still wore its shaggy winter coat—which was fair enough, given that icicles were still hanging from the eaves of the barn. Chestnut hair stuck out in tufts and whorls all over the animal's solid body, fading to a contrasting cream under its belly, where the girth of a therapy saddle disappeared into a nest of shaggy fuzz. A notably pretty face—with a fine, tapered muzzle—poked out from beneath a voluminous flaxen forelock, through which Andie was able to make out the friendly gleam of one steady brown eye.

Will, almost falling out of Rhys's arms in his eagerness to get to the horse, squealed and flapped his hands in its face. The horse, standing squarely on its four sturdy legs, didn't even blink.

"I'm starting to feel better about this," Rhys said. He turned to Andie and added in a stage whisper, "Do you think we could smuggle her into the back of the car and take her home?"

"Um, 'she' is actually a he," corrected the woman standing on Andie's other side. She was an attractive woman in her midfifties with a distinctive snowy-white bob that cast a flattering light on her neat features. "Not that you can tell under all that fluff. This is Ace. He's our favorite hippotherapy horse for the under-fives."

"I can see why," Andie said. "Ace is adorable. It was so kind of you to fit us in at short notice, Mrs. Mulcahy."

"Please, call me Maisie."

Maisie and her husband, Ed, were the owners of the farm, Andie had discovered in her calls leading up to the visit. Maisie, a speech therapist by training, had been hospitalized the previous week, when Andie had first shown up at the farm.

Andie smiled. "I hope your leg is feeling better." She gestured to the forearm crutch the woman was using to support her weight.

"If only it were just the leg," Maisie sighed. "But we don't need to talk about that. Tell me about your little boy here."

"Rhys's little boy," Andie corrected.

"Of course. You said on the phone that you're his OT, right?" Maisie stopped to steady herself, leaning more heavily on the crutch. Andie noticed Ed's eyes narrow in concern.

"I'm fine, Ed," Maisie assured him. "But would you call Carol and Emily over here? We're almost ready for their help."

Andie offered to take Ace's reins, and they walked slowly toward the indoor arena while Ed headed in the direction of the main barn. Andie and Rhys took turns filling Maisie in on Will's history and development, describing the therapies he was already receiving.

"If he takes to this, you'll want to be in touch with his regular speech therapist," Andie pointed out. "But I should be part of the conversation, too."

"Andie is coordinating all of Will's care," Rhys said, and his glance felt like a caress, his implicit trust like a hand at her back.

Every time she looked at him, her mind swam with a dizzying mix of fear and elation. She'd tried to come clean with him about her concerns on the way back from the playground the day before, but there was no way she could fully explain the alarm she felt over her attachment to him and Will, or the dangers of the emotional and ethical minefield she found herself traversing. She'd planned to retreat to her room last night to buy herself some space. They'd given Will his bath before Rhys took him to the library to meet with Karina, so technically her evening should have been her own. But Rhys sought her out on some pretext or other, and, sure enough, she'd wound up in his arms and in his bed. Whenever she got within a twenty-foot radius of him, her traitorous body seemed determined to throw itself up against his, like a bobby pin stuck to an MRI scanner.

She could live with the straightforward honesty of their physical attraction. Surely it would ultimately burn out, and they would be free once more. It was the rest that she fretted about. The way he watched her with that uniquely Rhys-like mixture of wonder and hope, completely unaware of how unworthy she was of the honor.

"Ah, here are Carol and Emily." Maisie's voice broke into Andie's thoughts.

She introduced a tall woman in her late forties as Carol, one of the farm's volunteer side walkers. Carol's daughter, Emily, in her early twenties and the spitting image of her mother, was one of Saddle Tree's part-time riding instructors, who also helped out with the hippotherapy program.

Maisie began explaining the basics of the first session and ran through the standard safety rules while Rhys held Will, who was resting one outstretched hand on Ace's shaggy neck. Andie couldn't help but notice that Will wasn't fretting and fussing the way he often did when the adults around him were occupied in conversation. He kept his gaze fixed on the placid horse, tentatively rubbing his fingers through his thick coat.

When the time came to get Will up on Ace, Rhys was the one who deposited him in the saddle. Will clutched at his father's arm, his vestibular sense triggered as he was lifted through the air. Once on board, he leaned forward in the deep, padded seat, and Emily guided his hands firmly around the sturdy handlebar. His eyes were wide as Carol and Emily took up their positions on either side of him, fitting his feet into the stirrups and holding his legs steady with a gentle, even pressure as Maisie gave the order to walk. He continued to crouch forward with a mystified, blissed-out look on his face, as he felt the unfamiliar rhythmic motion of Ace's gait.

Andie was so overcome with emotion as she watched that she barely noticed Rhys slipping his hand into hers. She had to incline her head away for a moment to contain her tears, focusing on Will and Ace's methodical progress down the length of the arena. Maisie stood in the center, resting her weight on her crutch as she assessed Will's response. There was something therapeutic about just watching the horse's repetitive motion, the pattern of his steps, the predictable bobbing of his serene blond head. By the time they'd done two circuits of the arena, Will's posture had loosened and straightened a little, and he gave an excited half squeal, half laugh as he passed by.

Maisie directed Carol and Emily to bring Ace closer to the center in ever-decreasing circles, and she started to walk slowly alongside, talking to Will in a soothing, singsong voice and introducing some simple games to focus his attention. Andie felt a shiver of concern as she watched the older woman's progress—the stiffness in her gait and the way she favored her left side. *She's in pain.*

Maisie persevered with the therapy session nonetheless, focusing on Will's receptive language, engaging him in reciprocal activities so she could gauge his level of functioning. By the end of the session, only one of his hands gripped the saddle's handle. He'd woven the other into the pale strands of Ace's mane. He squawked when he was lifted down from Ace's back but was pacified when Maisie asked Carol to help him brush the horse.

"I have to make a couple of calls while they finish up," Maisie said, "but would you like to join me in the house for a cup of coffee afterward?"

Andie agreed enthusiastically and offered to carry Ace's saddle back to the tack room while Rhys stayed to watch Will. She inhaled the smell of clean leather and horse as she slid the saddle back onto its rack, hung up the girth, and then wandered back out into the yard. It was a gorgeous day, bright and blazing, and the red barn stood out against the backdrop of snow-covered paddocks and dark evergreens. The icicles had started to thaw and drip, and Andie leaned against a post-and-rail fence, closing her eyes and basking for a moment in the resplendent light.

She yelped when a blast of warm, moist air and the brush of bristles against the back of her neck announced the arrival of the black mare she'd noticed on her first visit to Saddle Tree Farm.

"Hello there!" Andie laughed, turning to marvel at the large beast. A child's shriek echoed across the yard, and both Andie and the mare turned to watch a preschool-age boy dart across the half-frozen ground, chasing after the barn cat. A girl of about ten or eleven followed, her ponytail bouncing as she giggled and skipped, swinging her riding helmet from one hand.

"Jake, Becca, get in the car!" A woman's harried voice trailed after them. "Jake, you have soccer in fifteen minutes, and you have to change on the way, remember?"

Andie flung a sympathetic smile at the woman who emerged from the barn's center aisle, laden with coats, backpacks, and snack bags. Jake's and Becca's hearing had apparently been compromised by the overpowering cuteness of the ginger cat, who found a dry patch of ground and started writhing exuberantly.

"Kids! We're going to be late!" The mom's increasingly strident tone fell on deaf ears as brother and sister laughed and exclaimed, both bent low over the cat's fluffy belly.

A long time ago, Andie had been the same way with Gus, she remembered with a wistful smile. They'd always found it so easy to get on each other's wavelength, aware of their mother's stress only in that distant, myopic way of children. They'd been that way on Gus's very last day.

The disastrous chain of events had started with the abandoned piano lesson, Andie remembered, a sick feeling churning in the pit of her stomach. It had been raining—actually, sleeting—and she'd plopped down next to Gus on the couch after school to watch one of his favorite cartoons, succumbing to the guilty lassitude that makes cabin fever its own kind of pleasure. Too much TV. Too much of the same four walls.

She was supposed to go to her lesson, but lethargy had taken over, and she hadn't practiced enough that week. Like Jake and Becca in the farmyard, she didn't want to switch gears and follow the schedule. She didn't want to spend an hour seated on the wooden bench at Mrs. Murphy's, her back ramrod straight as she tried to wing it, hoping the teacher wouldn't chafe at her slow progress.

So she'd complained of a stomachache and begged her mother to let her stay home. Whined, actually, with a relentlessness guaranteed to wear Susan down. Susan usually brought Gus along to piano and had him play in the waiting room while Andie did her lesson, and there was no chance of her being able to wrangle two recalcitrant kids into the car. So Andie had won. If only she'd known what a Pyrrhic victory it was.

Soon the relative quiet of the house was shattered by the shouts and giggles of the two youngest Tilly siblings. Gus was in a rambunctious mood, throwing himself on Andie's supposedly ailing stomach and causing her to dissolve into laughter and squeals as she tried to defend herself. Susan's face was sharp with irritation, her warnings increasingly strident, but Andie and Gus were unable to contain their high spirits, innocent hilarity tightening its grip the more they tried to suppress it. Adult displeasure had no power to penetrate their childish communion. They were giddy and punchy, and the tide of their raucous play would not ebb. Finally, Susan, stiff with tension, had ordered them to get their jackets and rain boots on and ushered them outside, headed for tragedy.

"I see you've met Shanti." Maisie's voice startled Andie back to the present, and she turned to watch Jake and Becca's mom ease her car into the snow-lined road, the children safely buckled inside. Andie's left hand was clenched in the mare's thick mane, but even the coarseness of the strands against her fingers seemed less real to her than the sleet and fog of that distant evening.

She forced herself to attend to Maisie. "Yes, she's incredible."

"She's my baby," Maisie said fondly. "She's been with me for almost twenty years. Since before I got sick."

"Sick?" Andie echoed, the fog in her mind receding as she focused on the woman in front of her. "Do you mind my asking . . ."

"It's MS," Maisie said. "You should know, because my health could interfere with the continuity of Will's treatment if you decide to pursue therapy here."

She gestured to her cane and the stiffness of her right leg as they walked back to the stable. "Much of the time I do okay, but when I have a bad spell, I can't get around like I used to. Hippotherapy can be rather physical work if you do it properly. Our side walkers are wonderful, but I'm the only accredited therapist we have."

"I'm sorry." Andie wasn't quite sure what else to say. "Are you sure—"

"I'm not throwing in the towel just yet," Maisie said with a shaky smile. "If you'll bear with me, I'd love to work with Will."

"I think Rhys would agree that we'd jump at the chance to work with you whenever you can do it. And of course we're happy to be flexible."

"Then we'll make it happen." Maisie's smile broadened. "I'll look at the schedule. A lot of the timing depends on when our side walkers are available. I have to rely on volunteers to keep the program going."

"I might be able to help you there." Andie explained the undemanding schedule she was lucky enough to have while in Concord, with hours free while Will was at preschool and his other therapies. "I know my way around horses, and I'd love to volunteer."

"Today's my lucky day, then." Maisie's brown eyes gleamed. "Come in and have a coffee, and I'll get you scheduled in for a training session before you change your mind."

CHAPTER NINETEEN

Andie stood in the upstairs kitchen, soaking in the sounds of the house. Her childhood home had always vibrated with noise and movement. The slamming of doors. The incessant clanging of steam through heating pipes. The shouts of squabbling girls. The bristling awareness of her parents' moods, which she could gauge just by the pressure of their footfalls on the creaky wooden stairs. Rhys's house was so expansive and well insulated that she often had to strain to tell where the other occupants were and what they were doing at any given moment, if she could tell at all. She knew Mrs. Hodge was downstairs with Will, getting his dinner started. Rhys was due home any minute.

Her chest tightened with anticipation. It was almost Pavlovian, the exhilaration that possessed her when she heard the tread of his footsteps in the corridor at night in the large house, or when he appeared beside her unheralded in the kitchen or the OT gym, offering to pitch in as she finished a task. Her rib cage would suddenly feel too small to contain the surge of emotion that overcame her. Her breath would turn fast and shallow at the merest suggestion of his touch. She felt mildly unhinged—in the nicest possible way, of course—her body alternately jolted with adrenaline and bathed in pleasurable endorphins.

She was now exactly halfway through her contracted time at the house. Just six more weeks and she'd be gone. This crazy flight of fancy would end, and she could go about putting her life back together. She wondered if her infatuation with Rhys would have loosened its grip by then, or if she'd have to suffer the full effects of withdrawal.

She was torn between the hope that she was growing as important to him as he was becoming to her, and the equally fervent wish that his feelings for her were far more tepid. How else would she be able to bear the inevitable guilt when she wrenched herself away—as she knew she must?

But there was nothing tepid about the way he touched her each night, or the way he looked at her when they lay basking in each other's arms afterward, laughing and sharing stories about their day. The joy of it was enough to sweep her along in its inexorable current.

She craned to look out a window that overlooked the driveway, listening for the crunch of wheels on gravel, but was summoned instead by the chirping of her cell phone stuffed into the pocket of a jacket slung over a nearby chair.

"Jess!" she cried, fumbling as she picked up the call. So much had happened since she'd last seen and talked to her sister. "How are you feeling?"

"A bit pukey, but fine." Jess's cheerful voice sounded close enough that she could almost reach out and touch her. "Are you ready for Sunday?"

Sunday. The maple-sugaring event. Her mother had left a message several days ago, and Andie had texted back a response and then put it out of her mind, eager to slip back into escapist bliss with Rhys. But she couldn't deny that her childhood had never been far from her thoughts in recent days, her memories awakened by her visits to Saddle Tree Farm, her dreams haunted by half-formed images that she didn't know whether to attribute to recall or sheer imagination.

"Yeah, I told Susan I'd be there."

"And what about Rhys and Will? Are they coming?"

"I haven't asked them."

"Why not?" Jess pressed. "This is your chance to show Susan how good you are at what you do. What better way than for her to see the trust Rhys has in you?"

"Susan is *my* problem, not Rhys's. I don't really think it's going to help anyone to expose him to the Tilly craziness." Or to enmesh Rhys even more deeply in her life than he already was.

"Well, then, let's end the craziness," Jess insisted. "The way she undermines you . . . it has to stop."

Andie's heart swelled painfully. Typical Jess, campaigning for her as tirelessly as ever. She loved her for it, but part of her wished her sister could let things be. There was one question that had been nagging at her, though.

"Jess, I need to ask you something." Andie's voice was small. "How did Dad used to act toward me when I was little? You know, before . . ." She didn't have to say before *what*.

"Jim? How did he act toward you?" Jess sounded surprised. "You don't remember?"

"Well, not really, no," Andie admitted. "The accident was kind of like this dividing line. It's hard for me to remember how things were before. Or, at least, I sometimes think I remember, and then I wonder whether I'm just making it up."

"You were so young when it happened." Jess sighed. "I know he was hard on you afterward, but before that, he worshipped the ground you walked on. You really don't remember?"

"No. Tell me what he was like, Jess."

"Well . . . he was different with you than he was with the rest of us. I don't know. They were so young when Susan got pregnant with Louisa, and then Rose and I came along, and for him I think we were just more of the same. An obstacle to the life he'd planned."

"You mean law school?"

"Yeah, that, and the idea of getting away from Camden for good. There he was, stuck with small kids, and he couldn't shift onto another track. He was kind of locked into the same life as Pops." Their grand-father had been a career cop in the Camden PD.

"So he took it out on Susan," Andie commented, her tone bleak. One of her few persistent memories of her early life was of huddling on her bed with Jess, the air around them thick with rage, fear, and whiskey fumes as Jim bellowed at Susan in the bedroom next door. They would cringe, waiting for the splintering of wood or the sickening thud of a blow.

"You remember that," Jess said softly. "Well, how could you not? It was awful. But then they'd make up, and she'd be walking on air and suddenly pregnant again, ready to pop out yet another kid they couldn't afford."

"He was a regular small-town Henry the Eighth, desperate to get his son."

"Yeah, basically," Jess snorted. "Louisa, Rose, and I were a sore dis-appointment to him. But with you, something changed. I don't know if it was that he was finally coming around to the way his life had turned out, or if it was that you were just so darn gorgeous and funny and endearing—"

"Please!" Andie scoffed. That was most definitely *not* how she'd felt as a child.

"But you *were*, Andie." Jess's voice softened. "You were the cutest thing I'd ever seen. And you were such a tomboy. You were always up a tree or on a roof or on a horse. You drove Susan to distraction, but in Jim's eyes you could do no wrong. You might not have been his boy, but you were the next best thing."

Andie's thoughts skipped back to the memory of being in the kitchen with Jim and Susan, held on his lap like a pawn smuggled behind enemy lines, safe under his protection while others suffered as the targets of his malevolence—Susan, most of all. She shuddered. It was a dynamic she'd never understood, of course. She'd been a young child. She'd never asked for Jim's favoritism. But she'd needed affection from somewhere, as her mother always seemed to have precious little to give her.

Of course, everything changed after Gus's death. Her father became a broken man. He had nothing left for her. No emotion left inside him at all. Just a vacuum that could never be filled, even by the amber-brown contents of a bottle. Andie's heart churned with a strange melancholy, a sense of mourning for all of them. For Susan, for Jim, for their three eldest daughters, for Gus—always for Gus—and for herself as well, the once-vibrant child Jess had described.

"I feel sick," she said.

"Like I've said before, you don't have to come on Sunday." Jess's voice was rich with compassion.

"No, I do," Andie said with renewed certainty. She was galvanized by the sense of a horizon coming into view as the first layers of long-sedimented assumptions were finally scrubbed from her lens. It was not a comfortable sensation, but now she knew things had to change. She couldn't cling to her opaque understanding of the past and allow it to continue to shape her future. She needed to see Susan. She needed to go.

"Promise me you'll think about bringing Rhys and Will. Show Susan how highly Rhys thinks of you. Think about how it would feel to finally turn up to this thing with reinforcements."

"I'll think about it." It was all Jess could get out of her, and they eventually said their farewells, promising to see each other in a couple of days.

Andie leaned against the kitchen counter, her head in her hands. She racked her brain, trying to remember a time when she and Susan had not been set against one another—by Jim, by circumstances, by nature. There was one uncorrupted memory, but it felt so fleeting and tenuous she was afraid it would dissolve into tatters if she looked at it head-on. She saw the yard behind the farmhouse, its patchy grass over-run with clover, the white heads bobbing in the breeze. She and Susan were reclining on a picnic blanket, making daisy chains from the clover blossoms, the minute plastic cups and plates of Andie's childhood tea set laid out before them. She remembered delicate little cucumber sand-wiches cut into triangles without crusts, and dainty bite-size cupcakes.

Had Susan really made that miniature feast and packed it into a basket? Had the humorless woman she now knew really consented to pour orange juice from a child's teapot and sip it from a tiny pink plastic teacup? It felt like a dream, but she knew it was real. She could taste the unfamiliar crunch of the cucumber and remember her delight when Susan had placed the circlet of flowers in her hair. Andie must have been around four years old, she realized. It was before Gus, and it must have happened while the three older girls were in school. The memory was so piquant that her eyes stung.

Could she bring Rhys and Will to Camden? It was hard enough for her to reconcile the two halves of her childhood—before the accident and after. Dragging her present into her past, superimposing the two by bringing Rhys and Will to the farm, might just be enough to tear a fatal hole in the fabric of her own personal space-time continuum.

Her relationship with Rhys was a secret thing, a guilty pleasure, budding within the climate-controlled bubble of the house. Other than their trips to Saddle Tree Farm, it hadn't been tested in the outside world, exposed to public view. Was it something she dared to claim? And would it hold up if she bared it to the harshness of Susan's scrutiny?

She took a deep breath, preparing herself to go downstairs.

"Oh, there you are, dear." Mrs. Hodge appeared in the doorway. "Mr. Griffiths is home and was asking where you might have got to. He's giving Will his dessert."

"Thanks, Mrs. Hodge. I'll go down now."

"I wanted to say one thing, if I may."

"Certainly." Andie's curiosity was piqued.

"Well, I feel I should caution you against making yourself too . . . *convenient*," the woman said, all maternal concern. She even reached out to take one of Andie's hands in hers and gave it a little squeeze.

"I . . . er," Andie stammered, completely flummoxed.

"I would just hate to see you get hurt," Mrs. Hodge finished, curling her fingers over Andie's and holding her in place for an extra beat before she let go and allowed Andie to slip by her into the corridor beyond.

Convenient? Andie walked shakily toward the main staircase, hot waves of humiliation washing over her. But embarrassment turned to anger as she stopped at the head of the stairs. Is that what Mrs. Hodge thought? That Rhys was dallying with her simply because she was *there*, because she could tack on some free, personal services after her day with Will was done?

If Mrs. Hodge had been purely censorious, that would have been one thing. Far worse was the fact that she looked concerned, knowing, and faintly *pitying* of Andie's assumed plight. Not unlike Susan, with her weighted sighs and her constant admonitions not to take on responsibilities that were supposedly beyond her depth. As if Andie were a perpetually hapless, naive child who could never quite measure up to the demands of the real world.

She stood rooted to the spot, her anger expanding with the gratifying rush of a gas flame igniting. *I've had it. I've had enough.* She was sick of the guilt. She was sick of always being the second-class citizen.

Her whole adult life, she'd done nothing but strive to be the most conscientious, responsible human being she could be. She'd graduated at the top of her class. She'd dedicated her career to helping children. She volunteered. She gave to charity. She recycled. Hell, she even felt vaguely guilty about hanging up on robocalls. Where relationships were concerned, she was careful to tailor her hopes and expectations to the modest limits she'd set for herself, always burdening her feelings with so many self-imposed footnotes and disclaimers that she was surprised she could even see for the fine print.

Nobody could be harder on her than she was on herself. The sheer audacity of her mother's relentless second-guessing, her put-downs in the guise of concern—and Mrs. Hodge's, for that matter, with her transparent attempt to hoist Andie by the petard of her own retrogressive sexual double standard—suddenly filled her with a combustible, righteous fury she'd seldom been privileged to enjoy.

To hell with being meek. To hell with always needing to do the right thing. She wanted to raze her mother's quaint red barn to the ground. She wanted to wipe that troubled, earnest look off Mrs. Hodge's face for good. She was even inclined to give herself a temporary pass on her feelings for Rhys and Will, for daring to want something from them— love, approbation, a sense of belonging—instead of always being the one who simply gave.

Convenient, huh? She was too incensed to join them downstairs and risk further exposure to the condescending look in Mrs. Hodge's eye. She might do something she'd regret. Instead, she paced into her bathroom and impatiently cast off her clothes, craving the cooling jets of the shower. Set to bracing cold, the spray sluiced through her hair and drummed against her shoulders and back, but it couldn't touch the indignation that simmered in her veins. The worst thing was that, from a purely objective standpoint, the nanny's scruples made sense. From the outside, Andie *was* just the latest player in an age-old tragicomedy: the employee who falls into a physical relationship with her employer. Her actions looked every bit as tacky and reckless—not to mention unoriginal—as Mrs. Hodge had implied.

What that equation didn't account for, however, was Rhys himself. Rhys, who never seemed to do anything that wasn't passionate, honest, and well meant. Rhys, who never stopped insisting on elevating their bond to transcendence, even as she tried to reduce it to the merely physical.

Convenient? How wrong Mrs. Hodge was, and how thick the irony. As Andie stood beneath the shower jets, anger and frustration twined with the bottomless, insatiable longing that was always her first response to Rhys. It wasn't fair. Why wouldn't he simply allow her to be convenient? She felt a wild urge to punish him for his genuineness, his kindness, his goodness. *How dare he make me feel this way? How dare he make me want more than I ever presumed to ask for?*

She stood under the force of the spray for untold minutes, lost in the turmoil of her thoughts, stoking her fury by replaying in her mind the solicitous touch of Mrs. Hodge's hands on her own. Finally, she toweled herself off with rough strokes and, still brooding, went to find Rhys.

"Andie!" Relief and puzzlement dawned on his face when she discovered him in the kitchen. Will had been already settled in bed, and the house was dark around them. "I was wondering where you were. I asked Mrs. Hodge—"

"I know," she said, letting her hands drop to her sides so the plush, white, unbelted bathrobe she wore fell open to reveal the inner curves of her breasts, an expanse of smooth, pale midriff, and the provocative dark triangle at the juncture of her thighs. Her core was molten with desire, the force of her yearning almost painful as she studied him: the furrow between his blue-heather eyes, the sensuous lines of his mouth, and the telltale ridge already pushing at the front of his jeans in immediate response to her. According to Mrs. Hodge, Andie might be powerless, but at least there was a transitory power in *this*—the power to put that sharp hitch in Rhys's breath, to make his pulse pound hot and fast with the same need that consumed her.

"What . . . ?" His question was choked off as she slid to her knees in front of him, shrugging the robe into a heap on the floor. Her deft fingers permitted no argument as she unfastened his belt and made short work of the buttons on his fly, giving a primitive grunt of satisfaction as she reached through the gap in his boxer shorts, and his turgid length sprang into her hands. *I'll show you convenient.* She licked her lips, gratified by his white-knuckled grip on the edge of the granite as he leaned back against the counter.

He was musky and silky, and as hot as if his blood were spring fed from some volcanic source. A small moan escaped her as she went to her hands and knees and fitted her lips around him, slipping over the smooth head to tease him with an elaborate delicacy before taking him deeper in rhythmic, demanding pulls. She could feel the wetness pooling at the entrance to her body as her flesh swelled and ached to have him inside, tormented by the stimulation she was performing with her mouth.

As if sensing her desperation, he stretched forward, running a shaky hand along the arc of her spine, over her buttocks, and dipping lower to find the slickness that awaited him. His groan as his fingertips found her was the sexiest thing she'd ever heard. She shuddered, craving the thrilling invasion of his fingers but knowing that if she allowed him access, she'd be undone. This was about him, not her. A dark, subversive part of her wanted him to *use* her, just as their uneven power dynamic suggested she'd been used all along. So she shifted out of reach with an impatient growl, her tongue painting relentless, teasing trails down the glistening wet length of him, before her lips resumed their suction.

"Andie, God . . ." Rhys's voice splintered as he braced himself with both hands once more, his hips bucking as he drove into the welcoming vortex of her mouth. Her hands roamed over the bunched muscles of his thighs, rock hard beneath the denim, only his cock exposed in quick flashes as her lips pumped, while she was fully bared to him and to the coolness of the night.

See? This is what convenience looks like, she thought with a grim sense of vindication. *It's really not so bad, is it?* Her anger stoked her desire ever higher as she goaded him to take his pleasure from her body and prove, once and for all, that their connection was but a fleeting thing, and not the soul-deep bond she feared it was.

Triumph flared and made her throat thicken with a paradoxical disappointment as he cried out, seemingly on the verge of release. But he pulled clear of her insistent mouth, hauling her to her feet. Was he going to bend her over the countertop and expend himself in a final, urgent flurry of thrusts? Her eyes flashed in challenge as he drew her face-to-face with him. *Go on. Finish this.*

His resolute gaze met hers, and, to her immense surprise, he smoothed the still-damp strands of hair from her brow and planted a gentle kiss there before lifting her onto the edge of the countertop. Frustration boiled beneath her skin as she lured him in for a devouring, openly erotic kiss, nipping at his bottom lip as he pulled away. She parted her thighs, aching to draw him in, but he pushed her firmly back to lie on the polished granite.

Protesting, she braced against him, trying to struggle upright. "But I wanted to—" she began.

"I know, and now I want to," he said simply. His hands were firm bronze bands around her wrists, holding her arms by her sides as if he instinctively understood she needed something to push against. And push she did, the tension in her muscles met by the resisting force of his in an unspoken battle of wills as he anointed her belly and hips with lingering kisses. The coldness of the smooth stone beneath her was reminiscent of the rush of the shower, but equally incapable of soothing the fever of her flesh. She squirmed in torment, both loving and hating the control he exerted over her as his mouth zeroed in on its target.

When his tongue brushed over the exquisitely sensitive bundle of nerves at the peak of her cleft, she jolted in shock, straining against her confinement. *Oh, the terrible, melting pleasure of it*—the cool whisper of his breath and the heat of his tongue, lapping and teasing in an intimate caress she'd never accepted from anyone.

"Wait." Her plea escaped on a fluttering exhalation. *This was all wrong.* She'd wanted to be used, not worshipped. But there was reverence in his hooded gaze as he watched her, and in the absorbed sweep of his lips and tongue. With a sigh that blended surrender, protest, and a deep, hidden joy, Andie made herself relax against the bonds of Rhys's hands, implicitly signaling him to continue.

It wasn't long before the tension mounted within her again, but he held her firm, anchoring her body so her senses could escape in a flight of pleasure she'd never before imagined. Her fingers clenched as she scaled the blinding peak of sensation, shuddering beneath the voracious tribute he paid with his beautiful mouth, a thorough homage that was anything but cursory or convenient. She was almost delirious when he finally released her, and it was then that he turned her over the now-warmed counter's edge, covering her body with his after hastily stepping out of his jeans and sheathing himself.

His fingers wove through hers as he entered her with one slow, deep thrust that completed the job of turning her legs to jelly. His cheek pressed against hers as he moved with her, fused as one, and she was dimly aware that the fear and fury that had consumed her when she'd come to him had dissolved into nothingness. She trusted him—even more, perhaps, than she trusted herself. Soaring, she let him take her over the edge once more, propelled by the escalating rhythm of his sure, urgent strokes.

And by the time they were spent, and had gathered the strength to creep—damp and smiling—up the staircase to the big, cool bed, Andie had come to a decision. She *was* going to invite Rhys and Will to her mother's farm. She was going to show up there with someone in her corner, at long last. She was going to demand her mother's absolution. And if she didn't get it, she was going to forge her own path, once and for all.

CHAPTER TWENTY

Rhys pointed the Range Rover in the direction of Camden, Massachusetts, his thoughts full of the woman who occupied the seat beside him. Over the past few weeks, Andie had become a fixture in his bed. But she was so much more than that: a balm to his doubts, a magnet to his senses, and a singing effervescence in his blood. Although they'd settled into something of a routine, there was nothing routine about his days when he knew that her hot, sweet kisses and the oasis of her body were waiting for him at the end of them.

This must be some sort of addiction, he told himself. He'd never felt this powerful sense of elation in the company of another person, the conviction that they could draw the shades and erect a barricade and be perfectly content in their own private union, drinking in the satisfaction of each other's company—nothing further required. He only hoped she felt the same way.

Will had dropped off to sleep in his car seat a half hour into the ride, and Rhys placed a warm hand on Andie's nearest jean-clad thigh. As the car ate up the miles, her anxiety visibly ratcheted up, her eyes becoming a storm of green, brown, and gold. He snuck surreptitious glances at her delicate profile and the solemn set of her lovely mouth.

She had paired her jeans with her red sweater and pulled her hair into a low ponytail at the nape of her neck. He imagined loosening the elastic later that night and encouraging the dark waves to ripple over her shoulders.

Andie sucked in a tense breath as they passed a traditional white sign announcing their arrival in her hometown: ENTERING CAMDEN, INCORPORATED 1786. The outskirts of the town were indistinguishable from those of its neighbors—small and in many cases dilapidated farmhouses lining the main road, separated by large expanses of frost-glazed fields. Then came the usual run of automotive and tractor-supply stores, interspersed with a stretch of fast-food restaurants, gas stations, and strip malls. Finally, more densely settled blocks heralded their entry into the older town center.

Antique homes, including some large Victorians, graced the perimeter of a traditional village green. Farther on, beyond an intersection where train tracks passed through the town, were all the ingredients of a classic Main Street: two white-steepled churches, a redbrick post office, a library, a regional bank, a funeral home, a barbershop, a hardware store, an insurance office, a real-estate office, and a general store. There was even a restored Art Deco movie theater, and a thrift shop with a glamorously styled window display to appeal to students from the surrounding colleges.

"Nice town," he commented mildly. It was only then that he noticed Andie's unnatural pallor and the grim tension in her hands as she clung to her armrest.

"Andie, are you okay?"

"Just a little carsick," she murmured, fending him off with a wave of her hand as she settled back into her seat and turned her face to the window. She let her eyes flutter closed altogether as the final few blocks of the town center flashed by.

What is it that's unsettling her? Rhys wondered. He felt an overwhelming urge to muscle in between her and the threat she faced, to defend her bodily, if need be. But if the source of her fear was internal, what then? The idea of whisking her back to his bedroom and distracting her from her demons held tremendous appeal, but that was too easy. She'd come through for him when the going got tough, and he would do the same.

He was touched she'd invited him today, in spite of her palpable unease about making the trip out here at all. Rhys couldn't help but feel a fierce curiosity about her background and what today's visit might reveal about the childhood that still held her in its powerful grip.

As the GPS counted down their imminent arrival at Andie's mother's farm, the houses once more became fewer and farther between. Andie sat straighter in her seat again, her expression resolute. Their destination loomed in the form of a large and picturesque red barn set back from the road beside a neat white farmhouse. A driveway opened into a large, paved turning circle and parking area beside the barn, where a number of cars already sat. An open field allowed for spillover parking. An arrow with the words "Petting Zoo" pointed from the parking lot to a collection of smaller outbuildings huddled beside pens that held a menagerie sure to take Will's fancy. On the opposite side of the barn was a weathered, pitch-roofed building with a chimney belching maple-scented steam.

Will stirred, attuned to the slowing motion of the car as they pulled in.

"Good timing," Rhys commented, reaching back to give his son's leg an affectionate squeeze.

"Here goes," Andie murmured.

"Hey." Rhys reached out and took her hand. "It'll be okay."

"Thanks." She smiled and squared her shoulders, her determination evident in her burning eyes and the set of her jaw. "Yes, it will."

She broke free and headed for the main barn. Rhys lifted Will out of his car seat and hoisted him up on his shoulders to follow the others walking toward the rustic building.

A large, engraved sign proclaimed TILLY'S FARM STAND in antiqued gold lettering above the barn's double doors. It was a relatively temperate day—in the midforties and sunny, despite the large piles of snow still on the ground—and one of the doors was propped open to reveal an expansive, airy space with clean-swept, wide pine floors dotted with folding tables and chairs set up in clusters.

The far end of the large, open room was set up with trestle tables loaded with heated catering trays and large coffee urns. Another table nearer to the doorway was lined with glass bottles of amber liquid and small tasting cups next to a sign that invited guests to sample the farm's bounty of maple syrup in its various colors and grades. Andie, head down, made for a corner to drop off her bag so she could help finish setting up. Will, clutching his trains, tilted his head back to inspect the raftered ceiling.

"Andie!"

A tall, angular woman with pale, freckled skin, shoulder-length red-brown hair, and amber eyes crossed the floor to intercept them. There was something about the vivid intensity of her well-formed features that marked her as Andie's sister. She swept into their path, her attractive face alight with curiosity.

"Jess!" Andie hugged her eagerly, and both faces turned to Rhys and Will.

"You must be Rhys," Jess said, eyes gleaming, too impatient to wait for Andie to make the introductions. "I'm so glad you could come. And Will." She leaned in and gently squeezed Will's knee.

"Andie has told me a lot about you," Jess volunteered, her face full of mischief. "And, I must say, you don't disappoint in person."

"Ah, thanks? I think." Rhys cast a questioning look at Andie, but she just shrugged and elbowed Jess in the ribs.

Will chose that moment to reach out for Andie. He did the classic toddler lean, pitching himself toward the object of his desire as if basic physics had nothing to do with his own safety. He teetered precariously for a second before Andie stepped closer, completing his transfer into her embrace. Her ponytail trailing over one shoulder was an irresistible lure to the toddler, who cooed and chortled as he stroked the cool strands.

It was then that Rhys looked down the wide corridor formed by the rows of tables and saw at the far end of the room a figure watching them. How long she'd stood there he could not know, but once he spotted her, he couldn't shake the strange idea that perhaps she'd been there forever, as still as an effigy, her features a study in conflicting emotion—as if a gifted artist had set himself the task of depicting disdain and fascination, resentment and longing, and love and hatred in one woman's face. And she was staring straight at Andie and Will.

Rhys froze as the murmur of Jess's and Andie's voices rose up around him. He had to fight the sudden urge to throw himself between this woman and the pair who stood by his side, as if her laser focus had a cutting edge that could actually harm them. He couldn't tear his eyes away, until a passerby crossed between him and the woman and momentarily blocked the invisible current that bisected the room. Rhys shook himself out of his daze and rubbed his eyelids. She was still there, a handsome woman in her midfifties with salt-and-pepper hair and delicate features that had been sharpened, not softened, by age.

"Who is that?" he blurted, already knowing the answer.

"Oh, that's Susan, star of today's show," Jess replied drily. "You must come over and meet her."

Rhys shot a quick look at Andie, but her expression was unreadable. She followed Jess and Rhys, hugging Will close as they made their way to the other end of the barn.

"Hello, Andrea," the woman said with a tight smile. She held still as Andie leaned in and gave her a dutiful kiss on the cheek and made the introductions.

"How nice." Susan fluttered, her eyes turbulent. "I didn't expect to meet your employer today."

Out of the corner of his eye, Rhys saw Andie's shoulders stiffen.

Susan turned her focus directly on him. "Mr. Griffiths, we're honored you came to our little celebration. Of course, it's usually only family and friends, so I hope you'll forgive the modest scale of our little spread."

What to say to that? Think. Think. Rhys's head spun as he took in the double-edged meaning of the woman's pleasantries, branding him an outsider even as she extended her disingenuous welcome. Andie's eyes flashed a warning.

"At this point, Andie is like family to both Will and me, and I hope she would say the reverse is true," he managed. "So I'm sure we'll do just fine."

Jess smiled like the Cheshire cat and looped an arm through Rhys's.

"I can tell I'm going to like you," she announced as she led him off to meet her husband and Andie's other two sisters.

~

Andie looked longingly after Rhys and Jess as they walked arm in arm to the other side of the barn, which was filling up with guests, including some familiar faces from her school days. Will lifted a hand to play with her hair, cooing softly, and Andie smiled and rubbed her cheek against his.

"I suppose you think it's funny to flaunt that poor child in front of me," Susan said, her eyes narrowed.

So this is the way Susan is going to play it. Andie tucked Will even tighter against her, fuming at her mother's characterization of him. "I invited Rhys and Will here because they're part of my life."

"Well," Susan sniffed, "I don't know how you expect to keep him out of harm's way while you help with the breakfast."

"It's not a problem," Andie said, tamping down her anger, forcing herself to be upbeat. Let it not be said that she wasn't willing to give it one last try before changing tactics for good. "Rhys and I will trade off. Rhys offered to take a turn at the serving table. He might be able to sell some maple syrup, too."

A teenage boy shuffled up, carrying a heavy coffee urn. Probably one of Susan's farm-stand employees. "Mrs. Tilly, where do you want this extra urn?"

"This way, David." Susan beckoned. She stopped for a moment, turning on her heels to look back at Andie. "Well, for God's sake, keep an eye on that child. As if I don't have enough to do today without worrying about what you've gotten yourself into." She gave a martyred sigh and bustled off toward the tables.

Andie felt her fury solidify and pulse, like a coal glowing at her core. But better that than the anguish that had overcome her when she, Rhys, and Will had passed along the busiest section of Main Street twenty minutes earlier. The tremor still hadn't quite left her hands, and it was hard to swallow around the lump lodged in her throat. She'd almost asked Rhys to turn off and take the maze of back roads she would have chosen if she'd been driving herself. Anything to avoid that corner. The corner where it had happened.

But she'd pulled herself back together and even survived Rhys's first brief encounter with her mother. Later, she was going to get Susan alone, and they were going to talk. For now, she pressed her lips against the smoothness of Will's cheek.

"C'mon, Will. Let's grab your dad and go see some animals before I need to start playing waitress."

She followed in the direction Rhys and Jess had taken, slipping out the side door of the barn.

Predictably enough, the blond miniature horses were a huge hit. They looked so much like Lilliputian versions of Ace from hippotherapy that Will was simultaneously baffled and beside himself with excitement. He shrieked and chortled, his happy cacophony echoing around the animal pens and earning a heavy-lidded look from a nearby llama before it went back to chasing the chickens that had wandered into its enclosure.

Next, they braved the warm confines of the sugar shack, where Andie was surprised to see a familiar figure sporting Susan's faded and stained old leather apron over jeans and a sweatshirt.

"Officer Hendrix?" Andie murmured in confusion. The woman was perhaps fifty, with a face that radiated good-natured calm. A few deep laugh lines grooved skin that was otherwise smooth, bronzed, and set off to advantage by cropped gray hair brushed forward in a pixie cut that suited the proud angles of her cheekbones and her pointed chin.

It had been easily ten years since Andie had seen the woman, who'd been one of the first officers to arrive at the scene of the accident on that distant night of sleet and fog. She could still remember the strength and warmth of Officer Hendrix's arms around her, holding her back from Gus's body as the flashing lights of the cruisers penetrated the gloom with lurid spokes of color.

"It's Chief Hendrix now, actually."

Denise Hendrix had always been a friendly, capable presence in town. Connected to the Tilly family by the tragedy of Gus's death, she was more than just a familiar face glimpsed at police picnics and other gatherings. During her lonely teenage years, Andie had been keenly aware of Denise in the background as something of a guardian angel—making visits to the house to check on the family. Making sure Andie didn't fall in permanently with the rough crowd after her self-esteem plummeted like a stone to the bottom of a well as she entered adolescence.

"Congratulations." Andie remembered her father's dinner-table tirades when Denise had joined the department, the first woman police officer in Camden's history. Jim had been a card-carrying member of the old guard, out to ensure that Denise—or any woman who tried to penetrate the male-dominated bastion of the Camden PD—more than paid her dues. Looking into the woman's steady, intelligent brown eyes,

Andie felt a wave of admiration. "But what are you doing here? I didn't know you were a maple-syrup aficionado."

"A person's gotta have a hobby." Denise shrugged. "I hear you're an occupational therapist now. It sounds like you've done great."

Andie looked at her searchingly. It was not a conclusion Susan was likely to have cultivated. Andie couldn't help but feel a flash of curiosity about what her mother was to this vibrant, generous woman. Denise moved around the sugarhouse with a familiarity that was almost proprietorial.

"Yes, in fact, this is Will, one of my clients, and Rhys, his dad." Andie wondered how else she should introduce Rhys. She wasn't sure she could even define their relationship for herself. It was a constant electricity in her veins, a warm fullness in her chest that could tip her into laughter or tears in an instant, and a vertiginous pull in her stomach—a bittersweet yearning that left her perpetually off balance.

Greetings were exchanged, and Rhys peppered Denise with questions about syrup grades. Then he wandered off to peer curiously into the boiling trays of watery sap while Andie held Will at a safe distance.

"From what I can tell," Denise said quietly to Andie, "Susan's still wrestling with a few ghosts, and they're not going down without a fight."

Andie stilled, not taking her eyes off Rhys. "Well, I think I'm done waiting."

"You know . . ." Denise paused, considering. "I'm glad. It's past time."

Andie nodded, a little taken aback to be speaking with a nonfamily member about the Tilly family's demons.

"Oh, there you are, Andrea." Susan's voice interrupted from the doorway. "I could use some help in the barn." She raised her eyebrows at Denise, who responded with an infinitesimal twitch of eyes and lips in a funny little exchange that hinted at an emotional shorthand of long use.

Susan might not have been thrilled to have Rhys and Will at her pancake breakfast, but she knew a good marketing opportunity when she saw one. Soon Rhys was stationed at the serving table, doling out short stacks and doing a booming side trade in bottles of Susan's maple syrup. Andie did the rounds of the tables with the coffeepot, watching Rhys in action.

The line that snaked across the barn from the serving table featured a conspicuously female clientele. Everyone from her old high school principal to the prom queen of Andie's graduating year to the octogenarian town librarian was represented in the excited group, eager to come within a few feet of the most attractive man ever to cross the Camden town line.

He was pretty spectacular, Andie conceded, her rib cage suddenly stretched to bursting. Not just his commanding physical beauty but his kindness. She could tell it was an effort for him to play up to the twittering throng, but he did it valiantly. A muscle twitched beside his left eye as he tried to avoid looking down the spray-tanned cleavage of prom queen Jean Marie Stokes, who now ran Jean Marie's House of Dance on Oak Street.

Rhys, spotting Andie, raised bewildered eyebrows at her, forcing her to suppress a breathless laugh. She could hardly believe they'd had another erotic interlude in the laundry room last night. His presence was like some surprise gift that never lost its luster. With each taste of bright, narcotic joy he delivered, she wanted more. And more.

It felt surreal to see him in public and at a distance. Their life at the house was so intimate, so seamless, she could almost believe she'd conjured him by a sheer act of will—a figment of her imagination or her desire. And yet there he was across the room, a flesh-and-blood figure whose magnetism acted on others besides herself. He was a man whose presence changed things, made ripples in the wider world. Could she really ever have this Rhys? The public Rhys?

Gathering herself, Andie craned to see Will, who'd found Rose's youngest, Luke—a fellow toddler and train enthusiast—and was on the floor by the serving table with his new playmate and a cluster of toy engines, watched over by all three of Andie's sisters. Andie headed slowly toward them, strangely shy in the presence of Louisa and Rose.

"Be still, my beating heart," Louisa cried, her eyes drinking in the vision of Rhys surrounded by his admirers. Her warm laughter drew Andie into the sisters' conspiratorial huddle.

"It's a good thing Eric's up to his ears in pancakes right now," Rose chimed in, "because I haven't been able to take my eyes off that man since he got here."

"So, what do you think?" Andie asked Jess in an undertone.

"He's incredible." Jess's eyes gleamed. "And we had a *very* enlightening chat. He told me how it came about that you started working for him. I've just been sharing the story with Louisa and Rose, seeing as how none of us are ever going to get any information out of *you*."

"I've never heard anything so romantic in my life," Louisa sighed. "Will picked you, and only you, to help his dad."

"You've been hiding your light under a bushel," Rose said, her tone puzzled and almost hurt. "I never knew you were some sort of child whisperer."

"Back off, Rose," Louisa laughed. "I was going to ask Andie for help with Finn's pencil grip. I have seniority here. I ought to get a perk or two. Get in line."

Louisa and Rose want me around their children? The entire barn seemed to reel for a moment and come to rest at a different latitude. And Jess kept looking at her with that gleeful twinkle in her eye.

"So, spill," Jess demanded half an hour later, when Andie had been relieved of beverage duty, and they'd taken an overexcited Will outside to sit in a sunny, sheltered spot by the barn for a few moments of quiet. Rhys was still drumming up business inside. "What's going on between you and Rhys?"

Andie balanced Will on her lap and held a paper plate laden with bite-size morsels of syrup-soaked pancake for him. As finger food, it was messy, but it was certainly keeping him happy. "Who says anything's going on?"

"I'm saying it," Jess said, rolling her eyes. "That man is so into you it's written all over him. If Ben looked at me that way, I think my clothes would burn right off."

"Okay, maybe my clothes have gone up in smoke a few times," Andie admitted. "Maybe even more than a few. But Jess, I have no idea what I'm doing, and it scares the hell out of me. I like him too much."

"And that's so terrible because . . . ?"

"It feels too big," Andie said softly. "Too important. He's the real deal, Jess. He's a grown-up, and I'm still on my training wheels."

"Andie, from where I stand, you're doing just fine."

"I really did mean to leave it at friendship, but I . . . *feel* things. Now the stakes are too high." Andie swallowed, hard. "I can't follow where this might lead."

"Why not? Because of your self-imposed prohibition on the whole family thing?"

"Jess, you know I can never be a parent."

Jess gave a strangled laugh, eyeing Andie up and down. "I don't know," she said. "If it looks like a duck, and it quacks like a duck . . ."

Andie stared at her sister. She'd become so accustomed to Will's weight snuggled in her lap, the tickle of his curls against her cheek, and the little-boy scent of his neck, that she was no longer consciously aware of the subtle shifts in her posture, her movements—and her psyche— that made this feel like second nature.

"As far as I can tell, parenting is something people just get up and do every day," Jess said. "It's not like they wait around for anybody to give them a certificate telling them they're qualified to do it." She rubbed her hand over the place where her belly would soon swell. "And even if they did, they wouldn't be looking for an endorsement from

Susan, of all people. You're the one who encouraged me to believe I could do it in spite of her, remember?"

Just then, a tractor passed the barn, pulling a large red-painted hay wagon lined with bales for seating. It stopped beside the animal pens.

"Next ride to the maple grove in five minutes," announced the sixty-something-year-old man driving the tractor. "All rides free today." The guests milling around the animal pens started to form a line, waiting to take their place in the hay wagon, their faces wreathed in smiles. Andie felt an uncomfortable flash of pride. There was no doubt Susan was contributing to the local economy by making the farm a destination and creating jobs in the community.

She smiled and, raising her hand to her eyes, squinted into the sun to look at the man driving the tractor. Something about his face was familiar, but for some reason the clues didn't add up, until his smile fell when he looked straight at her.

Her breath whistled inward with a sharp stab, and she gripped Jess's sleeve.

"Jess," she said urgently, "is that Earl Peterson driving the tractor?"

"What?"

"It is. It's Earl Peterson." Andie's lungs were suddenly incapable of processing the breath she'd sucked in, and she choked out a painful series of coughs, her eyes stinging, her head reeling. The man had looked so different seventeen years ago, his shoulders drooping, his eyes desolate pits. Now he seemed restored to himself, herding the crowd with jocular ease, the weathered smile lines carved around his eyes suggesting a man at peace. Until he saw Andie.

Realization finally dawned in Jess's eyes. "I had no idea she'd hired Earl Peterson," she said, shocked.

"I need a few minutes," Andie gasped hoarsely. "Would you do me a huge favor and take Will back inside to Rhys?"

"Of course," Jess said. "But are you sure I shouldn't stay? Are you really okay?"

"I'll be fine," Andie said, her cheeks hot, her eyes watery. "I'm just a little freaked out. I need to be by myself. I'll be back inside in a few minutes. Thanks, Jess."

Susan hired Earl Peterson. Andie stumbled off in the direction of the farmhouse, circling around the back to the small, private patch of lawn where a tree stood within a circle of stones. Gus's tree. One look at Earl Peterson's face had hurled her back in time seventeen years, and at this moment Gus's tree was her only anchor.

Her brother had always loved dogwoods. He would point in jubilation when the spring sunshine filtered through their waxy petals, making them glow like a beacon. Gus's dogwood was pure white. She remembered the day they'd planted it as if it were yesterday, the remaining members of their family united for an hour in their sorrow, the quiet eye in a storm of blame, remorse, and recrimination that would rage on for years.

In a couple of months the tree would bloom again, heralding the arrival of another summer Gus would never see. Andie sank to her knees on the damp ground. Her pulse raced as the images and sensations flooded in. The shape of Gus's hazel eyes. The cowlick that caused a cheeky chestnut tuft to stick up in front, even when his hair was freshly trimmed.

How she'd loved him. The pain threatened to break her, snapping her at the waist with a tremor so engulfing that she barely noticed the rough bark of the dogwood pressed cold against her forehead as hot tears trailed down her cheeks.

She wasn't sure how long she knelt in place, her hands tensed into claws, her nails sinking into the moss at the base of the tree as if to get a purchase on reality.

"Andie?" Rhys's voice broke through the haze, and warmth spread down her spine as he pressed one large hand between her shoulder blades. Before she knew it, he was beside her on the ground, heedless of the cold and damp—hauling her into his lap, lifting her up and folding himself protectively around her as she shuddered and heaved with racking sobs.

"Wh-where's W-ill?" she asked through torrents of tears.

"With Jess. He's fine. What is it? What happened?" The deep timbre of his voice resonated beside her ear, warm and rich. "Jess said you were upset, but she wouldn't tell me why." One of his hands caressed the nape of her neck, and she gave a convulsive sniff. His heady scent curled into her nostrils, and she inhaled deeply, breathing in his comfort, cherishing it even if she could not yet respond. The front of his shirt had soaked up an ocean of tears by the time her cries finally subsided.

"Oh G-God," she hiccuped. "My little brother—"

"Your brother? What . . . ?"

"My brother d-died when I was eleven," she said, still trembling. "H-he wasn't quite four years old. He was barely bigger than Will. H-he was hit by a car on Main Street."

Tears began to leak again. "We passed by the spot this morning and I . . . then I saw . . . I saw . . ."

"It's okay, my love, I'm here. Take a deep breath." His broad chest was a shelter against the onslaught of fresh pain, and she found she could breathe more freely pressed up against it.

"I saw the man who drove the car that struck Gus. He's here, at the farm."

"What?" Rhys sounded perplexed. "Why would he show his face here?"

"You don't understand. It wasn't his fault. He d-did nothing wrong." Another sob racked her body. "And he's here because . . . because my mother hired him."

She tilted her face up to look into eyes that glowed with the hot blue of a gas flame. "I'm upset because it means she forgives him . . . but she still doesn't forgive me."

Rhys seemed to freeze in shock for a moment. "Doesn't forgive *you*? What are you talking about, Andie? What would she need to forgive you for?"

Andie had thought that if the occasion ever arose where she had to tell Rhys about Gus, she would feel trepidation—anxiety at the risk of losing his trust. But she was strangely calm as she began to talk about the events of that awful evening.

She told him about shirking her piano lesson and about the giddy mood she and Gus had spiraled into. Gus was prone to hyperactivity even without provocation. He was delightful—smart, funny, sweet— but hard to manage, and from her adult vantage point, Andie realized how Susan must have resented her riling him up.

She didn't understand why her mother had done it—dragged them into town to run errands. She could still see the grim, determined set of Susan's jaw as she'd announced that Andie and Gus wouldn't get to lounge around giggling and shrieking in front of the TV all afternoon. They would damn well come into town with her and behave themselves while she tried to salvage something productive from the day. Christmas was in less than two weeks, and she still had gaps on her shopping list.

"Gus was whining and complaining even before we got to town," Andie said, her tears still wet on her cheeks. The windshield wipers had carved a small pair of arcs in the freezing drizzle as their headlights cut through the murk. It was already getting dark, but the town glowed as they entered the busiest stretch of Main Street. White Christmas lights twinkled from storefronts, and the streetlamps up and down the street were hung with festive "kissing balls" fashioned from balsam fir, pinecones, glittering baubles, and tinsel. An atmosphere of excitement prevailed, despite the fog and sleet.

"He cheered up when we saw the decorations. They looked so magical, with the tinsel and the lights shining through the fog."

They'd accompanied Susan into the first store on her list, the prim little stationery and gift shop, Andie explained.

"Susan was trying to pick out some letter-writing paper for Aunt Mary, and she was all uptight about us not touching anything. She'd brought the stroller, but Gus never wanted to sit in it anymore. I tried to buckle him in, but he yelled, so I played with him, trying to keep him quiet. He was hanging off my arms, begging me to spin him around, so I took him into the corner to do it, but he let go of my hands and almost knocked over a cabinet full of china ornaments. Everyone turned around and stared at us.

"Then we had to go to the toy store to get stuff for our cousins, and that was better because there was a train table. But Gus saw a Ninja Turtles play set he wanted and started begging. Susan snapped at him, and he completely melted down."

Andie winced at the memory of a frantic Gus, blood sugar crashing, melting into a puddle on the floor. Telling Andie to pile their packages into the stroller, a white-lipped Susan had finished paying amid a crescendo of screams, then carried Gus bodily out onto the sidewalk on Main Street, where the drizzle had turned to sleet, and the pavement was starting to become slick.

"I was so relieved to be back outside, away from the comments and the looks from the other customers. I figured we'd finally be able to head home, but Susan had other ideas. She made us stop at the bakery and tried to console Gus with a treat." Andie had been surprised her mom was offering sugary snacks so close to dinner, but she'd cheered up at the idea of getting to have one of her favorite cider donuts.

Twenty minutes later, cinnamon and sugar still sticking to her jacket and sweetening the corners of her mouth, Andie had slumped a little when Susan announced that they still had to stop at the convenience store to get milk, and the hardware store for a new latch for the rabbit hutch.

Gus veered from sugar high back to sugar crash as they made their way along Main Street, finally reaching the busy corner where the windows of Dolan's Hardware blazed with holiday finery. Dolan's maintained a friendly holiday rivalry with Jeffers & Sons Insurance on the opposite side of the main thoroughfare, each vying to outdo the other with their brightly lit, captivating window displays. Andie felt a thrill of pleasure as she moved toward the warm light of Dolan's window.

"It was incredible," she sighed. "Dolan's Christmas window was one of my favorite things."

But, to Andie's dismay, Susan had hustled them past the display and into the narrow aisles of the hardware store, where Gus scooped up loose handfuls of shiny screws and bolts from open boxes on the lower shelves and ran them through his fingers, delighted by the sound they made as they cascaded back into their containers. Startled by a warning from Susan, he missed the box he was aiming for and let a shower of steel pieces spray the floor of the aisle. With a calming word, Andie bent to help him gather them up as Susan went to the counter, shaking her head in exasperation.

Finally, they were done, and Andie wrestled the stroller back out through Dolan's door, onto Main Street.

"I begged for just a minute to stop and look at the window, but Susan was looking at her watch, suddenly all stressed out about getting home."

The matter was settled by Gus, who—pushed to his absolute limit—refused to either budge from the window or get into the stroller. His feet were tired, he moaned pitifully, and he wasn't going to walk another step. Every time Susan tried to budge him, he melted down into screams and tears.

Andie, seduced by the lure of the window, was happy enough to stay put. She'd inched closer to the display, a miniature winter wonderland featuring brightly lit cottages, horse-drawn sleighs, a model train, and a tiny skating pond crisscrossed by mechanized model skaters. It was pure magic.

She couldn't quite remember how the subsequent negotiation unfolded. Susan, spitting mad at their noncompliance, announced she was going to walk the few blocks to the car and pull it around so they could bundle Gus directly in. She extracted a promise from Andie to watch him while the feat was accomplished. At least, Andie must have agreed, as Susan had certainly stressed the fact in the aftermath. In truth, Andie would have been happy to agree to anything in order to prolong her chance of following the mesmerizing figure eights carved by the tiny skaters in the glittering surface of that miniature pond.

"I promised I'd watch him," Andie said, her voice small.

Gus calmed a little as Susan strode off. Andie remembered looking down at his face, lit by the display. She looped her fingers through his, but he soon wiggled out of her grasp. He was in that testing phase, constantly wanting to assert his independence. Certain he was as transfixed by the window as she was, Andie had allowed herself to focus on the costumes of the skaters, decked out in Victorian coats, hats, mittens, and muffs in rich shades of plum, cherry, and emerald. Ragamuffin children held snowballs poised ready to throw, and courting couples leaned toward one another as they made the pond's circuit, the smooth arcs of their movement accompanied by the faint chime of carols that poured from a small speaker over the store's entrance.

"I was so distracted by the scene in the window that I lost track of Gus," Andie whispered. "I forgot about him."

Then, like a nightmare, the terrible scream of brakes filled the air, and the music was gone. There was nothing but the sickening thud of Gus's body and the sound of Andie's own howls of anguish echoing in her ears. And the pitiful figure of Earl Peterson, retching his shock and remorse into the gutter as his old Buick, driver's door hanging open, stood skewed across one lane of Main Street.

The minutes and hours that followed the accident remained a blur, Andie told Rhys. Somehow Susan had reappeared. Her stark cries were the most terrifying thing Andie had ever heard, because they confirmed to her that the scene in front of her was real, not just some grotesque misunderstanding. Andie could still remember disjointed images from the hellish tableau. Gus's small hand clutching a spray of silver tinsel. One rain boot tossed aside, revealing his foot in its white cotton sock.

He'll be cold, had been her irrational thought as the first responders cordoned off the street. But Gus would never feel the cold again. Or, instead, was it true that cold was all he would feel as he lay in the ground and the years wore on?

"There was a piece of tinsel that had fallen from one of the streetlamps," she said softly. "And he ran into the road to pick it up."

Gus, a dark, low, indistinct shape in his hooded navy jacket, must have been practically invisible as Earl Peterson, who—they later learned—had only ventured out to buy a gallon of milk, turned onto Main Street. And, in the space of one awful moment, everything changed forever.

For years afterward, Andie confessed to Rhys, she'd been too terrified to really sleep. Night after night, she would stare at the stained ceiling of her childhood bedroom—frozen in place, too frightened to move her eyes in any direction. Tormented by the idea of Gus laid out in his small casket, his tattered blue baby blanket and his favorite toy nestled by his side, the cab of one small yellow truck containing a secret note she'd tucked inside on the day of his funeral. *I love you. I'm sorry.*

CHAPTER
TWENTY-ONE

Rhys clutched Andie, feeling the soft whisper of her hair against his cheek and the tremors that shook her body, cursing his own helplessness because he didn't know how to make this better. He didn't even know where to begin.

The most powerful loss he'd ever experienced was the wrenching pain of Will's diagnosis, the cruel dissolution of the dreams he held for the child of his imagination. But the heavy weight on his chest—the terrible anxiety that had dogged him as Will missed his developmental milestones, and the grief that crushed him when the diagnosis was confirmed—had lifted over the past several weeks. Will was alive. Will was whole. Will was a miracle in his own right. He was brave and beautiful, and as full of potential as any other child. He was not lost forever. Not like Andie's little brother.

He hardly knew what to do as she trembled against him. He wanted to pour his strength into her, give her every scrap of the resilience she'd restored to him. His chest hurt, as if she had somehow crept into a secret inner chamber of his heart, and her tears were scouring him from the inside. And, in a way, that was what had happened, he realized with a start.

He was in love with her. Definitively, irreversibly in love with this woman whose fear and reticence now made an awful kind of sense, but whose strength and kindness had managed to change him anyway.

The knowledge of it sank in, bone deep. *I love her.* Of course he loved her. She'd captivated him, ever since her first day in his house, with her generosity and her sweetness. There was an enchantment about her. Will had seen it from the start, and it had worked its magic on Rhys—cracked him right open. Made him see things that were never possible before.

Oblivious to the cold and damp seeping through the legs of his jeans, he cupped her face, pushing back fallen strands of hair from her wet cheeks and pressing feverish kisses to her forehead, her earlobes, her closed eyelids. *I've got you. Just hold on, and we'll ride this out together.*

No wonder she'd reacted with such horror when Will had pulled free from her grip in the crosswalk weeks ago. God, her blood must have run cold. And yet she'd stayed, in spite of the terrible tug of grief and dread. In spite of the fact that doing so meant waking up each day to face her worst fears. She'd stayed to help him, because he had asked. Now, he wanted more than anything to return the favor.

"Andie, you were eleven years old when it happened," he said. "It was a terrible accident, but it wasn't your fault."

"I took my eyes off him," she declared. "I said I'd watch him, and I didn't. If I hadn't pretended to be sick to get out of my piano lesson, we never would have been there in the first place. And if I hadn't let myself look at Dolan's window . . ."

"What if your mother hadn't dragged the two of you out that afternoon?" Rhys countered. "What if she hadn't decided to leave her two young children on a street corner so she could get the car? What if Earl Peterson had left his house thirty seconds later? What if his wife had bought the milk? It was an *accident.* It wasn't your fault."

"Susan blames me," Andie said starkly. She pulled slightly away and started to gather that familiar shell of grim stoicism around her. She wasn't done blaming herself, either, apparently.

"You were an eleven-year-old child," he repeated, frustration clawing at his insides. "You should have been playing catch and focusing on your long division. Not shouldering responsibility for matters of life and death."

"That doesn't matter to her."

But does it matter to you? Rhys looked at her intently, wondering. Would Susan Tilly have been able to get away with her torturous seventeen-year mind warp if Andie hadn't been so willing to carry the burden of guilt? But then, Andie could hardly have done otherwise. She'd been a mere child—vulnerable, impressionable—forced to bend and conform to a cruel set of circumstances beyond her control, to grow in a shape that fit them, like a tree buffeted by an ocean gale. Trained to view herself as culpable. More culpable than the mother who left her eleven-year-old to wrangle her hyperactive, overtired toddler brother on a dark street corner. More culpable than the man who drove the car that hit her brother, if Susan's magnanimous hiring decision was any indication. Rhys burned with a blast of fury.

"What do you want from her now, Andie?" he asked urgently. Whatever she needed from her mother to mitigate her pain, to make her whole, he was determined to get for her. "Does it even matter what she thinks anymore? Hasn't she forfeited any right to pass judgment on you?"

"I want her forgiveness." Andie's eyes glittered. "It might be stupid after all this time, but—God help me—I still want it. I don't think I'll ever have any peace until I get it."

"Then that is what you will have," Rhys responded. "I'll talk to her—"

More tears trickled down Andie's cheeks, but now she was smiling.

"No, Rhys," she protested. "That's probably the sweetest thing any-body has ever offered to do for me, but this is my battle to fight. I need to do it myself."

"Okay, then." Rhys helped her to her feet and stood facing her, run-ning his hands from her shoulders down to her fingertips and back up again, trying to warm her. "I suppose it should be now. Today. What do you need? Coffee? Wine? I could take you for a drink first. We passed a bar on the way through town. Do you think it's open now?"

"It's after twelve, so I suppose so." Andie was laughing now, her cheeks still wet. "But, no. I don't need anything extra. Just you in my corner."

"That, you can count on." He looked at her red, blotchy face, puffy eyes, and bedraggled ponytail, and felt his heart squeeze.

"And chocolate afterward?"

"Consider it done."

～

"We need to talk." Fortified by a cup of tea and an impassioned pep talk from Rhys, Andie had gone in search of Susan. She felt strangely buoyant, the impression of Rhys's arms around her still making her skin tingle. *My love.* She wondered whether he realized what he'd said, or whether the words were just the generic endearments of a fraught moment. And if he'd meant them, what should she do? Half of her wanted to soak them up, like drenching rain to her thirsty heart, while the other half wanted to bolt in fear. She couldn't think about it now.

She found Susan in the storage room in the side aisle of the barn, a room that had once been Bingo's stall. Her mother had completely overhauled the barn ten years ago, and pristine poured-concrete floor-ing and tiers of shelves partially obscured the room's original function, but the wall facing the breezeway, with its barred window and sliding door, was unchanged. Andie gazed at the familiar nicks and dents in the stall door, trying to conjure the gentle presence of her beloved chestnut horse. Now the space was sterile, smelling of cardboard and coffee grounds. She stood in the doorway, ensuring that Susan would have no choice but to face her.

"Oh, it's you, Andrea." Susan tore into a bulk box of coffee-creamer tubs and loaded a fresh supply into a Tupperware container to bring out to her guests. Her task completed, she stepped forward expectantly, poised for Andie to let her by. "Can this wait?"

"No, actually, it can't," Andie said. "We need to deal with this now."

"Deal with what?"

"Your attitude to me, the way you treat me. It has to stop."

"Really, Andrea." Susan shook her head wearily. "There's no need to be so melodramatic. I don't know what you're making such a fuss over. I call you. I invite you here."

"Once a year, to wait on your friends," Andie pointed out. "To keep paying off my debt, isn't that right? But I never deserve my own seat at the table." Andie couldn't even count the number of family events she'd been excluded from over the years. Louisa's and Rose's children barely even knew her as their aunt. "Let's just get it out in the open, for once. You still blame me for what happened to Gus."

Susan's head came up, her eyes glinting dangerously, as if Andie had no right to speak his name—as if that were Susan's prerogative alone.

"Do you think I don't mourn for him?" Andie demanded. "Do you think a single day goes by when I don't feel his loss with every cell in my body?"

"You don't know the first thing about it," Susan snapped. "He was *my child*."

"And I was your child, too. Eleven years old. I've already served a sentence that's lasted my whole lifetime over again, and more, since it happened. How much longer do I have to wait until you'll forgive me? You apparently have no issue with Earl Peterson. You hired him as a driver, for God's sake! But I'm still a lost cause?"

"Earl . . . that's none of your business." Susan placed the container of creamers down on a shelf and put her hands on her hips, her stance wide, emphatic.

"I think it is," Andie retorted. "There was more than one factor involved that night. Yes, I looked away when I should have been watching Gus, and I'll spend my whole life being sorry for that. But I was just an exhausted eleven-year-old who'd been dragged around for hours on a fool's errand. You know what Gus was like. You couldn't handle him under those conditions. How did you expect me to? Why were we even out so late that night anyway? In the dark and the sleet?"

Fear streaked through her veins. It felt dangerous to be asking the questions. Making the demands.

Susan lowered her head, her shoulders rounding as she braced her hands on her thighs for a few moments. Her rib cage heaved as she took a series of harsh breaths. When she finally straightened, her stare was flat and dark.

"I'll tell you why we were out," she said, her voice low and deadly. "Because it was *Tuesday*, and your father was trying to sleep off a mean buzz, like he always did after coming home from third shift and holing up with his Old Crow. Your piano lesson was a safe place for us to break up the afternoon so the two of you wouldn't go stir-crazy at home and wake him up. But that day we didn't go."

She gave a smile so bitter it should have puckered her mouth. "You were only too happy to go purring up to your father when he was in a good mood—like you were his pet cat. But he wasn't so crazy about you getting in his face when it didn't suit him. Gus, either. I was the one who had to look out for you, keep everyone safe. But what would you know about that? Huh?"

Andie quailed to see the anger in her mother's face, hard and unyielding. The way Susan said it, *purring up to your father*, made her want to retch. Like there was something dirty in it. But, thank God that had never been the case. Still, something about Andie's bond with

Jim obviously provoked a visceral reaction in her mother. *My child* was how she'd referred to Gus. As if Andie weren't a part of her, too. As if she were simply Jim's child—co-opted to his side as his ally, his favorite daughter—and therefore exiled from her mother's affections forever.

"Do want to know what he did, the time before that, when I couldn't keep you kids quiet, and he was sleeping off a hangover?" Susan's expression was frighteningly avid, obscene with the hurt she knew she was inflicting and the gruesome satisfaction of it.

No, Andie thought, she really didn't want to know. She really didn't need to know more now.

"He shoved me so hard into a doorframe he dislocated my shoulder. He made me tell the doctors I'd slipped in the shower."

Andie flinched, and a ripple of triumph passed across Susan's face. "So that's why we were out in the dark and the cold. And that's why, when it finally hit six thirty, I had to get you and Gus into the goddamn car, because if that man's dinner wasn't hot and on the table by seven, things could go south pretty darn quickly."

Andie ached for her mother, hemmed into that volatile world of banality and violence, focused on the singular goal of survival, with no room for softness or joy, no room for compassion or gentleness—certainly no room for the magic of a Christmas window. Hopelessness fluttered in her chest, along with a painful yearning for her mother to see her as the child she once was, not just as an instrument of tragedy or an extension of the man she'd loved and had come to hate. She needed Susan to finally recognize her as the daughter she still wanted to be, if given half a chance.

"I'm sorry," Andie said softly. "And you're right. I didn't know. What he did to you was unforgivable. But, Mom, he's been gone for ten years now. And I'm still your daughter. I need to hear from you that when you look at me you see more than just the person who let go of Gus's hand."

Andie dropped her hands to her sides and waited, looking straight at her mother. *Remember the tea set and the daisy chains,* she willed. *Please, Mom.*

Susan looked right back, something in her expression softening for a moment as she looked at Andie's flushed cheeks and her messy ponytail. But then the brittle screen shuttered her eyes again, and she looked away.

"You promised you'd watch him," she said, her voice faltering for an instant as she repeated the old refrain.

Andie froze. "So, that's it, then." She felt like she was deflating, the breath departing her body, like the fleeing inhabitants of a town in the path of an advancing army. But when she next inhaled, she was surprised to find that she did not feel desolate or cowed. She felt strangely cleansed. All hope of reconciliation with her mother might have fled, but the ghosts had fled, too. The tension that had simmered between them for seventeen years was out in the open, put into words, and deprived of its ability to draw power from the shadows. "I'll be on my way."

Susan picked up the tub of creamers and hugged it to her chest, a strange expression on her face.

"I won't expect an invitation next year," Andie said, her resolve solidifying. "I can't do this anymore."

She turned away, skimming her fingers along the barred door of Bingo's stall. *Good-bye.* Stepping into the aisle, she looked back through the bars of the stall at her mother, still frozen in place.

"I'm proud of what you've done with the farm. You've made it into a place that makes people happy."

With that, she started walking. Long, deliberate paces, trying to ignore a new, ferocious burning in her chest. Would this really be the last time she set foot on the Tilly farm? It would have to be, if her decision was to stick.

She emerged, slightly disoriented, into the happy din of the barn. Rhys, who'd been pacing with a tired Will in his arms, rushed toward her expectantly. It almost broke her heart to see the hope and concern in his eyes. She gave a brief, quashing shake of her head to signal the failure of her mission.

"It's okay," she assured him. "I'll be fine. Let's get out of here. I just have to go to the house first to get something."

Rhys reached one arm out, pulling her close to press his lips against her flushed forehead. "I'll say good-bye to your sisters."

Andie trudged toward the modest white farmhouse. More than 150 years old, it was the product of a former age—unassuming and functional. She pushed open the unlocked front door and stepped inside, her tread making the floorboards creak exactly where she knew they would. The house's familiar smell engulfed her, but she stopped in surprise as she looked around. She couldn't remember how long it had been since she'd set foot inside, but the changes were striking.

The wall dividing the living room and dining room had been knocked out, and the space, while still far from grand in scale, was open and comfortable. The walls were a warm dove gray, and a bold tomato-red sofa took pride of place against one wall, adorned with splashy cushions in white and red. It felt as if a hand other than Susan's had been at work in the decorating style. Through a sleek cutout in the dining-room wall, she could see a gleaming new kitchen, one that displaced the ghosts of her childhood from their familiar seats.

If she and Susan had any kind of a relationship, she should have known about this transformation of the farmhouse, Andie realized. For years, her connection with her mother had been a fragile, insubstantial thing. And yet, for so long, she'd allowed Susan's view of her to remain the organizing principle of her life—dictating who she was, what she was entitled to, where her hopes could lead. She'd submitted to Susan's imperative that her dreams be cut down to size, parceling the different facets of herself into boxes as confining as the poky rooms of her childhood home. And all the while, Susan had been renovating and expanding, turning the farm into a successful business, allowing her vision free rein.

Andie felt a stab of regret. For time wasted, for decisions made through a contorted lens. She turned and ran up the narrow staircase to her childhood bedroom on the second floor. It, too, had changed. The twin beds had been taken out, the carpet pulled up. The refinished hardwood floor gleamed, and a large desk stood in the corner near the window. Anxiety clutched Andie's chest. *Where is it?* She scanned the changed landscape of the room, her heartbeat drumming frantically until her gaze finally landed on the worn spine of a photo album bound in blue gingham, nestled in the far corner of a bookshelf.

She plucked the album from the shelf where it sat beside other, similar volumes. This one was hers, the place where she'd painstakingly gathered her memories of Gus, and of her childhood before the accident, as well as a few later photos. She'd never been able to have it in her apartment, but now she was ready to claim it.

Tucking the album under her arm, she headed back downstairs and straight out the front door, pulling it shut behind her.

Rhys had the car idling in the driveway, Will already buckled into his car seat. Andie ran over and jumped in, settling the photo album on her lap.

"Ready?" Rhys asked.

"Never readier," Andie said firmly. As Rhys pulled the car out, she turned to look back at the barn.

Denise Hendrix emerged in the doorway, a frown on her face. She walked out toward the parking lot, still wearing Susan's old leather apron, scanning the area. She caught sight of the Range Rover just as Rhys turned onto the road and, her pace picking up, raised her hand as if to flag them down. But the car was already speeding away from the farm. Andie watched as the red barn and small white house receded in the distance, the figure of Denise outlined against the shrinking back-drop of her childhood.

~

"She *what?*" Rhys sputtered on the drive back to Concord, as Andie gave him the gist of what Susan had said to her. He supposed he must be a complete innocent, but it cut him to the quick to hear of a parent treating her child that way.

"Don't worry," Andie said. "I'll get over it. At least I got it out in the open and asked for her absolution, point-blank."

"Sure," Rhys conceded, frowning. It might be an improvement, but it was hardly a satisfactory result. She was putting a brave face on it, but she looked small and wan, and her hand quivered slightly as he enfolded it in his.

"Rhys?" she said tentatively.

"Yes?"

"I need to tell you something."

"Okay." The serious look on her face set his heart thumping.

"When I took this job with you and Will, I didn't do it for the purest of reasons."

"Oh?" Not sure where this was going, Rhys could do nothing but facilitate whatever it was she needed to get off her chest.

"I guess in a way I was looking for absolution through Will—just like I wanted it from Susan. For what happened with Gus, I mean. When Will said my name, I felt capable and wanted for the first time in a very long time."

"What's so bad about that?"

"It was a selfish reason to take the job. It shouldn't have been about me." She looked at him drowsily, worn out from the intense emotion of the day. "*And* I wanted him to come to me instead of Karina that day on the log bridge at the playground. I was competing with Will's own mother. Do you understand how messed up that is? I'm an awful person, and I'm woefully overinvolved with your family. I should probably hand back my therapist badge before someone gets hurt."

Rhys had to chuckle. "That's your dreadful confession?"

"That's it," Andie confirmed in a small voice. As she spoke, her eyelids drooped to half-mast and then closed completely, as if she could finally rest now that her revelation was out. Her chest ceased its tumultuous rise and fall as her breathing settled into a regular rhythm.

Rhys looked over at her calm in sleep, and his heart soared. *Overinvolved* sounded pretty damn good to him right now. Will dozed in his car seat, and Rhys snatched glances at him through the rearview mirror, his chest stirring with an almost-painful fullness.

~

"What's that?" he asked later, when Will was tucked in bed, and he came down to the den to find Andie sitting in front of the fireplace, the gingham-bound book she'd taken from the farmhouse sitting in her lap.

"It's a photo album. Pictures from when I was a kid."

"May I?"

He sat beside her, producing a bar of imported Cadbury Dairy Milk from behind his back, and shifted her so she sat nestled between his legs, leaning back against his chest. He broke off a row of four chocolate squares each to fortify them for what he expected was to be a bumpy trip down memory lane.

Andie held the album and began to turn the pages. She sat still and solemn as the images from her past appeared in sequence, tears occasionally leaking from under her lashes. There were photos of her as a baby, large-eyed and serious. One showed her as an infant cradled in the crook of her father's arm while her mother stood with the older girls lined up in front of her, her hands on the shoulders of a russet-haired preschool-age child who could only be Jess.

Jim Tilly was tall, clean-cut, and imposing, not quite the image of the dissolute man Rhys had imagined from Andie's description. Those images came later, the man's eyes receding into puffy pouches of flesh, his mouth settling into a mean-spirited downward tilt on one side.

There was a photo of Andie at around age five, her hair in braids, an oversize backpack hooked over her skinny shoulders as she held Jess's hand—probably on her first day of school. She was a soul-crushingly beautiful child, her eyes uncertain, her blouse half-untucked, and her skirt slightly askew.

At some point, she'd clearly been given her own camera, as the album was loaded with slanted, slightly fuzzy shots of horses, and many photos of a happy toddler with cropped chestnut-colored hair and a spray of freckles across his nose. *Gus.* There he was dressed up in his best for a family gathering, laughing as he threw bread crumbs to ducks in a pond, and running around the Tilly's yard in just a diaper. Another photo showed him, slightly taller and slimmer, turning to look over his shoulder as he peed into a deflated wading pool, an expression of pure, wicked glee on his face. Probably his last summer, Rhys guessed, his heart plummeting. Within a year, Will would take on that longer shape, losing his toddler squatness.

"He was a cheeky kid," he observed with a melancholy laugh.

"Yes," Andie agreed. "He was a handful." She seemed to grow stronger as she told Rhys about Gus, about his fierce affection and his curiosity, and about the bond they'd shared as the two youngest children of the family, often left to their own devices as the relationship between their parents deteriorated, and the older girls found refuge in clubs, sports, and boys. Gus had been Andie's pint-size sidekick, shadowing her everywhere. Many preteen girls might have chafed at the constant demands of an adoring younger brother, but Rhys heard delight kindle in her voice as she described small adventures and run-of-the-mill childhood mishaps.

"He would have been twenty-one this month," Andie said, raising a hand to wipe her cheek. "He would have been tall . . . and funny. I'm sure he would have been funny. He always used to crack me up."

Rhys pressed a kiss to the back of her neck and looked on with interest as she turned the remainder of the pages. The photos of her after age eleven were fewer. It would not have been a time she was keen to document. There were a few photos of her in her teens, looking miserable and ill at ease. In one image she looked almost anemic, her eyes bleak, the color leached from her lips. Her hair was so lush by contrast it appeared to have stolen her vitality, draining the life and joy out of her to feed its own dark profusion. Sadness wended through his veins.

"Enough of that," she declared uncomfortably, flipping forward to graduation photos of both Jess and her.

At Jess's graduation, Susan, Louisa, and Rose clustered around, dressed to the nines and smiling proudly. Andie was probably behind the camera, he guessed. At Andie's graduation ceremonies, for both her bachelor's and master's, there was only Jess. *His* parents had flown all the way from Wales to see him get his doctorate from MIT, he reflected.

His whole body smarted with outrage on her behalf. He wanted to correct the injustice done to her, right the imbalance in the universe, but—as the day had shown—wanting it would not make it so. All he could do was love her and move forward with her, helping her find new joys to crowd out the old sorrows.

He was in love with her, and he ached to tell her, to kiss the words into her skin, but it felt wrong to announce his feelings when she was still working through the shock of her break with her mother. He wanted the moment to be perfect, memorable, not just another emotional ambush on a day that had been packed with them. He hugged her close, dreaming. Waiting.

CHAPTER
TWENTY-TWO

Ten days later, the spring thaw had finally arrived, and it was all action on the playground. Rhys marveled at the transformation that had taken place since the day of Karina's surprise appearance at the log bridge. Now, like Chaucer's pilgrims, a phalanx of suburban mothers filed by in the clear April sunshine, bent on sacrificing a few hours to the whims of their small charges.

Karina actually begged off their weekly meeting, saying she had a doctor's appointment, so Rhys invited Andie to join him for the outing. He carried Will from the car, with Andie by his side, as they headed for the colorful oasis of slides, swings, and climbing structures. The breeze whipped a tendril of hair across Andie's cheeks, and she swiped it away, her eyes bright with pleasure at the gorgeous day. She was still fragile after the confrontation with her mother, but she was gradually recovering her spirits, in large part thanks to the time she was spending with Will at Saddle Tree Farm.

Every evening, Rhys was galvanized by the desire to declare himself to her, to let her know he loved her, but a note of caution kept his impulses in check.

Will let out a squeal and took off as Rhys lowered him to the ground, his sneakered feet pounding across the playground mulch.

For a gratifying period of time, Will was just one of the toddlers, operating the levers of the excavation toys in the sandbox, squealing to be pushed by Andie on the swings, flexing his first countercultural muscles by insisting on climbing up the slide rather than going down.

Rhys began to relax and let his guard down, too, sipping his takeaway coffee in the perfect warmth of the weak spring sunshine—not too hot, not too cold. Until trouble developed at the seesaw.

Instead of the traditional lever-and-fulcrum design with one long, flat board to sit on, this seesaw had springs, molded seats, rubber handles, and a four-way design that, on a busy day like this one, meant a sizable crowd of small patrons waiting to claim one of the coveted four spots. Sniffing out potential conflict, Rhys and Andie wandered over.

Will had held the east-facing seat for a good eight minutes, according to Rhys's calculations. He would have to give up his place soon or face mutiny from the crowd milling around the structure, which sat in a shaded corner of the playground lined with fragrant cedar chips. While the more sanguine parents sat back and sipped their lattes on sun-drenched seats, others stood around to referee and offer assistance.

A red-cheeked boy of about four hovered near Will's perch, poised to move in as soon as he glimpsed the first sign of hesitation. For all the progress he'd made lately, Will understood as much about turn taking as he did about nuclear physics. He bounced with blithe unconcern, his smile so pure and enraptured that it sent an arrow through Rhys's heart.

Taken aback perhaps by the deepening scowl of his red-cheeked compatriot, a few moments later Will let the pace of his bouncing slow down. The other boy, sensing weakness—or at least opportunity—reached out a hand to grasp one rubberized handle, his hand coming down right beside Will's.

Will's face went from bliss to bewildered rage in a few seconds flat as the other boy edged closer and prevented him from continuing his bouncing.

"Will!" Rhys broke into a jog and closed the remaining distance to the seesaw. "It's time to get off now and let someone else have a turn."

The red-cheeked boy now had both hands on the handlebars beside Will's and was angled across him in such a way that Rhys couldn't bodily extricate Will from the equipment without jostling him, too. The boy started yelling at the same time Will did.

"It's not fair! I want a turn!" The boy's voice rose rapidly to a crescendo. "Mom-eeeee!"

Every female head on the playground not already turned toward the melee now swiveled in their direction. A few people stood up uneasily, looking around for the mom in question. A woman with a neat brown bob turned away from a younger toddler installed in a baby swing and—asking the mom beside her to keep an eye on the child—headed for the seesaw.

"Josh!" she called.

Oh, no! Not again. Rhys cringed. Andie moved in, poised to do damage control.

"It's my turn!" Josh cried, weeping hot, angry tears as Will's screams echoed in his ears. "This baby needs to get off."

Will broke off to inhale a deep breath, readying himself to hit a new octave. But when he gathered himself, an extraordinary thing happened. Instead of the inchoate scream Rhys was expecting, Will's little mouth worked to produce something quite different. A word: loud, clear, and perfectly formed.

"No!" Will looked almost startled at the exotic utterance that had just burst from his lips, but he quickly made his peace with it. "Nooooooooo!"

Rhys looked wide-eyed at Andie, who froze, a stunned smile dawning across her features. She let out a laugh, too happy and astonished to produce words of her own.

"My turn!" Josh cried again.

"Noooooooooo!"

Josh's mom was almost upon them, backed up by a small cluster of friends who weren't inclined to jump into the fray but—by the same token—were a little bemused by the sight of Rhys and Andie beaming giddily at the rapidly escalating conflict.

"Um, I think it's probably time for them to switch," said one of Josh's mom's friends snippily.

Rhys, overcome with love and outright jubilation, was hopelessly tickled by the funny side of the scenario. Swiping tears from his eyes, he laughed helplessly and bent down to kiss the top of Will's head.

"Good for you, Will," he said, unable to wipe the grin from his face. Andie was overcome, marveling as she leaned in to give Will a hug.

"What is it?" asked Josh's mom, scowling slightly.

"Will has autism," Rhys explained. "That 'no' is only the second word he's ever said."

"Oh my God!" "That's wonderful." "Amazing." "Way to go, Will!" A chorus of cheers and supportive comments erupted from the group. Josh's mom peeled her son's hands off the seesaw's handlebars so Rhys could extricate Will, and he placed him down in the middle of the small crowd as the celebratory mood deepened. Moms with no previous acquaintance shared their happy astonishment at the turn of events. A dad with his curly-haired toddler daughter perched on his shoulders came up to give Rhys a pat on the back and shake Andie's hand.

One mom offered juice boxes to Will and a couple of her charges. Another dug through a designer diaper bag and handed around individually packaged baggies of baked, organic snacks. "I'm Noreen," she said with a friendly smile. "My eldest has Asperger's."

Rhys marveled as he and Andie slipped easily into conversation with Noreen and her friends, swept along on a tide of goodwill. Andie's advice about Will, spoken months ago, after another toddler conflagration, echoed through his mind. *He will be exactly who he is. And you'll just have to try to keep up.*

She'd spoken those words in the dead of winter, when confusion, grief, and angst had still been the dominant features of his emotional landscape. But she'd been right. His fretting and soul-searching—all those nights sitting by Will's bedside in a fever of worry, all those days of comparing his son to his typically developing peers and pining for the moment he would catch up—were of no use to Will. All Rhys had to do was love him, and Will would be who he was. Beautiful. Miraculous. All Rhys could ever ask for in a son.

On the way home, Rhys insisted on stopping at the supermarket for a cake. He had a particular design in mind, featuring a very unnatural shade of cerulean and a stenciled image of Thomas the Tank Engine. Andie ushered Will up and down the aisles, retrieving grocery items for therapy as they waited, and then all three bore the cake home, bursting into the house in a flurry of cheers and laughter.

"Mrs. Hodge! Jillian!" Rhys called. "You must celebrate with us."

Mrs. Hodge brewed a pot of her best Earl Grey, and they all sat around the kitchen island savoring blue cake on bone-china plates, except for Will, who ate his straight from the high-chair tray and managed to get a good portion of the frosting in his hair. Rhys had experienced some pretty exceptional days in his life, but this one was turning out to be one of the greatest.

～

"You barely touched your cake," Andie commented to Jillian as they carried the plates over to the sink.

"Oh, but what I did eat was worth it," Jillian enthused. "All that blue hydrogenated oil and sugar makes me feel like a kid again."

"You are looking particularly svelte this week."

"I've lost close to sixteen pounds," Jillian said jubilantly. "Last night I went shopping for my mother-of-the-bride dress, and I almost fit into a size ten. I haven't been a size ten since I was a teenager."

Andie let out a little whoop of celebration and gave Jillian a hug.

"I knew you could do it," she said with a grin.

"I'm thrilled," Jillian enthused. "And I'm so happy for you, too."

"For me?"

"Yes, for all of your success with Will. And because of how things seem to be going between you and Rhys." Jillian's eyes sparkled. "I've worked in this house for a long time, and I have to say it's never been like this. It's just so wonderful to see Rhys happy and Will doing so well."

"Well . . . thanks," Andie responded, not really sure what else to say. It would be disingenuous to deny that there was something between her and Rhys, but she wasn't yet ready to define for anyone else what that something was. Still, she had to admit she was starting to feel stronger and happier than she'd ever been. Her despondency over her confrontation with her mother was fading as new, positive developments crowded in, and at every turn Rhys was her biggest supporter.

"How's the post-Susan rating scale today?" he would ask each morning.

"The needle is hovering between acceptance and abject self-pity," she'd joked over breakfast that day.

Sometimes he would just offer a word or two to remind her he was in her corner, and on other occasions he'd listen at length as she analyzed and cried and picked over the rubble of her relationship with her mother. Most of all, he encouraged her to take on new challenges, to dream and plan for a future that she wanted, not one that she was just prepared to settle for.

That morning, before the momentous trip to the playground with Will and Rhys, she'd done another of her many volunteer stints at Saddle Tree Farm. She was still on a high from working with the horses and the kids—today, a four-year-old girl with cerebral palsy and a teenage boy with Down syndrome—and from Maisie's enthusiasm about her plan to earn a hippotherapy certification, and to formalize an arrangement with Saddle Tree Farm that would enable her to build a practice mixing traditional occupational therapy with equine-assisted therapy.

Rhys, too, was hatching ideas that were footholds to the future. He shared with her his progress in setting up a foundation to help autistic children. He wanted her to be on the board and to advise on the areas where needy families were most likely to fall through the cracks of the medical system.

Zephyrus Energy was being honored with a corporate philanthropy award at a black-tie autism fundraising gala the following week, and Rhys couldn't wait to show up with Andie on his arm and introduce her to his friends—not to mention his contacts in the business community. She hesitated a little at the idea of taking on that kind of role. It felt so public, so mature. But, with Rhys by her side, she was prepared to give it a try.

And to have Will add a new word to his repertoire was a wonder beyond reckoning. She still chuckled in delight when she recalled the look on his face as he'd uttered the significant syllable. It seemed that the whole world had come alive with possibility.

Rhys *knew* her, really saw her in a way nobody else ever had before. He saw her pain, her guilt, and her fears. He saw her imperfections, her failings, and her triumphs. He'd looked into the deepest core of her and accepted what lay there. He'd seen the sordid reality of her family life growing up—with its mortifying callousness and casual violence. He'd actually trodden the earth of the farm, walked among its ghosts, and his only response was to embrace her with a fervor that made her tremble with the wonder of it.

And his passion, the way they melded together each night, was a shining grace note that made everything subtly different, even how it felt to inhabit her own body. She had never known that the slide of skin against skin, the intimate mapping of the topography of another's form, and the laying bare of her wants and needs could be a miracle in which she could not just lose herself but find herself.

I'm falling for him. She'd practice the declaration sometimes as she moved about the house. If she said it enough, she might desensitize herself to the panic that the realization brought on. *Deep breaths.* But, in her heart of hearts, she knew that "falling" didn't quite capture it. *If there's a fall to be taken, I've already crash-landed.* She loved him. She loved who he was to the marrow: a heart-melting combination of warmth, decency, awkwardness, kindness, and riveting intensity, all wrapped up in one breathtaking package.

~

A few days later, in the spirit of optimism that seemed to have taken over lately, Andie was actually motivated to pull on her running shoes while Will was at preschool. Rhys had left for a whirlwind business trip to Silicon Valley the day before to finalize a licensing agreement with a small tech company whose software was an ideal fit with Zephyrus's wind turbines. In the absence of her habitual Rhys-induced high, she was prepared to take the bull by the horns and chase the ever-elusive runner's high.

Unfortunately, she was thirty minutes out from the house before she was reminded of just how passionately she loathed running. With a stitch in her side, an elusive pebble migrating around inside one of her shoes, and her hair falling in her face, she turned around and began to hobble back up a hill that seemed to have magically increased its gradient since she'd jogged down it blithely just minutes before.

With music blaring from her earbuds as she swilled the last mouthful of water from a big, clunky bottle, she cut across Rhys's acreage from the road rather than go all the way to the long driveway. She put in a final burst of effort just in case Mrs. Hodge or Jillian was watching her approach the house, jogging up to the garage doors even as she wilted on her feet.

Just as she entered the four-digit code on the garage door keypad, an insidious finger of scent drifted around her, jabbing at her olfactory system with a sharp bouquet of bergamot and jasmine. *No, don't turn around. You're imagining it, the same as always.* The garage door began to rumble open.

She froze, convinced now that she actually felt the exhalation of a breath against the back of her neck. Taking out her earbuds with a show of methodical calm, Andie turned, bracing herself for what she would see.

"Agh!" She couldn't repress a cry as she came face-to-face with Karina, who had crowded up so close that Andie would have been hardpressed to fit a hand's width between them. Based on her appearance, it was hard to believe the woman had slept a single night since Andie had last set eyes on her on the wintry playground a few weeks ago.

Andie stepped back, only to find that Karina looked no better from a slightly more socially acceptable distance. Her skin was thin and dull, a trace of fine blue veins visible at her temples. The dark circles under her eyes had deepened. She also appeared to have lost weight, something that on Karina—already as fashionably thin as a whippet—was not auspicious.

Concern rippled through Andie. Karina's reason for not meeting with Rhys and Will on the day of Will's "No" breakthrough had been a doctor's visit. *Is she terribly ill?*

At least she's under the care of a doctor. She smiled weakly, trying not to show her shock. She racked her brain to remember whether Rhys had mentioned anything important in the wake of his other visits with

Karina since the log bridge incident. Karina had started pushing for one-on-one time with Will, Rhys said, but she'd backed down when he insisted she needed more time to acclimatize first.

Andie also recalled one throwaway comment from Rhys that Karina, at least, seemed to have ditched the silk outfits for more practical playground attire. Perhaps she was having trouble keeping up with the dry cleaning while camping out on a friend's couch, he'd speculated. Now Andie worried that she was having trouble keeping up with a lot more than that.

Karina stepped forward threateningly.

"You're a liar," she spat. "A black-hearted, scheming, traitorous liar."

"What? No . . . I—"

"You tried to hide the fact that you and Rhys are together, but I know what you've been up to."

Her eyes shifted, as if her view of Andie was drifting in and out of focus. Andie had no idea what to say. She'd never made any claims to Karina about the status of her relationship with Rhys. Karina had simply assumed. But it was a detail she sensed it would be foolish to argue. Karina was way beyond that.

Despite the temperate weather, she was swathed in her black wool coat, which was marked with a couple of visible stains. She picked at a sleeve, pulling at a loose thread and winding it around one finger, only to unwrap and rewrap it a moment later in a frenetic motion that left Andie deeply unsettled. A reddish-purple line was scored in the flesh of Karina's finger where she'd drawn the thread tight over and over again.

"I told you I intended to get our family back together," she said. "But you don't care about that, do you? You and Rhys have been plotting behind my back. *Laughing* at me."

"No, Karina. That's not true. Please. Let's sit down and talk about this."

She had the presence of mind to jab at the keypad again so the door rolled back down. The last thing anyone needed was Karina barging into the house in this state. Andie gestured to a neat patch of lawn that overlooked the front of the property, a pleasant, calming place to sit.

"Oh, sure. Now you deny me access to my own home?" Karina scoffed. "Any minute now you'll be trying to stop me from seeing my son."

At that moment, Andie reflected, she would do practically anything to prevent Karina from seeing Will. A familiar flicker of guilt danced in her belly. Of course, if she were not in the picture, Karina might never have been pushed to this strange impasse.

"Karina, please. I'm not out to stop you from continuing your visits with Will." *Provided you're emotionally stable,* Andie amended silently.

"How big of you," the woman snapped, backing away. "You won't win, you know. You won't take my son from me. I'll make sure of that."

"Wait—"

But Karina spun around and stalked off to the car she'd parked just to the side of the garage-bay entrance—a yellow Mini Cooper with black racing stripes and checkerboard side mirrors. The vehicle looked altogether too cute to contain the human maelstrom that whirled toward it.

Andie watched the cheery little car as it shot down the driveway. When she was certain Karina had departed the premises, she turned back and reentered her access code, trembling slightly as she ascended the basement stairs. She had to call Rhys. But, first, she needed some more water. The troubling encounter with Karina had parched her, leaving her throat tight with tension.

As she headed into the kitchen, the sinister scent of jasmine and bergamot seemed to grow stronger. *Did she get in somehow? Am I losing my mind?*

Over in the highest-traffic area of the room, between the kitchen island and the sink, Jillian wielded a mop and hummed to herself. Andie was so relieved to see a well-balanced human being that she sagged with relief.

"Jillian," she said, wrinkling her nose, "do you smell that?"

"You mean the floor cleaner?"

"No, it's more like a perfume."

"Oh." Jillian brightened. "Do you like it? It's my new eau de toilette. A friend of mine gave me a bottle because I admired it on her."

She moved closer, holding out her wrist to give Andie a sniff. Andie recoiled as a blast of the scent hit her limbic system. She supposed there was nothing wrong with the perfume in its own right. It would just always fill her with a primitive aversion.

"I love it," Jillian enthused. "My friend is acting as my weight-loss trainer, and it's been driving me crazy how much I've wanted the fragrance. I think I'll wear it to my daughter's wedding."

A horrible suspicion dawned, but Andie was uncertain how to voice it.

"Um, Jillian?" she began. "This might be a strange question, but is your friend and weight-loss coach by any chance Rhys's ex-wife?"

Jillian looked confused. "Yes, why? She was the person I reported to when I first worked here. She got back in touch because she wanted to talk to me about her postpartum depression. I went through it, too, years ago, with my daughter. She was just so nice, so apologetic about how she'd behaved to me when I worked for her . . ."

She trailed off, halted by the look on Andie's face. "Is something wrong?"

"I'm afraid so." Andie described the run-in she'd just had with Karina outside.

"Oh, goodness." Jillian's face fell. "She never said anything to me that seemed off. She seemed so humbled by what she'd gone through, and so happy about Will starting to do better."

"Have you mentioned anything to her about what has been going on in the house? She showed up at the playground once when she should have had no way of knowing where we were. And somehow she found out that Rhys and I are . . . together."

"Oh, dear." Jillian wrung her hands. "I believe that must have been me." She looked at Andie beseechingly. "I didn't mean any harm by it. She acted like you were all friendly with each other. She seemed to know enough about your plans that I was convinced. Oh, Andie," she cried, gulping down her upset, "I've really made a mess of things, haven't I?"

"You didn't know," Andie said. "But Rhys is going to want to talk to you about what Karina has told you since she's been back." She wondered how Rhys would take it.

"Oh, dear." Jillian looked stricken. "I suppose I might lose this job."

"Well, I hope not, but I guess it's up to Rhys." Andie squeezed her hand.

Another thought struck her. "You're not the friend Karina has been staying with all this time, are you?"

"No." Jillian shook her head. "Karina would hate it at my place. I have two yappy little dogs and—"

"Well, that's one good thing, at least." Although it crossed Andie's mind that if Karina were staying with Jillian, she'd be easier to track down.

Jillian looked relieved that she hadn't compounded her offense by harboring the troublesome Karina, on top of everything else.

"I'm going to call Rhys now," Andie said. "I'll talk to him first, but then I'll need you to get on the phone. Let's get this sorted out."

She led the way into the den, Jillian trailing behind her, sending out insinuating wafts of jasmine and bergamot with every step.

CHAPTER
TWENTY-THREE

Rhys hurtled in from the airport that night like a Force 12 hurricane, all harried concern and rumpled beauty. Seeing his headlights sweep across the front of the house, Andie went to greet him, reaching the top of the staircase as he emerged into the foyer.

"Thank heavens you're back," she called, the pronouncement morphing into an exclamation of sheer relief as she raced down the stairs. He ran up to meet her and engulfed her in his arms, pulling her into a kiss that tasted of coffee, spice, and cold nighttime air. When he finally pulled back, she saw that he was carrying a bunch of deep-purple tulips.

"These reminded me of you." He handed her the flowers.

The tulips were so . . . *perfect.* Their clean, unfussy shape and streamlined leaves didn't demand attention but somehow earned it anyway. Their subtly gleaming purple hue was both serious and sensuous.

"I don't want you to worry about Karina," he said urgently. "Tom and I have sent the message out to all of the engineers at the company. We're going to find out which of Karina's old friends she's staying with.

In the meantime, she obviously won't be seeing Will. We'll deal with this, I promise."

"You've tried her phone again?"

"She's still not picking up." He frowned. "I talked to Mrs. Hodge about what to do if Karina approaches her when she's out with Will. Tom's also talking to his family-law contacts."

"Oh God, Rhys," Andie fretted. "She was in such bad shape."

"I know," he soothed, pressing his lips to her hair. "But we'll get to the bottom of this. We'll find her and make sure everyone comes out of this okay.

"I talked to Jillian," he added.

"I know. She told me what you said." Andie planted a kiss at his throat. "I'm so glad you didn't let her go."

"She didn't know she was doing anything wrong," Rhys said equitably. "Karina can be a master manipulator."

"It just feels so wrong, knowing she's out there and in such a state. I do feel for her, you know? If my presence here is what pushed her to this, then—"

"It isn't," Rhys said grimly. "Or if it is, then that in itself is just a symptom of a bigger problem."

"Let's go look in on Will," Andie suggested, eager to repeat a ritual she'd performed a dozen times since the toddler's bedtime. It was just so comforting to watch him, to see those chubby fists flung out against the pillow, and to hear the steady rhythm of his breathing. They climbed the stairs together, and Rhys placed a reassuring hand on her shoulder as they gazed down at Will, his fingers playing with the fine, silky hairs that had escaped from her ponytail.

The evening before Rhys's trip to California, they'd draped themselves on the couch, and he had retrieved his own photo albums to show her. She'd lost herself in idyllic images of him fishing with his cousins in the River Teifi and grinning around the table at family events held in a formal dining room the likes of which the Tilly family had never seen.

She particularly loved one photo of Rhys and his mother, taken before he left for MIT. She had soft brown eyes that glowed when she looked at her beautiful, geeky son, whose wardrobe and hair had definitely seen some positive transformations in the intervening years.

Rhys also pulled out an album from Will's earliest days. One image showed an infant Will curled in sleep against his shoulder. Rhys rested one large hand over the tiny cocoon of Will's body, his face that of a man in love with the world.

Seeing the breadth of his life, so different from hers, Andie had started to believe that maybe this was meant to be. That maybe Rhys had found his way so far from the place of his birth for a reason. That somehow their paths had crossed because he needed her and she needed him, and Will's first word was a catalyst, bringing about the consummation of a perfect inevitability. She wished she could reclaim that sense of surety now, but in the course of a single day, the tide had turned, and nothing seemed inevitable anymore.

"Come to bed," Rhys said much later, breaking her trance and guiding her away from Will's bedside. She tipped her head against his shoulder, warm in the circle of his arms as they made their way slowly to the master bedroom.

"Andie, I have something to tell you," he said solemnly, sitting her down on the edge of the big bed.

Andie froze. *What now?* Yet more bad news? *Oh God.* He was moving to California. He'd been diagnosed with a fatal illness. He *had* fallen in love with a work colleague, after all. It was all over. *Over.* And she'd been a complete fool.

"I hate to put this on you now, when all that stuff with your mother is still so fresh, and you've just been accosted by Karina," he said, his eyes serious. "But I can't wait any longer."

It's even worse than I suspected. He's throwing me out.

"I love you."

His brow creased, and his fathomless eyes—so familiar, so dear to her—were as apprehensive as if the fate of the world were at stake.

Her breath escaped in a rush of disbelief, and she choked and gasped.

"*What?*"

It was a startling thing to hear put into words by this impossibly beautiful man. And yet she was surprised to find that his declaration did not alarm her. She knew, through her daily experience of his care, his warmth, and his spirit, exactly what his love was. She knew its taste, its touch, and its texture. She knew what it was worth. And she knew, too, that it had changed her. She was no longer the terrified, reticent girl she'd been when she'd arrived at the Griffiths home. His love had nourished her, lifted her up, transformed her. No, what she felt was not fear but happiness.

"I said, 'I love you,'" he repeated, his face exquisite in its seriousness, its gravity.

The dim cavern of the bedroom suddenly seemed to glow like the sunrise, and she was certain the incandescence was coming from her, from the unfiltered joy that was somehow pouring out of her, in spite of the rigors of the day, the shock of Karina's accusations, and her troubled awareness that the woman was still out there somewhere, beyond their immediate reach.

"Um, wait—" she spluttered again, her heart fluttering and her brain not quite able to formulate a response.

"I know. My timing is awful. It's—"

"Stop that right now!" Finally, she regained what was left of her composure. She was weak with a paralyzing mixture of agony and mirth, like her heart was being torn from her body, never to be truly her own possession again, but she couldn't quite bring herself to mind losing it.

His eyes were still uncertain. "You're making a fresh start. It's too much to think you'd want to take on me and Will, when Karina—"

"Rhys, Rhys, stop!" She reached out, framing his face in her hands. "I don't care about Karina. That is, I'm worried about her, and I hope she's going to be okay, but she has no bearing on how I feel about you and Will. One hundred Karinas wouldn't change how I feel."

She smiled beatifically. "I love you, and I love that little boy of yours. It's a done deal."

"It is?" She watched his face as her conviction finally penetrated the fog. His chest expanded, along with a smile that seemed to touch the very corners of the room. "Well, then." He scooped her up into his arms and placed her in the middle of the bed. "I think there's only one thing to be done about that. I love you," he said again.

Just like the first time she heard it, she was conscious of a brittle layer around her heart dissolving. She could get used to this, she decided, as their mouths danced together, and they were enveloped in a spreading veil of heat.

"We're going to be okay, you know," he said.

"You promise?"

"I promise."

He was playful and indulgent, unwrapping her with slow jubilation, like she was an outlandishly sumptuous gift that he had all the time in the world to savor. And he was right, she thought, shivering under the path of his hands. They did have time—and the luxury—to explore where this momentous new reality might lead them.

"I want to taste you," he declared, peeling the waistband of her leggings down and anointing her hips with hot, moist kisses. She felt her inhibitions, her need for control, slipping away once more. She trusted him, would go anywhere with him, even into the crucible of an obliterating pleasure. And that is where he took her, with his mouth and his hands, as the moon rose high over the house, and all around them the earth sighed and awoke, rich with the promise of spring.

"Maisie called." Andie walked downstairs into the kitchen the next morning, clutching her phone, her expression troubled. "She sounds upset."

Rhys glanced up from his own phone, angling it to hide the screen from her as she walked over to the coffee machine. It was corny of him, he knew, and drastically premature. But he couldn't help himself. He'd been browsing diamond rings. He had something in mind—an elegant straight-edged cut with long, simple facets rather than a round stone with a confusion of tiny sparkles. An emerald cut was what he was after, he discovered, browsing on the Tiffany website. Although he had only declared his love the previous night, the idea wouldn't let go of him.

Precious little in Andie's life had been rock solid. Not the affection of her parents. Not the commitment of those old boyfriends of hers, the merest mention of which made his hackles rise. But Rhys's commitment to her was as unshakable as bedrock, and if his persistently literal mind insisted on seeing his devotion represented in an actual rock, what was wrong with that? *Women like that kind of thing, right?*

He'd intended to wait before confessing his feelings for her. He'd meant everything he said the night before. He knew she'd only just begun to recover herself, to examine her own wants and needs, finally liberated from her mother's brutal seventeen-year assault on her self-worth. And then to have Karina accost her . . . but, God, he'd missed her when he was out in California. Those three thousand miles were a tipping point, and the momentum of the return trip had sent him rushing headlong into a declaration. He loved her. And she, to his eternal wonder, loved him, too. It was tough to think over the buzz of exultation churning through his brain.

"Huh?" he said finally.

"Maisie called. She wants me to go over there early this afternoon, but she wouldn't say why."

"Why don't I ask Mrs. Hodge to bring Will directly over to Saddle Tree after preschool and meet you there for his therapy session?" he suggested. "That way, you can help Maisie out and do Will's session right after."

"Sounds good," Andie agreed, a worried frown still fixed on her face.

"Hey," Rhys said, "don't worry about Karina. As soon as I finish this coffee, I'm going to start making calls. We'll find her."

And he would, he vowed. Even without his newfound happiness, he would have reserved a generous cup of compassion for his troubled ex-wife. But first he needed a few more moments to relish the way Andie had transformed his life. With her settled on the opposite side of the table, he was able to go back to browsing rings. He savored his coffee, thinking he might call Jess to ask for advice about Andie, and to see whether her sister would accompany him on a very important shopping trip.

~

The perfection of the day teased Andie as she drove the familiar back roads to Saddle Tree Farm that afternoon. Everywhere she turned, there was evidence of spring. All along the roadsides, patches of previously bare earth had erupted into clusters of purple-and-gold crocuses. Here and there, frothy yellow sprays of forsythia blazed against formerly monotonic vistas of still-bare branches and shrubs.

Rhys loved her. Her life had burst its meager confines and taken on a color and luster she never could have imagined before. And yet Karina still cast a long shadow over their future, one she wasn't convinced Rhys was taking seriously enough. He hadn't seen the desperate look in Karina's eyes the day before. He hadn't seen the deep red-purple indentation in her skin where she'd wrapped and rewrapped that loose thread from her coat like a Mafia-style garrote.

Nothing could blunt the elation she felt at loving Rhys and being loved by him, but now she had way too much to lose.

Turning into Saddle Tree Farm's familiar driveway, Andie parked and went in search of Maisie. She saw her sitting in an Adirondack chair to the side of the stable yard, watching the black mare, Shanti, with a strange intensity.

"Maisie!" Andie called, waving as she stomped across the yard in her paddock boots.

Her friend waved in return, but her face looked peaked, her smile not quite reaching her eyes.

"You sounded so upset in your message this morning. I wanted to head over here right away," Andie said, as she drew closer.

"I'm glad you didn't," Maisie responded. "Ed would have been in the way."

"What's going on? Is everything okay between you two?"

"Fine." Maisie heaved a weighty sigh. "But the time has come for me to face facts, apparently. At least that's what Ed tells me."

"Oh, Maisie. Your health?"

"So it seems . . . when I was first diagnosed, in my late thirties, it was with relapsing-remitting MS." Maisie tracked the movement of the large black mare as she meandered across the yard. "It was almost inevitable that at some point it would transition to secondary progressive MS."

"What does that mean?"

"It means no more remissions—no more periods of improvement." Maisie shook her head, her face a heartbreaking blend of strength and resignation. "My last stint in the hospital should have been a wake-up call, at least according to Ed. It's over." She gestured at Shanti, at the barn, and at the surrounding gardens and fields, to indicate what, exactly, was over.

"But, the hippotherapy practice? The horses?" Andie knelt by Maisie's chair, unable to process what she was hearing.

"I'm sorry, Andie. Will is doing so well with his therapy, and I was so excited about the idea of bringing you on here as a therapist, but I don't think we're going to make it for that long. We're hemorrhaging money. We're going to have to sell up."

"No!" Andie was horrified. "This place means everything to you. The horses—"

"Will have to be sold," Maisie said, her eyes welling. "I looked at the books last night and realized that over the last couple of months, I've had to cancel fifty percent of my lessons, thanks to one MS-related crisis or another. I kept telling myself it would get better, but it appears the jig is up."

"But I can step in and help out more," Andie protested. "I can be here—"

"You'd need one hundred hours of experience and a certification before you could take over as the primary therapist here, and then there's the regular riding instruction I'd been handling," Maisie pointed out. "Ed is worried about me. He's not prepared to watch me do this anymore. And he's not wrong. Apart from my health, neither of us is getting any younger. It isn't easy for him to maintain this place, and we can't afford to hire more help."

No, Andie repeated to herself. There must be some way to rescue the situation.

"That's why I asked you to come while Ed was out," Maisie explained. "He has a meeting with the bank today, and I need you to help me with something. He'd make a big fuss if he knew what I had in mind."

"I'll do whatever you need me to do," Andie said fervently.

"I need you to help me ride Shanti one last time. There's no way I can get up on her myself, with this weakness on my left side. I don't need umpteen side walkers and a body protector, like Ed would insist on, but if you could work the hoist and make sure I don't come to grief . . . it might be my last chance." Tears rolled down Maisie's cheeks, despite her best efforts to swipe them away. "I love this big girl."

No, no, no, this is all wrong. Maisie should be able to get up on the big black mare whenever she wanted, to keep her beloved horse for as long as there was breath in either of their bodies.

As Maisie spoke of assisted living—a small unit and long-term care she and Ed would be able to afford once the farm was sold—her ambivalence was palpable. Andie sensed her relief at finally being forced to admit she could no longer hold the entire operation together, but she understood her sorrow, too, at having to say good-bye to her horses and work she was not yet ready to leave. She shouldn't have to face this predicament, to see everything she loved scattered to the four winds.

"Of course I'll help you ride Shanti," Andie assured her. "It would be my honor. But there must be some way—" Andie's mind raced.

"Let's focus on the things we can control," Maisie said gently. "Riding her again . . . well, it would mean the world to me."

Andie went to fetch Shanti's tack, then easily caught the mare and slipped on her halter. Maisie held the lead rope through the fence rails as Andie laid the saddlecloth on the horse's broad back and cinched the therapy saddle in place, then replaced the halter with Shanti's bridle.

Maisie's progress toward the indoor riding arena was slow, but they made it to the hoist, and Maisie seated herself in the metal-framed chair attached to the winch.

"So much for my pride," she laughed. "I used to be able to get up on her without even using the mounting block." Andie had to sniff back tears as she tethered Shanti and set the contraption in motion, lifting Maisie through the air onto the horse's back.

"Ah, that's it." Maisie sighed and closed her eyes as she settled in place, straddling the large mare. "I should have been doing this all along, but I was too proud to ask."

"You never tried hippotherapy for yourself?"

"It would have seemed odd, and there was never enough time or enough hands to help." Maisie chuckled sadly. "Physician, heal thyself."

"Where do you want me?"

"If you could just stay on my left, I'm fine with the reins, and I feel pretty stable in this saddle."

Andie walked quietly beside her friend and the big black mare, concocting desperate schemes one by one and then throwing them out as the pitfalls of each one became apparent. How could she do it? Save the farm? Save the horses? Keep this wonderful place functioning for all the families who came for hippotherapy here?

She was struck by an awareness of how much she'd come to love Saddle Tree Farm—every corner of the rambling garden, every inch of the classic barn, every 1950s bronze sparkle in the laminate kitchen countertops. She'd been so excited about growing this new branch of her career here, working with Maisie, forging something real and important in this place where she felt completely at home. It was a blow, but nothing compared with what her friend must be going through. Andie would have to find a new hippotherapy practice for Will when the time came and would need to search for a place to establish her own practice, if that would even be possible now. But all she could think about now was Maisie.

They made slow circuits of the arena, falling into a meditative pace. Andie hovered beside Maisie's left leg, reaching out every now and then to touch Shanti's powerful neck. If she hadn't burned her bridges with Susan, Andie might at least have been able to prevail upon her to provide a new home for the mare, she thought ruefully. Maybe Louisa or Rose could help persuade Susan, she thought, with a faint glimmer of hope. It would be a huge relief to be able to offer Maisie that much, at least.

"Let's take her outside," Maisie said. "I want to feel the sunshine on my face."

"Good idea." Andie nodded and helped direct the mare to the outdoor arena. It was a perfect moment, as they stretched and moved in the heat of the spring sunshine, the breeze kissing their cheeks, the sun bringing out rich tones of mahogany and claret in Shanti's coat.

"She's such a beauty," Maisie sighed.

Andie agreed. The gentle strength of the horse and the beauty of the day even conspired to work their magic on her, loosening the hold of the angst brought on by Karina's appearance at the house the day before. There were still certainties, she reminded herself. There were still things that were solid and honest and good, even in the face of illness and sorrow and adversity.

"Andie!" Will's voice piped in the distance, and Andie saw a flash of his face before Mrs. Hodge leaned into the car to start unbuckling his car seat. Another car door closed, as Emily arrived, right on schedule, to help with Will's session.

"Oh, I lost track of the time," Maisie said sorrowfully.

"Should we go back in and use the lift to get you down?"

"No, I think I can dismount. In this case, gravity is my friend." Maisie pulled Shanti to a halt and, leaning forward, was able to swing her right leg over the horse's back, with Andie's help. Andie braced herself and held the older woman steady as she slithered down to solid ground. Maisie stood there for a moment, gripping the stirrup leathers and supporting her weight against the mare's barrel body.

"That was incredible, Andie. I'll never forget it." Maisie's eyes were luminous as she reached to hug her. "Thank you, my dear."

"I wish—"

"Hush now," Maisie said gently. "Now, if this were a movie, I'd make a dignified exit and slink off to lick my wounds, but I'm afraid you'll have to help me over to that chair and then bring me my crutch. I'll wait here while you turn Shanti out first."

Maisie stood holding the fence rail as Andie led Shanti back to her yard and untacked her. Will, running ahead of Mrs. Hodge, reached them just as Andie was helping Maisie settle back into the Adirondack chair.

"Andie!" He fastened one hand to each of her jean-clad legs, looking up imploringly. His eyes were wide and smiling, his cheeks shining with sheer vitality and unadulterated glee. Wispy little spikes of hair fell forward onto his forehead, like a fluffy starfish had taken up residence on his head.

Andie opened her mouth to speak but found that the words were knocked aside by an inarticulate flood of sheer adoration. She bent to pick him up, hoisting him onto her hip, loving his squawk of happiness and the way he reached out to lay his—admittedly slightly sticky—hands on her cheeks.

"It's a good thing you have strong arms," Maisie said fondly, reaching out to tweak one chubby toddler leg.

Mrs. Hodge appeared, picking her way across patches of mud in her crepe-soled shoes, a note of curiosity in her expression as she took in the scene.

"I should make the introductions," Andie said with a smile. "Mrs. Hodge, this is Maisie Mulcahy. Maisie, this is—"

"Margaret," Mrs. Hodge interjected. "Margaret Hodge."

Andie looked over in surprise as the woman reached out to shake hands with Maisie. Mrs. Hodge didn't usually start her acquaintance-ships on a first-name basis—in Andie's experience.

"I would get up," Maisie apologized, "but . . ."

"Nonsense," Mrs. Hodge boomed jovially. "No need to stand on ceremony."

"Um, I'll go get your cane, Maisie," Andie said. "Come on, Will. We'll take a walk to the arena. Then we'll go get Ace."

The two older women were quickly swept into what sounded like an enthusiastic chat, and, before she turned away, Andie glimpsed their side-by-side expressions as they regarded her—Maisie's face solemn and fond, Mrs. Hodge's softened by a warm curiosity. She set Will down and, taking his hand, led him across the yard, aware of the sensation of both of them watching until she disappeared into the shadows of the indoor arena.

CHAPTER
TWENTY-FOUR

"I don't know, Jess," Andie hemmed and hawed into the phone. "Do you really think I can get away with it?"

It was the evening of the autism fundraising gala, and she stood in front of the floor-length mirror in her room, assessing herself in the silver-gray Badgley Mischka dress. She wasn't sure whether she should wear the gorgeous confection to the charity event she and Rhys were attending that night. Her other option was a functional black jersey dress with three-quarter sleeves that could be dressed up with a necklace but would hardly set the world on fire.

"Andie, if you can wear that gown in my living room at next year's Oscar party, you can sure as hell wear it to an event at a fancy hotel with a bunch of corporate bigwigs."

"Perhaps," Andie conceded. "But maybe it would be better for me to stay low-key."

She'd confided in Jess about her declaration to Rhys, and his to her, a week ago, but she hadn't truly settled into the reality yet. It was hard to comprehend the magnitude of their implicit promise to each other when she was still on a knife-edge over Karina. The woman seemed to have truly gone underground. Rhys must have spoken to every one of the Zephyrus engineers, but nobody had fessed up to billeting a very angry, jittery—albeit glamorous—black-haired woman with vengeance on her mind.

"Relax, Andie," Jess laughed. "Enjoy yourself. Don't fret about Karina. Enjoy your first public event with Rhys. He's the perfect man."

"I know he is," Andie agreed. That was never in question. It was herself she was worried about. No matter how she looked at it, in her secret heart she occasionally still felt like an impostor. The way Rhys looked at her, like she was the wellspring of all things great and providential, still had the power to scare her. She had changed, it was true, but it would take time to settle into the skin of the person she was when they were together. The woman she was becoming was strong, but the very newness of this love, this sense of belonging, opened up a fissure of vulnerability. How could she possibly live up to Rhys's image of her, she sometimes wondered? And how could she embark on this new phase of her life when Karina was still out there? Wretched. Strung out. Hurting.

"I mean it," Jess enthused. "Enjoy yourself. Wear the dress. Take pictures."

Andie glanced at the clock. It was only half an hour until they were supposed to leave for the hotel. She might as well leave the silver-gray dress on and brazen it out. She finished her makeup and pulled her hair into a loose braid and twisted and pinned it up, creating a look that was part farm girl, part Greek temple maiden.

Andie had not had a date to the prom in high school. She'd forgone that particular tradition, going instead with a motley group of girlfriends. Hearing Rhys's voice in the foyer below as she arrived at the top of the stairs, she felt oddly like this was her chance to do the time-honored slow parade down the staircase. Only, instead of a pimple-faced teenager waiting for her at the bottom in a baby-blue cummerbund, there was—*good God!*—Rhys in a tux.

She'd never quite understood the point of male formal wear before, except to prevent the sloppier half of the species from detracting from the much more interesting and splendid spectacle of their mates' evening gowns. But Rhys in a tuxedo made it all very clear. In fact, it seemed in that moment that the form had been invented solely to set off his astounding masculine beauty.

The deep white V of his shirtfront outlined by his shawl-collared tuxedo jacket blazed against the caramel tones of his skin and made his eyes do their bewitching gas-flame glow. The sharp, tailored lines of his jacket and trousers set off the length of his legs, the breadth of his shoulders, and his trim waist and hips. He looked edible. In fact, as she drifted down toward him, Andie had to fight the impulse to throw herself at him and start nibbling at his neck. If only Mrs. Hodge weren't standing right by his side. It was really too much to bear. All thoughts of Karina were summarily ejected from her mind as she reached out and took his hand.

"Andie . . ." Rhys himself seemed to be struck speechless. Andie was confused for a moment, having completely forgotten—in the face of the spectacle that was Rhys—that she herself was dressed in anything out of the ordinary.

"You look quite lovely, dear." Mrs. Hodge beamed. Her view of Andie seemed to have softened considerably since her trip to Saddle Tree Farm.

"Um, thanks," Andie said shyly. She looked at Rhys, her gaze tangling with his. She couldn't look away. All she could do was match him smile for smile, locked in a strange, wordless communion as they headed for the door.

~

"You look incredible. I have mentioned that, right?" Rhys's voice caressed her ear—far more potent than the champagne that coursed through her bloodstream.

"Rhys, stop," Andie protested. "You're freaking me out. I didn't realize we were going to attract this much attention."

She was still getting used to the opulence of the hotel ballroom. Chandeliers twinkled overhead, gilded mirrors gleamed, and rich oriental carpets softened the footsteps of the guests coming and going in their evening finery. Andie tried to calm her nerves as she inhaled the scent of spring flower arrangements and expensive perfume, hearing the tinkle of crystal glasses and the low murmur of sophisticated conversation. She sensed a strange, electric energy in the room, which could probably be attributed to the buzz that followed Rhys as he moved through the crowd.

People murmured and smiled as they passed, dazzled by Rhys and inordinately interested in her. One woman had actually cornered her by the bar while Rhys was fetching them drinks, and congratulated her on the coup of arriving here on his arm.

"I'm famously antisocial," Rhys laughed when Andie told him. "That's the only reason they're interested."

"Yeah," she responded drily. "That must be it." But she had to admit she was having fun.

Rhys introduced her to a parade of new faces, making a point of singling out his friends from MIT and Vision, Inc. Noah, Rhys's head of engineering, was a tall green-eyed man whose insouciant golden stubble did nothing to detract from the sharp figure he cut in his tuxedo. Their mutual friend Ashutosh—Ash, for short—introduced by Rhys as a mathematical genius, was a graceful dark-eyed man with an accent that mingled Indian with British and American. He was forged on a much smaller scale than his friends, but had an outsize charisma that drew the eye of every woman in the room.

"Ash's net worth is in inverse proportion to his size," Noah joked as his friend slinked off to take one of a seemingly endless series of calls.

"You're just jealous, Noah," retorted Minna, a slight, elegant woman, whom Rhys seemed to regard with a brotherly affection.

"No question," Noah agreed, handing a glass of champagne to Rory, a tall woman who watched the room from behind a pair of heavy-rimmed glasses, her flyaway hair caught back in a wispy sable ponytail. Minna and Rory were heading up a lab pioneering a new breed of DNA nanomachines capable of detecting disease antibodies, Rhys told Andie in a whispered aside. All of these friends had willingly flocked to the charity event to support Rhys, and Andie was touched by the easy affection the group obviously shared.

A little intimidated by the brainpower assembled around her, she took a deep gulp of her champagne. As if aware of her discomfort, Rhys leaned in to press a kiss to her temple.

In a fleeting gap between the crush of new arrivals to the ballroom, Andie thought she saw a pale face staring at her with eyes of blue fire. She stood transfixed for a moment by the unearthly intensity of those eyes, the shock like a cold jolt between her shoulder blades. As Rhys stepped back to address a joke to Noah, she blinked and looked again, but the gap in the crowd had closed. Now she saw nothing but flashes of satin and silk and benign smiles—Boston's business elite arriving with checkbooks open. It must be the champagne and the nerves, she told herself, suppressing a shiver of disquiet.

She caught Tom's eye, and he gravitated to her side without missing a beat.

"How are you doing?" he asked.

"A bit overawed," she said faintly, wondering if he'd think her crazy if she told him she thought she'd seen Karina.

"Don't worry," he assured her. "I don't think there's anyone in this room who isn't in awe of you. Rhys is a notoriously tough nut to crack. Everyone here wants to know more about his beautiful mystery woman."

"That's probably why this whole thing feels so weird," she said, waving away the compliment. "I'm not used to being stared at."

She glanced over to where Rhys, Ash, and Rory were deep in conversation.

"Actually, I'm going to duck out for a few minutes of quiet before the dinner starts," she announced. "I'll be right back."

She walked from the ballroom into the hotel lobby, spotting the restroom on the far side. Already she was able to breathe easier, away from the wafts of perfume and the weighted glances. She set her evening bag down on the bathroom counter and ran cool water over her wrists, dabbing a few droplets at her throat and behind her ears to cool herself down.

She was contemplating freshening her lipstick when the only closed stall in the bathroom banged open, its door rebounding against the wall with a tremendous crash as a figure from Andie's nightmares stepped out, her eyes blazing with the zeal of an avenging Fury.

Her dramatically pale skin was framed by a low-cut black velvet gown that seemed to absorb all light. Her tousled mane of black hair swirled past her shoulders. Her face was blanched, highlighting sharp cheekbones and bitten red lips. And her eyes. *Oh God.* Her dark under-eye smudges were exaggerated by a heavy coating of mascara applied with a shaky hand. She looked even more disturbed than she had at their last standoff.

"Karina!" Andie exclaimed, backing up against the counter.

The tension Karina exuded the week before had ripened into visible tremors. Andie watched, aghast, as the woman's hands quivered, and her breath came in quick rasps. *Why was she here? What was she thinking?* Andie wanted to help her, but she was frightened of her, too. Karina gave off a manic energy mingled with a raw despair. Tears stood out on her cheeks, even as her mouth stretched into a strange, knowing smile that made Andie's stomach curdle.

Andie stretched out a tentative hand, reaching instinctively to calm her. "Karina, please. Talk to me for a minute. I want to—"

"Don't," Karina practically spat. She wrenched her arm away and marched to the door, flinging one more damning look Andie's way before she shouldered her way into the lobby.

"Oh my God." Andie braced both hands on the edge of the countertop. The loathing in Karina's gaze, the contempt: both were agonizingly familiar companions. It was as if the blood racing through her veins had been transformed into a gelid substance.

Andie made her way back to the ballroom, almost stumbling in her haste. Rhys, seated at their table, stood as she approached. She must have looked shaken, indeed.

"Andie, what is it?"

"Karina is here."

"Now?"

"I saw her in the restroom less than a minute ago." Andie held a hand to her churning stomach. "I tried to get her to calm down and talk to me, but she shook me off. She's really upset, Rhys. I'm worried what she might do."

"I'll go and find her." Rhys beckoned for her to take a seat at the table and strode out into the lobby, vigilance hardening every line of his body. Noah joined him, the two of them cutting briskly through the crowd.

Minutes later, Rhys stalked back into the room. "She's gone. I didn't see any sign of her," he reported, taking Andie's hand. "We're just going to have to get through this. Tom, Noah, and Ash are going to watch the doors of the ballroom in case she tries anything during the awards ceremony. She probably just wants to embarrass us."

"Oh, no," Andie said grimly, "I think she wants a lot more than that."

Just then, the evening's master of ceremonies called the room to attention for the live-auction portion of the fundraiser. Rhys pressed a reassuring kiss to Andie's forehead and took his seat beside her.

Andie forced herself to settle back and train her eyes on the proceedings, even as her mind continued to race. *It's fine,* she told herself. *You can't ruin Rhys's evening because Karina is decompensating. This charity means a lot to him. He's getting an award, for God's sake. Get a grip.* She took a gulp of the white wine a waiter poured into her glass, but it burned like acid on her tongue, and she switched to water.

Her own hands trembled slightly as she clutched her glass. She knew Karina had no claim on Rhys, but she felt guilty anyway about the way things had unfolded. Worthless. Culpable. Like the impostor she'd always known herself to be.

She smiled through interminable auction items. Trips to Bermuda and Tuscany. The use of a private box at Fenway Park for a dozen guests. A week of spa treatments at Canyon Ranch. Noah, Tom, and Ash made periodic circuits of the ballroom and checked the lobby, returning each time with the all clear.

Finally, the awards were handed out, Rhys looking awkward and gorgeous as he stepped up to the dais to accept the organization's Leaders in Philanthropy Award on behalf of Zephyrus Energy. Minna slipped into Rhys's vacated seat and squeezed Andie's hand as everyone at the table cheered enthusiastically.

"He's something, all right," Minna chuckled. "I'm glad he's finally met his match."

When, after lengthy good-byes, they finally stepped outside the hotel's entrance to get the car from the valet, the night had turned cold. Andie's head pounded and her feet ached—and the vision of Karina's dark-rimmed eyes still swam in her mind. She still couldn't shake her sense of unease. Not wanting to deflate Rhys's mood, she huddled in her jacket and half dozed to block out the image of Karina's wild stare as Rhys took I-90 West.

"Andie, wake up." Rhys gently shook her awake as the car's headlights swept across the front of the house.

"That's odd," he said, a moment later. "I don't remember leaving the garage bay open."

"What?" Andie struggled awake through a haze of dread and fatigue, his words plucking a discordant note in her brain. *The garage door. How could I have been so stupid?* She rubbed a hand across her eyes, remembering the disastrous end to her attempt at running. The earbuds that had blocked out the sound of Karina's car pulling up behind her. The waft of that infernal perfume as she'd entered the garage code.

Karina had been standing so close when Andie turned to face her that Andie was practically able to count the pores of her skin. Karina was certainly close enough to see the combination for the keypad. But in the drama of the ensuing confrontation and the surprise over Jillian's connection with Karina, Andie hadn't thought about it. She hadn't thought. Period.

"Will!" She shivered with the chill of premonition, suddenly fully awake and bolt upright in her seat. The open bay of the garage yawned before her, its aperture dark with foreboding.

"Will? What? Why would you think . . . ?" Panic flared in Rhys's eyes in response to her stricken look.

"Karina surprised me when I entered the key code last week," Andie confessed with a sob. "I didn't think about it at the time, but she probably saw the code I entered."

"And you didn't say anything?" Rhys's tone was hard, incredulous. His face was carved granite, taut and unyielding in its anguish, except for a telltale muscle that pulsed along his jawline.

"I warned you about her," Andie said weakly, her defense sounding pathetic even to her own ears. "But I wasn't specifically focused on the key code. Karina's accusations and the shock of seeing her like that kind of pushed it out of my mind." It wasn't just an error of judgment, she reflected. It was a complete absence of judgment.

Rhys didn't say anything else. He pulled up the car with a lurch and was out in a flash, leaping the flight of concrete steps to the interior door, which was unlocked, as usual.

Andie ran, struggling against the slim-fitting cut of her gown. She ended up hoisting it up around midthigh in careless handfuls and kicked off her high heels to bolt up the stairs after Rhys.

Fear mingled with a desperate, last-ditch hope. Perhaps she was wrong. Maybe Karina had not been here tonight. Maybe they would push the door open to see Will safely slumbering in his bed, his sleep-flushed profile outlined against the pillow.

Careering down the hallway, she reached Will's door at the same time as Rhys. There was no need to even turn the doorknob. The door was ajar, and the rumpled white sheets were drawn back to reveal nothing but shadows. The room evoked a barren emptiness, the same emptiness that resonated in the pit of Andie's stomach. The space felt sterile, apart from the lingering aroma of jasmine and bergamot. Will was gone.

"Mrs. Hodge!" Within seconds, Rhys was pounding on the nanny's door.

They stood for endless moments, waiting for a response, Rhys's jaw clenching, his gaze sliding past Andie's.

He couldn't even look at her. Not that she was surprised. She made herself sick, all dressed up in her silver finery—triumphal, almost bridal. *What a joke!* He'd thought she was the making of him, of his happiness, but now he was learning all too well that she was nothing but his undoing.

Finally, the door swung open to reveal a bleary-eyed Mrs. Hodge, a robe flung over her flannel nightgown.

"Mrs. Hodge, is Will with you?" Rhys's face was haggard, pleading.

"No. Why would he be?" The woman looked perplexed, like he'd taken leave of his senses, when really he was just grasping at straws. "Wait, what do you mean?"

"Was anyone else here tonight?"

"No." Mrs. Hodge's eyes widened. "I heard the sound of the garage door at about ten thirty, when you got in, but that was it. I was already in bed, and Will was fast asleep, so I didn't come out. What's happened?"

Andie slumped hopelessly while Rhys explained the situation. It was now almost midnight, meaning Karina had a ninety-minute head start to take Will wherever it was she chose to go.

"Oh my Lord!" Mrs. Hodge's skin took on a tinge of gray. "How . . . ? Oh, no . . . *oh, no.*" She shivered suddenly and swayed on her feet. Andie reached out a hand to steady her, then—knowing the woman always felt calmer with the kettle on—suggested she make a cup of tea, but only after calling Jillian to make sure Karina hadn't somehow shown up on her doorstep.

Rhys pulled his cell phone out of his pocket and dialed Karina's number, already aware that it was a futile exercise. He paced down the corridor and then turned back, shaking his head in desperate frustration.

He wiped the back of his hand across smarting eyes and then thrust his phone at Andie. "Keep trying. Don't let up. I'll use the house phone to call the police."

He stormed off down the corridor to find the phone. Andie longed to run after him, to wrap him in her arms and tell him everything would be all right, but she couldn't bring herself to so much as lay a hand on his shoulder. Her touch would be anathema to him, her words nothing but fatuous nonsense. How could she assure him everything would be okay? There was every chance it wouldn't. She knew nothing. She was nothing. Nothing but the hapless girl Susan looked at with such contempt.

A chasm opened up inside her as she paced and dialed, paced and dialed. Everything she was, everything she thought she'd started to become, began to shake loose and slip toward the abyss. The phone continued to ring and ring. Andie was barely hanging on by her fingernails. She thought of Will, stolen from his home—his routine, the people he loved—by a woman he hardly knew. *He must be terrified.* He was so small and vulnerable, and Karina—as Andie had seen her at the hotel that night—was nothing if not terrifying. She was powerful in her torment, Maleficent back for revenge. And Andie had been the one who'd unwittingly unleashed Karina's vengeance upon them all by giving her the tools to fulfill it.

She could barely breathe. This pain was strikingly familiar, the agony of having the very structure of her existence—its most beloved and familiar contours—torn away. She was eleven years old again, and all certainty in her life, all security, had been razed to the ground. She stood in a desolate wasteland, everything she'd built since revealed for what it was: a ghost city built on the shakiest of foundations.

Rhys appeared again, the house phone pressed to his ear. He raised his eyebrows at her questioningly, but she could only shake her head. Karina was, predictably, not responding.

"Her car?" Rhys frowned into the phone and then looked at Andie. "What was she driving when she came here last week?"

Andie was relieved to be able to offer some useful information. "A yellow Mini Cooper with black racing stripes and a black-and-white checkerboard pattern on the side mirrors."

"Wait, that's Allison's car."

"Allison?"

"My assistant at Zephyrus." Rhys swore under his breath and paced faster. "That was the present she bought herself when her first shares vested. It's so distinctive it has to be the same one. Maybe Karina has been staying with her."

Rhys relayed Allison's full name and Framingham location to the officer on the phone, then ended the call, vowing to go immediately to wherever Will might have been taken.

He reached out a hand. "The Concord police are getting in touch with Framingham," he said. "Can I have my phone back? I'm calling Allison."

Andie felt annihilated by guilt and self-loathing. Who was this beautiful, brisk man with the shuttered expression and stern jaw? What right did she have to know him, to touch him? She handed the phone over, careful not to let their fingertips brush.

He turned away, on the move again. Andie could hear the urgent timbre of his voice as he interrogated Allison on the other end of the phone.

"I think Karina's at the hotel," he announced a couple of minutes later. "She was planning to sit at the Zephyrus table tonight, for some reason, and stay over after the event. And she *was* using Allison's car tonight."

"She was there to get you back," Andie said with dreadful certainty. "And when she saw me there, she must have decided to snatch Will."

"I'm calling that officer back, and then I'm going to the hotel." Rhys's expression was dangerous.

"I'm coming with you." Andie had to see this through. She would see Rhys reunited with Will if it was the last thing she ever accomplished. But, after that, she was leaving.

It was time to end this fantasy. She followed Rhys back downstairs, the certainty of it solidifying with every step. Her life wasn't frothy silver tulle and lace, champagne toasts, children's laughter, and a passion so grand that the very air that touched her skin was charged with it. Her life was the four walls of her Boston apartment, minor affairs with little risk and less reward, and the institutional corridors of a place like Metrowest, filled with children she could aspire to help but would always have to leave—even the ones she grew to love. Her mother was right. It was foolish to reach for anything else.

She pulled her own cell phone out of her evening bag as Rhys tore down the driveway in the Range Rover, Will's empty car seat in the back a symbol of their intent. They would be bringing him home tonight. "We should confirm that the Mini is at the hotel," she said. "Make sure she hasn't taken Will somewhere else."

Rhys nodded, every muscle in his face tight. Andie called the hotel's main number and asked to be connected with the valet desk.

"Um, yes," she improvised when a male voice came on the line. "I dropped off my yellow Mini Cooper with you a short while ago, and I had my hands full with my son. I wonder if you'd mind taking a peek at the backseat to see whether I left my jacket—"

"Of course, ma'am." The man paused awkwardly. "I hope the baby is feeling better. Hold on a moment." Andie heard a rustling sound as the man put the phone down.

"They're there," Andie told Rhys. "It sounds like Will was upset when they arrived."

Rhys's eyes clouded with distress, and the car shot forward another ten miles over the speed limit.

"Sorry, ma'am," the valet said, returning to the phone. "No sign of a jacket, but the backseat is a mess. The vomit . . . would you like us to send it out for cleaning and detailing?"

"No," Andie said. "Thanks for checking on the jacket."

She hung up, frowning. "The valet mentioned vomit in the back of the car."

"Will sometimes throws up when he's really upset. When we find him, I'm having a doctor check him from head to toe, and if she has harmed even a hair on his head—"

"I don't think she'd hurt him," Andie said lamely. "She might be angry at us, but she loves him."

The memory of Karina's appearance in the hotel restroom rose up to smite her. She honestly had no idea what the woman might do. She'd looked desperate, undone, not really in her right mind. Andie should have listened to her first instinct and insisted on heading home right then. But she'd ignored her gut response, allowing herself to be lulled by the chandeliers and candlelight, by the effervescence of the champagne and the happy, self-congratulatory mood in the ballroom. Just like she'd been lulled by the window at Dolan's Hardware.

She snuck surreptitious glances at Rhys, taking his intense silence as an implicit rebuke. Eyes blazing like a wild man, he trained his sights on the illuminated vista of the city as it drew ever closer.

CHAPTER
TWENTY-FIVE

Rhys spotted the two Boston police officers as soon as he and Andie entered the hotel lobby. His urgency propelled him across the expansive space. Every nerve in his body jangled painfully. It felt so wrong not knowing exactly where Will was—*how* he was—that it was like the entire universe had been unplugged and then rewired the wrong way.

He lost no time in greeting the police, then quickly proceeded to fill them in. "We called from the car, and the hotel valet confirmed that my ex-wife and son arrived here a short while ago, and her car is still in the lot."

"Would your wife have registered under her own name?"

"Ex-wife," Rhys corrected. "Yes, Karina Novak. We think this was an impulsive thing. She wouldn't have any reason to have booked under another name."

The concierge tapped a few keys on her keyboard. "Yes, it looks like Ms. Novak is—"

Another hotel staffer behind the desk disconnected from a call, a worried frown creasing his brow. "That's the third call of a disturbance

on the fourth floor," he reported. "Apparently a child is screaming
and—"

"Ms. Novak is in 416," the concierge confirmed.

Rhys and Andie ran toward the elevator bank.

"Hold on a moment, sir, ma'am," one of the officers cautioned, his
face impassive. "This is a tense situation, and we're not sure what we're
going to find up there. If you'd kindly hang back—"

"Of course," Rhys said tightly, unable to think of anything but
closing the distance between Will and himself. He stood back while
the female officer punched the elevator call button, but after only a few
seconds of waiting, all four gave up and headed for the stairs, the concierge—with a master key—following close behind. Two hotel security
guards joined the group as it proceeded up the stairs.

The cries were audible as they reached the third floor, even through
the heavy fire doors that separated the stairwell from the interior corridors of the hotel. By the time the group emerged onto the fourth floor,
the echoing screams were inescapable. All along the hallway near room
416, doors opened and closed as guests looked out, shaking their heads
or congregating in disgruntled clusters. It was after one in the morning.
No wonder they were upset.

On the way down the corridor, the police officers peppered Rhys
with questions. What was Karina's state of mind? Had she ever done
anything like this before? Was she likely to be in possession of a firearm?

"Of course not!" Rhys spluttered, his heart practically seizing at
this last inquiry.

He had to force himself to stay calm. It sounded for all the world
like Will was being tortured in there. But, then again, Will quite often
sounded that way in the loving and diligent custody of Rhys himself,
so it would be a mistake to jump to conclusions. All Rhys wanted was
his son back in his arms.

Nodding briskly at her partner, the female officer rapped on the
door. "Boston police, ma'am. We need you to let us in."

Will's screams continued, and the door stayed closed. His voice produced an echo that chilled Rhys's blood. Did Karina have him in the bathroom? Were they barricaded behind yet another door?

The concierge produced her key card from her jacket pocket and handed it to the female officer. Rhys's hand had somehow found Andie's, and she gripped him so tightly his bones hurt.

"Ma'am, we're coming in." The officer signaled for everyone to stand back as she and her partner stationed themselves before the doorway.

She was about to swipe the card when the door fell open, revealing a startling vision. Karina staggered into the doorway. Mascara and copious tears had scored sinister black tracks in the matte pallor of her cheeks, and her hair formed dark, tangled cobwebs that emitted an acrid bouquet. The pristine cloth of an Egyptian cotton hotel bathrobe made a striking contrast to the overall image of dishevelment she presented. As she swayed toward the group, a corner of the robe fell open, revealing that she wore only sultry black-lace underwear underneath.

"Rhys! Andie! Thank God!" she exclaimed, her voice otherworldly but strangely hospitable, as if she'd invited the whole motley group in the doorway to a cocktail party. "He won't stop crying." She swayed on her feet as she stepped aside to admit them.

On the floor behind her, laid out like a corpse in a TV crime scene, was a bedraggled black-velvet dress plastered in vomit curds—obviously the main source of the odor that hung like a pall over the room. In a haphazard trail that led to the bathroom door were an evening bag, black high heels, and a pair of toddler pajamas printed with happy sheep.

The police pushed past Karina and went to check the bathroom. Within seconds, they emerged, the female officer carrying a swollen-eyed, red-faced Will. He was clad only in a diaper, and Rhys scanned every visible inch of his body for signs of harm.

"Andie!" Will croaked, his voice sounding like he had contracted a case of croup. *"Dada!"*

Rhys couldn't help it. That was the moment that broke him. He moved forward, almost as unsteady as Karina herself, and took Will from the officer's arms. *The relief of it. The shattering, overwhelming relief.* Tears streamed down his face. His hands shaking, he hugged his clammy, hiccuping little son, pressing kisses into his hair, knowing with absolute certainty that he'd never seen anything so magnificent—so perfect—as that exhausted, bewildered little face.

"I needed him. He's mine, and I needed him, but he wouldn't stop crying." Karina's voice was hollow, bewildered. "The screams . . . I couldn't make them stop. I thought maybe he needed a bottle, but then I couldn't remember if he still takes one . . . I couldn't remember . . ."

Rhys watched, aghast, as his ex-wife drifted over to the king-size bed and picked up an unopened bottle of red wine that lay half-enfolded by the covers. With a strange, glassy expression, she scooped the wine bottle into her arms and gazed down at it as lovingly as if it were an infant in swaddling clothes. "Does he still take a bottle, Rhys? A bottle?" She lay down, wrapping herself protectively around it, still murmuring.

He stared at her, horrified. What had happened to his whip-smart, driven ex-wife? How had he not seen this coming? He was reminded of her jittery, panicked mood in the wake of Will's birth. Her grandiose assumption about being able to resume her place in their family upon her return to Concord. And her deteriorating appearance on her succession of visits with Will.

And then there were Andie's dire warnings. She'd pegged it. Karina was sick, in desperate need of help, and he hadn't taken Andie's admonitions about her mental state seriously enough. The woman had obviously been unraveling before their eyes.

Anger gave way to guilt as Rhys wrestled with his conscience. Five minutes ago he would have happily seen Karina imprisoned for what she'd put Will through that night, but now he saw it was quite possible he'd failed her, and—in doing so—failed Will. The police wanted to know whether he wished to press charges for parental kidnapping, but Rhys declined. What Karina needed was help.

A team of EMTs filed into the room, and there were questions to answer and decisions to make. After checking Will over, one of the crew pronounced him unscathed, apart from a minor case of dehydration. Karina, on the other hand, would have to be admitted to a psych facility for observation. She actually seemed relieved by the idea when the issue was put to her, in one of her brief patches of lucidity.

Bracing himself, Rhys placed a middle-of-the-night call to Karina's mother in Sacramento to learn his ex-wife's recent medical history. Karina had been diagnosed with bipolar I in the wake of her stint at Stanford, her mother, Danika, revealed in distressed, accented English. Karina's depression and mania were well controlled by the medication she'd been prescribed, and she'd regained her strength under her mother's care, but her doctor had not heard from her since she'd returned to Massachusetts.

This was Will's grandmother, Rhys reflected as he spoke to the woman, feeling chastened by the love and worry in her voice. He had never troubled himself to be in touch with her, to enable her to share in Will's life. He wondered to what extent Karina's faithlessness truly absolved him from this fuller set of responsibilities, especially in light of what he knew now.

A contrite Allison added her impressions to the general picture of Karina's last several weeks. Apparently his ex-wife had inveigled herself into his assistant's favor way back, before Will was even born. Allison was a mild, amenable person, dazzled by Karina's glamour and flattered by her overtures of friendship. "How could I say no to my boss's wife?" she'd asked, confessing to long-ago coffee dates and shopping trips.

Even after Karina and Rhys's marriage had ended, Allison had stayed in touch, sending Karina updates and occasional photos of Will. She realized now what poor judgment she'd shown. She would have plenty of time to think about that in her new position in reception at the company's gym. Rhys genuinely liked the woman, but he could no longer trust her with access to his e-mail and calendar. He suspected she might not stick around long in her new post, as she preferred to be at the nerve center of the company. He wished her well but wasn't open to keeping her in a position in which she was privy to sensitive information.

It was Allison who'd relayed the news of Will's official autism diagnosis, triggering Karina's return to Massachusetts. She'd willingly assented to Karina's request to put her up for a week or two when she first arrived back. But a week or two had stretched beyond three months, and tensions had started to rise.

At first, his ex-wife had seemed fine, Allison reported. She'd barely even thought twice about it when she came into the bathroom one morning to find a cluster of pink-and-white capsules sitting in the unflushed toilet and an empty prescription bottle in the trash. But, as the weeks went by, Karina's behavior started to change.

Allison's couch, which Karina had initially straightened up each morning, became a perpetual nest of tangled sheets, blankets, and clothes. Karina's makeup littered the bathroom, and she left dirty dishes in the sink and a trail of discarded clothes on the floor every time she returned to the apartment. She never lifted a finger to clean and had the unfortunate habit of wandering around in her underwear when Allison's boyfriend came to visit. Lately, her troubled state of mind had started to show in more obvious ways. Allison would emerge from her room in the middle of the night to find Karina pacing around the apartment, murmuring, eyes glazed.

When Karina had announced her intention to stay at the hotel for a night or two and asked Allison to procure a ticket for her to attend the charity gala, Allison jumped at the chance to finally spend some alone time with her boyfriend. She had no idea what Karina had been planning. She should have told Rhys about her link with Karina right from the beginning, she admitted tearfully, but she got in too deep and never quite knew how to bring it up.

The sun had risen by the time Rhys and Andie, with Will slumbering in his car seat in the back of the Range Rover, finally made it back to Concord.

"You tore your dress," Rhys said as they turned away from Will's bedroom door. It was the first chance he'd had to really look at Andie since their ordeal had begun. Her face was wan, and her pinned-up braid had fallen down and started to unravel. A side seam of her dress had opened to the thigh, no doubt from her vigorous leaps up flights of stairs.

"I don't care," she said softly. "The only important thing is that Will is back."

"And now I can fall asleep with you in my arms."

Rhys, wrapping himself around her, was dismayed when she stiffened against him, resisting the usual slow melt against his body.

"No," she said. "That's not a good idea."

"Okay," Rhys said gingerly. "It's been a tough night. It's understandable that you might want to get some rest in your own bed." *No, it wasn't.* He didn't understand it at all, but he didn't like the fatalistic look in her eyes as she stepped away from him. He needed to prevent this from escalating. Something was eating at her, and he sensed that if he let it continue to corrode her thoughts, it could have a dire outcome.

"Andie, please, I know what happened tonight was upsetting. I know I reacted harshly. I was just so afraid—"

"I'm leaving," she interjected. "And no, before you ask, this isn't some ploy. I'm really going, and if you have any respect for me at all, you won't try to stop me."

"Of course I'll try to stop you," Rhys declared. "I love you." He wasn't just saying it. He was tearing his heart out and handing it to her on a silver platter.

"It doesn't matter." Her tone was almost bewildered. Like she couldn't quite believe she was saying it, either.

This wasn't happening. She wasn't turning away from him and walking stoically toward her room, the soles of her bare feet flashing with each step. He wouldn't allow it to be true. He loved her. He needed her. He closed his eyes and reopened them, expecting the world to reconfigure itself to the way it should be. The way he'd thought it was just a few days ago when he'd bought the diamond solitaire nestled in the black-velvet box in the safe in his bedroom—*their* bedroom.

God, how happy he'd been on that secret shopping trip with Jess, running off at the mouth about Andie and her virtues, fantasizing about a life graced by her love. And now she was walking away from him. He watched her half-undone braid sway between her shoulder blades like a metronome, marking out the tempo of her desertion.

He quickened his pace, overtaking her and standing in the doorway to her room so she couldn't pass.

"I've never known you to be a boor, Rhys," she said, her chest heaving with barely restrained emotion. "Or the kind of man who doesn't credit a woman to know her own mind. Don't make me think badly of you now."

He wanted to yell in frustration. He figured he knew why she was doing this. That it had to do with her brother and her screwed-up relationship with her mother—that her flight was some sort of instinctive response to the horror of Will's disappearance. But he couldn't point it out without doing exactly what she warned him against. Besides, she was an intelligent woman. She had a more intimate knowledge of her innermost fears and motivations than he did. If instinct told her to desert him, and she obeyed the impulse, she knew what she was doing. She was choosing to walk away.

"What about Will?" he demanded. "He loves you. He depends on you."

"I promised I wouldn't let anything that happened between us interfere with my care for Will, and that still stands." She jutted her chin at him, her eyes lustrous with unshed tears. "I'll be here each day for Will's therapy sessions for the remainder of the time I agreed to. Then we can figure it out."

"Why? Why are you doing this?" He was going to force her to say it. *You will look me in the eye, goddamn it, and voice your convictions, not slink away coddled in a haze of denial.*

"I'm sorry. I'm not cut out for this. I never was." She was retreating behind her walls again, going back to her ghosts, refusing to see the flesh-and-blood man in front of her. A man whose life would never be the same without her in it.

Stop it, Andie. Just stop it. You're wrong. Dead wrong. Rhys wanted to sit down on the floor and grab her ankles, like a thwarted toddler. *Let's see you walk away manacled to close to two hundred pounds of recalcitrant man. Especially in that dress.* But he had to admit it wasn't a long-term solution.

He gripped the doorframe to steady himself. He couldn't do this anymore, couldn't pit himself against her ephemeral foes—not when she was so determined to keep them alive, to give them succor. The night had been too long, and he was too drained. "Fine," he said heavily, stepping aside so she could enter her room. "Leave, if that's what you're so determined to do. I'm not going to stop you."

Andie gave him a long stare, then nodded and walked past him, into her room, to pack her bags.

CHAPTER
TWENTY-SIX

Andie fled directly from Rhys's house to Saddle Tree Farm. To her great relief, Maisie invited her to hole up there for a while so she wouldn't be far from the Griffiths house and could return each day for Will's OT sessions. The woman subleasing Andie's apartment in the city wouldn't be moving out for at least two weeks, and the farmhouse had plenty of extra bedrooms. In turn, Andie offered to help Maisie with sorting, decluttering, and packing up the farmhouse. A FOR SALE sign had sprouted up on the grass verge out front, its ominous presence further darkening Andie's mood as she pulled Ernie into the yard.

She felt sick, her whole body rebelling against the desperate decision she'd made, even though she knew she'd done the right thing. She would never forget the look on Rhys's face when she'd finally come to the realization about Karina and the garage code. In that instant, the hard-eyed, stern-jawed Rhys had taken his place in the pantheon of vengeful deities that ruled her psyche—her mother and father chief among them—each more unforgiving than the Old

Testament God. She would never measure up, no matter what she did. No matter how hard she tried. The shame of it was unendurable. And the sight of Will's empty bed had stripped years from her life.

The thought of Karina driving twenty miles in a state of dysphoric mania with Will basically unrestrained in the car was enough to make her hyperventilate even now. All manner of unthinkable outcomes still flashed before her eyes.

But nothing could compare to the agony of missing Rhys and Will. She thought she would find a measure of relief at leaving the house, at setting in motion the only logical solution she could grab on to. So why did it feel like her heart had been pulled from her body and was being torn apart like carrion pecked by a murder of crows?

Everything that was important to her—essential to the very composition of her being—was being wrenched away, and she wasn't sure how she would go on.

Watching Maisie with the horses was enough to make her want to double over in sorrow. She had to hold herself together, to try to mitigate her friend's pain at the dissolution of her life's work and her imminent parting from these magnificent creatures she loved so well. Over dinner each night, the three of them—Andie, Maisie, and Ed—would fantasize about finding a buyer who would take on the farm wholesale, with the intention of continuing to operate it as is. But each knew the chances were slim.

The work of cleaning and decluttering had done even more to reveal the gorgeous bones of the house, the harmony of its lines, the grace of its high windows, and the charms of its many nooks, crannies, and beautifully crafted details.

Each morning, all three would wake early and have breakfast together in the glass-walled conservatory that looked onto a gently sloping lawn, with a view of the stable yard and a grove of trees beyond. In the morning light, the trunks of the trees, still budding with light spring foliage, created a barcode pattern of vertical shadows and stria-tions through which one could glimpse the piquant green of a distant pasture. Andie shuddered to think of all that beauty being razed to make way for a development of McMansions.

As if to underscore how dire things really were, Mrs. Hodge actually hugged Andie when she showed up for Will's first therapy session since leaving the Griffiths house.

"You're a good girl, Andie Tilly," the woman pronounced gruffly. "Things haven't been the same around here since you left. I don't know what went wrong between you and Mr. Griffiths, but—"

"Thanks, Mrs. Hodge." Andie didn't want to give her false hope. There was really nothing more to say. She squeezed the woman's arm and went to find Will.

Seeing him was an exquisite form of torture. He threw himself upon her, all gurgling laughter and happy relief at her reappearance. Being with him seemed to engineer a shift all the way down to the level of her electrons. An elemental force bonded them, and at the end of the session, it was almost impossible to tear herself away. On the way out of the house, she couldn't even look in the direction of the den, where she and Rhys had whiled away so many happy hours.

Rhys. Echoes of him were everywhere. In the house. In Will's face. In the landscape and buildings of the town. In the traitorous corners of her own mind. She supposed it would be easier when she was back in the city, but—at the same time—she had to admit she didn't want to leave. This was where her new life was meant to be. Packing up Ernie and driving east would be the final admission of defeat.

~

Rhys wanted to tear his hair out in frustration. Every cell in his body screamed at him to go after her. Mrs. Hodge confided that Andie had taken refuge at Saddle Tree Farm, and at least five times a day his fingers itched to turn his steering wheel in the direction of those familiar country lanes.

"How does she look?" he asked Mrs. Hodge, a few days into this untenable new reality.

"A little peaky, to be honest," she said, brow furrowed. "I don't think this new setup agrees with her."

Rhys had to suppress a grim smile as his stomach churned. At least she was feeling it, too. How *could* it agree with her? It was a travesty, an abomination, a violation of nature's laws for them to be apart.

But in his darkest hours, one disturbing notion haunted him. Maybe walking away was exactly what Andie had intended to do all along. *When this thing between us runs its course . . .* Even their mutual declaration wasn't necessarily a promise of forever. For him, it had been, of course, but Andie herself had talked about drifting from one short-lived affair to another during her life in Boston. Maybe he meant no more to her than those infuriating boyfriends of her past. *I love you* was not a permanent inoculation against the death of a relationship. Maybe the shock of Will's abduction had simply hastened the bitter end.

Instead of blazing a path to the farm to confront her, he headed into Boston. After work, he made a beeline for Vision, Inc., where he could rely on his friends to talk him out of doing anything rash. Tom called an emergency meeting, and by the time Rhys got down to the Seaport District, they were all arrayed on couches in the expansive warehouse space, pondering his dilemma. Ash pressed a beer into his hand and ushered him into a prime spot at the center of the gathering.

"Do you know what she said to me when she left—to make me let her go?" Rhys asked them, slumping back into his seat. "She said she's never thought of me as the type of man who doesn't credit a woman to know her own mind."

Minna inhaled sharply. "Oh, no. She's *good*," she said, eyes wide.

"That's like Kryptonite," Noah agreed.

"I can't go after her, can I?" Rhys said. "She's tied my hands."

"You're hamstrung by your own basic sense of decency." Minna furrowed her brow. "That was canny of her to use it against you."

"If I tell her she's wrong, I'm a big, disrespectful jerk—"

"And if you don't, you're a big, stupid jerk," Ash chimed in from where he sat, cross-legged on the floor.

"So what do I do, Einstein?"

"You go after her," Ash decreed at the exact same moment Noah piped up, "You give her space."

Rhys looked from one to the other in bewilderment, then buried his head in his hands. "Maybe she's right," he said. "Maybe she just doesn't have the stomach for the kind of drama I've put her through. God knows Andie has more than enough baggage from her own family. Why would she want mine as well?"

"Why, indeed?" echoed Tom drily, a long-suffering look on his face.

Rhys took a long slug from the neck of his beer bottle as silence settled over the group. Rory, whose frown had been getting progressively deeper over the course of the conversation, now practically had her eyebrows knotted together.

"She did have three months to get to know exactly what it was she'd be walking away from," Rhys continued bleakly. "She knew what her leaving would do to me, and to Will, but she walked away anyway."

"You can't argue with that," Noah intoned.

"*Bullshit!*" cried Rory, exploding to her feet. "I don't know about you pussies, but if the guy I loved insisted on holding me to a bad decision I made under duress—at the end of one of the most stressful nights of my entire life—because he was too *decent* to challenge me on it, I'd string him up by the balls."

"So I *should* go after her?" Rhys, electrified by the prospect, braced himself against the couch cushions like an athlete about to spring from the starting block.

"And this man is at the helm of a publicly traded company." Tom shook his head.

"Hey," Rhys protested, "I pay you to advise me, so bloody advise me!"

"Of course you should go after her!"

Brightening, Rhys levered himself to his feet only to be brought up short by Minna's restraining finger pointed at his chest.

"You can go after her," she said, "but you can't go off half-cocked. You need to give her time. And you need a plan."

So Rhys settled in to wait—and plot. In the meantime, he was still busy cleaning up in the aftermath of the other grand error of his lifetime: *Karina.* He regretted how cold he'd been to her during Will's infancy. If he hadn't thrown up his hands in frustration and dismissed her as simply fickle and faithless, he might have paid more attention to her mental decline in the months after Will's birth. He might have been able to support her better and prevent her downward spiral. But he'd been hurt and angry, and her decision to run off to California had only compounded his resolve.

Now he was in regular contact with Danika and Lukáš, Will's grandparents, who would be coming out to visit Will and to whisk Karina back to Sacramento to recuperate under the care of her psychiatrist. There was no reason Karina couldn't have a full and rewarding life, provided she committed to staying on her medication and avoided major stressors. Over the last few weeks, Rhys had visited her several times on the psych ward, and after she'd been stabilized, he could see signs of the woman he'd once so liked and admired.

"I'm sorry, Rhys," she said one morning as the sunshine slanted across the tattered couches in the patient's lounge. "I screwed things up royally, didn't I? Finding out about you and Andie kind of set something off in my head. It was so obvious you belong together."

Hearing that, Rhys crumbled inside. Fortunately, Zephyrus Energy was providing all kinds of distractions. He and the other company officers had decided to establish a business presence in Beijing, and Rhys was going to have to go there to sort out the red tape involved in setting up a representative office. He'd decided to make a fuller trip of it. He would bring Will and Mrs. Hodge, leaving Will in her care while he was tied up in meetings. Then, Mrs. Hodge would fly directly back home while he took Will to the UK to visit his parents. In all, they would be gone for around two weeks. Enough time, perhaps, for Andie to think things through. He had to hold on to a glimmer of hope or else lose himself to desperation.

Perhaps rashly, he'd decided on another big change. He no longer felt at ease in the Monument Street house. It had never been his choice, and it had Karina's character and tastes stamped all over it. It was too big, too glossy, and too new. In the midst of all the emotional currents of the past several weeks, he'd found himself missing the pale stone walls of his family home in Wales and the way the house sat in the valley, like it had belonged there for centuries. He wanted a home with that sense of permanence and continuity. He wanted it for Will. And—if he was completely honest—it disturbed him to have Will sleeping in a room from which he'd once been stolen. Even if Karina was no longer a threat, the sense of violation lingered. So he'd started talking to real estate agents about putting the behemoth house on the market.

He needed a fresh start. Now he just had to figure out how to secure the one thing that would make it the start he wanted.

~

Her overnight bag packed, Andie eased Ernie out of the Saddle Tree Farm driveway. She wasn't heading east but west, to take up Louisa's invitation to stay for a long weekend in Camden and visit with her family and Rose's. Mrs. Hodge had called to say that Rhys and Will were going on a two-week trip, to Beijing, of all places, followed by Wales, so—with Will's daily OT sessions temporarily suspended—Andie had decided it wouldn't hurt to get out of town.

Beijing. She'd been sitting in front of her laptop when Mrs. Hodge called, and had idly Googled "Zephyrus Energy" and "Beijing," only to turn up an article in the alternative energy trade press about Zephyrus opening a Beijing office. She quailed to think of Rhys and Will so far away, doing unknown things in a strange, teeming city. Like she had any right to feel so proprietorial, she admonished herself. She had no claim on them. They could go where they wanted. As long as they came back.

She took her usual route toward the center of Concord, which led down Monument Street. The ache always set in on the last half mile of the approach to the Griffiths driveway, when the house loomed to the left, set back from the road in all its grandeur. She remembered sledding on that gentle hill, her arms wrapped around Will's padded middle. Now, as she drew closer, she saw an unfamiliar splash of white and red by the front fence of the property.

No. It couldn't be. Her heart leaped into her throat as the unfamiliar object proved to be a realty sign hanging jauntily from its white frame. She pulled Ernie over with a violent yank of the steering wheel and stopped by the side of the road. *No.* It was too much. First Saddle Tree Farm, and now this. It was like her future was being sold out from under her. Except that it was a future she'd rejected, a future she'd disqualified herself from embracing.

A disturbing thought flashed into her head. *They're moving to Beijing.* What better way for Rhys to assuage the hurt of her abandonment, she thought with racking pain. A new life. New horizons. Why should she be surprised that he would take her decision as final? She was the one who'd insisted that he not second-guess her. There was nothing stopping him from pursuing a new life on a different continent. He was a cosmopolitan kind of guy. Why should he be tethered to Massachusetts if his company was growing internationally?

The more she thought about it, the more certain she became. She imagined him and Will installed in a Beijing high-rise. There would be lots of glass and sleek surfaces, and a sweeping view of other glass towers veiled in smog. They would have to find an expatriate community and probably a new nanny. Mrs. Hodge likely wouldn't want to move to China when her daughter was in Connecticut. Most critical, Will would need a new set of therapists. Andie's anxiety spiked as she thought about it.

By the time she pulled in at Louisa's house, she was convinced their move was practically a done deal. They would gaze upon the same sun and the same moon she did, but they would always see them from a completely different angle. The vistas and experiences of their lives would be unimaginable to her. The idea of it hurt so badly that she wanted to put her head down on the steering wheel and sob.

"You look like you need a beer," Louisa commented, hugging her as she welcomed her inside.

"Let's crack open a cold one," Steve, Louisa's husband, agreed jovially, kissing her on the cheek.

"Okay, then," Andie agreed. There would be no more Rhys, with his mellow red wines and urbane tastes. A beer on the back deck was more her speed. It was how she'd been raised, after all. She followed Louisa and Steve out the back, where their two youngest boys, Finn and Zach, were kicking a soccer ball around their small patch of yard. The boys mumbled shyly when Andie went to greet them, a little taken aback by the sudden appearance of this mystery aunt who'd always been nothing but a ghost in their lives.

"This is nice," Louisa said, once they were settled and engrossed in catching up.

"We should make a habit of it," Andie agreed.

"About that," Louisa said, her brown eyes sorrowful. "I feel terrible that I let us drift apart. I always sent my invitations through Susan—"

"And she would conveniently forget to pass them along," Andie supplied. "Or she'd go a step further and imply that you weren't comfortable having me around your kids."

"She always told Rose and me you weren't interested," Louisa confided. "That you'd left Camden behind for your life in the city, and you didn't care about our ordinary little families."

"None of that is true." Andie felt tears gathering, and they brimmed over when Louisa placed a gentle hand on hers.

"That's what I get for letting Susan curate our relationship." Louisa shook her head ruefully. "Well, that's all over now. We have a lot to make up for."

Soon Rose and Eric and their children, preschooler Lila and toddler Luke, arrived. The children giggled as they played tag with Andie in the backyard, while Steve and Eric fired up the grill, and Louisa and Rose threw together some salads in the kitchen. They all enjoyed a noisy, hearty meal out on the deck in the warmth of the spring evening. This was life in Camden as it should have been all along, and Andie couldn't help reflecting that—even if she couldn't have Rhys and Will—Rhys had delivered her own family back to her. Her gratitude was fulsome and real, and almost consuming enough to help her forget, for a few moments, what she'd lost.

~

The morning of the last day of her visit in Camden, Andie and Louisa strolled to a donut shop on Main Street to pick up fresh treats to bring back to the house. As they walked, Andie kept her eyes trained on the patch of sidewalk outside Dolan's Hardware, still a block and a half away. Could she go there? Was it necessary for her to look her ghosts in the face at such close range?

A florist had opened its wide glass windows to the open air, and tubs of colorful blooms were lined up on either side of the yellow-painted doorway. In one tall bucket were slim boughs laden with pink-and-white dogwood blossoms. Andie knew, at that moment, what it was she needed to do.

"Hold on a minute," she said to Louisa.

Minutes later, she emerged from the store with an armful of beautiful, waxy white blooms wrapped in tissue paper and cellophane, set off by one hopeful spray of pink.

"Pretty," Louisa murmured with a smile as they continued toward the café.

They stood in line at the bustling donut shop, laughing and chatting fondly, Andie holding the flowers with reverent care. In the line ahead of them, she spotted a woman with a silvery pixie cut.

"Denise!" Louisa called out when the woman turned away from the counter with her purchases.

"Hi, Louisa, Andie." Denise's smile was warm. She reached out to hug Andie, around the obstacles of their cups and packages. "I didn't realize you were in Camden. How long are you staying?"

"Um, I'm actually leaving in an hour or so." Andie looked around nervously, wondering if Denise's presence meant Susan was also in the vicinity. "I came to hang out with Louisa and Rose for a couple of days."

"I'm so glad." Denise looked at the bundle in Andie's arms. "Those are gorgeous flowers. Is it a special occasion?"

"I was planning to visit the cemetery on my way out of town," Andie said. "It's a long time since I've been to Gus's grave."

"Oh, that's why you chose dogwood flowers," Louisa said with a flash of understanding. Her face grew solemn. "Would you like me to come with you?"

"No, it's okay. I actually think I need to do this by myself. But thanks, Lou."

"Next time you come to town, I'd love to see you," Denise said as they parted at the door. "Give me a call, okay? Louisa has my number."

"They're together, you know," Louisa said as they turned to retrace their steps back to the house. "Susan and Denise."

"I suspected," Andie admitted, "when I saw Denise at the farm on the day of the pancake breakfast."

"What do you think?" Louisa's eyes were wide.

"Truthfully?" Andie paused. "I think Susan should kiss the ground every day in thanks. Denise is good people."

Louisa laughed, giving Andie a comradely shoulder bump. "That's kind of what we think," she agreed. Then she looked up under one arched brow. "So there's no ambiguity in your opinion of Susan, then?"

"Where Susan is concerned, ambiguity is a luxury I can't afford anymore."

CHAPTER TWENTY-SEVEN

When Andie pulled up at the cemetery on the outskirts of town an hour later, having said her good-byes to Louisa and Rose and their families, the grounds were deserted. She closed Ernie's door with a tinny clunk and surveyed the manicured paths that led from the parking lot. She could have found her way to Gus's grave with a blindfold on, even though she only visited once a year these days, when she came to town for the maple-sugaring party.

She cradled the dogwood blooms as she struck out across the undulating hills, sticking to the center path until she reached a grove of trees and took a smaller trail to the left. She stopped when she reached the crest of the hill that led down to the plot where Gus lay. She could already pick out the granite headstone from among its neighbors. Her gaze didn't waver from it as she stepped onto the fresh spring lawn and walked slowly down the hill.

AUGUSTUS JAMES TILLY. It was a big name for a small boy. She reached out and traced the engraved letters with a finger, still unable to quite believe he was interred in the ground beneath her feet. She'd blocked the day of the funeral from her mind. All she could remember now were impressions:

how it had been unseasonably, indecently warm for December, and how the sky had opened and rewarded the mourners with a surprise drenching, as if God were either crying—or, as Andie now preferred to think of it, playing a practical joke on them all, like Gus would have wanted.

One by one, she draped the dogwood branches around the headstone. *I hope you like them, Gus.* Then she sat cross-legged in the grass at the foot of the grave, surprised to find that she felt calm. She closed her eyes and let her memories of her little brother emerge of their own volition. She drifted peacefully, one palm held flat against the ground where he lay.

Slowly, imperceptibly, her thoughts turned to Will, her lips curving in an unconscious smile as she thought about his innocent trust in her, and the love he'd bestowed on her and conjured within her, ever since she first laid eyes on him at Metrowest.

It's too late, she realized in a headlong rush. She could no more decide not to love him than the snow could decide not to melt in the spring. In walking away, in seeking to mitigate the risk to her heart, she'd made a false choice. By trying to sidestep the potential pain of loss, she'd inflicted the loss upon herself.

Wherever in the world Will was, she would always love him—would always be connected to him by a cord of affection so sensitive that it could tip easily into pain. But that's what love was: the courage to endure having a piece of your heart walking around outside your own body, exposed to the vagaries of fate and the world's incipient cruelties. Love was having the ability to comprehend that risk, but the faith to embrace it anyway. Rhys had that courage, and she now recognized its spark in herself as well.

Rhys. The very thought of him was enough to undo her. He was a man who knew how to love. The image of his face upon the discovery of Will's empty bed flickered before her. What she saw now was not the face of an avenging deity but of a father in pain. He was not at all like Susan. He'd been upset with Andie, yes. Even, perhaps, infuriated. But, much as his displeasure had felt like an annihilation at the time, it had been fleeting, and it had not meant the withdrawal of his love.

She'd never really learned that, she realized now: that unconditional love didn't mean never getting upset, never getting angry. That you could be furious with people and still keep loving them. In her life, the withdrawal of approval had always meant the revocation of all rights: to love, to comfort, to security. Rhys had declared his love for her as dawn broke at the end of that disastrous night, but she'd been unable to comprehend it, unable to hear anything but the tumult of her own fear.

What have I done? The true extent of her mistake was shockingly clear to her. Rhys had given her a priceless gift—the only thing she'd ever really wanted—and she'd thrown it back in his face. *I'll go to him,* she thought feverishly. *I'll find him and explain.* But he was in Beijing. The thought was enough to stir not just melancholy but outright panic.

"Gus, I've really blown it," she moaned piteously.

Just then, on the crest of the hill, Andie glimpsed the flash of a blue shirt and a mop of salt-and-pepper hair. *No. It couldn't be.* Susan.

She stared in disbelief as her mother picked her way down the hillside, around gravestones and flower arrangements. As she approached, Susan raised her hands placatingly.

"Before you say anything," she said, "you shouldn't blame Denise. She did everything short of locking me up to prevent me from coming here. She said I'd be ambushing you."

"Well, she's right."

"But, Andie, I had to see you." Susan knelt beside her and looked at her with pleading eyes. "It's been eating me up, how I treated you at the farm that day."

Andie looked away, shivering with aversion. She wanted to leap to her feet and run out of there as fast as her legs would carry her. The only thing stopping her was Rhys. He would want to hear about this conversation, she realized. That is, if he ever spoke to her again.

She remembered his sweetness and concern at the maple-sugaring event, the way he'd prepped her for her confrontation with Susan like an old-time boxing coach readying a prizefighter for a match. He would want to know that the hurtful way Susan had left things that day hadn't been the final outcome of their showdown, after all.

"I'll listen to what you have to say," Andie said warily. "But make it quick."

"I was surprised you confronted me," Susan admitted. "And a little angry, and quite scared."

"Why scared?" Andie was puzzled.

"Because I wronged you so badly all those years ago, and all along I've been waiting for the other shoe to drop. I panicked."

Andie nodded slowly. She understood panic. But she still didn't understand why Susan sought her out now. "What are you saying?"

"You . . . you weren't to blame for Gus's death," Susan said, her voice quavering. "Of course you weren't. But I put the blame on you to save my own skin.

"Jim loved you, you see, and by then he hated me. What I told you about the dislocated shoulder was true. And another time, he broke my wrist. He was a monster, and I was terrified. I . . . I let him think Gus's death was your fault, when really . . . it was mine."

Andie froze. "What do you mean?"

"I didn't tell the truth about what happened when I left you outside Dolan's." Susan's eyes were dark pools. "I didn't go straight to the car. I was frantic with worry about what your father would do if I didn't get dinner on the table. That part is true. But then I remembered he'd asked me to get him a bottle of Old Crow . . ."

Susan shook her head in disgust. *"Asked,"* she laughed bitterly. "Actually, I should say *ordered."*

Andie kept her eyes trained on the thick veins of silver in her mother's dark hair.

"Back then I'd do anything to keep the peace," Susan said. "And booze trumped dinner—no question. I should have gone back to Dolan's and had you come with me, but I couldn't take it. I couldn't drag Gus on one more errand."

Susan's hand shook as she plucked compulsively at a tuft of grass by her feet. "There was a line at the liquor store. I should have left, but I was weak. I just had to get that damned whiskey. I knew what kind of state Gus was in—fed up and hyper—but I left you to deal with it. *You*, an exhausted eleven-year-old.

"When the accident happened, I didn't even hear it." Susan's mouth was a brutal slash of grief. "Can you believe it? My only son was . . . *killed* while I was buying cheap whiskey for a man who despised me. I didn't even realize anything until I came back out and saw a crowd gathering on the corner outside Dolan's. I dumped the bottle and ran."

Andie couldn't say anything. She'd never known how long she'd stood before Dolan's window or how much time had elapsed before Gus dashed into the road. She'd always taken her mother at her word that she'd only stepped away for a minute or two. But even if this new version of events was true, it was still just a tragic accident.

"I was so ashamed—frantic," Susan confessed. "I knew how people would look at me if they knew the truth. So I told the police I'd only just walked away to get the car. The lie just . . . slipped out.

"And Jim—I *know* he would have killed me." Susan's voice was hollow. "So I let the lie stand. I knew it would destroy your relationship with him, but I . . . I did it anyway. I'd always been jealous of the way he loved you, and the way Gus loved you, too. I'd poured my whole life into them, but they didn't care. Your father resented me, and Gus—well, I didn't have a way with him."

Susan shivered, her eyes bleak. "Pretty soon, part of me even started to believe the words coming out of my mouth. I had to, you see. But it didn't stop the guilt, the terrible guilt. I even started to resent you for the way it made me feel. It makes no sense, but that's how it was."

"Why?" Andie croaked. "Why are you telling me this now?"

"Because I love you," Susan cried, her eyes imploring. "In spite of everything I've done, I love you. I just got so bogged down in the lie I didn't know how to let it go. When your father died, I wanted to tell you, but by then you'd become a young woman—so driven, so self-possessed. And yet, when you looked at me, you were still that wounded little girl. It tore me up inside to see you, so I made sure it only happened once a year."

Susan took a deep, weary breath. "When you confronted me at the farm, you forced me to take a hard look at myself."

She looked sickened, her expression raw with self-loathing. "Believe me, I wasn't proud of what I saw. You were my littlest girl . . . you deserved my love and my protection, no matter how Jim treated me." Susan reached for her throat, tugging at the silver chain of a locket she always wore, so familiar to Andie that she'd long since ceased to notice it. With shaking hands, Susan opened the face of the locket to show Andie something nestled inside: a small dried-out husk of a pressed flower. A clover blossom, aged and brown.

The daisy chains. Andie had to stifle a sob.

"I don't expect you to forgive me. I know that's too much to ask. But I needed to tell you anyway."

Andie was queasy, disoriented. She knew that, by rights, there was no reason for her to care about Susan's pain, but somehow she did anyway. She couldn't help it. And she knew for a fact that she didn't want this hanging over her anymore. She'd been through too much, learned too much, seen too much. Mostly, what she felt was exhausted. Like she could go to sleep and not wake up for a thousand years.

"I'm not saying I'll be able to see you after this," she said softly. "I don't know. But I do forgive you."

Susan's tears finally came, bubbling out of her like a wellspring from the newly thawed earth. Andie couldn't touch her, didn't have enough left in her to transfer any more of her strength to assuage her mother's grief. But she sat beside her until the shadows over the graveyard shifted, and peace settled over the hillside. Then she got slowly to her feet and, legs still trembling, walked back to the car and set off for Concord.

CHAPTER
TWENTY-EIGHT

Rhys had spies everywhere. He still hadn't decided quite how to approach Andie, but that didn't mean he was ignorant of her movements. Jess, Louisa, Rose, Maisie, and even Denise Hendrix had all become accustomed to his regular check-ins. Minna and Rory were on hand whenever he needed a pep talk. And Mrs. Hodge and Jillian were now his active coconspirators. The important thing, the one fact that gave him hope, above all, was that Andie was still in Concord. She'd extended her stay at Saddle Tree Farm and continued to see Will each day. It was like they were all in suspended animation. They'd reached the point where her officially contracted work with Will had terminated but kept on going regardless.

"She knows she made a mistake," Jess had confided immediately upon his and Will's return from their trip. "She's confused and upset, but she regrets leaving. She told me she loves you and Will so much."

The relief was immense. He'd fretted and stewed over Andie through each of his back-to-back meetings in Beijing. Fortunately, things had gone well in spite of his inattention, and he'd already handpicked a cluster of people to get the new office off the ground once the lease was signed.

His visit with his parents had only reinforced his urgent need to get Andie back. Their easy, loving relationship inspired him. Decades down the line, he still intended to place a kiss on Andie's lips each time he left the house—even if it was only to run out to buy a pint of milk. It would be a matter of policy. He would still want to walk down the street holding her hand, even when both their hands were wrinkled and spotted with age.

Jess's words infused life back into his veins. Andie and Susan had been through an emotional confrontation at her little brother's grave site, Jess reported, after some secretive calls with Denise. Andie was still raw from all she'd been through, but Jess detected a new certainty in her as well, an undeniable peace and clarity about what was important to her—Rhys and Will.

Rhys's heart soared. Not just for himself but for the woman he loved. He realized that, for Andie, Will's disappearance had reopened a wound that had still been only partway toward healing in the aftermath of their visit to Tilly Farm. Andie had wrested control of her worldview and her self-esteem back from her mother, but her confidence was still new and tenuous in those first weeks after the pancake breakfast. He cursed himself for declaring his feelings for her so precipitously. She wasn't ready—he'd known that. But he'd been so eager he hadn't been able to stop himself. He'd wanted to claim her, to cleave her to him forever.

Now, reported Jess, Andie had found solid ground.

What Rhys needed was to pave the way for her return, to show her how loved she was—how essential to his future, and Will's—and he still hadn't figured out just how to do it.

It was Mrs. Hodge who found the solution.

"We'll throw Will a third birthday party nobody will soon forget," she declared, beaming.

Rhys grinned. The woman was a genius. He scooped her into a hug and spun her with such exuberance that her feet left the floor.

"Oh, my," she cried, patting her careful iron-gray curls back into place when he deposited her back down. He gave her a smacking kiss on the cheek for good measure and stalked off humming to himself.

He had logistics to organize and calls to make.

~

The invitation arrived care of Saddle Tree Farm, printed on heavy, expensive card stock. Will's third birthday party. Despite the formality of the presentation, the notice was short. The party would take place that weekend, in only four days' time.

Andie's heart pounded in trepidation, but she knew she had to go. She couldn't miss Will's birthday. Besides, she owed Rhys an apology. Even if she'd destroyed things with him, she couldn't leave their relationship the way it was when she'd fled from the house. She owed him and Will so much more than that.

It had been the privilege of her life to know them, to love them, and Rhys needed to hear it. He deserved that acknowledgment from her because it was the truth. And because she was ashamed of the way she'd treated him, rejecting the love she now understood to be the most precious gift she'd ever received. It would hurt beyond reckoning to see them, to come face-to-face with what she'd lost, but she would do it. She would make sure their last memory of each other was worthy of all they'd shared.

She called to give her RSVP to Mrs. Hodge and then drove all over the Boston suburbs, tracking down the perfect present for Will: a selection of rare Thomas trains and accessories that were as yet missing from his collection. She bought a woven basket from a craft store and spent hours lovingly wrapping the gift in a way that displayed the trains to advantage through shiny cellophane. She hand-drew a card and fastened it to the basket with a strand of blue curling ribbon.

As she worked, she thought about Susan. Denise had brokered a phone call between them in the two weeks since their meeting at the cemetery. On the other end of the line, Susan had sounded timid, deferential—a far cry from the woman whose skepticism and constant aspersions had always ravaged Andie's peace of mind. It was as if the woman's armored shell had fallen away, exposing a pallid, tentative creature unused to the light and the open air.

Andie knew it would take time to sort through her feelings toward her mother. One day, they might find their way back to some sort of relationship, if Andie could stomach it. After all, there must be something redeemable in her mother if Denise felt the way she did about her. But right now Andie's focus was elsewhere: on making amends to Rhys and Will.

When the day of the party dawned bright and sunny, she dressed simply but carefully in jeans and a fresh emerald-green blouse. She wanted to push the image of the ungrateful harpy in the torn silver-gray evening dress out of Rhys's mind. She left her hair loose and wore a pair of silver flip-flops embellished with elephant charms she knew Will would love.

She was ready way too early and paced around the empty farmhouse, her pulse hammering. Maisie and Ed were out running an errand that had something to do with staging the property for its next open house. Soon, this phase of her life would be over. She wandered out into the stable yard to spend a few moments with Shanti before she left, resting her hand on the mare's glossy black shoulder.

"Wish me luck," she murmured.

Colorful balloons and ribbons festooned the red-and-white realty sign outside the Griffiths house, mocking Andie as she turned Ernie up the driveway. The house looked like something out of a brochure, its red brick immaculate, its white trim gleaming. More balloons and streamers bedecked the front portico, and colorful swags of bunting hung from the twin Juliet balconies. A bouncy castle sat on the side lawn, next to long tables laden with food and drink. Farther down the hill, a temporary corral housed a pony that looked a lot like Ace.

Andie pulled Ernie up just outside the garage bay, next to a group of other cars, and stepped out tentatively, clutching the cellophane-wrapped basket to her chest. She walked in the direction of the lively crowd that milled around on the lawn.

Scanning the crowd, she stopped stock-still, an aura of unreality descending. Rhys's Visionaries were there, of course. She spotted Ash and Noah on the lawn, Noah apparently insisting upon teaching his friend to throw a football, while Minna and Rory mingled with Will's preschool classmates and their parents. But, interspersed through the laughing, chattering group were also a number of strikingly familiar faces.

Surely that wasn't Jess and Ben over there, admiring the cake, and—*wait*—Louisa and Rose, with Steve and Eric chasing their kids around the lawn. The woman propped in the picnic chair closest to the drinks table bore a startling resemblance to Maisie, and that looked like Ed hovering nearby. *Well, of course, they're here to provide the pony rides—which they could have mentioned, by the way . . .* But that didn't explain the Tilly family reunion taking place on the lawn. *Why are they here?*

Andie shook her head to clear it, and that's when Rhys appeared, emerging from the center of a cluster of party guests. *Oh, the gorgeousness.* Was it possible that in the weeks since she'd seen him, his charisma had been honed to an even finer point? He strode toward her, bearing Will in his arms, and she trembled at the sight of those two beloved faces, side by side.

"Andie!" Will called. Why was it that his dimples made her want to cry?

"Hi, Will," she said, clearing her throat. "I can't believe it. You're three!"

"Let me take that, dear." Mrs. Hodge materialized by Andie's side and dislodged Will's present from her arms, freeing her to greet Rhys and Will properly. Andie leaned in to ruffle Will's hair and deposit a kiss on his cheek. Then she backed away, flustered by her proximity to Rhys.

"Andie," Rhys said, "thanks for coming." He didn't look angry at her or disappointed. He looked downright magical. His eyes were soft, his smile warm.

Out of the corner of her eye, Andie saw a handsome woman with short silver hair lift a toddler who looked identical to Rose's daughter, Lila, into the bouncy castle and then follow her inside. Andie looked around warily and was relieved to see there was no sign of Susan. It was as if someone had waved a magic wand and assembled a living tableau that depicted her world exactly as it should have been, populated by versions of the people who were most important to her—all of them chipper and on their best behavior. *I must be hallucinating.* Clearly, she needed to head back to the farm to lie down. Maybe she had a migraine coming on.

"Hi, Rhys," she said faintly. "I feel a bit . . . strange. In fact, I think I just saw Denise Hendrix climb into the bouncy house, and I know that couldn't be happening."

"Oh?" He gave a charming, lopsided smile.

"I wanted to give Will his present and . . . see you. But I think I need to go home and lie down."

"Okay," Rhys said mildly, apparently seeing nothing odd in her declaration, in spite of the fact that she'd only just arrived. "Will and I will walk you to your car. But, first, I need to get something."

Okay, then. I guess this is it. He's letting me walk away. Even the epic hallucination unfolding before her eyes couldn't distract her from the jab of pain. Rhys was acting like they were nothing more than old friends. Her presence might be a pleasant addition to the soiree, but her departure wouldn't provoke even the merest ripple of regret. Her heart sank in dismay. Had he already moved so far beyond what had happened between them? *Does he really think there's nothing more for us to say?*

Rhys walked over to one of the tables and said a few words to Tom, who was looking festive in a Hawaiian shirt. Tom handed Rhys an emerald-green party-favor bag with silk rope handles, which Rhys carried over to Andie.

"You'll need this," he said with eerie good humor. He waved the bag in her direction but didn't hand it over. "You forgot it when you left."

"I did?" Andie was mystified. Even though she'd been upset, she'd made sure to pack thoroughly, and she hadn't noticed that any of her possessions were missing during the last few weeks at Maisie's house. *What could I have left behind?* Whatever it was, it was small. An earring, perhaps? With leaden steps, she followed Rhys as he led the way to the car.

"Well, then . . ." She stopped by Ernie's driver's door, unsure of what to say next. All the heartfelt apologies she'd rehearsed had been driven from her head by confusion and a growing sense of disappointment.

"I suppose I'd better take that." She held out her hand for the favor bag, but Rhys moved it out of her reach.

Then he closed one hand around the handle of Ernie's nearest back door. *Wait. What is he doing?* If he intended to gallantly open the door for her, then surely it should be the driver's door. But, no, he looked quite purposeful as he swung the back door open with an embarrassing creak. Then, even more strangely, he leaned in and deposited Will on the backseat and climbed in beside him. He settled into the seat, pulling Will onto his lap.

Ernie's roof was too low for Rhys's long proportions, so he stooped as he sat there, framed by the backdrop of torn upholstery and flimsy plastic fixtures. He looked incongruous and utterly silly. *What is this?*

Andie's skin prickled with annoyance. If Rhys was going to usher her out of his life so blithely, the least he could do was stop playing games and let her go without rubbing it in. Surely their final parting warranted a little solemnity, a little dignity. But there he was, smiling up at her with the world's goofiest grin.

"Rhys, what are you—" She stopped as he grasped her hand and pulled her in beside him. The familiar aroma of old vinyl enveloped her as she was jostled up against Rhys's body.

"I told you. If you're leaving, then you'll need to take what's yours," he explained, looking way too pleased with himself. He paused for a moment and gazed at her, his eyes alight with warmth and mischief. "I'm just helping you load up the things that belong to you. Me and Will—your family."

"What?" Bliss broke over her like a starburst as she looked at the two shining faces beside her. She imagined this was what it felt like to be the circus performer who was shot from the cannon. She was soaring, pumped full of the purest exhilaration as her entire future expanded before her. A hopeful future. A future full of boundless joy. To her immense surprise, tears sprang from her eyes and started dripping onto her blouse. She'd had no idea they were quite so close to the surface.

"And you'd better have this," Rhys added, raising his eyebrows wickedly. He thrust the favor bag at her, the movement causing something to rattle around inside.

Frowning, Andie took it and plunged her right hand into the bag's narrow opening, feeling around for the elusive object. Finally, she pulled her hand out, with something glinting on the end of her index finger. The most exquisite emerald-cut diamond ring she'd ever seen.

"What?" she cried again.

"Andie." Rhys shook his head, his eyes playful. "You should know it goes on the other hand. Like this." He plucked the ring from her finger and reached across to pull her left hand close. The light that flashed from the elegant facets was almost blinding as he slid the diamond onto her ring finger.

His hands were gentle and strong as they closed around hers. He was solid, so solid, his warmth and substance ineffably more precious than the jewel that glittered on her finger. And Will—he was a gift so transcendent she would never stop marveling at her good fortune. There would be challenges; she knew that. Plenty of them. But she and Rhys would tackle them as they'd grown accustomed to doing—one at a time, together.

"Oh, Rhys, I'm so sorry," Andie sobbed. "I can't believe I walked out on you like that. I should have known how much it would hurt you . . . after Karina . . . but I was so scared . . ." She continued to blabber. The sudden turn of events seemed to have unleashed an exotic verbal cocktail, in which the words "harpy," "Beijing," "Susan," and "Will" featured prominently.

"It's okay, Andie. It's okay," Rhys laughed, wiping tears from his eyes. "I love you."

"Oh my God, I love you, too," she announced, like it was a revelation. "So much more than you could ever understand."

"So you're in?" He grinned and flicked at the bauble on her left hand.

"Yes, Rhys," she said with a watery smile, happiness infusing every word. "I'm definitely in. All the way."

With a satisfied nod, Rhys cranked down the window on his far side, straining and grumbling as the handle stuck. Then he poked his head out and bellowed one word.

"Success!"

A great cheer went up from the crowd on the lawn, and—as if the floodgates had opened—they all came traipsing across the hill, laughing and hooting, bearing champagne bottles and glasses. Rhys and Andie pushed Ernie's doors open to let in some air as the crowd swirled around them, all color and light. They each accepted a glass of champagne from the boisterous throng, which was led by Tom, who'd added a purple lei to his Hawaiian ensemble, and Mrs. Hodge, who had one orange lei and one pink one draped across her starched bosom. The nanny handed Will a sippy cup filled with apple juice for his part in the festive toast.

Noah, Ash, Minna, and Rory, beaming broadly, hovered at the edges of the crowd, refreshing glasses left and right, while Jillian handed around cupcakes.

"I have one more question," Rhys said, his glass raised. "I was planning to make an offer to Maisie and Ed for Saddle Tree Farm, but I wanted to check with you first."

"Rhys, now you're messing with me."

"Not at all," he demurred. "I've been sneaking over there a lot lately while you've been out, to plot with Maisie, and I love the place. It reminds me a little of my parents' home in Wales."

Andie looked around in confusion, seeking out Maisie's face in the crowd. Her friend raised her glass, tears shining in her eyes. Andie's heart was so full she worried it might constitute a medical emergency.

"Yes, Rhys." She clinked her glass against his. "A thousand times, yes! Now kiss me before I explode."

Rhys was only too happy to oblige, and the fizz of champagne on her tongue had nothing on the shock of elation that sparked through her as their lips finally met.

ACKNOWLEDGMENTS

This book is very special to me because I gave my hero, Rhys, the same challenges I confronted when my child received an autism spectrum diagnosis. As Rhys's son, Will, moves from his first word to his second, his father learns to let go of the panic and to make peace with the traits within himself that have led to a harder-than-usual path ahead for his brilliant, beautiful, non-neurotypical son.

I am thankful beyond words for my own funny, loquacious boy, who is now king of the tween rejoinder and whose MLG nerd persona is pitch-perfect. And for my amazing daughter, who has staked out her own quirky territory.

Enormous thanks to my mum, a librarian who raised me to be a bookworm. I'll never forget any of the libraries that have been my refuge over the years, particularly the Epping branch library, where I first discovered romance novels as a teenager. Thanks to my dad, who didn't panic at having two creative daughters but instead took us on some grand adventures. And thanks to my wonderful sister—my companion on countless flights of imagination growing up.

I owe a huge debt of gratitude to my critique partners, London Setterby and Alexa Rowan. Your insights have helped me recalibrate, solve plot holes, and think about my writing in new ways.

Thanks to the romance community for providing a wealth of resources for aspiring writers, second to no other genre. Through writing contests, I have benefited from the advice and encouragement of RWA chapter members all over the country. My several-book-a-week reading habit continues to open new vistas on our diverse, ever-evolving genre and has introduced me to the work of incredibly talented writers who inspire me to write more and work harder.

This book's life in the real world would never have been possible without the incredible representation and guidance of Victoria Lowes Cappello and Jenny Bent. Thank you for plucking *The First Word* from the query pile and steering its fate. I couldn't be happier that the book has found a home at Montlake Romance, where it has grown immeasurably stronger under the guidance of Maria Gomez and the rest of the Amazon team. I am particularly grateful for the guidance of Andrea Hurst, who taught me not to be afraid to use my antagonist to full effect, and for the meticulous work of copy editor Paul Zablocki.

Finally, I thank my wonderful husband and fellow writer, Rob Vlock. I love that we are always each other's first readers and biggest supporters.

ABOUT THE AUTHOR

Photo © 2016 Caroline Alden Photography

Isley Robson is a word lover who, when not reading, spends her time writing about colorful characters and the people who love them. After earning a degree from the University of Technology Sydney, she moved to the Boston area to continue her studies and eventually took a job in corporate communications. Through it all, she continued writing and has now won a variety of romantic-fiction awards, including the Orange Rose 2015, the Fire and Ice 2015, the Catherine 2014, the Laurie 2014, and Show Me the Spark 2013. Her debut novel, *The First Word*, is book one in The Visionaries series.

Robson lives in New England with her writer husband, two children, and two dogs. For more information, visit her at www.isleyrobson.com.